COUNTER

ASSAULT

MICHAEL
STEPHEN
FUCHS

First published 2012 by Complete & Total Asskicking Books
London, UK

Copyright © Michael Stephen Fuchs

The right of Michael Stephen Fuchs to be identified as the author of this work has been asserted by him in accordance with the Copyright, Designs and Patents Act 1988.

ISBN: 1522785590
ISBN-13: 9781522785590

For Anna

"Not even Hell can lay a hand on the invincible."
- Parmenion, Macedonian General to Alexander the Great

"The AO's a graveyard," says Master Sergeant Eric Rheinhardt, call sign Little Bo Peep, peering into his hand-held Blue Force Tracker unit. A black cloth, draped over his head, masks the glowing screen. "No friendly signals. Nothing."

Beside him, the mission commander, and for whom Rheinhardt works as 2IC (second-in-command), keeps his eyes plugged into his binocular night optics. A biker moustache traces the contours of his mouth and a curl of sand-colored hair flips out the back of his lightweight tactical helmet. Still scanning, he spits tobacco juice into the dirt a foot in front of his face.

"Not enough transmitters at the FOB," he says, profile unmoving in the near-blackness.

The two men lay side-by-side, belly-down, on a low ridge overlooking the southern edge of a town in the western desert of Iraq.

Rheinhardt absorbs this in silence. "Got eyes on their glint tape?" For night ops, which are pretty much all their ops at this point, they usually slap a lot of infrared reflective tape around on their packs and helmets. This makes them light up like glow-sticks in friendly night optics. Midnight gunfights go more smoothly when you can tell who the good guys are.

"Not really," Tucker says. "Pretty much out of IR tape tonight, too."

Rheinhardt clenches his jaw in silence. He flips up his blackout cloth after checking the signals of the rest of their own team, who are deployed on the surrounding ridges. He then checks comms with the AC-130 Spectre gunship on station a half mile above them and five clicks to the east. The response comes back almost immediately.

"That's a solid copy, Rage One-Niner. Skippy Five-Five is on station, loaded for bear, and going nowhere. Response time: zero-point-five mikes."

Zero-point-five mikes, Rheinhardt thinks, amused. Half a minute flight time – that's good service, and good to know. The AC-130 is basically a flying gun platform, lingering over the battlefield while its crew scours the ground through a massive sensor suite of video, infrared, and synthetic-aperture radar. On command, its 20mm Vulcan miniguns, Bofors 40mm auto-cannon, and 105mm howitzer can reduce to splinters and smoky barbecue anything, or anyone, on the ground below.

Rheinhardt's team tonight is charged with JTAC duties – joint terminal attack controller, i.e. directing the on-call death from above. This should only come up if the assault team in the town below gets in trouble, or the mission otherwise goes south. Barring that, they will simply provide overwatch, plus C2 (command and control) – light duty for an American Tier-1 special operations force.

Their dark digital desert camo-pattern uniforms show no unit insignia. But they are veteran operators with what is officially known within the Department of Defense as the Combat Applications Group, or CAG. When it was founded, nearly 30 years earlier, it was designated the 1st Special Forces Operational Detachment-*Delta*.

2

Everyone in and around it just calls it the Unit.

* * *

In the town below, the team preparing to take down a sprawling and ramshackle IED factory is not American, but Israeli. They are from Sayeret Matkal, the Tier-1 SOF unit of the Israel Defense Forces (IDF).

The Israelis got involved because they had critical intel on the targets: two master bomb-makers from Lebanese Hizbullah, who were trained, financed, and most likely smuggled into Iraq by the Iranians. It's an open secret that the IRG (Iranian Revolutionary Guards) have been training and arming the Shi'ite militias throughout the Iraq insurgency. These guys live to fuck shit up, both regionally and globally. Even worse is their Quds Force, a special unit tasked with exporting Iran's Islamic Revolution, which means arming and training extremists and insurgents in terror tactics around the globe.

There's also the small matter of where and when they are running this op – dead in the heart of al-Anbar bandit country, at the very bloodiest moment of the raging Iraq insurgency. The lid for this powder keg hasn't even been seen in months. And on any given night, virtually anything can happen.

"Don't worry, man," Rheinhardt's commander says, flipping up his NVGs and checking his watch. "Those motherfuckers down there have got themselves a prenuptial agreement with Death."

Rheinhardt realizes something terrifying: he can't say for sure whether his boss is talking about the jihadis who run the

IED factory – or their own SOF partners who are going in to kill them. Something about the man's attitude to the Israelis leaves him very uneasy.

He starts to say a silent prayer on behalf of the soldiers down below, then realizes the invocation might not make it any further than the man beside him. His commander's call sign is Heat Rash. But he is known throughout the Unit as Sergeant Major Rod "the God" Tucker, a seemingly all-powerful deity, vengeful and jealous. Rheinhardt has learned a dizzying amount in two years serving under him – about how to kill, how to stay alive through hell and back, how to function as a supremely skilled and dangerous operator. But to Rheinhardt, when he's honest with himself, Tucker always just seems like he's on the verge of either getting the whole team killed – or else lighting up everyone on the planet, just to watch them burn.

Rheinhardt switches freqs and checks in a final time with the team below.

* * *

In the black and sleeping town, Captain Natasha Akhilov holds up a mud wall with the curve of her back. Stretching away into the darkness on either side of her are a dozen frozen figures – a whole statuary of poised, black-clad, heavily armed badasses. Akhilov has served in the IDF long enough to no longer think about being a woman leading men into combat. Israel needs, and uses, everyone.

"Assault team, Overwatch," Rheinhardt's voice speaks in her ear. *"Send sitrep, over."*

Rather than speak aloud, she puts her gloved hand to an arm-mounted keyboard and presses out her response: STACKED UP ON TARGET.

"Solid copy. We show clear on visual and thermal. No radio chatter. You are GO to breach."

This whole town may seem to be asleep. But Akhilov knows that it is also nuts-to-butts crowded with hostile militia, plus their Iranian advisers. A single gunshot might bring a thousand or more fighters out of this woodwork. And she commands a single squad. They're exquisitely skilled and trained, and equipped with the very best in military hardware and technology. But still only twelve men.

She and her team must get inside this building, take it down, and kill everyone who carries arms or presents with hostile intent. They must then grab explosives or residue samples for forensics, snatch one or more prisoners for interrogation (including, ideally, the Hizbullah master bomb-makers), and then wire up the whole place for a peaceful remote detonation.

And every piece of this must happen in total silence.

Akhilov makes a hand signal to her long-time 2IC, Lt. Ari Dayan, who picks the lock, pulls the door open and stands aside. Akhilov steps inside first.

Tip of the spear.

* * *

Rheinhardt hunkers down in the dirt, pulls his weapon into his shoulder, and sweeps the area with the rifle's night optic. He can make out very dim IR glints in the three other perches on the perimeter where the other members of their five-man

5

team lay up. A scan across the buildings and alleys below reveals nothing. Glowing green dick.

Out of the corner of his eye, he sees Tucker jamming a fresh wodge of tobacco into his cheek and looking preternaturally relaxed. It's one of only two moods the man has, the other being ice-cold murder. In any case, there's nothing for the two of them to do but sit in the chill blackness, scan for targets, and wait for the Israeli team to complete mission and exfil.

Rheinhardt exhales quietly.

Nearly half of the target building goes up in a Hindenburg-sized fireball.

The hot breath and pummeling roar of the blast wave hits them a quarter-second later, tearing at their skin, uniform edges, and eardrums.

Then one second of silence, during which Tucker spits, audibly, into the dirt.

And then Rheinhardt's radio goes hectic.

"Overwatch, Assault." It's Akhilov, speaking in her Slavic-sounding accent, and panting like a sprinter. *"We've triggered an IED of some sort. I have multiple casualties. Over."*

Rheinhardt flips his night optic over and out of the way. With half the fucking town on fire, the lighting is pretty good now.

"Roger that, Assault. Can you exfil your wounded?"

Akhilov answers, *"Wait one."*

And that's when the small-arms fire starts up, multiple AKs and RPM light machine guns, all firing on full-auto. Either this was a trap, sprung with total surprise and success; or else the locals sleep spooning with their weapons – locked, cocked, and ready to rock.

"Huh," Tucker drawls, getting around to bringing his own weapon up. He carries an extremely old-school M14, favoring it because the 7.62mm rounds it shoots are big and heavy and knock people down; and the stock is wood, so it won't take a bullet and shatter on him at a bad moment. Sighting in, he says, "Looks like our boys down there, and their girlfriend, are a little bit fucked."

"No targets," says Rheinhardt, sweeping his barrel in both directions. His radio squelches.

"My seriously wounded are KIA," says Akhilov. *"We are walking out. Over."*

"Roger that. We have overwatch. Exfil path is clear."

But no sooner does he say this, than it stops being true. The incoming fire doubles in intensity. And from the muzzle flashes, Rheinhardt can make out a pattern of gunmen closing a loop on the building. The first Israeli pops out of the front door, and is instantly cut down.

"Fuck," Rheinhardt mutters. He quickly puts out two dozen rounds into the thickest area of muzzle flashes (the Israelis' weapons are suppressed, and will not flash), then does an instant tactical reload.

Invisible hands pull the felled IDF commando back inside the building. Rifle barrels appear now in window openings, spitting out thick, muffled waves of bullets in orthogonal directions. Withering fire comes back in. Mud walls spit chips as they take high-velocity punishment and begin to disintegrate.

Rheinhardt switches frequencies to Akhilov's squad net. He needs to know what the hell is going on. But she's not going to have time to brief him. *Fuck.* The radio chatter's all in Hebrew. But he guesses from the tone and intensity that she's about to lead a breakout.

He's right. Covering fire from the building ramps up and the first group of shadow figures sprint from the front door. Each is forced under cover again within twenty meters. They are pinned down in the deadly warren of the town. Rheinhardt can see a half-dozen mini-engagements taking place – a little fire and movement from the Israelis, but their positions are poor.

Rheinhardt remembers what a training cadre member in the Unit told him once: "If you survive one ambush, go home, get in your rocking chair, and thank God for the rest of your life." It's usually that bad, and looks like being so tonight. Rheinhardt gets a look at the back of an ambusher, takes the shot. Kill. Then another, and another kill.

He hears Tucker speaking into a hand mic, above the noise of the battle.

"Skippy Five-Five. This is Rage One-Niner. Stand by for fire mission."

"Rage One-Niner, Skippy Five-Five, send fire mission," the Spectre crew replies. Rheinhardt's got the same channel still open, continuing to fire while listening in.

"Requesting CAS," Tucker says. "Package as per pre-sighted target grid and solution. Requesting 105, over."

"Rage One-Niner, I confirm, 105 on pre-sighted grid. Please confirm cleared hot, over."

"That's a-ffirm. Fire for effect on—" He turns to face Rheinhardt, who has grabbed his arm.

"Sarge," Rheinhardt says. "Friendlies down there."

Tucker gives him a lethal look. He pauses one beat, then flexes his powerful arm, bringing the mic back to his mouth, and Rheinhardt's hand along with it.

"That's a-ffirm," he says into the mouthpiece. "Fire for effect on target."

"Roger that. Coming around and starting gun run."

Rheinhardt can't believe what he's hearing. "For God's sake. At least give them a chance to break contact."

Tucker pins him with an unamused eye. "Those klutzy motherfuckers down there have got about thirty seconds to break contact."

Rheinhardt persists. "Call in precision fire with the Vulcans and 40 mil. It's not too late…"

"Not happenin' man. Those IED-makers are killing fifty-plus Americans a month, and wounding three hundred. They ain't gettin' outta here."

Rheinhardt wants to tell him they don't even know for sure the ambushers are the same people as the bomb-makers. But they're out of time. He turns away and resumes firing, while hailing Akhilov.

"Assault, Overwatch! You have incoming fires your position. *Exfil immediately*. Break contact. Repeat, break contact and exfil *now*."

"Anyway," Tucker says, sitting back, "precision fire won't help. Bird can't tell who's who."

No shit, thinks Rheinhardt, picking out targets and dropping them as fast as he can fire and reload. *No BFT transponders – or fucking IR tape.*

* * *

Captain Akhilov sights in and empties the magazine of her bullpup TAR-21 assault rifle. The robe-clad man in her sight disappears, along with the flimsy crate he concealed behind.

She looks one position over to her lieutenant. He's still on his feet, and also going cyclic – firing full-auto until empty, reloading and going again.

Doctrine in an ambush is to unload and then assault through the ambush lines – the only alternative being to sit around with your faces hanging out until you get picked to pieces. Akhilov slams a fresh mag home and braces to give the assault order. They're getting out of here now or never.

Then she hears traffic from the American team, but can't make it out over the full-auto roar.

"Say again, Overwatch." She presses her palm to her ear. The drone of the AC-130 coming on station overhead never even breaks through the noise of the gunfight. Akhilov feels the first 105mm artillery round hit before she hears the sound of it.

That was too close, she thinks. Then another – *way too close*.

She feels the air compact, twist, and superheat around her body.

Her visual field goes bright white.

* * *

Rheinhardt's radio perks up, underneath his gloved hands, which are covering up his head.

"Rage One-Niner, Skippy Five-Five, fire mission complete. You just got love from above."

With the explosions settling, Rheinhardt dares to uncurl and look up again. Where the target building used to be, and within a hundred meters in every direction, is just a kind of hell. Nothing lives in there now.

Flipping his night optic back into place, he scans out to the edges of the destruction, where the darkness is lapping back in. He can just make out one or two palsied figures, face down, trying to drag themselves away from the inferno, glowing a faint and pixilated green. The dying – much less lucky than the dead.

"Pack up," Tucker says, pulling his wad of tobacco clear with thumb and two fingers as he gets to his feet. "Exfil to rally point one, then we're RTB."

Rheinhardt stands and blinks slowly. The ghostly green figures of the dying commandos linger as an after-image in his mind's eye. And they won't be going away for a long time after.

Eric Rheinhardt, now Sergeant Major, once again looks through advanced night optics, once more lighting up a deathly black and desolate landscape. He watches the near sentry at the outside security station check his phone, then light a cigarette. The lighter flares wide and bright on the light-amplified green field.

The other sentry makes a warning gesture, and the first cups the ember inside his hand.

Rheinhardt brings up his crosshairs, places them on the first sentry's left temple, and fires. The man's head stops existing, and the rest of him slumps to the ground like a dropped sack of cement. The second guard sits frozen, open-mouthed, covered in blood. Rheinhardt smoothly pivots his aim to the right, fires again.

"Bo Peep to Alpha," he says over the radio to the rest of his team. *"You're clear to approach."*

Three human figures, slithering and silent, assault rifles at their shoulders in the low ready position, slip past Rheinhardt's field of vision. Just behind, a four-legged form pads smoothly after them – a combat assault dog, and like them also wearing body armor, and a radio earpiece, tuned to the same squad net. As the group passes the guard shack, one of the humans recovers a guard's radio and security card, then follows the others to the exterior wall of the structure. The building shows only a single story above ground. But five more extend deep below the surface of the dark and hulking mountain.

Rheinhardt watches the others take up positions to either side, while the one with the security badge squares up to the door. Staff Sergeant Javier Roque is five-foot-eight, of medium build, with dark skin, black hair, and boyish features, usually including an amiable grin. He puts an electronic listening device to the surface of the door, withdraws it, then waves a hand-held IR transceiver around the edges. He then makes a hand signal behind his back, to the dog.

The armored dog – who is a massively oversized and scarily intelligent beagle known ironically as Mr. MacSnuggles, but usually just Mac – darts forward and performs an elaborate series of sniffing operations around the doorway. He then turns and puts his muzzle in Javier's hand. This means the entrance, and its immediate vicinity, are free of explosives. Javier finally slides the keycard through the reader and presses open the door. In two beats, the team slips inside – making way for and led by a hulking giant.

Master Sergeant "Uncle BJ" Johnson takes point now. After slinging his assault rifle behind him, he produces a six-inch Spyderco Warrior knife in his right hand, and a suppressed custom Kimber .45 pistol held forward in the left. The latest Enhanced Night Vision Goggles, with four barrels, 120-degree vision, and thermal imaging, extend down and out from the edge of his black tactical helmet, not quite reaching his sandy moustache. At six-foot-five and 260 pounds of hardwood-like flesh, he is a demon descending into the worst nightmares of the Iranian mullahs.

Seeing dim lighting up ahead, Johnson silently flips up his NVGs. He makes a "hold" fist over his shoulder, then accelerates smoothly down the hall, silent in his size-14 assault boots. At a security station by the elevators, he kills a guard half-dozing behind the desk and lays him on the floor without ever waking him up.

While Javier swipes the keycard at the elevator, the third team member slips behind the desk, sits at a computer station, and begins typing. Sergeant First Class Aaliyah Khamsi switches channels to her secure SATCOM radio and adjusts the rock-star mic that curls from her helmet around her wide and angular cheekbones. She darts her intense and nearly black eyes up to the other two, who now disappear into the elevator.

"Ops, Bette Noir," she says into the mic. "On station."

With no delay, a voice responds crisply in her ear: *"Bette Noir, Ops. Go ahead."*

"I've got a log-in prompt. And I've seated the USB device. But no joy. Presume the port's been disabled."

"Roger that. No problem, Ali. We'll do it the hard way. Just pop the CPU case for me."

"Roger that. Wait one."

And with that a young computer science PhD in a high-tech Ops Center in North Carolina proceeds to walk a deployed special operator through the process of penetrating a secure network in a nuclear research facility in northern Iran.

When the elevator door opens again, Johnson and Javier now flank a third man – dark-skinned, with a bushy gray moustache, and wearing actual pajamas. He clutches a small shoulder bag and looks warily up and down the corridor.

Their radios chirp up. It's Rheinhardt, reporting from outside.

"Yeah, guys, I've got visual on a medium ground transport approaching – approx two-zero enemy personnel. Break." The radio squelches once. *"And they look pissed."*

Johnson looks sharply at Javier. "You miss something? An alarm you didn't catch?"

"No, man," Javier says. He wrinkles his brow – then pulls the newcomer's satchel from his hand. He sweeps it with a small electronic scanner, which lights up. "Tracking device." Not bothering to search it, he simply launches the bag skidding down the hall. Without another word, the four put their shoulders down and make for the exit.

* * *

Rheinhardt watches the initial approach of the truck on a live video feed from an RQ4 Global Hawk, a large unmanned aerial vehicle (UAV) loitering at 40,000 feet offshore over the Caspian Sea. Once the truck rounds a bend and clears the edge of the building, he's got a direct look at it himself. But by that time it's only 100 meters away.

He puts his crosshair on the grill and fires a round through the engine block. That stops the vehicle dead. The soldiers in the bed of the truck begin to pile off.

As Rheinhardt pauses to check his background, he sees the rest of the team spill from the front of the building and sprint in his direction. The angles are good, so he sights in and starts pouring giant 50-cal slugs into the crowd fanning out from the back of the truck.

His team reaches him seconds later. As the enormous and grinning Uncle BJ dashes by, he kisses his hand and plants it on Rheinhardt's night-vision lens. It leaves a big fucking smear.

Rheinhardt clocks the disposition of the enemy – mainly diving for cover – then risks spinning round 180 degrees to track the team. They reach a hide and begin unspooling a tethered helium balloon, which they inflated earlier and covered with a blanket and rocks. Now they unreel it 60 meters into the sky, all within seconds. Rheinhardt can also hear Javier on the air mission net.

"Lunchbox One, this is Thundernuts One-Zero – we are three pax, one K-9, one PC, requesting immediate STARS pick-up from primary extraction point."

Almost immediately, the rumbling roar of an MC-130W Combat Spear SOF transport (known as the "Combat Wombat") swoops down toward them from the blackness above the coast. Rheinhardt watches the team clip onto snaplinks on a stretch of rope, after helping the newcomer into a nylon harness. They duck their heads while doing so, as sporadic fire now whistles in from the survivors around the truck. Javier speaks Mac's name into his chin mic. The dog has been standing five meters back, facing away toward the enemy. He now turns and darts up to Javier, who clips him in as well, and straps on his "doggles" to protect his eyes in the air. Each member of the group double-checks the fastenings of the next, hands clapping backs, finishing with seconds to spare.

The dark predator shadow of the aircraft thunders in overhead. A V-shaped yoke mounted off the back ramp of the plane hooks the tether just below the balloon. And one after another, the four figures are powerfully lifted off the ground and up into the sky. The plane disappears from sight, as the crew chief begins to reel in three operators, one dog, and one precious cargo (PC) – all courtesy of the surface-to-air recovery system (STARS).

Rheinhardt spins back toward the truck just as the remaining infantry work up the necessary sack to approach his position. Their facial expressions, large and plain now in the night-vision, go from terrified to bemused. Rheinhardt is out of ammo, but it doesn't matter now. Shaking his head at the smear on the glass left by BJ's parting kiss, he detonates the thermite charges.

"Damn, that's gotta hurt," says a voice behind Rheinhardt. A hoary hand comes down on his shoulder.

Rheinhardt removes his head-mounted VR goggle display, through which he has just remotely led this operation 6,500 miles away in Iran, and places it on the console.

His station is near the center of the Unit's Tactical Operations Center (TOC). Overhead, at the front of the room, three large video screens display airborne camera views and real-time mission data. At similar stations all around him, another dozen soldiers type on keyboards, talk into headset devices, or page through documents on tablet computers.

The smaller screen before Rheinhardt has gone black. This is because the SWORDS unit he was remotely operating – a two-tracked Talon robot, mounted with cameras, sensors, and a Barrett 50-cal rifle – has melted into a twisted pile of smoking steel and rubber from the intense heat of the thermite charges he detonated upon it.

Rheinhardt's commander, Colonel Richard E. "Dick" Havering, appears from behind him. He swings around and leans up against Rheinhardt's desk. He wears the standard Army Combat Uniform (ACUs), tan fatigues with a digital camo pattern. A gray crewcut, steel-framed oval glasses, and a Bluetooth headset frame his lean and weathered face. He speaks with an amused southern twang.

"That was a pretty expensive hunk of robot you just blew up there."

Rheinhardt's dark green eyes crinkle as he smiles. He is six feet tall with a medium, muscular build, and wears tan cargo pants and a long-sleeve synthetic tactical t-shirt. Clipped to the right side of his belt are a smart-phone, a Leatherman multi-tool, and a small LED Maglite. He leans back and runs his fingers through his dark, wavy, and not-quite-military-short hair.

Still smiling, he says, "I commend you to Dan Schilling's Five Lessons of Combat, the first of which is: 'Never risk your life for an inanimate object.'"

"Fair point," Havering says. "Still… your own last mission. And you don't even show up for it." He points at the bank of screens and the VR goggles.

Rheinhardt laughs. "At least I was driving the robot. Soon it will be an autonomous, networked robot army. And you and I will be out on the street with 'homeless vet' scribbled on scraps of cardboard."

Havering straightens up. "Best thing, maybe. Can you keep your eyes open for thirty hours without blinking? That Reaper drone you hear buzzing overhead can."

"Yeah," Rheinhardt says. "I suppose the robot is our answer to the suicide bomber. You wanna blow stuff up? Go for it. We'll build more."

Havering nods. "Still… I've got to think a human team is always going to want their leader to have some skin in the game."

"Hey, C2'ing this one remotely was *your* idea." Rheinhardt pushes back in his chair. "You wanted me spending the time doing handover documentation, not making my hundredth trip out to CENTCOM. Anyway, it's BJ's team now. I'm just a ghost in these halls."

"Hell of a thing," Havering says, his gaze going slightly out of focus. "You leaving."

"Well… I've got no regrets. Except one – not giving out my drinks at the Parachute Club."

"Yeah. Gotta die for that. Just about the only thing you *haven't* done in this unit." Havering straightens up. "When you've finished playing with your robot here, come see me in my office. One last debrief."

"Now's good," Rheinhardt says.

He logs out of his station, stands, and takes one last walk with his commander out of a room that for him is filled with many memories – and ghosts.

Dr. Azad Sultan sits shivering on the bench seat of the shuddering Hercules turbo-prop airframe. The outside night air was not that cold, even at 120mph. But the experience of being dragged through the lower atmosphere like a human kite tail has left the Iranian nuclear scientist, and underground dissident, shaking like a centrifuge.

To his left, "Uncle BJ" Johnson unstraps himself and begins checking Sultan out.

Master Sergeant Johnson is a veteran Delta assaulter with 13 years in, including four as 2IC to Rheinhardt in Alpha team, with multiple deployments to Iraq, Afghanistan, Libya, and the Horn of Africa. He's physically enormous and imposing, an habitué of the Unit weight room, and a devoted Harley rider. Last but not least, he's husband to Army Captain Kim Johnson (headquarters staff, 82nd Airborne), and father of two small, blonde, and angelic children.

"You okay, man?" Johnson says to Sultan. "No bullet holes? No propeller amputations?" In addition to being incoming team leader, due to Rheinhardt's retirement, BJ is also the squad's most trained-up combat medic. As Javier once put it, if you got shot, you'd rather have BJ working on you than your GP – he can do it under fire, or while wounded himself. Plus he knows a lot more about trauma care for blast and bullet wounds.

From Sultan's other side, Javier helps the newcomer with his buckles. Staff Sergeant Javier Roque is the son of Mexican immigrants who entered the U.S. as migrant laborers. He enlisted at 18, earning his citizenship by serving in uniform and under fire in Afghanistan, taking his oath of citizenship at a ceremony at Bagram Air Base. An assaulter with additional expertise in comms and tech, Javier is the most junior member of the team. He's also primary handler for the dog, Mac, having gone with him through most of the top military K-9 schools, as well as the Unit's own Combat Assault Dog program.

"Dr. Sultan," Javier says, unstrapping the older man. He checks his watch and glances out the porthole. "Welcome to Free Iraq." Sultan permits himself a weary smile. He has been kept under detention by the Iranian regime since the 2009 post-election uprising. He leans in closer to Javier, to make himself heard above the engine roar.

"I don't understand how we're able to just fly out of Iranian airspace like this…"

Javier smiles, a boyish grin. "Basically the same way the Israelis were able to fly straight in and bomb the Syrian nuclear reactor in 2007. We own their air defense radar."

Javier looks to BJ, who is finishing his medical once-over. "Go ahead. I think once it's been in *Newsweek*, it's not really classified anymore."

Javier explains. "Air Force program called Big Safari. It sends network packets in on their air defense radar beams, hacking and taking control of the systems. After that, we can insert misleading data, false positives, or ghosts. We can even take control of the radar dishes themselves, steering them away from friendly aircraft."

Azad looks awed. "*Ma'shallah*," he says.

"Yes, sir," Javier agrees. "What wonders God hath wrought."

"But won't there be an international incident? With the men you shot, and the explosions?"

"What? You mean from our raid on the mullahs' nuclear weaponization facility?"

"Yes."

"I suppose there might be... if the mullahs *had* any such weaponization work going on."

"*If* they had?"

"Yes. As you will know, theirs is solely a peaceful nuclear energy program."

"I see your point," says Sultan. "They can't protest a raid on a program they deny having."

"*Ojala*, Dr. Sultan. God willing."

"Yes. *Inshallah.*"

The third member of the team finishes a secure sat-phone call with the Unit TOC, then returns to the rear of the plane and pins Sultan with her large, luminous eyes. Sergeant First Class Aaliyah Khamsi fled the civil war in her native Somalia at age 16, seeking asylum in the U.S. She then put herself through Cal Berkeley, earning a degree in political science. In the Army, she completed the rotary wing aviator course, later qualifying to fly Apache helicopters in combat. She was shot down twice, once in Iraq and once in Afghanistan, walking away both times. Now she serves as one of the Unit's top snipers, also occasionally flying Alpha team away from death's door in small planes and helos.

"Dr. Azad," she shouts over the engine roar. "How are your connections with the dissidents these days?"

Azad nods in answer. "Pretty good. I was able to stay in touch with the movement online, even after they locked me up."

Ali smiles. "Well, you're a free man now. Your family will be very glad to see you."

The plane begins its approach to Kut Airbase in western Iraq. From there, they will cross-load to a faster bird, then fly non-stop back to Pope Air Force Base (AFB) in North Carolina. And then back to "the Ranch" – their usual term of affection for the sprawling Delta compound at Fort Bragg.

"Tell it to me again," says Havering. He stretches his long legs out beneath his desk, and holds a lit cigar beside a wheezing desktop air filter. "Help me understand."

"You already understand," says Rheinhardt, twirling his own cigar, unlit. "You just pretend you don't."

"Yeah. Hardly needs saying, I suppose. Twenty-two years in. Fifteen in the Unit. You've by God done your bit. Plus the next dozen guys' bits."

"It's just my time," Rheinhardt says. "I'm going to be forty next month. I've brought back a lot more people than I've gotten killed. Time to call it a day. Before the Black Chinook comes for me." The Black Chinook is a special operations legend, a mythical helicopter that descends to whisk you away when you've screwed up too badly. It says your services are no longer required by the SOF community.

"Plus," Havering says, "you're still breathing. That's a definite plus."

"True." Rheinhardt pauses, his smile fading. "Also, I don't know... maybe I've done all the killing I can do, and still get to look myself in the face every morning."

Havering nods, but frowns. "You don't need me to remind you we count success in live hostages and civilians, not dead terrorists. But I might suggest you try to count the number of innocent people who are still sucking oxygen, solely because you've put your ass on the line every day for

25

years. Your job has most assuredly been that of *saving* lives. And you hold your head up every day God gives you, Eric."

Rheinhardt nods once. "I suppose. But eventually it all starts to feel like shoveling seaweed against the tide. And the bad guys always just flood back in again."

"You've made a difference, believe me. But it's time to lay down your burdens. Let someone else fight the war for a while."

"Yeah. The rest of my war will be in a chair."

"Tell me about your Pentagon posting," Havering says.

"Adviser to the Assistant SecDef for Special Operations and Low Intensity Conflict."

"And, as such, liaison to…"

Rheinhardt shifts in his chair and looks slightly defensive. "Liaison to a number of allied spec-ops organizations."

Havering smiles. "One of them being the Israeli Special Operations Directorate. Where a certain lady friend of yours happens to be employed."

Rheinhardt presses his lips together. "I'm on terms with some of their people. That's part of how I landed the job. The working relationships."

"Fair enough," Havering says. "Fair enough. I hope you get to have many very fulfilling professional interactions in your new role."

Rheinhardt stands. "Colonel. It's been an honor to serve under you."

Havering stands and grasps his hand. "The honor is utterly mine. Commanding men like you has been the great honor of my life. Godspeed, Sergeant Major."

Havering salutes first.

Rheinhardt returns it, turns on his heel, and walks out the door.

Inside the small Alpha team ready room, three tired and dirty commandos stand or sit, peeling off weapons, ammo, gear, and dirty clothing. Already unburdened of his body armor and headset on the plane, Mac the beagle lies off to the side with his head on his paws.

Johnson, Javier, and Ali each have their own yawning weapons and gear lockers. After a mission, but before an operator does anything else, he re-arms: fresh batteries go in NVGs and gun sights; weapons are cleaned with solvent and high-pressure air, followed by a light coat of oil; team radios are charged; rifle and pistol magazines reloaded; ammo and grenade pouches refilled. Once that's done, and the operator is ready to go out again on the usual moment's notice, he can see to himself.

A Delta operator can represent anywhere from a half million to upwards of ten million dollars in training, depending on stage of career. And that's aside from the wealth of operational experience had by veterans. So, because their time is so incredibly valuable, operators get a lot of support and outsourced services. But weapons maintenance isn't one of them. Everyone from the newest recruit out of the Operator Training Course (OTC) to the Unit commander cleans his own weapons. Some things you do for yourself.

With their kit squared away, the three operators nod their goodbyes and head in separate directions. They've got a couple of hours to themselves before their next assignment, an after-action briefing on the mission just completed. After that, the new workday begins. In theory, they were able to sleep on the plane.

* * *

Javier heads out of the main building complex, walking Mac over to the small kennel facility. There, he will be fed, watered, and washed, as well as provided with any other care he needs. Then he'll rack out for a while. Javier will come and get him the next time he's off duty, or assigned to tasks where Mac can hang out.

"See you, buddy," he says, scruffing the dog's head. Mac trots through the doggie door.

Javier reverses course, swings by the cafeteria for breakfast in a box, then heads home to the Bachelor Operator Quarters. After swiping himself into his small suite, he strips and showers off nine time zones' worth of grime. He towels off, puts on sweats, takes a quick look at e-mail – and then plops down on the bed and starts eating and making phone calls. First, always, are his parents. They still live in Midland Texas. And they will still be up well before sunrise.

"*Hola, mama. Bien, bien, bien. Totalmente seguro, por supuesto.*" He spends a lot of time reassuring her that he's safe. He listens to her warm and comforting chatter, while stretching out and into his bed, enjoying both its softness and cleanness. He also savors the delicious feeling of being out of danger, which never loses its charm, however many missions a soldier returns from.

"*¿Y cómo está mi padre?*"

Javier listens to the news, unwraps his warm food, and smiles with his dark eyes. As a background task, he also tries to decide if he has the time and energy for a workout and run before the morning briefing.

* * *

Uncle BJ hits the weight room straight away. He's found that if you start letting anything get in the way of your workouts, then everything gets in the way of your workouts. And it is understood to be the personal responsibility of everyone in the Unit to maintain a razor edge of physical fitness. At their level, it's a lot like being a professional athlete. But with no off-season.

After lifting, he showers and changes, goes out to the parking lot, hops on his bike (a Harley-Davidson Fat Boy cruiser, complete with leather bags and fringe) and drives home through the thin early-morning light. Home is a three-bedroom, two-story house in the small town of Southern Pines, about six miles from base.

He pulls in the driveway, lets himself quietly in, and finds Kim already up making breakfast in the kitchen. She never knows when he'll be back. So she always cooks for four.

"Hey, baby," he says, wrapping his arms around her from behind, as she flips French toast.

"Hello, beau," she says back, reaching behind them both and scratching the back of his head. "Welcome home. Can you do the school run this afternoon? Captain Johnson's got a CAPEX today that is *fore-ordained* to run late." A CAPEX is a "capabilities exercise," a dog and pony show put on for senior brass or politicians. And Captain Johnson is her, BJ's wife. She finds outranking her husband to occasionally be useful.

"No problem," he says, nuzzling her hair.

He kisses her cheek, then pulls away. She knows where he's going, as his routine never changes. He pushes silently into one bedroom, and then the other, standing and watching his children, first Nathan (eight) and Marissa (eleven), as they sleep.

The peace in there, the dimness, and the slight and steady rising of their breathing, is like nothing else for him. It makes everything he does make sense. And it allows him to explain to himself why he does what he does, even though it entails such risk and sacrifice.

To make a better world for them.

* * *

Ali ends up only a couple of doors down from Javier, but gets there quicker without the doggie detour. After showering, she puts on a tan t-shirt underneath ACUs, with her rank insignia on a Velcro patch in the center of her chest.

Like all other Delta operators, Ali has total latitude with regard to what she wears. She's also free to flout the Army's general grooming standards, not least because operators frequently work undercover, where it's helpful not to look like GI Joe (or Jane). Also, in an outfit devoted to unconventional warfare, you tend to get a high proportion of unconventional people. Finally, with so many life-and-death tasks, working against such steep odds, Mickey Mouse army crap is just not something they make a lot of time for.

But here's the thing. Ali *likes* the uniform. She had a hell of a long way to come, and a lot to fight through, to earn the right to wear it.

Born into a traditional Muslim family in Hargeisa, Somalia's second city, young Aaliyah was raised to be obedient, to be modest, and to study the Koran. But her grandmother was non-traditional and, after the death of Ali's mother, sent the girl to a secular school, going against the wishes of her father. Here her natural intelligence and curiosity were given free rein, and she learned English and French (on top of Somali and Arabic) and began reading widely and voraciously.

When she was 16, her father decided she'd had more than enough of education and literature, and arranged a marriage for her to a cousin in Toronto, whom she had never met. He put her on a plane, which unfortunately for him connected through New York. Ali got off the flight, swallowed her fear, committed herself to leaving behind everything she'd ever known, and marched up to passport control and requested political asylum.

The asylum application process lasted a year, during which she hopped a bus going west. She passed through twelve U.S. states, gawking at the immense space, the cleanliness and good order, and the palpable freedom. She hopped off again when she hit the San Francisco Bay. Within days, she had work as a translator at a shelter for abused women (many of whom only spoke Arabic, and a few who spoke Somali). Within two years, she had earned a spot to study at the University of California at Berkeley, majoring in political science.

There, she took up hiking, rock climbing, and target shooting, all of which she excelled at. It was these physical pursuits, plus her continuing desire to learn and achieve, that first led her to consider a military career. But there was something else – a growing sense that she owed something to her adopted country, which had taken her in and saved her from a life of subservience. And a feeling that she had some debt to the world, to try and make these blessings possible for others.

A few days after graduation she swore her oath of enlistment. After Basic Training, she was accepted into Army Helicopter Flight Training, where she finished so high in her class that she was invited out to selection for the Apache.

The Apache helicopter gunship, with its 30mm electric cannon (slaved to the pilot's retina), pods of anti-personnel rockets, and laser-guided Hellfire missiles, is perhaps the deadliest fighting machine in the world. "Riding the dragon," as Apache pilots call it, requires simultaneously dealing with the flight instruments, four different radio frequencies, the weapons-targeting computers, the defensive suite's threat reports, and the cameras and radar. Taking an Apache into battle has been described as "like playing an XBox, a PlayStation, and a chess Grand Master simultaneously – whilst riding Disneyworld's biggest roller coaster."

Ali nailed it, finishing near the top of her class yet again. She went on to serve both in Afghanistan and Iraq, surviving two shootdowns while heavily engaged, in both cases bringing the bird down via auto-rotation to a more or less controlled crash.

When the Special Operations Command needed a female, Somali-speaking soldier for a high-risk mission in the

Horn of Africa, she volunteered – in exchange for a guaranteed spot in Delta Selection. The Army made the deal, not thinking she had a prayer of completing the course, never mind being selected. But they obviously hadn't studied her docket very well – she'd never failed at anything. And so she became the first woman ever to complete the world's most grueling (and lowest pass rate) military assessment and selection process.

And the first woman Delta operator. Ever.

So wearing the uniform has nothing to do with the fact that her briefing today is for a whole room full of very senior people. Delta operators are invariably as smart and well spoken as they are deadly, and more than capable of interacting with people at any level. No, the uniform simply symbolizes for her how much she has made of her life, and how far she has come.

After brushing it down carefully she sits at her laptop to review her after-action report, which she wrote in the air, and which will form the basis of her briefing. She also has no one to call on the phone this morning. Her father will not speak to her, and her sister is not allowed to. Her grandmother was buried years ago.

And Ali was not invited to the funeral.

Rheinhardt zips closed his last duffel bag. Everything else is already boxed up in the back of the truck. Not much to start with, even after cleaning out the one-bedroom apartment. The divorce, two years earlier, had him traveling light again. Since then, he's stayed deployed so much he never really did settle into the new place.

Divorce rates in the Unit remain stratospheric, despite all the marriage counseling and family services the Army throws at them. It's probably a result of the surprise alerts, the deployments on 60 minutes' notice, and missions that can go on for months – with the end date rarely announced. Guys would finally show up at home again, only able to say, "Where have I been? Someplace hot. What's for dinner?"

Rheinhardt slings his bag and pulls the door closed behind him, not bothering to lock it.

Outside, the day is gray and drizzly. Climbing into the truck, his mood wistful, he consoles himself by thinking that at least the hardest part is over: driving off the Delta compound for the last time. Passing the gate, surrendering his security badge to the unsmiling MP, then watching the buildings disappear into the pine trees in his rearview mirror, was one of the hardest things he ever did.

He's still a soldier. But no longer an operator. Back in the Big Green Army. Leaving his home of a decade and a half. And his truest family – his brother operators.

* * *

But he does now have one last covert op to execute.

Backing out of his driveway, he spins the wheel and turns onto a narrow two-laner snaking through the Carolina pine forests. And without any GPS devices, or map and compass, or any of his commando tracking skills, he sets off on a heading toward… his ex-wife's house.

This morning he's got a hostage to rescue: a very nice hound dog named George, whom Rheinhardt lost in the divorce. He'd probably feel a lot worse about the dognapping – if his wife hadn't left him while he was on an overseas deployment, and then turned up with a new boyfriend about .005 seconds afterward. In any case, George, whom Rheinhardt feels very sure loves him more, is about to be liberated from his long captivity.

"Ops, this is Little Bo Peep, over."

Rheinhardt is now parked in the rain at the end of another residential street. He's only talking on his cell phone, to a buddy back at the Ops desk. But radio protocol is a hard habit to shake.

"Bo Peep, Ops. Send it, over."

"I'm at the staging point for Op Precious Pooch. Interrogative: is enemy pax in target structure?"

His buddy has already been briefed on the mission. Basically, he's tasked a high-altitude UAV to track the ex-Mrs. Rheinhardt's movements through the afternoon.

"Bo Peep, Ops. That's negative. Enemy pax is Oscar Mike." On the move, i.e. not home. *"Target vehicle is now pulling into, uh, Safeway. Seems to be a grocery mission. How copy?"*

"Bo Peep copies all. Interrogative: have you got eyes on the PC? Over."

35

"That's affirmative, Bo. George is in the doghouse."

Rheinhardt adjusts the windshield wipers to clear the drizzle. He starts the engine, reverses fifty meters down the road, then cuts the wheel and backs into a driveway. He exits the vehicle, trots around the side of the one-story stucco ranch house, and approaches a tall wooden slat fence. With a hand-held mechanical breaching tool, he removes the gate from its hinges, then whistles once for George.

The dog sticks his sad brown-and-white face out of a paneled doghouse – then, spotting Rheinhardt, gallops joyously out of the yard and straight into the passenger side of the truck. Rheinhardt presses the door closed behind him, then spares a couple of seconds to rub George's lovely, floppy face.

"Hey there, old man. Ready for a road trip?"

George barks once, happily. And with that, they peel out of the driveway, then race out of the neighborhood through the drizzle. Free and clear.

"Ops, Bo Peep. I have the PC and am mission complete, over."

"Bo Peep, Ops. Roger that. Great job." Rheinhardt imagines the voice on the other end of the channel getting a little misty now, like the air around the pine trees. *"You go well, Bo. And take care of yourself. Molon labe, brother."*

"Molon labe" is the motto of his squadron. At Thermopylae, when Xerxes II told the 300 Spartan warriors to lay down their weapons, this was what King Leonidas said in reply: "Come and get them."

"Roger that, Ops. Little Bo Peep... out."

And after that there was only the hiss of the tires on the wet road going north.

Aaliyah Khamsi stands at the front of the arena-style conference room.

The lights in the room glow dimly and a projection of a computer screen fills the front wall. Most of the thirty seats are taken by Alpha team (minus Rheinhardt), Colonel Havering, the Unit intel and ops officers, and a handful of representatives from other three-letter agencies (TLAs) up and around the national command authority (NCA) and the intelligence community. Azad Sultan sits in the front row. Ali flashes her laser pointer onto his bald head.

"I think you all know Dr. Sultan, at least by reputation. Nuclear physicist, PhD from Imperial College London, senior scientist in the Iranian nuclear program. However, when he was caught taking to the streets during the 2009 protests, the mullahs locked him up in a room and threw away the room. Or, rather, since he's too valuable for that, they locked him in a room next door to his lab, and forced him to continue working.

"Since then, he's been heroically sandbagging. That is, doing as little productive work as possible, while maintaining his ties to the underground dissident movement, and carefully feeding us information about the state of their nuclear program."

A hand goes up in the audience, attached to one of the TLA guys. Ali laser-points it.

"So how come he's sitting here now?"

"We had reason to believe they were on the verge of killing him, or torturing him, or both. So we went in yesterday to extract him."

"And where does that leave us fixed for HUMINT inside the Iranian nuke program?"

Ali nods. "Not great. But the same op did allow us to install significant signals intelligence assets in the heart of their Chalus facility. We're going to give you a demo of those today." Ali nods to a uniformed, dark-haired, somewhat pale, and lanky young man seated just in front of her, hunched intently over a laptop.

The young man is Warrant Officer One (WO1) Mike Brown. He was recruited into the Delta Signals and Support Squadron directly from the Department of Homeland Security (DHS) a year earlier. As a civilian DHS employee, he had been posted onto Rheinhardt's Alpha team to help take down a high-tech Islamist terror cell. They were so impressed with Brown's work and his skills that they invited him to stay.

Despite the initial gig very nearly getting him killed in several fascinating ways, Mike now works his high-tech magic full-time in Delta's sprawling computer and network facilities. He's also been semi-attached to Alpha team, since their technical genius team member, Tim McDonough, died in the same campaign.

* * *

"As you'll know," says Mike, clearing his throat quietly, "in 2010, the Stuxnet virus attacked computer networks at Iran's nuclear enrichment facilities in Natanz and at their Bushehr reactor. The damage was so severe they had to literally throw away most of their computers. Stuxnet is fiendishly hard to clear up once it's gotten infested, and in the end they also had to rebuild their centrifuges and buy a new turbine. This incursion set their nuclear program back at least two years, maybe as much as four.

"And a virtual attack like that one is every bit as effective as a military strike, and a whole lot less messy. Not to mention less likely to get condemned on the floor of the U.N. General Assembly. So, whoever pulled that off, it was a pretty good job."

Someone speaks up from the floor. "Who *did* pull that off?"

"Whoever. The Israelis. Us. Us working with the Israelis. Hard to say."

"I get it," the man says.

Mike continues. "But the problem with such an attack, especially a really successful one, is that they hunker down against the next one. Basically, at this point, all of the systems in or near their nuclear program are air-gapped. No connections to outside networks, no way to get in over the wire. So we had to go there physically this time. But our new exploit, which is even more advanced than the last one, should have them pulling out their hair and getting nothing done for at least another two years." He looks over at Sultan. "Maybe enough time for the Iranian people to retake their country."

Mike flips through command-line windows onscreen. "Basically, we've breached the network and implanted code that will monitor all network traffic going in or out, silently send the results back to us, and propagate itself out to other machines and networks that connect to the first one. It vacuums up documents, monitors keystrokes, takes screenshots, and records audio. It's got code to conceal itself, plus its own onboard anti-virus software to clear out any competition."

Another one of the TLA guys raises his hand. He wears a jacket with leather elbow patches, a square-end knit tie, and corduroy pants. He looks like a high school chemistry teacher.

"If their network's air-gapped," he says, "and you had to go onsite to get into it... then how are you getting data back out again?"

"That's classified," Mike says. "Suffice it to say, our outgoing comms are LPI – 'low probability of intercept'."

"Yeah, I know what LPI means, Scooter."

Mike didn't know, but now guesses, that the man works for the NSA. He doesn't respond to this, but just flips to a video window.

"We've also got control of nearly two dozen onboard webcams and microphones. These provide us with real-time viewing and listening into the labs, barracks, and administrative areas." On the screen, a woman in a white coat types and sips coffee in fish-eye view. Just as Mike finishes speaking, she disappears – the screen goes black.

"Hmm." Mike flips windows. Also black. A third is black. "Uh huh. A little technical difficulty." He looks uneasy, but goes on.

"We've also got malevolent code, a logic bomb contained as the payload of a second virus. With this, we can start doing damage in small increments, degrading their efforts a bit at a time, but never enough that they start ripping the guts out looking for the source. For instance, this PC will start hard-rebooting three times a week, at varying intervals. It begins… now."

A Windows desktop appears onscreen. Mike types in a terminal window below, then leans forward, squinting. Nothing happens. He types the same command again, then a third time. Nothing. Silence fills the room.

Finally, Havering stands. "End briefing. Thank you all for coming." He descends the aisle to Ali. "Screw the wrong goat there, Sergeant?"

Ali looks down to where Mike is still typing and flipping windows. "Perhaps this one didn't go as brilliantly as we thought. Well, at least Eric isn't here to take the beatdown for it."

Mike stands and turns to them. "Rheinhardt's gone? He didn't even say goodbye."

Havering stares at the younger man, unamused. "This is the Unit, son. We don't do goodbyes. Now get your ass back on into your Matrix there and figure out what went wrong. Yer makin' me look bad here."

Mike salutes, scoops up his laptop, and hoofs it out.

"This is you." The civilian staffer holds open the door for Rheinhardt. She's mid-twenties, pretty, well-spoken, and perfectly turned out. Georgetown grad, Rheinhardt figures. She leads him into the private office.

His office. He quickly notes an actual, traditional darkwood desk. Plus a window, with classy drapes. The view is only of an interior courtyard, one of the many that separate the rings of the enormous structure. Still, it's natural light. Not bad, considering the Pentagon is the world's largest office building, with 6.5 million square feet, and 17 miles of corridors.

The young woman gestures at the desk and Rheinhardt sits. From this vantage, he can see a large cabinet in the back of the room. It holds a flat screen with video camera on top.

"That's your telepresence unit," she says. "You can control it from the desk console here. The directory is pre-loaded with connections to your opposite numbers in every special operations unit in your area of responsibility, which is Central Command." She smiles. "But I'm told you're career Army. Which means you'll already be acronym immunized. So that would be 'every SOF oppo in your AOR, CENTCOM'."

Rheinhardt smiles back. "Yes, ma'am. So it's your basic Charlie Foxtrot."

She laughs. "Yes, it is." She pauses before going on. "Vic is going to meet you here in ten."

Rheinhardt's eyebrows rise slightly.

"He's not one for putting things off. And it's generally first names around here."

"Okay, then."

"Don't sweat this one too much. It will be just a quick greet and gab. We'll be bringing you up to speed in various directions over the next few weeks – briefings, introductions, tours, welcome packs. Lots more briefings. Do you need anything else for the moment?"

"… Um, where's the latrine?"

Her smile makes a return appearance. "Just left down the hall. And I'm just down the hall as well, if you need me for anything."

* * *

Rheinhardt allows himself to exhale after she exits, and has another look around. The natural light, from a warm spring Virginia morning, really is pretty. And the air smells very clean. He mentally contrasts this with his old Squadron ready room, never mind the Unit gym locker rooms. He supposes he's moving up in the world.

Though "Vic" seemed an oddly casual way of referring to his new boss, Victor Mitchell, Assistant Secretary of Defense for Special Operations and Low Intensity Conflict. As such, the man reports directly into the SecDef himself, with responsibility for counter-terrorism strategy and operational deployment of all U.S. special operations forces.

Which includes pretty much everyone Rheinhardt has ever served with.

Even more dauntingly, Mitchell is a legend himself in the spec-ops community. He served in Army Special Forces (the Green Berets), first as an NCO and later as an officer. After he left the Army, the CIA recruited him in as a paramilitary officer, putting him in their elite Special Activities Division (SAD). While in Delta, Rheinhardt did significant work, both training and operational, with SAD. He knows firsthand that they are top-drawer. So, Mitchell has definitely earned the right to make life-and-death decisions about when and how to send the nation's elite soldiers into harm's way. Or, more often, straight down harm's throat.

The door knocks, not gently.

"Sergeant Major," Mitchell says, striding in with a full head of steam, his hand extended. "Welcome to Fort Fumble – where general staff and civilian DoD employees have been working overtime to make your life difficult for twenty-two years and counting."

Rheinhardt stands and takes the man's hand. "Oh, I'm pretty sure the enemy's caused one or two of my problems along the way."

"Fair enough." Both men sit. Mitchell is fifty-ish, thinning brown hair, oval glasses, easy smile. "You know what, since I've been in this job, about seven years now, I've had access to virtually all of your mission profiles and after-action reports. I even read one or two of them."

"Nice to know someone has. It was a lot of paperwork."

"Some outstanding accomplishments in there. More than outstanding. Superhero stuff."

Rheinhardt shifts slightly. "You've been operational. You know how it is. You get it done."

Mitchell shakes his head. "Did you really engage and defeat a half-dozen hardened Chechen AQ fighters in indoors CQB? Using only your side arm? And with your tibia sticking through your leg?"

Rheinhardt looks down. "I had help."

"From eight hundred yards out! What about the leg – and the pistol?"

"I had expended all the ordnance for my primary weapon. It had been kind of a long day. And the leg wasn't nearly as bad as it sounds."

Mitchell leans forward. "I could talk about that kind of stuff all day, believe me. But there's never any time. We'll talk again soon. And it'll have to be soon, because we're planning to get you in the air, and keep you there. The TP's good, but not enough."

"Couldn't be more travel than my last job."

"Good point. Okay. Enough for today. Welcome to the team."

They both stand.

"Captain," Rheinhardt says.

"No, I'm just Vic now." Exiting, over his shoulder, Mitchell adds, "You have a good one."

Clearly the man knew his Delta lore. "Have a good one" has been the folksy, signature Delta parting, ever since the founding days.

* * *

Rheinhardt drops back into his chair. His eye is drawn to the telepresence control console.

Curious, he turns it on and calls up the directory. Sure enough, there's a listing for "IDF SOF Directorate, Sirkin Ops Center, Israel."

He hovers his pointer over the "Call" button.

What the hell? he thinks. *Might as well range the weapon, before I need to use it in anger...*

Havering, Ali, Javier, and Johnson converge on the Squadron Ops Room after Mike texts them. A smaller and less high-tech facility than the TOC, the Ops Room is used for Squadron-level operational activities, which are usually, but not always, less time- and mission-critical.

Mike sits at a station in the corner with his laptop.

"Brown," Havering says, quick-marching across the room. "Put us in the picture."

"Colonel," he says, nodding to the rest of Alpha. "My gut tells me we've been counter-hacked. That's what it feels like."

"What's your evidence?"

"My evidence is there's no evidence."

Havering sighs. "Okay. Break that down for me."

Mike flips through a series of windows onscreen.

"I've pulled and scoured every system logfile on this machine, the one Ali got us into. It was the initial vector of our infection." He scrolls through a few screens of standard syslog entries: system events, user logons, programs starting and stopping. "I've also pulled ghost versions of these from unwritten-over sectors of the drive."

"What are we looking at?" Havering says, squinting at the screen as if it were in fact the Matrix. He watches a few screens go by.

"Nothing," Mike says. "No evidence of anything clever being done on this machine since we breached it. More importantly, there's no evidence of the *really* clever stuff that would be needed to cover up their original cleverness. No tracks. And no track covering. Totally clean."

"And I'm guessing," says Havering, exhaling tiredly, "there's no chance that means nothing actually *was* done."

"No. Because they completely dumped us."

"What does that mean?" says BJ, muscling in for a closer look.

"All our surveillance, all our intrusive code. Gone. We're only looking at these forensics because I grabbed them before they kicked us to the curb. As of two hours ago, we're totally locked out of the Iranian systems at Chalus."

Ali taps a pen on the desk. "I thought the Iranians didn't have the kind of hacking talent – or cyberwar capability – to defeat our tech in this area?"

"They don't," Mike says. "Or didn't."

"Who, then?"

"I can't know for sure," Mike says. "But they not only detected and defeated our intrusion, but they left zero footprint in doing it. And that itself is a pretty clear footprint: I think it can only be the Russians, the Israelis, or the Chinese. Obviously, the Israelis are out. And by Russians, I mean either the military or the Russian mob. But to the best of my knowledge, those three are the only nations with cyberwar units advanced enough to beat us this badly, this quickly."

By moving from DHS to the Army's Joint Special Operations Command (JSOC, Delta's parent unit), Mike has essentially transferred from defensive to offensive cyberwar ops. The change seems to suit him. It's always easier – plus, Mike would say, more fun and less stressful – to attack than to defend. But only when you win.

Havering curses, not quite under his breath. "Okay. So we got out-geeked. Maybe the Iranians brought in some sharpshooters to help to secure their systems. God knows they've been cozy enough with both Putin and the Chinese Politburo these last few years. Nuclear reactor deals. Friendly votes, and timely abstentions, in the Security Council."

"Yes, sir," Mike says. "Russian FAPSI, their equivalent to our NSA, runs the world's largest and best hacker school in the south of Russia. And the Chinese military's cyberwar units have been good enough to hack the Pentagon, Lockheed Martin, and Google. They've verifiably broken into the personal workstations of German Chancellor Angela Merkel and SecDef Gates."

"Ballsy sons of bitches."

"Yes, sir. They're totally shameless. And the scale of their industrial espionage is epic. But the Russians, in the opinion of this soldier, have better skills."

"Any way to figure out which one we're facing?"

"Negative. Not at this time."

At DHS, Mike had to learn some key skills for operating in the bureaucracy of the federal government, such as extemporization, hedging, and glad-handing. But he's had to unlearn all of them here. In Delta, big-boy and no-bullshit rules apply at all times. Everything is reality-based. The stakes are too high, the operational challenges too big, and the margins between success and failure almost always too thin.

Havering takes this all in. "Okay. Got anything else to go on?"

"Yes, sir, one other clue. But I'm afraid you're going to like it even less."

Havering plops himself down in a chair, looking resigned.

"Well," he says tiredly, "we're not making Corn Flakes here."

Another old Unit catchphrase – for when things get difficult or complicated.

Which is almost all of the time.

Israel Defense Forces (IDF) Major Chaya Akhilov looks up over the piles of virtual paperwork cascading into her inbox. She tries to focus on the room. The young orderly is still standing there, looking at her expectantly. "Will there be anything else, Major?"

"No. Thank you, Private."

"And ma'am?"

Akhilov pauses to pull a band around her hair, which is wildly curly and shoulder length, the color of the desert at dusk. "Yes?"

"It's great to have you back, Chaya. Though I'm sorry your leave got cut short."

"Thanks, Rachel. This place is starting to feel more like home than the farm. Which I suppose is not so bad."

The orderly exits and Chaya collapses back into her chair, just staring at the door for a few seconds. Her wide and angular cheekbones, thin and sharply set mouth, and astonishingly deep green eyes, all makeup-less, are both beautiful and deadly serious.

She allows herself one mournful sigh before getting back to work. She is supposed to be on leave this week, helping back at home with the barley harvest. But flexibility is the first requirement of a military officer in Israel.

Another day, another existential crisis.

As of yesterday, Israel's most dangerous and bellicose enemy in the region, the theocratic regime in Iran, has edged closer to their goal of developing nuclear weapons. Or, rather, they have progressed more quickly than predicted, based on latest and best intel.

But scientific advance is a very tough thing to project, particularly inside of a paranoid police state. Though, there could be little doubt about the Iranian mullahs' end goal.

Nor, if one listened to the words that came out of their mouths, could there be much doubt about what they intended to do with nuclear weapons once they got them. Public statements that "Israel must be wiped off the map" and "Israel is a rotten, dried tree that will be annihilated in one storm" had become so commonplace as to draw no notice – particularly in the halls of the UN, where threats to nuke a member state evidently could be shrugged off.

The Israelis, and the IDF, and particularly their Special Operations Directorate, definitely did not have the luxury of ignoring such threats of a second, nuclear, holocaust. They had to plan for it.

And they had somehow to avert it.

And so here sits Chaya Akhilov, back on station, during what was to be her annual leave. But she can't really complain. Not when every Israeli is required to serve in the military for two to three years, from age 18. And not when so many others have paid such higher prices.

And also, in fairness, Chaya tries to remember, it is only fifty minutes by car to the base from her home. No place in tiny Israel is very far from any other. When off base, Chaya lives on a kibbutz in the Jordan Rift Valley, which has also been her family home ever since her great-grandparents emerged out of the rubble of the Holocaust in Europe. Like many others, they made the Aliyah (or "ascent") back to the homeland, both ancient and new, of the Jews.

They were Belorussians, who had survived the Nazi assault from Poland, as well as the subsequent methodical extermination, by fleeing into the forests. Thousands of the Jews of Belarus did the same. They lived in the forest camps for three years and served with the Jewish partisan forces. Chaya's great-grandfather fought in hit-and-run actions against the Nazis, while her great-grandmother cooked, sewed, repaired weapons, and otherwise tried to live up to the gift of one more day of life and freedom.

When the war ended, the Akhilovs were two of 250,000 displaced Jewish survivors who sought a new beginning in their historical homeland. They eventually settled in the brand-new Kibbutz Gezer, which had been carved out of the hard earth of the desert. Almost immediately, they had to fight again for their survival, in Israel's War of Independence. This was when the Arabs rejected the UN partition of Palestine – and the infant state of Israel was set upon by five Arab armies on the very day after its founding, in a war of attempted annihilation.

The outmanned and heavily outgunned Jews, many of them Holocaust survivors and WWII veterans, force-marched all night to protect their scattered and beleaguered settlements. Somehow, they successfully defended their tiny patch of land.

And the Jews had a state again – for the first time in 2,000 years.

The Akhilovs, Chaya's great-grandparents and their descendents, had stayed, worked the land, and built a life and a state. But the settlement was no longer called Kibbutz Gezer.

In 2006, it had been re-named Kibbutz Natasha.

Yes, Chaya's whole community, her whole world really, had been re-named for her fallen sister, the hero. Forgetting and moving on became that much harder for her after that. But, then again, Natasha had been killed in the largest single-day loss for special forces in IDF history – that terrible night in western Iraq. So nobody was forgetting very quickly.

And Jews have long memories. Sometimes, their history has been all they have.

Chaya glances from her screen down to the photo of Natasha on her desk. When that was taken, her sister was the same age Chaya is now. When Natasha died, Chaya was at the end of her original two-year mandatory service. She had never intended to make a career of the military. But, surprising every-one, including herself, she re-upped the same week as the funeral.

Somehow walking away didn't feel right.

Two years afterward, she got the nod to attend Selection camp for Sayeret Matkal – the IDF's most elite special forces unit, and Natasha's old outfit. Its specialties are counter-ter-rorism, deep reconnaissance, and intelligence gathering. So, along with the shooters, assaulters, snipers, and undercover operatives, Sayeret makes use of a lot of headquarters, intel, and other desk staff. Chaya's is nominally a desk job. But, then again, virtually everyone in Israel has to be ready at a moment's notice to grab a rifle and rush to defend Eretz Yisrael.

So Chaya's is a desk job, and it is not.

* * *

Her commander, Lt. Colonel Eshel, sticks his head through the plane of her office door.

"You have seen the new air strike mission profiles?"

The planning and ops staffs have had to put together new contingency planning, based on updated estimates of when the Iranians would go nuclear. As soon as that happened, things were going to get seriously grim all around. There were no good military options – none without grave dangers. Which is one reason they have explored all possible non-military options. Including cyberwar.

"Yes, sir," Chaya says. "I'm reviewing them now."

"And the brief on your new Pentagon liaison?"

Chaya pauses fractionally. "That one, too."

"But you already know this man, do you not? Rheinhardt? Former Delta shooter?" Eshel doesn't wait for an answer, already withdrawing his head. "Oh, and welcome back."

Chaya doesn't bother thanking him. He's already gone.

* * *

Yes, Chaya does definitely know the man – U.S. Army Sergeant Major Eric Rheinhardt. They met a month after Natasha's death in Iraq. Officially, anyone lost on a Sayeret mission has died "in a training accident." No more can be said publicly about it.

But, bizarrely enough, this American senior non-com, who had been there when it happened, used his own personal leave to fly across the world and meet with Chaya. To tell her how bravely her sister had died – in this "training accident."

Of course, he couldn't tell her what had really happened. At the time, Chaya had barely been out of adolescence, and the physical presence of the American commando had been overpowering. He'd been kind, and extremely respectful. Still, she'd been intimidated.

In the years since, and since Chaya's assignment to Sayeret, her and Rheinhardt's paths have crossed several times again. Regular cross-training ops. Contingency and joint ops planning for terrorist atrocities across the Middle East. And, once or twice, an actual joint operational mission.

On these occasions, there had sometimes been chances for Chaya and Rheinhardt to speak. Even a few moments alone. Chaya had instinctively recoiled from any relationship beyond a strictly professional one. But special operations are pretty dramatic affairs – charged both physically and emotionally. It was hard always to keep recoiling.

In between, she had kept in touch with him through (secure) e-mail. And they had formed something of a bond, something like a connection.

Now he is back. In a role where his very job will be to deal with Chaya on a regular basis. And she guesses he will be visiting at a faster operational tempo than the previous rhythm of about once a year. She finds herself with conflicted feelings about this.

And no sooner has she thought of the devil than he is named out loud – almost.

"TP for you, ma'am." The orderly has reappeared in her doorway. Before she says it, Chaya somehow knows. "It's the Pentagon."

She rises and moves at a measured pace down the hall to Sayeret's telepresence room.

And what will you be wanting today, Sergeant Major…?

"Okay, give me the worse news," Havering says to Mike. "What are we looking at now?"

He and Alpha team lean in toward Mike's laptop, where he has brought up a video window.

"This is guncam footage from the SWORDS robot Rheinhardt operated in Chalus." He hits play on a video window, then drags the slider forward to where the Iranian soldiers show up in the truck. "Okay, what do you see?"

BJ snorts. "I see a bunch of straight-leg infantry getting lit up by the goddamned Terminator."

"Seriously," says Javier. "I think the war on terror effectively ended they day they put weapons systems on those things."

"Pipe down," Havering says. "I've seen all this. Rheinhardt engages the infantry, covers the team's withdrawal, then hits the kablooey switch."

"Correct," Mike says. "But that's in the night-vision view. Rheinhardt wasn't using it, but the infrared camera was still on – and spooling video to disk. Check this out." He switches windows and the scene goes from shadowy green-and-black, to puffy black-and-white. The white represents areas of higher heat.

The truck comes into view, its cab almost fuzzing out the screen with engine heat. Then the troops scramble off the back, each glowing brightly. Several are shot and fall, their

57

prone figures slowly dimming. The view pans back toward the escaping team. Mike stops the video.

"There. On top of the structure."

The others follow his finger. There's a small, irregular heat signature on the rooftop. Mike zooms in. Silhouetted against the heat blob is what looks like a rifle barrel.

"Shooter on the roof," BJ says. "He should have smoked us. Why didn't he take the shot?"

"Moreover," says Ali, "why didn't our overwatch spot him?"

Mike puts the two windows, night-vision and thermal, side by side. "Because he's almost totally invisible in night-vision." Mike pauses and looks up. "Is that normal?"

A short but spooked silence passes. Ali speaks up. "There are some IIR-treated dyes and camo patterns that are partially effective against NVGs. I expect this is a case of that, plus the guy just kept a low profile. Look how close he is to the roof. And motionless. He's also broken up his profile with a blanket or hood. Solid sniper tactics."

"So he's good," Javier says. "Quds Force, maybe?"

BJ shakes his head. "Maybe. But those guys are only Iran's 'special forces' in their own small minds."

Mike points to the infrared window again. "Okay. Now check the rifle. At first I thought it was just an AK." He zooms in tighter. "But now I think the barrel's too long and thin. And the magazine's too straight…"

BJ and Havering actually bump heads leaning in at it.

"Motherfucker," BJ says. "Sir." He rubs his head.

"We know what that is," Havering says.

BJ: "It's an M14."

Javier: "What kind of Iranian carries an M14?"

Ali: "Could just be aftermarket. They're readily available, and still a solid sniper platform."

Havering, clenching his jaw and shaking his head, says, "No. Show me the other thing again. Those logfiles. On the machine we got kicked off of." Mike pulls them up. "There was something… Down. More. More. There – stop. I saw it, but it didn't register."

Mike scans the line Havering's pointing at. "It's a user logon event. From today. Admin user h-underscore-rash. That mean something?"

Nobody says anything. Havering and BJ regard each other.

"Yeah," says Javier. "That mean something?"

Finally BJ speaks. "Okay, I'll bite. What the fuck is Rod Tucker doing in Iran?"

Now Ali and Javier exchange pretty clear *Holy shit* looks. They obviously know the name.

"Brown," Havering says. "Give us the room."

"Sir," says Mike, standing and clearing out. He's pretty accustomed to being left in the dark about certain things these days.

* * *

"Rod Tucker?" says Ali, arching her eyebrows. "As in 'Rod the God'?"

Havering squints at her. "What do you know about Rod Tucker?"

"Almost nothing," Ali says. "It was a topic you just didn't bring up with Eric."

"Scuttlebutt only," says Javier. "How he was team leader, complete and total asskicker, and troop sergeant major... then one day, he was just out, PNGed – and dishonorably discharged." To be PNGed in the Unit is to be made persona non grata. You don't get invited to the barbecues anymore. But dishonorable discharge is almost completely unheard of.

BJ leans back in his chair now, locking eyes with Havering.

"C'mon, Colonel. Let's not let ourselves get treed by a chihuahua here. Until we have some context, there's no way to know what's going on. Much less operationalize anything."

Havering pauses a beat, then speaks in a flat tone. "Sergeant... there would be absolutely *no way* to overstate how dangerous this man is. Whatever Tucker is doing in Iran, it's already a disaster. I think you yourself know him well enough to know that."

BJ considers this for a moment. "Yeah. It can't be good." He scratches up under his Harley-Davidson ball cap. "But I still wouldn't be too quick about connecting the dots until we've collected more than one or two dots."

"Fair enough," Havering says. "I suppose the next step is the intelligence community."

"So called."

"Yeah. But ring up Langley anyway, see if they have any clues for sale."

"Will do," BJ says. "You also want us to start working on some mission concepts?"

"Absolutely. Kill or capture. Plus recon options. Get with Will in the intel shack. He'll pull down the area studies, plus shelved target folders for sites in Iran. Get him to put together some initial target packets and map boards."

"Roger that, Colonel," BJ says. "Let's hope this one ends up just going back on the shelf."

Havering exhales heavily. "Yeah, let's hope like hell… But you know how it is. Hope in one hand, shit in the other, see which fills up first."

Javier and Ali rise as if to leave.

But BJ stays seated, and speaks again, stopping them. "There's one other thing," he says to Havering. "And I think you know what I'm thinking."

"Yeah," says Havering, looking like he'd hoped to avoid this. "Rheinhardt served with Tucker longer than anyone."

"And closer," BJ says.

"Not to mention he was with him at the very end. I suppose if anyone knows what Tucker is capable of, and what the goddamned hell he might be doing in Persia, it's Eric."

Havering exhales heavily and makes a decision. Turning to Ali and Javier, he says, "Okay, you two have new assignments, effective now. Fly to DC and report to the C Ring of the Pentagon, second floor. And you bring Sergeant Major Rheinhardt right back here again."

"Seriously?" Ali says.

"Jesus, Colonel," says Javier. "He probably hasn't even sat down yet."

"Good. Then he won't have got too comfortable. I'm going to write you up some talking points while you're in the air. Check mail for 'em."

"Can't we do a TP?" Ali says. "Or just pick up the phone?"

"No," Havering says, sounding tired. "He's got to look into your eyes. Both of you. That's the only thing that will get him back here now."

Ali inclines her head. "So, basically, you're using us to get him back because he loves us."

Havering puts his palm to his forehead, but doesn't look at either of them. "I use you people every single day. That's pretty much my whole job description. Now get in the air. I want you wheels up in thirty."

Rheinhardt eases his truck into the too-small space in the dimly lit basement parking garage. This is the furnished corporate housing that DoD has arranged for him, presumably so that he could start work now, find a place to live later. These kinds of priorities are not foreign to him. Most of what his country has needed of him, it's needed yesterday, or earlier.

He kills the engine and sits in the near-darkness, letting his mind catch its breath.

His first day was a blur of paperwork, briefings, and administrative trivia. And he's now faced with the stark reality of having to do this kind of stuff full-time. There was no getting around the fact that his new life is going to be a hell of a lot more routine and sedate than his old one. Whether he could deal with this would probably only become clear with time. But he'd have to give it the time.

However, one episode stood out in sharp relief. This was his videoconference with Chaya. He's not sure how he expected her to react to seeing him. There had always been an awkwardness between the two. At first, he presumed it was because he knew what had actually happened to her sister. It was difficult for Chaya, knowing he knew, but never being able to ask.

For Rheinhardt, it went beyond awkwardness. There was an inner, crushing guilt. Because he knew Natasha never should have died that night. And he had stood there and let it happen. Ordinarily, Delta guys don't have a lot of time to sit around indulging guilt or regret. Of course, they review and critique their actions remorselessly. But always with a view toward improving performance next time. And they always, always take responsibility for their actions.

But not on that one. There had, as yet, been no reckoning.

It had just faded away.

* * *

He yanks the keys from the ignition and pulls his custom Vickers .45 from the glove box. This is his very favorite gun, the one he could never leave behind, nor go far without. Happily, he's been allowed to keep the federal ID that most Delta operators get issued. The one that allows him to carry a firearm out in public, onto planes, basically anywhere.

He clips the holstered weapon onto his belt and unasses the vehicle – mentally laughing at himself for still thinking in military slang. As he ritually scans the corners and shadows of the parking deck, then pads quickly up the back stairs, he realizes how completely his behavior and thought patterns have been shaped by his years in the Unit.

Many of these things about him will be a long time changing, if ever.

George greets him right at the door, sloppy dog kisses on his hands. It's either affection, or a desperate need to crap. Probably a bit of both. George is used to having the run of an open yard. So, being confined to an enclosed area is something they've both got to get used to now. Rheinhardt clips the leash on him for a quick circuit around the block, and they step out into the quiet, pretty, northern Virginia dusk. As they walk, he lets his mind range back again.

No, there had never been any reckoning over what happened in Anbar. But Rheinhardt had never quite been able to let it go, either. All he could do was try to be a friend to Chaya. But that was the second source of awkwardness — their feelings toward each other, which never felt precisely like friendship.

When he first laid eyes on her, on that trip of atonement to the Holy Land, he was struck by how much she looked like her sister. Beautiful and severe. And the resemblance, both physical and in her manner, her military bearing, only grew over time. He had hardly known Natasha before her death. And knowing her sister was, in a very strange way, like a second chance to learn about one who had been lost. Almost to commune with the dead.

What also grew over the years was the sharp, unfamiliar ache of his feelings toward her. As did hers, he at least imagined, toward him. Neither dared acknowledge this, much less do anything about it. Certainly not when their work together was on the training ground, and sometimes on the battlefield.

Now that he was out of the field, and both of them in desk jobs, could there be something between them? Or would he, one day, have to tell Chaya the truth about Natasha's death? And would she ever be able to look at him again?

Hell. It was hard enough for Rheinhardt to get his head around the fact of not being operational anymore. And not being married. And up north. Too much change, too fast…

Back inside now, suit off, cargo pants and comfy technical t-shirt on, he stretches out on the couch and watches CNN. Another old habit. Delta always monitored breaking news in real time, so whenever anything was attacked or hijacked, by the time they got the deployment order, their on-call squadron was already suited up, loaded out, and sitting on the tarmac with the engines running. The lead story tonight is about a new U.N. resolution against Iran, for more violations of the nuclear non-proliferation treaty.

Good ole U.N. resolutions, Rheinhardt thinks. *Those always help a lot.*

As does the NPT. It's done nothing to stop Pakistan from going nuclear, or North Korea. And it certainly won't stop Iran. Doomsday weapons and madmen. Hell of a combination.

Rheinhardt hoists himself back up, goes to the fridge, and deploys a frosty one. He figures he can treat himself to a beer tonight, maybe even two. He did survive his first day of work.

He plops back down in front of the screen, where the Iranian president is ranting on the world stage again. One day, Rheinhardt feels pretty sure, something is going to have to be done about Iran. In his career, he's gotten a special appreciation for the trouble that the Iranian regime causes around the globe. He's fought Iranian-armed Hizbullah in Lebanon, Iranian-financed Hamas in the West Bank and Gaza, and Iranian-backed insurgents in Iraq. In Afghanistan, he's narrowly dodged Iranian-supplied IEDs – explosively formed penetrators, actually, EFPs. Extremely deadly items.

He even once had a two-hour running gun battle with Iranian Quds Force operatives, for once doing their own dirty work, in Venezuela, of all places.

And all of this is aside from the agony of the well-educated and cosmopolitan Iranian people – living under a brutal seventh-century theocracy, which polices women's morality, and executes gays by hanging. And which put on a farce of an election in 2009, then remorselessly crushed the peaceful people's revolution that resulted.

Lying by the couch, George growls at the screen. Even he's got a bad feeling about this guy.

Rheinhardt drifts off to sleep where he lies, beneath the drone of the news, while trying to coax his mind onto more peaceful topics. Nonetheless, he dreams the dream again – the one that always comes back, with the burning green night-vision figures. They crawl after him, chasing him tirelessly, their fingers burned off, trying to grab on to him with the black and green stumps.

He wakes later in the night, to a knock at his door.

What the hell? he wonders, rolling off the couch. *Even I don't know where I live yet…*

Johnson sticks his mammoth and leonine head into Colonel Havering's office.

"Borrow you for five, Colonel?"

"Door literally doesn't close, Sergeant."

Johnson carries a tiny netbook, which looks even tinier with his huge hands wrapped around it. He pulls a chair over and sets the device on Havering's desk.

"You're going to love this," he says.

"Oh, really?"

"No. Not really." Havering looks completely unsurprised. BJ flips through a few windows. "These are CIA dockets on Tucker. Recent ones."

Havering sighs. "RIP inter-agency cooperation. Born 9/11/2001. Died about a year later."

"Yeah. Evidently they didn't think this stuff was important enough to pick up the goddamned phone. Anyway, look here – these are mostly from *this year*. Tucker went black for a long stretch after the thing in 2006. But then he pops up again in January. CIA assets either spot him, or pick him up on signals intercepts, in these three locations."

Havering leans in to the screen now, reading aloud. "Lebanon… Gaza… Ukraine… That's a hell of a travel schedule."

"Yeah. And each time, after he pops up, he goes straight back down again."

"They have any idea where he is now?"

"Nothing with any data behind it. But I'll give you one guess what my guess is."

"Yeah. Iran. And we've got the guncam footage to back that up." Havering pauses to look incredulous again. "Fuck."

"Yes, sir. But it gets much worse. Agency does actually have an entirely decent idea of what he was doing in Lebanon and Gaza: running training ops."

"Oh, please don't tell me he's been training Hizbullah or Hamas."

"Yep, on both counts. He was definitely spotted going into, or coming out of, known terrorist training camps near Gaza City, and in southern Lebanon. It is believed he was recruited and paid for this work by the Iranians. Agency thinks he was doing hands-on training in CQB, explosives, electronics, and comms. All of which he's hellaciously qualified to teach."

The two men sit in silence for a moment. Finally Havering speaks.

"So let me see if I've got this all straight. What we have is an extremely senior and veteran Unit operator – one who served as a trainer and cadre member in Selection and the Operator Training Course *for years* – out there teaching God-shudders-to-think-what to probably the first and third most dangerous Islamist terror organizations in the world?"

BJ nods. "That about captures it. Though, actually, at this point, I'd probably characterize Hizbullah as the world's first terror army."

"Yeah. An army without a state."

"They're determined, disciplined, well-trained, and well-armed. And Iran's best weapons go to them before they go to the Iranian army."

Havering nods. "And now these assholes have got access to Delta skills and know-how. Slightly out of date. But they could still pick up some pretty damned good tricks from someone like Rod Tucker."

BJ snorts. "Hell, the quality of the tricks is only the half of it. They'll be picking up *our* tricks. Not only will the geo-political scene and people in the region be fucked by a hyper-tactically skilled Hizbullah or Hamas. But we could very *personally* be fucked, when we next face these guys in the field."

Havering runs his hand over his crewcut. "And speaking of politics, how do you think Congress is going to react if they find out millions in taxpayer dollars have effectively gone to training terrorists in elite tactics?"

Johnson doesn't answer. They look expectantly at each other, until finally Havering says it.

"This could bring down the Unit."

Colonel Havering leans back, looking extremely tired. To Johnson's eye, there's also something unfamiliar about his mien. It looks like grave worry.

Or maybe even fear.

"Well, well," Rheinhardt mutters, eye to the peephole of his door, side arm in hand. It's impossible for him to imagine exactly what these two are doing here in the middle of the night. But it's very unlikely to be a social call. He undoes the locks and holds open the door.

Aaliyah and Javier, both in casual street clothes, walk in.

"Alright. Sit down, guys. Beer?"

A few minutes later, Rheinhardt sits in silence with Ali and Javier in his living room, the lighting low. They have just finished briefing him on current events. Rheinhardt knits his fingers together behind his head and leans back on the couch. He doesn't look disbelieving. Anything that comes out of the mouths of these two he's long taken instantly as the truth. But he doesn't look happy.

"Does the colonel realize I've already got a job?"

Javier nods his agreement. "Yeah. He does. But he's already gotten sign-off from the Assistant SecDef to have you posted back to the Unit, to consult for us on this one."

"The man doesn't waste any time."

Ali clears her throat. "The Colonel says, and I quote" – and here she puts on a credibly gruff southern accent – "'The Pentagon has muddled its ass along for many years without the services of Sergeant Major Rheinhardt. They'll make it a couple more weeks. Goddammit.' Transmission ends."

"Nice," Rheinhardt says. "That everything?"

"No." Ali's smile melts gently away. "He also wants us to tell you: this is one hell of a mess, and you may be the only one who can help us clean it up. And if you don't…" She lets that hang.

"Jesus," Rheinhardt says. "With this guy, I don't know, maybe so. The colonel's convinced it's really Tucker? Working for the mullahs?"

"Both him and BJ," Javier says. He pauses. "They say Tucker was a real master blaster."

Rheinhardt nods. "Yeah. He was. But it's not so much his skills that make him dangerous." Rheinhardt looks expressionlessly at his midnight visitors. "It's his soul."

* * *

"Tucker was sergeant major of 3rd Troop, B Squadron, where I served under him. He had a lot of years in. A lot of time in, and a lot of hats left lying on the ground."

Rheinhardt leans forward and puts his elbows on his knees. The level of his voice drops.

"We were deployed to Iraq in 2006. Height of the insurgency. You remember the wheels were just coming off the wagon at that point. The country was on the verge of civil war. You'll also probably remember the combined Task Force. Us, DEVGRU, SAS, the 160th, all working under General McChrystal. Operating out of Balad AB, north of Baghdad.

"And we were just doing this incredible tempo of operations. Out every night, sometimes twice a night. Kill or capture on insurgents, safehouse takedowns, vehicle interdictions. Whatever intel we brought back got crunched during the day, to plan the next night's raid. Then we did it all again. We had persistent eyes in the sky, tracking insurgent networks in real time. We confiscated weapons, explosives, cash, training manuals, bomb-making kit, maps, intel. We just kept sprinting. And we were methodical. We killed thousands. And arrested many thousands more."

Javier nods. "Some think that was what turned the tide of the war. If I recall correctly, AQ suicide attacks dropped from a high of a hundred and fifty a month to, like, two. No one left alive to blow themselves up."

Rheinhardt shrugs. "Was that our doing? Maybe. Surely some of it. But I also think the Iraqis themselves had a lot to do with it."

"The Anbar Awakening," Ali says.

"Yeah," says Rheinhardt. "That. And that was where this thing happened." Rheinhardt pauses. "We were way out west in Anbar, doing a takedown of a bomb factory. This was a joint op with an Israeli team, Sayeret guys. But there were some comms problems. And it resulted in a serious blue-on-blue. A bunch of people died – all Israelis. Later, an inquiry concluded no one was at fault."

"And *was* no one at fault?" Ali asks.

Rheinhardt seems to ignore this for the moment. "A few weeks later we rotated back States-side. I wasn't privy to it at the time. But someone in JSOC decided the incident warranted more of an investigation. A quiet but very deep look into Tucker and his background. Like the rest of us, he had already been cleared to Top Secret/SCI level. But this time they found some things the earlier security checks had missed."

"Like what?"

"Some unsavory associations. Ties to so-called patriot groups. Anti-government paranoia, anti-UN stuff. The black helicopter crowd."

"Hell," Javier says. "I'm pretty anti-UN. So are you, last time I checked."

"And we do," Ali adds with a twinkle, "actually fly quite a lot of black helicopters."

Rheinhardt nods. "True. But not just that. Also anti-Zionist, anti-Israel. Probably anti-Semitic. People who think the U.S. Government is controlled by Jews."

"Hell. How'd he keep that under wraps so long? With all of the security checks?"

"God knows. He was very careful, probably. Kept his life exquisitely compartmentalized. All of us know how that goes."

Ali nods as she takes all this in, then looks thoughtful. "Anti-Semitism. And then, however it happened, a bunch of Israelis get killed in his op. Doesn't look good."

"No. And it started looking much worse, soon afterwards. He must have known he was being watched. Certainly the investigators were worried about getting made, surveilling him. I mean, you don't just park across the street with a pair of binoculars. Not with a guy like Tucker. You'd be dead before you got the parking brake on."

"Good point," says Javier. "I wouldn't want the job of spying on one of us."

"No. They didn't take any chances. When they went out to bring him in, they did it with a CIA para team. SAD guys. All very tight. Extremely tactical."

Javier: "He was still one of ours. They should have sent our guys to get him."

"Maybe. But they didn't."

"And what happened?"

"He killed the team. Half in a booby trap, the other half in a clean-up firefight."

"Holy shit."

"Then he blew the apartment – the whole building burned down – and just winked out of existence. Bye bye."

Ali and Javier take this in silently. Javier's phone goes off.

"Go for J-Dawg," he says. "Roger. En route." He closes the phone and stands. "Unrelated, need to know. Ali, I'll jump on a commercial flight, and leave the P-12 on the tarmac for you."

Rheinhardt gives her a look.

"My orders," she says, "are to not come back until I've got an answer from you."

Javier stands, shakes Rheinhardt's hand, and lets himself out.

* * *

Rheinhardt and Ali regard each other silently over the coffee table, in the dim light.

"Your orders," he says, "aren't really to wait for an answer from me."

"No. My orders are: not to come back without you."

Rheinhardt laughs once, mirthlessly.

"And what you just told us," she says. "It wasn't everything that happened in Anbar, either. Not the whole story."

He looks down and regards his hands. After a moment, he speaks again, more quietly.

"It *was* a building takedown, out in Anbar, like I said. The Israelis as the entry team, us on overwatch. That much is true. But things went bad. An IED, then an ambush. The

Israelis were heavily engaged, down in an urban area, beneath our OP. Tucker called in air – 105 rounds from a Spectre. He just blew the shit out of everything. Schwacked everybody. He killed them all."

Ali takes this in, lips parted. "He must have had his tactical reasons…"

Rheinhardt looks up again. "Sure. Ostensible ones. There were some high value targets in the mix, ones Tucker said he wasn't willing to let get away. Lot of American blood on their hands. And we didn't have Blue Force transponders for the Israelis, so there was no picking them out from the enemy personnel. Also, Tucker claimed he gave them time to break contact."

Rheinhardt runs his fingers through his hair and exhales.

"I wasn't privy to everything they found out about him. But he evidently suspected Jews were involved in the 9/11 attacks. And he was convinced that unconditional U.S. support for Israel was getting American service people killed – in Iraq, across the Middle East."

"Well, half the country's college professors probably believe that last part."

"Maybe." Rheinhardt shakes his head. "Maybe that's why he did it. I don't know. But it's not the point. Because I not only stood by and watched it happen. Afterward, I also backed his story. I lied to protect him."

Ali doesn't know what to say to this. She puts her hand on his.

"When we got back, in the after-action report, and in the inquiry, he came up with the story about fried comms, saying it caused the blue-on-blue. It was plausible enough. But of course they asked me to confirm it. And I did."

He stares hard at nothing. Ali squeezes his arm.

Finally, Rheinhardt stands. "Listen. I have to go to work tomorrow. You're welcome to the couch." He can personally think of about a hundred places he's made her sleep in that are much, much worse. "And, honestly, I'm going to need a few hours to think about this one. I think there might be some linens in the closet." He waves vaguely over his shoulder as he disappears into the bedroom.

Ali watches his back disappear in silence.

Rheinhardt looks up just in time to see the flashing beacon at the top of the Washington Monument come on. The last purple light is fading on the horizon. And it's very peaceful here. He resumes strolling, hands in pockets. He's managed to get through his second workday – a half-dozen briefings with staffers, both military and civilian, then reading or scanning enormous piles of documents. And now, day done, finally, he's taken himself here. To walk and to think.

He's always liked the stateliness and grandeur of DC – "the new Rome," at the heart of this Great Republic in the New World. It certainly seemed like the right place to come to do some thinking. Including thinking about duty.

No sooner had he gotten out of the Unit, made the big change, than they try to drag him back in again. Just when he thought he had done his duty, all that could be asked of him. He'd been lucky to get out when he did – alive, healthy, and with an official record, at least, that any soldier could be proud of. But this Tucker thing…

The military has always had a small percentage of psychos. But as long as they stayed in service, at least they were *our* psychos. And very, very few of them ever had anything like Tucker's training and skills. Now that he's off the reservation, there's no question that he could be catastrophically dangerous. If he really was somehow working for the Iranian mullahs, then nothing could be more important than that he be stopped.

But was it Rheinhardt's job to stop him? He's undertaken so many world-saving missions he's lost count. No one person can keep saving the world for ever. On the other hand, maybe this was something only Rheinhardt could do. From a certain perspective, it might even look like... unfinished business.

* * *

Letting his mind run, Rheinhardt also finds bigger questions burbling up to the surface. Questions that had lived down inside him for a long time, but which he had managed to keep under wraps. Thoughts about his purpose, and about the futility of the works of man.

For over twenty years, he'd worked hard every day to craft himself into the best and most useful instrument he could be. An instrument for fulfilling his duty. And for opposing evil, for trying to uphold some principles of freedom and of civilization. To stand at the gates. For most of those years, he had also been teamed with the best thousand or so such battlers of evil in the world. Guys who were at the very top of every category you could rank them in: skills, bravery, intelligence, savvy, endurance, resolve. Honor. And in so many ways, it had been just what he was meant to be doing – the great purpose and culmination of his life.

But all that's over now. And what had he got at the end of it? A tiny store of possessions in a rented apartment. A divorce settlement. An aging hound dog, who needed daily poop-scooping. A few thousand dollars in savings. And an expensive but now largely useless pistol, tucked into the back of his suit pants.

And he is basically alone.

Alone, and suffering a serious crisis of faith. One he'd kept at bay for a long time, while he focused on doing the work. But every year the doubt crept a little closer to the surface.

Did anything he'd done, in all those years, really accomplish anything? Evil was still rampant, the world still at war. Profoundly wicked people still plotted to kill and destroy, preying on the innocent. So many years they'd been fighting the War on Terror. When did it end?

He'd survived it all himself. And somehow never gotten seriously hurt, despite the staggering risks every Delta operator runs. But, mentally, he was not so sure he was unscathed. Nor was he sure he could count his honor among the survivors of his operational career.

That had gotten badly singed, if not burned up entirely, in the flames of that Anbar air strike.

* * *

His path takes him off the Mall and through more white marble government buildings he hasn't been here long enough to name. Stirring from his reverie, he reads that the huge stone structure ahead of him is the Ronald Reagan Building. As he wanders into the spacious plaza out front, threading around the statues and the fountain, he notices how quiet and empty the area has gotten. Federal DC really shuts down at night.

He also notices two National Park police officers, in their distinctive foresty-green uniforms, who have followed him out from the Mall. Not followed. Just going the same way.

Aren't they?

For half a beat, Rheinhardt wonders if maybe his handgun is printing through his suit jacket in back, and drawing attention from the officers. But he instantly discards the thought. His instincts are too finely honed to be misled on this. Changing his angle of approach toward the building, he steals a look over his shoulder. The Park Police officers are obviously taking no notice of him, while closing the distance.

Way too obviously taking no notice of him.

And they're not right. It doesn't matter in what way. One fact obtrudes: they are wrong, and so is the whole situation. Rheinhardt hesitates for one more beat, considering a last time whether his assessment might be off. He is in a new place, a very different environment. Could he be spooked over nothing?

No. He couldn't.

In peripheral, he clocks the motion and geometry as he heads into the lee of the building.

Everything after that happens in fractions of seconds.

Knowing whatever he knows, with whatever level of certainty, Rheinhardt has no choice but to let the other two make their move first. Drawing and firing on men in police uniforms, in the middle of downtown DC, is simply off the menu.

However, the necessity of drawing second, but shooting first, poses no problem for him.

Rheinhardt has put out somewhere around a million rounds at the pistol range in his career with Delta. Virtually all of this has involved instinctive fire at ranges of 5 to 75 yards, much of it snap-firing from a holster quick-draw, and most of it while moving – running, leaping, falling, rolling, sighting in on moving targets, at full speed, and then faster. And they are skills that he's had tested in combat, literally hundreds of times.

He watches the two "officers" pick up their speed of advance.

He alters his trajectory to tweak the angles.

The rest happens too fast to follow, much faster than can be described. It is pure surprise, speed, and violence of action. Delta's three pillars.

The two men draw first – chunky auto-loaders, the 9mm SIG P225s that are National Park Service standard issue. Their guns do get clear of leather. By about an inch.

Rheinhardt draws second, turning in to them.

He draws, raises, and fires his weapon in a single fluid motion, a blur on rails, four rounds triggering off, two times two, all four of them dead-center headshots.

The two men drop like bags of sand, their animation evaporating instantly. All that remains are the inhuman motions of meat obeying gravity.

Rheinhardt continues advancing, gun up and forward.

Everything has now gone slow, serene, and razor vivid for him.

And he knows he has to beat the tunnel vision.

Because the backup team will be around here somewhere, probably behind him.

* * *

He closes on the two bodies, scanning in 360. There are a few evening strollers within sight on the surrounding streets. One or two look around curiously. But the four shots sounded like nothing so much as two car-engine backfires. It ended too quickly to draw any real notice. A strange quirk of psychology, but a reliable one: if it's over before you can figure out what it was, most untrained people will decide it was probably nothing.

Reaching the corpses on the ground, he deals with his second problem – that of having only four bullets to his name. While he would definitely feel naked without his side arm, spare magazines seemed overkill, especially working in what's probably the second most secure building in the world after the White House. Also, he'd had enough crap already on his belt, bulging underneath the summer-weight suit.

He picks up one of the SIGs from where it dropped and tucks it into his waistband. He then pulls the four mags from the duty belts of the dead men, and drops them in his jacket pockets. Finally, he hefts the other SIG in his left hand, while keeping his .45 in his right.

He doesn't bother checking the bodies. There was no chance or uncertainty in those killing shots. He knew those two were dead before the bullets even reached them.

He turns to see two figures exiting from the double glass doors that front the building, a man and a woman. Tourists, if judged by their clothes and bags. But these "tourists" are obviously the backup. Rheinhardt instantly clocks them.

Not hesitating, he starts to walk them down, accelerating like a cat, as they begin to haul H&K MP7 sub-machine guns out of their identical backpacks.

* * *

Rheinhardt's aggression, closing instantly with the targets, is meant to unsettle them, to put them back on their heels. It works. They are uncertain and shaky in bringing their weapons out. Rheinhardt has a chance to see that they carry the Heckler & Koch MP7A3s, PDW-class, with the body-armor-penetrating 4.6mm round.

Advancing on them, dual pistols held akimbo, he checks his background, then briefly checks fire. Behind his targets are building windows, reflective and opaque. They could have anything, like babies, behind them. He steps to the right to fix the angles. He's got plenty of time to work with. The MP7s are far too slow in coming up, and will never beat him, even with the margin of safe shooting he's working for.

That's when he takes the round to his upper right torso, creasing him between shoulder and neck. He hears the report a fraction of a second later – a rifle round, 7.62mm, and from extreme elevation. He probably didn't need to be told that. But he definitely wasn't expecting the sniper.

And Rheinhardt hates snipers. He has a special loathing, borne of several episodes of being pinned down and made helpless by capable snipers. It's like being attacked by the weather. A special powerlessness. It makes his eye twitch.

Looking down, he sees his .45 lying on the deck. His whole right arm is buzzing and numb. And the two backup guys are now beginning to open up with the MP7s. He considers continuing to engage the two in front of him, who are, in truth, still the most immediate threat. But he can't coexist with that sniper raining down fire on him from above.

Rheinhardt puts his head down, rolls out, and crashes into the lee of one of the statues that flank the plaza. It's a reclining woman, set on a huge stone pedestal. Excellent cover, from both the machine gunners on the deck, and the long rifle up above.

But because the building facade is a crescent, the sniper was able to emplace out on the edge of the roof and get excellent coverage of the plaza. Moreover, the two teams now have partially interlocking fields of fire. And the short-gunners will only have to fan out about 20 meters to each side to spread his cover on the flanks.

And then gun him down.

* * *

While he's got a second here, wounded and pinned down, Rheinhardt somewhat idly ponders who it is that might be trying to kill him. But of course it could be virtually anyone. In fifteen years with Delta, Rheinhardt tangled with, and in most cases seriously bloodied, virtually every important terror organization in the world. Plus not a few hostile intelligence and security services, and foreign militaries.

It's not completely surprising that someone would have a go at him, now that he's out of the security bubble of Bragg. He wasn't expecting it. But perhaps he should have been.

He pauses to get a quick reading on his wound. It's only a crease, really. But judging by the near total paralysis of his right arm, the round must have grazed his brachial plexus, the nerve that serves the whole appendage. He's also bleeding moderately. But it's not really in a wrappable spot, and he definitely can't spare a hand to clamp down on it. He's only got the one, and it's got to do all his shooting now. And all of this will almost certainly be over, one way or another, in the next minute or two, long before he bleeds out.

He considers his next move. The textbook play would be to put out suppressing fire on the left and right, to limit the mobility of the two ground shooters, and their ability to split his cover. But his training and tactics aren't so much about throwing the textbook out, as making it totally beside the point. Transcending the rules.

Also, he has no intention of continuing to fight under that enervating sniper cloud.

So instead of going left, or going right, he instead goes over the top – straight up and onto the back of the statue. This confuses and complicates the sight lines of the two on the ground long enough for him to make a tough shot up to the roof. And it's a beautiful shot. Nearly 150 meters, and about eight stories up.

He's already dropping back down again, when a mental review of the sight picture he took reveals a troubling fact: it was actually the spotter he shot. He wasn't expecting one, and the spotter's profile was bigger. *Son of a bitch*. Rifle rounds resume coming in from above.

Also, short bursts from the MP7s are chipping up stone around the edges of the statue.

And that's when two uniformed DC cops round the side of the building, straight ahead of him, at a dead run, weapons drawn. They skid to a stop, level their guns at Rheinhardt in their cute little modified Weaver stances, and scream at him to drop his weapon.

Rheinhardt shouts "Federal agent, undercover!" But he can't reach an ID. Also, the MP7s behind him are going cyclic now, drowning out his voice.

The cops panic and open up.

* * *

The updated tactical situation is: Rheinhardt is boxed in from above by the sniper; boxed in from behind and either side by the ground shooters; and the newly-arrived cops have a straight shot right down into his box, with Rheinhardt crouching at the bottom of it, bleeding.

Sorry guys, Rheinhardt thinks. *Nothing personal.* He pours the remaining thirteen rounds from his left-hand SIG into the cops' position. All thirteen hit stone, to their left, against the building. The ricochets shouldn't get them, but they do get peppered with sharp stone fragments. They quickly retreat out of view, eyes half closed, stinging, panicked.

Rheinhardt drops the empty mag out of the pistol. He jams the gun between his knees to reload it one-handed.

Now, he thinks, *would not be the ideal time to get rushed...*

The female of the backup team, a Gazan recruited by the Iranians into a sleeper cell in the U.S., grips her machine pistol with both hands, advancing one careful step at a time. With each step, she fires a short burst at the edge of the statue, to keep the man from popping up on her.

Because, despite her martyr's training, she has no intention of dying tonight. Her light skin, nearly accent-less English, and substantial Westernization were the qualities that earned her this assignment – and the extensive Iranian training that went along with it. And, while she can't admit it to anyone, she much prefers living in America to living in Gaza. She'd like very much to carry on doing it.

The man they are here to kill is clearly very good. He killed both members of the primary team in a heartbeat. It was that failure that called her and her partner out of the building and into action – and into very serious risk of death, or at least arrest.

The clock is definitely ticking. But this is not over yet.

She knows their target has been shot at least once. He may be dead or unconscious already. As she slowly swings out wide, around the right side of the statue, the crimson edge of a pool of blood comes into view, seeping out from behind. Another step, and she sees a shoe, pointing skyward toward the halogen-glowing night. Suppressing a smile, she wheels around the edge of the statue at full speed, depressing her trigger and firing flat out…

* * *

The man, her partner, holds his position before the fountain, gun held stiffly forward. He is watching the left side of the statue, hawk-like. He is also trembling markedly. And he is secretly very relieved to see the woman advancing up the right side. Partnering with the woman had been the idea of the Iranian special operatives. They claimed it would make them less suspicious, and would give them better opportunities and greater access in America.

He saw it only as an insult to his manhood. Now though… perhaps she is making herself useful. Let her flush out the dangerous American. Maybe she would get him. Maybe he'd get her but in so doing expose himself. Meanwhile, he will hold his position here. As long as he kept this side of the statue in his sights, the American could not get the drop on him. Now he sees the woman's expression change – and then she charges around the back of the statue, firing. The roar and muzzle flash of the tiny machine gun are transfixing. He watches it for a half instant too long.

He first feels the shock in the center of his chest, then hears the shots, and only finally sees the man in stocking feet running straight at him, from the left side of the statue, at lightning speed, triggering off rounds. And then the waters flow upward and envelop him, snuffing out the flame of his life.

He sinks down into nothingness.

There is a certain level of speed, skill, and physicality that is indistinguishable from magic. By being master of the physics and physiology of shooting and combat, the Delta operator is effectively the Neo of his own Matrix.

But trickery never hurts, either. Rheinhardt had the blood to spare; and the shoes were uncomfortable anyway. Now, swinging around the side of the statue, he hammer-throws himself forward, firing left-handed, and watches the second shooter tumble over backward, splash into the ornate fountain, and sink from view.

In the same electric motion, he blasts beneath a hail of rounds from the sniper above, who cannot depress his muzzle quickly enough to track. In a half-second he's safe in the defilade of the building front. As he reaches the front door, he skids to a halt, turns, and waits to see if the woman will follow him in a loop around the statue. But a hail of shouts and gunfire testify to her fate – shot down by the two police officers.

Rheinhardt launches himself inside the building, sprints across the lobby, and in seconds is leaping up a back service stairwell.

* * *

He kicks open the steel door to the rooftop and feints once with his shoulder, which draws a hail of rounds. He then crouches down and comes out lower, and puts two rounds into the shins of the sniper, who is on his feet and aiming a handgun. The man collapses, howling, draped over the body of the spotter.

Finally, you son of a bitch. Go down.

Rheinhardt advances, but the sniper comes up again with the handgun. *Motherfucker.* Rheinhardt fires into his shoulder and upper arm. The man convulses, but still keeps squeezing off shots, rounds snapping by Rheinhardt's head. Rheinhardt drops to one knee, and makes a difficult but instant decision: he abandons the wounding shots and drills the man twice in the head.

Rising and advancing again, he kicks away both guns, the pistol and sniper rifle. Rheinhardt curses the man, and curses his resolve. He needed a live capture, for interrogation. Because it isn't enough just to survive. Long-term survival requires knowing what the hell is going on.

Tossing the bodies, Rheinhardt comes up only with some currency, spare pistol mags, and a single page of printed notes. But they are printed in Farsi. Rheinhardt's Persian is exceptionally crappy. But he recognizes a transliteration of his own name.

As he's squinting at it, his phone goes off.

"Go for Rheinhardt."

"RHEINHARDT, HAVERING. Be advised: we have intel indicating you are in immediate danger. How copy?"

"Yeah, well… roger that, Colonel."

"I need you to move to a secure location, RFN."

"Yeah, I'm at one now."

"What is your location?"

"Roof of the Ronald Reagan Building, downtown DC."

"And how do you figure that to be secure?"

"Because I just secured it. Listen, I've engaged and killed six shooters, who came at me in public. And they were not amateurs."

"You hurt?"

"A little bit."

"The shooters?"

"All KIA. What is your intel?"

"Signals intercept. There was an anonymous tip about an Iranian sleeper cell in the DC area. NSA picked up their traffic this afternoon, saw your name, and took their time getting around to alerting me." Rheinhardt can hear voices in the background. *"Wait out, Sergeant."*

Still holding the phone to his ear, Rheinhardt steps to the edge of the building. A number of police are down in the plaza now, with more screeching up in cruisers. Given the gunfire, though, their SOP will prohibit them from entering the building. They will cordon and secure the area, until SWAT and senior leadership arrive on the scene.

Rheinhardt belatedly remembers his wound. He clamps his hand over it, managing to stop the light bleeding. He also finds he's already getting some feeling back in the arm. He guesses the nerve bundle was either just grazed, or pinched by swelling.

Since he's got the use of it now, he uses the free hand to pick up the sniper rifle, a scoped SR25. He drops the mag, and pulls the bolt back. The weight's not quite right. He absently checks the stock and notices the screws on the butt-plate are half-stripped. He reflexively reaches for the Leatherman on his belt, for its screwdriver…

"Eric."

"Sir." He places the rifle back on the deck.

"There is a Little Bird en route to your location now. ETA four minutes. Hold position."

"Roger that."

"We also have people talking to the DC police. They'll sort all that out after we extract you."

Rheinhardt can already see the speck of an MH6 Little Bird helicopter coming in low on the horizon.

"Colonel. You figure this has to do with Rod Tucker?"

Havering doesn't know what to tell him, so he doesn't say anything.

* * *

Rheinhardt watches the lights of federal DC recede as the bird gains altitude – the National Mall, the Capitol, and White House, and the clean lines of the boulevards spreading out below him. Wind pulls at his hair and his blood-splashed jacket through the open sides of the helo.

Before he's even aware of it, he realizes a decision has been made for him. Whether or not he goes back to the Unit, or goes after Tucker, or takes on this mission… all three have come looking for him. He mentally shrugs.

I guess Robert Frost had it right, he thinks. *The best way out is always through.* And this was unfinished business.

He plugs his cell phone into his cabin headset unit and dials Ali, speaking into the chin mic.

"Hey. Where's your P-12? Okay. Can you grab my go-bag from under my bed and meet me there? Oh, yeah – and my boots, from the closet, please. No, my last valet didn't die of anything. Ha ha. Out."

He switches channels to ICS and speaks to the pilot. "We're going to Andrews AFB."

"I was told to fly you to the Pentagon, Force Protection Agency."

Rheinhardt looks out at the lights scrolling by beneath them. He exhales slowly into the night air before answering.

"Change of mission."

"...Attempted Assassination On National Mall..." reads the news ticker at the bottom of the wall-mounted screen. CNN, it turns out, also plays non-stop in certain offices of the Quds Force, the special mission unit of the Iranian Revolutionary Guards (IRG). Brigadier General Qassem Suleimani, whose English is excellent, looks up from his pile of papers when the pretty news reporter begins speaking on this topic in pantomime. He hits the volume on the remote.

"—extremely dramatic scene tonight outside the Ronald Reagan Building, just off the National Mall in Washington D.C., as an unnamed Pentagon official survives an assassination attempt in the late evening..."

The video cuts to a crime scene on a stone plaza: police tape, flashing lights, and network news vans. Suleimani pushes his papers away and removes his reading glasses.

"Pentagon sources have so far declined to name the person or persons targeted. District police are reporting that all of the attackers, who are rumored to number anywhere from two to as many as ten, were killed in the thwarted attack. There's also no word as to the nationality or affiliation of the slain gunmen. We will of course keep you posted as news develops..."

Suleimani sighs out loud, and leans back in his chair.

Well, he thinks. *That could have gone better.*

* * *

On the other hand, he's certainly seen a lot of things go much worse.

During the Iran–Iraq War, as a lieutenant in the IRG, Suleimani watched boys marched out to clear minefields by rolling across them. He saw the First World War-style tactics, with trench lines, bayonet charges, and slaughter by machine gun. Before it was all over, he shared the searing national pain of an estimated one million Iranian casualties.

Suleimani had not, happily, been one of them. He instead became famous, a national hero, due largely to a few daring reconnaissance operations behind enemy lines. He then rose quickly in the ranks of the *Pasdaran*, or "Guardians" – formally known as the Army of the Guardians of the Islamic Revolution.

The IRG was founded in 1979 to prevent internal dissident and military uprisings, and now controls over 125,000 military personnel on ground, air, and water. They also control the paramilitary *Basij*, a plain-clothes militia force best known for enforcing public morality – as well as for helping to crush the 2009 uprising after the election that was, as Suleimani even-handedly thinks of it, disputed.

But even more aggressive than the Basij, and more elite than the regular IRG, is the Quds (or "Jerusalem") Force – a special unit tasked with exporting Iran's Islamic revolution, including what might be called "extraterritorial operations." This unit reports directly to the Supreme Leader, Ayatollah Ali Khamenei, and thus is above all reproach, and all meddling. And that makes Suleimani, since his appointment to command Quds Force in 2007, one of the most powerful figures in Iran.

An orderly knocks on the edge of his open door.

"General? The American is here."

* * *

The orderly makes way and another figure appears, pausing in shadow before striding into the room. He wears unmarked black fatigues, with a .45 autoloading handgun on his leg in a drop holster. His sand-colored hair is slightly curly and descends to just over his collar. A forked moustache traces a figure around his mouth like a Wehrmacht Eagle with down-turned wings.

As he enters, he walks from the waist, like the accomplished martial artist he is. Rather than conferring any serenity, though, this training has mainly made Rod Tucker meaner and faster. In his previous life, at 1ˢᵗ SFOD-D, he was known for his speed, agility, and brutality.

He approaches Suleimani's desk and stands with his palm on the butt of his pistol.

"You needn't go armed here," Suleimani says. "There will be no hostage rescue today."

Both men smile slightly at the reference, and the irony. The Quds Force headquarters was built on the site of the former U.S. Embassy compound in Tehran. It was a takedown of this very site, to rescue the 52 American hostages held there, that would have been Delta Force's very first mission after its founding, Operation Eagle Claw, in 1980. It *would* have been their first mission — if the helicopters for the insertion hadn't failed catastrophically in the desert, resulting in an aborted mission and national disgrace.

Tucker maintains his angled grin. "With respect, General, I go armed everywhere. You just never know when or where your enemies are going to pop up."

Suleimani nods. But his smile fades as he nods at the television screen. "Nor, evidently, does one know how capable one's enemies will prove to be. According to CNN, and also judging by their failure to report in, I've just lost half of my sleeper agents on the U.S. East Coast."

"Well…" Tucker drawls, looking over his shoulder at the screen. "I wouldn't worry too much about that. Sacrificing pawns is all part of the game." He looks back to the general. "And, anyway, their cell was already compromised."

Suleimani raises one eyebrow at this. "How do you know?"

"Because I compromised them. I dropped the dime on those guys."

The general doesn't know the expression about the dime. But he gets the basic idea.

"Don't worry," Tucker says, rubbing his moustache downward with thumb and forefinger. "Everything's going to plan. This was a provocation that Rheinhardt won't be able to resist. And Delta will follow with him, to their very great cost. With them hobbled, our biggest roadblock will be out of the way. And the others will fall in time."

The General takes this in without reacting. The American's plan is ambitious far past the point of brashness. So far, though, it must be admitted that he has delivered.

"And with the Great Satan hobbled?"

"Then the way will be clear for you to visit destruction on the Little one."

"The Zionist Entity…" says Suleimani, only half-seriously using the roundabout term the mullahs use for Israel. Suleimani is not a zealot. Nor particularly religious. And certainly not a Jew-hater – a perverse form of warped emotion that has humbled many otherwise clear thinkers and tacticians throughout history.

But he is a pragmatist. And ambitious. And he does see the effects on the regional power balance of having thousands of American troops on Iran's western border in Iraq. And thousands more on their eastern border, with Afghanistan. Only a monumental *coup de main* can restore Iran's place as regional hegemon.

The fall of Israel.

And of course Suleimani does work for religious zealots. Ones who desire nothing so much as a purge of the Jews from the Holy Land – and a quickening of the return of the Mahdi, the Twelfth Imam. Then this fairy tale figure, the mullahs believe, will usher in a return of the Caliphate and restore Islam as the dominant global religion.

For which a devastating regional nuclear exchange would be a small price to pay. Suleimani is not a "Twelver," as is the Iranian president. He doesn't believe in the Hidden Imam. And he's pretty sure a nuclear exchange can be avoided.

If only he goes about things in a slightly more clever way.

After an hour and a quarter in the air with Ali, a quick ground hop from Pope AFB to Fort Bragg, and a couple hours tactical sleep in his old Squadron ready room, Rheinhardt walks into Havering's office without knocking. He shakes his head slightly while doing so. It really is as if he never left at all.

"Good of you to rejoin us, Eric," the colonel says.

"I am an Army Ranger," Rheinhardt says, referring to his former unit. Rangers are always Rangers, regardless of what they do later in service or in life. "I go where I'm posted."

In a quick and efficient briefing, Havering brings Rheinhardt up to speed with the counter-hacking of their signals-intelligence assets in the Chalus nuclear weaponization facility; the possible involvement of Rod Tucker; and what they know about it all, which isn't very much yet.

Rheinhardt seems particularly interested in the M14 rifle on the infrared camera view, and the version of Tucker's call sign in the computer logfiles.

"*Two* telltales?" he says. "C'mon, Colonel. The man's not an amateur. He obviously wanted us to sniff him out. And unless he imagines that IQs have plummeted drastically around here, we're being played somehow."

Havering's smart enough not to pretend he already knew this. "Well… so much for that ten months at Command and General Staff College. I guess the question is, what's he playing at?"

Rheinhardt draws a deep breath. "I don't know yet. But I've got at least three threads we can pull on as we try to unravel this crapsack. First, I think I know where and how Tucker got hooked up with the Iranians in the first place."

"Oh, yeah?"

"You remember the Battle for Herat? In the west of Afghanistan, November 2001, during the initial invasion. We helped coordinate a local uprising in the district capital. The locals were Hazaris, but there were three different outside forces that came in and joined up. One was American. Second was some Northern Alliance fighters."

"Yeah, this is starting to ring a bell," Havering says. "And the third was—"

"Quds Force commandos. Under General Safavi, then-commander of the Iranian Revolutionary Guards."

"Jesus Christ."

"Yep. Hard to believe now, but that was about five seconds after 9/11. And we were happy to accept help from anyone willing to whack a jihadi."

"Yeah, and our interests and the mullahs' also aligned for about five seconds."

Rheinhardt nods. "I wasn't in Herat. I was still in C Squadron then, under Bad Bob. But, years later, Tucker would talk about it sometimes. He'd mention the Quds guys he'd met. And he'd hint that he was still in touch with them."

"Building contacts, maybe, for use later on in his career."

"This shit always happens when we make friends for special occasions."

"Yeah, blowback. Like the mujahideen. Our best buddies when they were fighting the Red Army. A bit less so after 9/11."

Rheinhardt nods and goes on. "The second thing is an ISR move we can make. I know for certain we've got enough video of Tucker, from guncams, headcams, and drones, from years' worth of ops, to put together biometric identifiers. Physicals and gait analysis, that kind of thing. Enough to have satellites and drones start searching for him. In Chalus, in Tehran, anywhere he's known to have popped up."

"Outstanding."

"I even know where the tapes are buried."

Havering pauses fractionally. The reference to tapes brings to mind something very dangerous – something he doesn't want to think about right now. "Make it happen," is all he says.

"Finally, I've got one more card I want to try out: Chaya Akhilov."

"Your IDF friend?"

"Yeah. They've got significant HUMINT and SIGINT assets in many or most of Iran's military units and operations. Whatever specific dirt Tucker's been rolling in, Sayeret may know something about it. I'd actually be surprised if they didn't. It's not the kind of thing they'd want to miss."

"Proceed on all fronts. Need any warm bodies?"

"The usual bodies, Javier and Ali, would do. Maybe BJ if things go kinetic."

"BJ's already working it. The other two are yours for the duration. I'll see that they're pulled from other duties."

"Wouldn't mind some tech support from Mike Brown."

"He's yours, too. Or mostly yours, anyway. I get a lot of requests for that man's time. But you'll get priority. Now you and your team go get us some answers."

"Okay, Colonel." Rheinhardt nods and turns to go.

But Havering speaks quietly, stopping him. "It's a hell of a thing."

"What? Me coming back again?"

Havering pauses, his mouth drawn. "Yeah, that. But I meant *Tucker* coming back again. And on the payroll of the mullahs. The leading state sponsors of terror in the world."

"Not to mention soon-to-be proud owners of a nuclear arsenal."

"And Tucker's a man who, I don't have to tell you, has one hell of a grudge against us."

"Yeah. It's pretty bad." Rheinhardt hesitates again before leaving. "Two guys in a room?"

Havering nods. "Two guys in a room."

"I think he not only wanted to be spotted. I think he wanted it to be me who did it."

"You think this is something personal?"

"Tucker always seemed to combine the personal and the professional pretty seamlessly. And not in a good way."

Rod Tucker feels the nightlife wash over him, as he walk̶ down along the main street of Amir Abad, one of downto̶ Tehran's trendier neighborhoods. Even on a weeknight, and under the watchful gaze of the Basij, Tehranis are out in force – flocking to the shisha cafes, eating lamb kebabs in open-air restaurants, and dancing to Western music. The beautiful Persian women are showing off just as much of themselves as they can get away with under the modesty rules – tight jeans, artfully done makeup and hair, and colorful tops and headscarves.

But there is also an undeniable wariness beneath the reveling. Tucker can feel it. He is an outsider. But he's also a highly trained observer of human behavior, across many cultures. And this is a nation curled up around wounds that have not yet healed.

He also knows he is only a few blocks from the spot where Neda Agha-Soltan, the beautiful young Iranian protester, was killed – shot down in the street during the 2009 protests. While she still lay bleeding out in a gutter, video of the whole thing was uploaded to YouTube. The world suddenly had a face to put with the suffering of the Iranian people. And Iran's Green Revolution had a martyr.

It was probably in that moment, Tucker figured, that the rule of the mullahs was doomed. But it would be a long time going through its death throes. And a lot could happen in that time – a lot of money could change hands, for one thing.

could change. All in
tton.

ne door, and threads
clocking everyone in
1984 – everyone's at
A all have agents on
, Shin Bet, IDF. Not
to mention every Arab and Sunni regime in the Middle East:
the Saudis, the Gulf States, the Turks, even the free Iraqis,
Libyans, and Egyptians. All of them terrified of an aggressive and nuclear-armed Persian hegemon, led by messianic
mullahs, preparing for their Day of Judgment.

Not seeing any immediate threats, Tucker pushes through
the swinging kitchen doors and takes the stairs two at a time.
In the back room above, the Chinese are already seated at the
table.

"*Wan shàng hao,*" says Tucker, bowing slightly to the three
men at the table. "*Nín hao?*"

The eldest of the three stands and extends his hand.
"Very well, thank you… Mr. Tucker."

Tucker takes a seat. He's not one for small talk, and he's
not a huge fan of the Chinese for that matter. But, after the
Iranians made the introduction, this has been his relationship to manage. For the kinds of transactions they need to
conduct, an American intermediary suits the mullahs down
to the ground. As it does the Chinese. On top of this, Tucker
knows the right questions to ask. And he knows how to keep
things covert.

"You will have seen the funds transfer," Tucker says, "for the last piece of work."

The leader of the Chinese nods politely.

Tucker leans in, his angular face severe in shadow. "I'm going to need your people to keep the Americans out of the Chalus computer systems. For at least the next week."

"That will not be a problem, Mr. Tucker. We have an entire tiger team, at our station in Cuba, dedicated to the active defense of those systems."

Tucker keeps a poker face. He knows the Chinese have *two* listening stations in Cuba – inaugurated in 2003 with their Operation Titan Rain, which extracted somewhere between 10 and 20 terabytes of data off of U.S. military networks. And Cuba remains an excellent location for deniable cyberwar ops. They can never be traced back either to mainland China, or to their clients – in this case, the mullahs in Tehran.

"Good," Tucker nods. "Now, as for the incursions we need into the IDF systems."

The man nods in turn. "A more challenging piece of work. But we have already made progress. This is Bob Li." He nods toward the man beside him. He is smaller, much younger, and totally Westernized in appearance. "We are putting him at your disposal for the duration."

"What up," he says, in California-accented English. Tucker is obviously bemused by this. "I did my PhD at Cal Tech," he adds.

"Fine," Tucker says. "What have you done lately?"

Li straightens up. "So far we've breached about half of the systems on your list."

"Only half?"

"The Israelis are incredibly security savvy. Virtually all of their systems are compartmentalized one from another. Every time I've cracked one, there's been no way to leverage that into access on the next. We've got to climb the hill again every time. The Special Operations Directorate systems have been toughest to crack. Impossible, actually."

"Don't worry about that one," Tucker says. "As I promised your boss, I'll get you in there. When the time comes."

"Whatever you say, man."

"Just as long as you're into the Military Intelligence Directorate systems. By my deadline."

"No guarantees in war, bro. Thrusts can be parried. That goes double for cyberwar. With the exploits we've already got in place, we can inflict some serious havoc on the Israeli systems, whenever you give the word. Will we be able to totally blind them? That remains to be seen."

Tucker debates with himself about whether to argue this point. In most of his career, failure was never on the table. But, then again, luck has always played its part. You could be the most elite special operator on any battlefield – but step in the wrong spot at the wrong time, and a stray "seeing eye round" could come out of nowhere and kill you just as dead as the greenest recruit out of Basic.

"Okay," Tucker says, leaving it at that. He turns back to the older man. "Now let's talk about the other thing."

With a nod, the older man dismisses the younger, who stands and leaves.

"The HEU shipment," Tucker says, for clarity. He is amused to note how he lowers his voice when he says this. It's irrational. But, then again, there are an awful lot of people, from the President of the U.S. down to taxi drivers in Tel Aviv, who would kill them just for having this conversation.

"The material is in transit now."

Major Chaya Akhilov replaces her desk phone in its cradle, gingerly, and with two fingers, as if she's handling explosives, or perhaps a snake. She looks up over her desk to her commander, Colonel Eshel, who sits in a chair opposite, legs crossed at the knee.

Eshel is tall and lean, with short brown hair tipped with gray, and piercing gray-blue eyes. He has an easygoing, self-deprecating nature about him; but you didn't want to cross the lines of professionalism or integrity with him. He's also one of the most experienced combat commanders in Sayeret. He was already in Chaya's office when this call came in.

"Well," Chaya says, weighing her words with care. "That was just about the most disturbing phone call I've ever had in my life."

"I wonder," Eshel says, "if I got the right end of that stick. Rheinhardt's back at Delta?"

"He is. And you're not going to like why. They have reason to believe a former Delta shooter has gone rogue. And may now be working for the mullahs. Not to mention training Hamas, Hizbullah, or both. All within the last few months."

Eshel frowns deeply. "And Rheinhardt wanted to know what we have on this man?"

"He did."

"And we have nothing."

"Correct. It's a total surprise to me."

Eshel's frown grows even deeper. "Very grim development."

"I'll query it through every database we have, and also have a few conversations." Chaya pauses, regarding her superior. "But what I'd really like to do is some prisoner interrogation. Who do we have in custody, who was out on the street recently?"

Chaya is referring to Palestinian militants from Hamas, who are fairly routinely captured in anti-terror operations in the occupied territories; or Hizbullah fighters, typically caught, when not killed, infiltrating over the border from Lebanon.

"Slim pickings right now," Eshel says. "With the peace process showing flickers of life, we've mainly been releasing Palestinians, not rounding them up… Wait a minute," he says, raising a finger in the air, while pulling out his mobile phone and speed dialing.

"Amit. Eshel. What is the status of your Qalqilya raid? It's been cleared by the courts? Okay. How would you like to launch tonight? Of course there is. A passenger, along for the ride. And some onsite interrogation. Major Akhilov. Yes. When can you stage? Yes? Done."

He puts the phone away, and pins Chaya with his gaze.

"A Hamas safehouse we've just identified, in Qalqilya. It's been under surveillance while Amit's team plans a takedown. I've just moved that up."

Chaya grows a grin at this.

"You can thank me by not being late. Or getting killed. Be at Kfar Saba by 0200. Body armor and tactical kit only, no rifle. No shooting for you. Once the site is secure, you can go in and talk to whomever there is to talk to."

"Thanks, Boss."

She's up and out the door before Eshel can rise.

Chaya sits in a lightly armored Land Rover, half a block down from the target house. She is in the passenger seat and, out of habitual security consciousness, cranes her neck to look up and down the dingy and poorly lit street. It is otherwise deserted. The entry team, in all black and full tactical kit, are stacked up in the alleyway and on an adjacent roof. When the site has been secured, Chaya will get the call to come in.

Qalqilya is actually a fairly modern city by West Bank standards. The town was badly damaged in the Six Day War, after which the cost of rebuilding was paid for by Israel. But, in the there's-no-such-thing-as-gratitude department, Qalqilya became a base for infiltrations and suicide bombings until, eventually, Israel had enough of exploding migrants, and built the West Bank barrier. This encircled the town and also separated its inhabitants from important farmlands nearby – thus pissing off the Palestinian populace, if possible, even more than before.

The mess, as usual, has been ongoing. As have the anti-terror operations.

It is very hard, Chaya thinks to herself in the dark, *to keep from adopting a does-this-shit-never-end? mindset.* One had to resist the enervating rot of cynicism, and of fatalism. Somehow.

"I have control," a voice speaks in her earpiece, the wire from which snakes into a hand-held radio in her lap. *"One, two, three – EXECUTE, EXECUTE, EX—"* Chaya knows

the sniper teams will take their shots on any visible, armed personnel on the second "execute." The third is drowned out by the explosion of breaching charges on the entrances.

A heartbeat later, every window, and the now-gaping front door, go solid-sheet supernova with the white light of flash-bang grenades, which have been chucked into every room in the house. Chaya realizes she should have covered up, despite the distance. Her night vision is seriously dinged.

Through the radio, she can hear the operators shouting familiar bits of "occupation Arabic": *"Don't move!"*, *"Show me your hands!"*, and *"On the floor! Arms and legs spread!"*

The raid seems to be going like clockwork – which is what Sayeret operators train so many thousands of hours to achieve. The goal is elimination of the always-lurking specter of chance from armed conflict. But a single word now erupts in Chaya's ear, cutting off other chatter.

"Detonator!"

Then a flurry of shots.

So much for the elimination of chance, Chaya thinks mordantly.

"OUT, OUT, OUT!!"

She can already see black-clad bodies tumbling out of the same entrances they went in through.

Then the upper floor of the house goes a rather more fluid and dynamic sort of supernova.

* * *

Chaya is hunching down in her seat, forearms over face, as debris begins to tinkle and thunk on the outside of the Land Rover. She's just uncovering her head when—

KA-SMASH!! A rather larger hunk of debris, an entire human body, crashes down across the hood and windshield. The bulletproof and shatterproof glass does what it's meant to – it spiderwebs and warps, but holds.

Being a Sayeret operator, even in the intel section, pretty much means being unflappable by definition. So Chaya doesn't panic when the man lands with a crash, rocking the whole truck, a foot from her face. Nor when he unexpectedly reanimates, shakes his head, and rolls off the car on the passenger side.

However, she does startle a little when he straightens up, locks eyes with her through the side window, swings around a pistol-grip AK that's stayed slung across his body through his aerial maneuvers and hard landing, and opens up in Chaya's face at point-blank range.

She crab-crawls to the opposite side of the passenger compartment, draws her side arm, and is debating whether to shoot back – the glass is buckling from the full-auto onslaught and won't last long – when a black figure appears out of the night at professional-athlete speed and body-tackles the shooter.

Both figures disappear below the window and out of view.

Chaya kicks the driver's-side door open and circles the vehicle, arms and pistol extended out and toward the ground. By that time, the man in black has flex-cuffed the flying Hamas guy at the wrists and ankles.

Chaya notes now that the latter is visibly smoking from his clothing and hair. He is not only a human cannonball, but a crispy critter as well. How he's still alive, never mind still fighting, Chaya can't imagine. How long he might keep breathing now is also a matter of speculation.

The man in black stands and peels off his balaclava, revealing himself as Master Sergeant Dov Levi. His bright smile gleams out from his Greek-God-like features. Rock-jawed with dark hair, wide shoulders, and a narrow waist, he is physically imposing, yet whimsical. He's always got a cheeky, and usually flirtatious, comment for Chaya.

"Hello, Dov," she says, holstering her weapon, and trying to steady her breathing.

"Hello, Sabra," he says, using the term that means both "desert flower" and "native-born Israeli." Dov is one of the third of current-day Israelis who are migrants from elsewhere. In Dov's case, it was one too many attacks on synagogues, Jewish cemeteries, and then actual Jews, in his native France, that sealed it for him. When he out-migrated in 2005, it had all started seeming very 1938 again across Europe. He took his incomparable skills, earned in the GIGN – the French Gendarmerie's elite special operations unit – and put them to work for his own people, where they were badly needed.

He pulls the trussed-up, coughing, and dazed prisoner from the ground, with a single vise-like hand. He arches one eyebrow at Chaya. "I heard you wanted to do... some interrogation?"

"Yes, please, Dov."

He turns to look at the man he holds, whose head is slowly lolling, and who is still smoking.

"You think this one might do?"

"Yes, I think he might."

"Where would you like him?"

"Just there on the curb would be fine."

Dov places the man in a seated position, hunched over in his own lap.

"Thank you, Dov."

He gives her another smile, and a wink, as he removes the bolt from the man's AK, pockets it, unslings his own weapon, and trots back toward what remains of the safehouse.

* * *

Somewhat to Chaya's surprise, her detainee is still alive and frisky when they cart him away. Perhaps even more surprising, he turned out actually to know something – fresh intel, both valuable and relevant. It wasn't a breakthrough. But he did have something to say about a "spooky American," sent by the Iranians, and known to be training Hamas fighters.

Now, as the Sayeret team races back over the border to the staging base in nearby Kfar Saba, Chaya is already dialing Rheinhardt. Getting him on the line, she has to shout, as well as strain to hear. The wind noise is pretty loud, what with the windshield lying back on the street where they kicked it out.

"I think you're going to like this!" she says. "Or maybe 'like' is the wrong word…"

Rheinhardt and Ali are going on their fourth hour of running archived video files through biometric analysis software. As the jobs complete, they upload the resulting data sets to a server farm at the National Geospatial-Intelligence Agency (NGA). NGA operates the Keyhole and Lacrosse satellites upon which the whole intelligence community depends, and also collects and analyzes geospatial intelligence (GEOINT). It was they who measured the shadow of the man in the compound in Abbattobad, Pakistan. At over six feet tall, they figured it was probably bin Laden. Delta's colleagues in SEAL Team Six verified that it was.

Rheinhardt is hoping that if they tell NGA's systems enough about what Rod Tucker looks like, how he walks, what sort of body heat signature he gives off, etc., they might track him down, too. Rheinhardt is rubbing his eyes, and stretching his fingers out, when his cell goes off.

"Go for Rheinhardt." His posture straightens. "Go ahead."

He flips windows on his laptop and starts tapping out notes at high speed.

"You're kidding. Seriously? Jesus. Akhil what? A-W-L-I-Y-A?"

Ali has pushed her keyboard away now and monitors one side of the conversation.

"Outstanding. Great job, Chaya. Really appreciate it. Bye."

He shuts his phone and regards Ali. She merely presents with a pair of sleek raised eyebrows.

"Ready for this?" he says. "Sayeret picked up a Hamas guy. One they hadn't seen before."

"Where from?"

"West Bank. You wouldn't believe the details if I told you." He shakes his head. "Anyway, under interrogation, the guy tells them about a new mil-trainer. American. Very serious guy. Wears all black. Blond hair, biker 'stache."

"That sounds tantalizing. Working in Gaza, as we heard?"

"There. But also in Sudan."

Ali, who is from the country next door to it, doesn't need to be told that Sudan, the largest and perhaps most lawless Africa nation, has for years been one of the world's most popular places to hide terrorist training camps. Algerians and Tunisians, Arabs from France and Belgium, Syrians and Jordanians, and all manner of armed Islamic groups have honed their havoc-wreaking skills there. Many of the camps have, by this point, been taken down by either precision guided munitions or unexpected visits from JSOC personnel. But they tended to pop up again nearly as quickly.

"A lot of Palestinian militants," Ali says, "have had little getaways to Sudan over the years."

"And the Iranians, particularly Quds Force, are known to favor Sudan for training foreign terror and insurgent groups. It all fits."

"Big country, though. Any idea where?"

"Akhil al-Awliya," Rheinhardt says, tripping a little on the pronunciation. "South of Khartoum. On the banks of the Blue Nile."

"Hmm. Why the Nile?"

Rheinhardt taps his stylus on the desk. "Some kind of maritime training?"

"That'd be unusual," Ali says. "There have been a few scattered small boat raids by Hamas on coastal targets in Israel. But not many, and not recently."

"I remember Hizbullah scored a missile hit on an Israeli frigate a few years ago. But it was an Iranian missile – and probably Iranians actually launching it."

"The Iranian connection again. Could they be planning more attacks on Israeli military or commercial shipping?"

"Maybe," Rheinhardt says. "Then again, the whole river thing could be a red herring. Maybe it's just a camp that happens to be on the banks of a river."

Mike Brown picks that moment to wander in through the open door. "Do we have any idea what Tucker was doing in Ukraine?" he asks, taking a chair. "CIA had him in Sevastopol, on the Black Sea, right? Seems like a strange set: Gaza, Lebanon, Ukraine."

"Keep going," Rheinhardt says.

"Well, I started trying to think what might take him there. First thing that jumps out at me – Sevastopol was formerly the headquarters of the Soviet Black Sea Fleet. Now home to both a Ukrainian naval base and a Russian naval base."

"There's that nautical theme again," Ali says.

Rheinhardt: "Two could be a coincidence…"

Ali: "But three's enemy action…"

Mike continues. "I checked all the intel feeds, CIA, NSA, DIA. Nothing. I set up an alert in case anything pops."

Ali pulls her foot up onto her chair, and her chin onto her knee. "Can't we drop a couple of Tomahawks into his training camp?"

"We could. But Tucker won't be there anymore. This intel's days old now. Given current events, I don't see him hanging out in one location for very long."

"Where then?"

Rheinhardt monitors the middle distance. "I don't know. He'll be making his next move. And whatever it is, it's sure to leave knives sticking out of the backs of people along the way."

"That dude," Ali says, "is racking up some serious bad karma…"

Captain Fyodor Kozhin, Ukrainian Naval Forces, tosses in the dark of his cabin. There was a time when he relished night watches. The black and endless sea, the aerial landscape of moving clouds lit by moonlight. And the dangerous thrill of possible enemy action. But that was long ago, before the end of the Cold War. Now… Kozhin is more tired than aggressive. He prefers to get his sleep. Leave the night watches to younger men.

Still, Kozhin has, late in his career, garnered a plum posting for himself. He is captain of one of only three *Neustrashimy*-class anti-submarine frigates in existence, and the only one in the Ukrainian navy. It is the most modern large frigate in the East – and one of the most advanced anti-submarine warfare (ASW) platforms in the world.

The *Tuman* ("Fog") is named after a WWII-era Soviet patrol boat that went down heroically battling three German destroyers. But she is rather more advanced than her namesake. Her integrated search-and-attack sonar system is capable of detecting and hunting down even the quietest of submarines at the most extreme depths. And after she runs them down, she can wreak sub-surface havoc with two types of anti-submarine guided missiles, sea mines, twin 55mm grenade launchers, and a 100mm deck gun.

If all else fails, she has a KA-27 ASW helicopter on deck – with a 980km range, nose-mounted search radar and 36 active sonar buoys. The helo also mounts a 7.62mm minigun, a 30mm cannon, sonar-homing torpedoes, and a weapons bay full of depth charges.

Basically, the *Tuman* is a submarine captain's very worst nightmare, a dark-night-of-the-soul predator lurking too close at virtually any range.

* * *

So, a terrifyingly capable warship. But with a series of increasingly stultifying missions. Endless patrols. Formation exercises. Pirate hunting in the Gulf of Aden if they're really lucky. And the odd distress call from a lost tour charter or fishing boat with clapped-out engines. It is the latter that causes Kozhin's executive officer (XO) to ring his wall phone tonight.

"*Da. Kogda? Da, pyat' minoot.*"

He throws off the wool blanket and gets his damp joints creaking. He wonders if he can even make it up to his bridge in five minutes these days.

When he arrives, they have not only reached the disabled vessel, but have also put three different deck spotlights on her. Peering out the Kent screens, Kozhin can immediately see that she's your standard shit-bucket Georgian trawler – barely seaworthy at the best of times, and subject to all manner of mechanical failure, due to horrifying maintenance standards.

Captain Kozhin can also see that she is listing badly.

"Well?" he says to his XO, who is also officer of the watch. He offhandedly takes a mug of black coffee from a junior officer.

"They were close when we got the call, ten minutes sailing. They report an explosion in their engine compartment. Dead in the sea. And taking on water – too much for their bilge pumps."

"Terrific," says Kozhin, pausing to blow on the surface of the coffee. "So this will not be the usual free high-seas wrench work. But instead a rescue."

"I'm afraid it looks that way, Captain."

Kozhin flips idly through the duty log on the console. "What do they crew?"

"Fifteen souls aboard."

"Well… may as well do it before we're throwing life preservers and fishing them out."

"Aye, sir."

Kozhin sips coffee and lets them get on with it. He can hear the slap as his sailors rig scramble nets over the port side, and hear the engines burble as the ship maneuvers in close. He can see the first fishermen scrambling onto the deck – and that's when he hears the popping of the spotlights going out.

What the hell? He steps out onto the gangway in time to see the last spot go dark, and the trawler plunged into darkness. With that, he makes out a handful of on-off flashes from the stricken vessel. Kozhin's eyes go wide.

Muzzle flashes.

He hears unsilenced gunfire now, as well as shouts – and senses more than sees a scuffle on the deck below him. He is already scrambling back into his bridge, lunging for the tannoy mic. But the General Quarters announcement dies in his throat as the hatch is kicked open again and a man in black steps in with an assault rifle at his shoulder. With a half-dozen shots, triggering off in no more than a second, everyone on the bridge is dead. Everyone but Kozhin.

The man in black steps forward as several other gunmen rush in behind him.

"*Kapitan Kozhin?*" the man asks, his cruel lips moving underneath a forked moustache.

"*Da.*"

Bewildered, Fyodor Kozhin hears the shots that kill him echo in the small steel cabin. He goes to his knees, then over on his side, as the control lights twinkle, then dim to black.

* * *

The man in black leans over the nav console with his two Gazan sailors, translating control markings from the original Russian. Peals of muted gunfire can still be heard from below decks. But the deck, and the bridge, are now secure. And they have already disabled the AIS maritime transponder.

It took Tucker several weeks of intense planning and training to take these Hamas fighters and turn them into a capable maritime commando force. But worth the effort, he now thinks.

In Arabic, he says to his two men, "Here – GPS coordinates for the mouth of the Bosporus." The men nod. "Distance is three hundred and fifty nautical miles. At our top speed that's about four and a half hours' sailing. It's important that we clear Istanbul before first light. You understand?"

"*Tayeb.*"

"Good. Then another hour through the Dardanelles, two to thread the Aegean. And then we are free and clear in the blue-water Med. Now get us underway."

"*Na'am, sayyidi.*"

He claps both men on the back, then hoists his rifle and heads below to help with the mopping up.

A hell of a prize, he thinks to himself. *Never thought I'd get to take down a Soviet warship… This job just gets cooler all the time.*

Rheinhardt lies in the dark, nowhere near sleep. His idea about grabbing a couple hours tactical rack is not coming to much. Stimulants can help in a pinch, when you have to function for fifty hours in a row, or across a series of twenty-hour days.

But it's also amazing how quickly and dramatically human performance deteriorates with sleep deprivation. Judgment goes, tempers flare, carelessness creeps into everything. And it doesn't matter if you're too jacked up or anxious to sleep. Insomnia is endemic in the Unit. Hundreds of guys with the weight of the world on their shoulders. It takes its toll.

At the moment, Rheinhardt is also worried he's at risk of something they call "target lock," a sort of blindness to everything outside of the movements of your prey. Movements which can be hypnotic – sometimes intentionally so. It's said that the most deadly animal to hunt is the human. Multiply that by about a thousand, and then you're hunting a Delta operator. In Delta, the man *is* the weapon. Now the man is also the enemy's weapon.

And this sword definitely cuts both ways.

But mainly in our direction, Rheinhardt thinks morosely to himself. *Particularly until we figure out what the hell this guy's doing.*

It's his job to assess the risks of a mission – and then make the final judgment about when those risks are worth taking. At Delta, an ironclad rule is that the people performing a mission are also the people who get to plan it. No top-down heroics by decree. And the mission commander makes the final go/no-go decision.

But can he still make those calls in this case? Is he too close to this one?

Another thing that's changed is the caliber of the enemy. Both Hamas and Hizbullah have fielded half-decent shooters at times. Of course, they've been most deadly when going up against schoolchildren on buses and elderly women at prayer. But now, if intel is to be believed, they have been trained by *a Delta cadre member.* A guy who used to be responsible for producing the very most cunning and fearsome commandos in the world.

Tucker's probably capable of taking anyone of military age and turning him into something extremely dangerous. A fighter skilled, at a minimum, in the three skills a commando must master to prevail in combat: how to shoot, how to move, and how to communicate.

So what's going to happen when Rheinhardt takes his people up against that sort of enemy? He had good luck in the last years of his career, in bringing people home alive. Will it hold? Or will he end up getting these people, about whom he cares so much, killed after all? And, if they are to die, will their sacrifice even make any difference?

He rolls over and carries on not sleeping.

* * *

His billet door knocks in the dark.

Rheinhardt clicks on his LED Maglite and splashes the door. "Yeah."

The door swings open, letting in the light from the hall. It's BJ. He's wearing an imprinted t-shirt that says, "Well, it's not going to suck itself." He's also carrying what appears to be a full bottle of Jack Daniel's.

"Room service," he rumbles.

Rheinhardt clicks off the light. "Leave it on the credenza, thanks."

BJ, already walking in, freezes and glares at him.

"Just kidding. You know you're welcome wherever I am. That much more so with Jack."

BJ pulls up the one chair, while Rheinhardt turns on the bedside lamp.

"Heard you were down here with the visiting dignitaries and shit."

"Home is where I hang my pistols." Rheinhardt nods to his gunbelt, hanging on the doorknob. "Glass?"

"No. Fuck it." BJ takes a quick pull and hands over the bottle. "It's sure good to have you back. Even if the circumstances are surreal."

Rheinhardt takes a slug. "Yeah. And I hate to admit it. But it's good to be back. Already."

BJ sighs quietly. "I never said anything. Didn't want to influence your decision one way or another. But you must have had mixed feelings about calling it a day."

"Mixed feelings like amputating something. But we always knew we couldn't do this for ever. One day it has to end. Better this way."

"Too true. You wound things down better than a lot of our brothers – in the ground, or in a wheelchair. And a whole helluva lot better than that Rod Tucker motherfucker."

Rheinhardt takes another drink, a longer one, then hands the bottle back. "I've got to tell you. Even after what he did, with everything we know about him, it's still hard for me to believe he's gone rogue. That he's shooting for the enemies of everything we've been defending all this time."

BJ nods. "And I gotta tell *you*. I wouldn't piss on that son of a bitch if he were on fire."

Rheinhardt laughs. "Not unless you'd been drinking grain alcohol."

"Probably not even then."

"Yeah… me neither."

Johnson seems to consider his next statement carefully. "The man chose his side. He's worse than an enemy – he's a brother who's betrayed us. And if we have to take him down, we cannot hesitate, *not even for a second*, just because we used to know the dude."

"Not least because hesitation would be fatal."

"Totally."

Rheinhardt nods, then frowns. "I've got a bad feeling about this one."

The two drink in silence for a while. Finally, BJ hoists himself up. Rheinhardt rolls his eyes at the other man's t-shirt. "It's not going to suck itself? Jesus, BJ."

"I don't know, seemed kind of appropriate today."

"What – for this mission?"

"Yeah. It's definitely going to suck. But, then again, it's not going to suck itself. So back to work." He stands and lets himself out.

And the whiskey finally does the job of putting Rheinhardt under for a few hours.

Tucker watches the lights of Beirut coming up as he and the driver of the truck zip north on the highway that connects Sidon, down the Lebanese coast, with that city of impossibilities, Beirut. The great black mass of the Mediterranean dominates the horizon out to their left.

This is not Tucker's first visit to Beirut. These days, the place is a far cry from the wild west show it was in the 80s and 90s. But it's still no place for the faint of heart. Or the slow on the draw. *This has got to be,* Tucker thinks to himself, monitoring the hodge podge of vehicles swirling around his truck, *the most beautiful and fucked up place on Earth.*

Start with a cosmopolitan city right on the Med, with the glorious Mediterranean climate that implies. Throw in gorgeous mountains all along the coast, plunging down into the same waters Homer immortalized. Put the capital city on a graceful strip of land thrust out into it. Mountains, sea, and luscious and fertile farmlands. Throw in some of the best-looking people in the world. Levantines, men and women both, are just beautiful.

But then picture a whole city, the whole country really, ripping itself into bloody ribbons, virtually non-stop for twenty years. A quarter million dead, mostly civilians. Another million wounded. And a million on top of that fleeing for pretty much anywhere else they could get to.

And that was just the *official* Lebanese civil war.

It all started when the PLO were kicked out of Jordan and decamped en masse to Lebanon, where they immediately got to work undermining the government. As lawlessness descended, Shiites, Sunnis, Maronite and Phalangist Christians, and Druze, all formed their own militias.

They fought one another to a bloody five-way standoff, occasionally pausing to take potshots at U.S. Marines, British and French soldiers from the multinational peacekeeping force, and the Syrian Army, which invaded under the pretext of restoring order.

And also of course at the Israelis, who were there on and off for decades, pounding the shit out of suspected PLO and Hizbullah positions. This they did anytime they thought the Lebanese Armed Forces (LAF) weren't doing enough to stop rocket attacks and border infiltrations into northern Israel. Which was virtually always. The LAF never had the power to stop those things.

No one was in charge.

* * *

Delta has a lot of history in Beirut. They've chased hostages and hostage-takers all over that battleground of a city. They had the impossible job of protecting the U.S. Ambassador, and accomplished it anyway, though they lost men when the Embassy building was destroyed by a truck bomb. That was one of the largest and most horrific suicide bombings ever – until the one six months later that destroyed the Marine barracks down the road, and vaporized 240 souls in an instant. It was one of the largest non-nuclear explosions in history.

And it was all pulled off by a Hizbullah bomb-maker. One trained and financed by... Iran.

How very little anything ever changes in this shithole, Tucker thinks to himself, watching the dark and sleeping city begin to encircle them.

Seemingly taking a page from Delta's playbook, the Hizbullah bombers built a whole mock-up of the barracks complex down in the Bekaa Valley. And they then rehearsed their attack on it, until nothing was left to chance. The Marines never had a prayer.

And this little stunt, this culmination of the horror and folly of America's years-long involvement in Lebanon, so impressed and inspired a then-unknown son of the bin Laden family, that he more or less duplicated the whole operation in bombing the U.S. embassies in Kenya and Tanzania fifteen years later, killing hundreds and wounding thousands more.

Including more U.S. Marines.

When the fuck would the elected idiots in Washington learn?

The core problem, Tucker knew, the one responsible for nearly a century of non-stop bloodshed across the Middle East, was the arbitrary national borders drawn for the convenience of European diplomats at Versailles. After its defeat in WWI, the Ottoman Empire was divided up in fascinating ways that had virtually zero regard for the ethnic, religious, or national affiliations of any of the people living there.

Just ask an Iraqi Christian, a Gulf State Shiite, an Afghan Baluchi, or a Kurd from virtually anywhere. Or especially a Palestinian. Because of course the whole mess was compounded massively, thirty years later, by the arbitrary creation of a settler state for the Jews – *Israel*. And by America's open-ended commitment to defend it, spending American lives every step of the way.

Europe, and the UN, had made these horrendous fucking problems. And America would never be able to fix them. But American military men would continue to die trying. Always, it was the soldiers who paid.

And it needed to end.

* * *

Post-civil-war reconstruction of Beirut had been going reasonably well, with the tourists even coming back in modest numbers. That was, until Israel fought another miniature war with Lebanese Hizbullah in 2006. For the first time, the "Army of God" fought the IDF, thought for decades to be unbeatable, to a bloody-nosed standstill.

It's amazing what Iranian arms and military advisers can do for a guerilla force, Tucker thinks. He's had the opportunity to see the effects of this firsthand. See them – and personally amplify them. Since then, Hizbullah has been getting ready for the next round, stockpiling over 40,000 rockets, many of which could now reach Tel Aviv. And there were additional reasons to think the next round would go even worse for the Israelis.

And while the non-stop artillery duels of the civil war had ceased for the moment, Beirut remains a frontier town – a good place for outlaws to move outside the law. And for smugglers to move the most coveted, and most remorselessly policed, contraband in the world.

Tucker checks his watch, then takes a quick look at the driver. Unbeknownst to the man (boy, really), he has been handpicked for this job, at the very last minute, for very particular reasons. The boy was told that the regular driver had been assassinated by the Israelis.

A plausible explanation. And unverifiable.

The kid, skinny arms draped across the wheel, steals a glance back across at Tucker. Neither smiles. Both are sitting on secrets. But Tucker's poker face is much the better one.

The truck angles off the dark highway, and they slip into the deadly warren of South Beirut.

* * *

Ultimately, the hand-off of the goods goes without any problem.

The material itself is only thirty kilograms in weight. But it's 30kg of something that takes years and an enormous industrial infrastructure to produce. The bulk of the package is actually the specialized transportation cask that holds the material. Ironically, it is labeled on the outside as being a "certified Type B package, which meets the International Atomic Energy Agency Safety Standard Series no. TS-R-1." Tucker isn't sure the people he's delivering it to give much of a shit about IAEA safety standards.

Then again, as the truck bumps west now, on another one of what in Lebanon is charitably termed a highway, Tucker thinks maybe he appreciates the safety rating. Now that they're back on the road, the border crossing into Syria is less than an hour away. After that, they are home free. Though, the boy driving, Tucker sees, is sweating rivulets down his face and arms. And it ain't that hot. Tucker steals a peak at his pocket radiation dosimeter.

Nope. Ain't hot in here at all...

The driver of the truck, Hakim, doesn't wait for the small prop plane to rumble down the dirt strip and lift off. Instead, he guns the truck's engine and spins dirt out from under its balding tires, just as soon as the cargo is cross-loaded from the truck to the aircraft. He then gives thanks to God that he is out of there. And especially that he is away from the terrifying American.

Hakim Maboob is nineteen years old, Shia Muslim, and native-born Lebanese. He is also a proud but very junior member of the Party of God – *Hizbullah* in Arabic.

Hakim's membership in Hizbullah, however, is with their Jihad Al Binna foundation. Despite the presence of the J word – guaranteed to cause hysteria and loathing in Westerners who know nothing about *real* jihad, the religious duty of all Muslims, and the internal struggle to be closer to and worthy of God – it is not a fighting group. Rather, it is a real-estate foundation.

Lebanon, particularly the south, has been devastated by decades of Israeli incursions, occupation, air strikes, and other violations of Lebanese sovereignty. It is the role of Jihad Al Binna to rebuild – schools, infrastructure, shelters for refugees. It is truly God's work. And Hakim's job is to help his people. So when he got the call from Al-Muqawama al-Islamiyya ("the Islamic Resistance," one of Hizbullah's military arms), and was told to report for duty, he did not know what it was about. But he knew he did not have the option of declining.

He dressed and crept out, taking care not to wake his mother, grandmother, or the dozen other relatives who shared their tiny house in the walled medieval city of Sidon. He walked in the dark to the address given him. And he took possession of the truck, where he also picked up the spooky American. Then into southern Beirut. And finally into Syria.

May God have mercy upon him.

* * *

Hakim waits until he is back over the border into Lebanon before he dares reach for his phone. And he dials the phone number given him by the Israelis.

He took the number, as well as the money they offered him, because, with the economy of southern Lebanon in ruins after decades of war, opportunities were few. And because his mother and the rest of his family were very poor and hungry. And because the small salary paid to him by the foundation was never enough to feed them all. No matter how much they scrimped, it never stretched far enough.

He had been told he need only provide small bits of information, only to allow the civilians in northern Israel to take shelter before rocket attacks. That wasn't so disloyal, was it? And all for his family. So he took the number, and the money. But now he finds himself in over his head.

And with his family in grave danger.

The risk of making this call today is grave. If anyone in the Party learns that he is talking to the Israelis, he will be hanged in public, at best. And at worst, his family... well, it doesn't bear thinking about. He dials with one hand, using half his attention to navigate the coal-black road.

The woman answers on the second ring, sleep in her voice.

Chaya, wearing only shorts and a sweatshirt, wails at the door of Colonel Eshel's quarters, a few feet down the hall from hers. He opens it bleary-eyed, in skivvies and an olive t-shirt.

"Dress," she says. "Ops. Now."

"Two minutes," he says, turning away but not closing the door.

Chaya, who has just gotten the call from her informer in Hizbullah, uses the 60-second walk to the ops center to speed dial Rheinhardt.

"Eric – it's Chaya." Even now, in this midst of all this, she pauses to consider that she chose first names. Not surnames, not rank. It seems natural, even at a moment of terrible crisis.

She flips on all the overhead lights in the Ops Center and starts making hand signals at the duty officer, while speaking rapidly into the phone and also logging in to her station. She puts her hand over the mouthpiece, and speaks loudly over her console.

"I need a full house. Get everyone in here. Now."

"Yes, ma'am." The duty officer grabs a phone and a clipboard.

"And I need to task air surveillance assets – drones at any altitude, spy planes, or sats. Whatever we've got that can look at the air between Damascus and Tehran. This trumps any other tasking. *Anything.*"

Rheinhardt has no way to appreciate the humor value in him wailing on Colonel Havering's door in the same manner, minutes later, on the other side of the world. However, it is eight hours earlier in their day, so at least Havering isn't in his skivvies.

Rheinhardt briefs him in rapid-fire tones while they half-trot, side-by-side, toward the TOC.

"An informant where?" Havering asks.

"Hizbullah. Bit player. Recruited recently, but believed reliable."

They round a corner, nearly crashing into two men rolling a chest-high pallet down the hall.

"Easy there, Colonel. Anti-tank rockets have right of way…"

Havering makes a palms-out conciliatory gesture. He and Rheinhardt flow around either side of the cart, barely breaking stride.

"So the CI's called up to be a driver," Rheinhardt continues. "Picks up someone who can only be Tucker."

"You're so sure?"

"As close to POSIDENT as makes no difference. They meet another vehicle, driven by ethnic Chinese, in South Lebanon. Tucker speaks Mandarin with them. They cross-load a large package, cross the border into Syria, then drive to a dirt airstrip."

"Where?"

"North of Zabadani they think. It fits the description, travel time, and geography."

"Fucking Syria." Havering shakes his head.

* * *

They reach the TOC now. Havering pushes a hand palm-out at Rheinhardt to pause him, then waggles the other at the duty officer, giving her orders before she gets there.

"I need to talk to the following people. Wherever they are, whatever they're doing. First – General Votel." Votel is the head of JSOC, Havering's immediate boss. "Then the National Security Adviser, the Langley liaison – no scratch that, make it the Agency Ops Director. And our Bureau guy. Start stacking 'em up. Go."

He makes a whirly motion with his finger at Rheinhardt, who resumes.

"They put the package on a prop plane, Tucker takes off with it. The kid clears out and calls Chaya from the road."

"And the package?"

"Nuclear materials cask, from the description. Almost definitely."

"How big?"

"About four by six by four. If it's HEU, with shielding, the cask could hold maybe 15 to 30 kilograms. Assuming enrichment to 90 per cent, and depending on the sophistication of the device, enough for two to four weapons."

"Couldn't be a dummy of some kind? Trying to head fake us?"

"Could be," Rheinhardt says. "But there's no motive for it—"

"That we've thought of yet."

"That we've thought of yet. And China's definitely got the material to sell. And there's no reason to think they'd hesitate to sell it to Iran, not if they thought they could do it without getting fingered."

"Yeah. They're worse than the goddamned French, as far as ruthlessly pursuing their own national interest goes." Havering pauses and squints. "But what about the atomic fingerprint? Isotopic purity, age of the fissile material? Something goes bang, forensics will pretty quickly tell us 'made in China'."

Rheinhardt shakes his head. "That's nice to think. But it's not necessarily so. First of all, we don't have fingerprint files for all of China's reactors. Hell, we don't even *know* about all of China's reactors. Second, North Korea. God knows the Chinese could buy or take HEU from their client state, and if something goes off and it says 'made in Pyongyang' on it—"

"That's a whole different geo-strategic deal."

"Exactly. And one that might even suit the Chinese Politburo."

Havering pauses, his expression growing even more grim. "I've got more bad news for you. I got the intel shack's report from your Iranian nuke guy. Sultan."

"Only now?"

"They had to hand him over to Agency, then wait 'til the spooks were done with him. Gave me their report today. I was just reading it when you barged in."

"And?"

"The executive summary is: Iran has basically finished their nuclear weaponization work. They've got a good design for a fairly sophisticated implosion device. Multiple weapons on-hand, ready to rock and roll. They just need the fissile material."

"And delivery systems?"

"They've got medium-range missiles from the North Koreans. But their Shahab-3's are already nuclear-payload-capable and everyone fucking knows it. They've also got Russian S-300s – sale of which was supposed to be prohibited by U.N. sanctions."

"Good ole U.N. sanctions."

"Yeah. Sultan says they've test-launched all three of them."

"Without us detecting it? How?"

"Down in SA. Venezuela. With their BFF Hugo Chavez."

Rheinhardt nods and clenches his teeth. "Huge country, spotty intel and sat coverage. So you're saying the only hold-up now is fissile material. Once they get that, they've got nukes."

"Exactly. We've been leaning on the wrong barn door. The state of their enrichment program doesn't mean shit, if they can just go shopping for it."

Rheinhardt shakes his head. "Sultan's sure about all this?"

"Nobody's totally sure about anything. But you can go talk to him yourself. He's back in the guest billets, four doors down from you. Come to think of it, I'm gonna bring him up here right now." He waves at somebody, anybody, in the TOC to come do that for him. "But listen, Eric—"

"Yeah?"

"You know where this goes now."

"Upstairs."

"No – *all the way* upstairs. Whatever happens now, all decisions are thirty pay grades north of us."

Rheinhardt exhales. "Roger that."

"Nonetheless… I've already initiated a Bowstring loadout."

Bowstring is the full Delta Squadron always on 60-minute alert, ready to gear up and take off for anywhere in the world they're needed. The duty rotates amongst the Delta squadrons.

Rheinhardt looks surprised. "When did you do that?"

Havering holds up his phone. "When you weren't looking. One touch alert. New IT kit."

"Who's on Bowstring?" Rheinhardt asks.

"B."

"Tucker's old squadron. Funny."

"No. It ain't."

Rheinhardt holds Havering's gaze. "I wanna go out with them."

"Negative. But you can help me C2 this thing here. Pull down the full mission profiles for the Chalus weaponization facility. Plus anything on anywhere they've got missile silos. God knows where we'll have to hit 'em now."

"Got it."

"Of course, there's not a chance in hell we'll get to operationalize anything… but, then again, our jobs are mostly about chance-in-hell types of things, aren't they?"

But Rheinhardt's already exiting. At a run.

Rheinhardt literally runs into Dr. Sultan, and the MP escorting him, in the last stretch of corridor outside the TOC. Rheinhardt's carrying an armload of binders, a laptop, and two tablet computers. By the time they step inside the high-tech chamber, where activity has exploded in the minutes since things kicked off, the two are in animated conversation.

"Yes, yes," Sultan says. "I've been trying to tell you. Implosion devices designed and built. Only needing the uranium. Enriched to eighty-eight percent or higher."

Rheinhardt pulls two rolling chairs up to an empty station. He looks up to see Havering in the elevated, glass-fronted command area, talking on three phones. Or holding them, anyway.

"You told this to the CIA interrogators?"

"I tried. They were very methodical. One thing at a time. When they returned me here, your men seemed to have a more suitable sense of urgency."

"What's your estimate for time to deployment? How long after they have the HEU could they put it all together and launch a nuclear strike?"

Sultan looks up, doing mental calculations. "Two to three days, if they worked round the clock. The work is delicate, very tight tolerances. And there are tests that have to be performed."

Rheinhardt is listening, but also logging in to his station and tabbing through several complexly colored and bolded screens — the current threat matrix board, the Executive Intercept Transcript Summary (XITS) provided daily from NSA, intel briefs from a half-dozen other agencies, plus his own secure e-mail.

"Needless to say," Sultan adds, seeming to sort of lecture off into the air, "they cannot know for sure that it will go bang until they test one — a real live detonation. And they can't do that without everyone detecting it."

Colonel Havering grabs the back of Sultan's chair and wheels him out of the way. "It's in the hands of the gods now."

"You mean the National Security Council," says Rheinhardt, half-looking up and typing.

"The NSC. And the president. Personally, I think if anything does happen, it's a hell of a lot more likely to be the Air Force, from 30,000 feet. Or Navy cruise missiles from 300 miles offshore."

Rheinhardt nods. "What are you going to do with B Squadron, then?"

"Stage 'em out of Balad in Iraq. If we do launch anything, we'll do it from there."

"When do they go?"

"They're wheels up—" Havering checks his watch — "right now. Well, another minute."

"They're still going to be almost eleven hours in the air. Who's at Balad now?"

"Half of C Squadron. Some detached DEVGRU and SAD elements. And a company of Rangers from the 75th. All those guys are on alert for a possible emergency assault into Iran. But they don't have the plans, they're not briefed for it – and never mind rehearsed it. Now where are you at with a deliberate assault plan?"

"Into Chalus? I need thirty minutes to get up to speed on the state of the shelved plans. Then I can give you a brief on how much work needs to be done."

"I know it's all vague at this point. What help do you need?"

"Ali would be good. She's actually been inside."

"Ali ain't here." Before Rheinhardt can ask, Havering jabs a thumb at the sky, meaning she's in the air. "I needed someone along for the assault who's actually been inside. Plus B's Third Troop is short a sniper at the moment."

"Who?"

"Slim got killed in Syria. Along with Hopper."

Rheinhardt pauses a reverent beat. "The rest of Alpha, then."

Havering nods. But he also sees something in Rheinhardt's face. "Ali's there, Eric. You're here. And I'm going to need you here until further."

"Understood."

"But if the clock moves up, I'll put you in the air in the Gulfstream. You'll make up some time that way. And then you can run things from the Balad JOC."

Chaya drops her desk phone back into its cradle. She's still on hold on her mobile, which is wedged between ear and shoulder. Her hands are glued to her keyboard. She leans in close to peer at two grainy video views on her monitor, both in night-vision green-and-black.

The first is from a small Hunter UAV zooming over Beirut, its camera locked onto Hakim Maboob's truck. They were able to acquire it very quickly, based on triangulation from cell towers. The Hunter is armed with Lahat laser-guided missiles. Unfortunately, it's not Hakim that Chaya wants to blow up right now. Because the nuclear materials are no longer with him.

The second view is from one of their enormous Eitan drones, which has enhanced night vision and forward-looking infrared (FLIR), which means it can see through dust and clouds. It can also stay in the air almost a day. But it's unarmed. This one was loitering over southern Lebanon at 40,000 feet when Chaya had it immediately haul ass due east, to try and track down one small plane in a very big sky.

That is what she wants to blow up. The plane transporting the uranium.

Chaya's already discovered that this aircraft has no transponder or filed flight plan. In all probability, it's flying too low for surface radar stations to catch. Now it will be a question of whether they can skin-paint it with aerial radar, or spot it on video – and do so before it lands again and disappears, probably for good.

But if Chaya can find it in the air, she can shoot it out of the air.

The lieutenant across from her is even now scrambling IAF fighters from Ramat David AB in the north – F/15 Eagles and F/A-18 Hornets, veteran pilots sprinting and pulling on their helmets, jet engines screaming and screeching down midnight-black runways.

* * *

Fixated on her screens, her attention divided eight ways, Chaya only realizes Colonel Eshel is behind her when he physically spins her chair around toward him.

"I said, 'I am going now'."

"Fine. Where to?"

"Beit Aghion, direct by helo." Beit Aghion is the prime minister's residence in Jerusalem. "We've given the night staff there a heads-up and summary. But this is something they're going to want to wake the whole cabinet up for."

Chaya nods once.

"You lead here. Fix and destroy that plane if you can."

"Yes, sir."

"If you can't... well, then we take it from there. But that's my helo landing now."

A lieutenant is now waving and shouting from across the room.

"What?" Eshel says above the general tumult.

The young man cups his hands. "That's not your helo, sir..."

"Then whose the hell is it?"

"The prime minister's, sir."

Thirty seconds later the PM walks in from the exterior door, trailing rotor wash and a handful of aides behind her.

Hakim Maboob is running full-out now, from the address where he first picked up and has now dropped off the truck, in the direction of home. The old walled city is just beginning to stir, the earliest risers amongst the merchants and artisans stacking produce and wheeling out carts. Fighting panic, Hakim doesn't slow as he sees his family's building come into view, all smudged browns and grays in the first faint light of day.

Rounding on the entrance hall, he skids into a beefy chest and set of arms. There are two hulking men blocking his way. Their full beards, black clothing, and Palestinian keffiyehs on their shoulders instantly identify them as members of Ansar-e Hizbullah – a splinter group of Iranian Hizbullah that Hakim has seen skulking around more and more in recent months.

Before he can react, a fiendishly strong hand grips him by his skinny upper arm. The man flips open a phone, speed dials, and speaks into it. His voice is both quiet and rumblingly deep.

"It's Ezzat, in Sidon. We have him. Okay."

The man hands the phone over. With a brief hesitation, Hakim takes it and puts it to his ear.

"…Hello?"

"Hello, Hakim." He instantly recognizes the lightly accented Arabic of the black-clad American. *"Did you make the call?"*

Hakim swallows dryly. "Yes. As you said." He tries to keep his panic in check.

"Tell me what you told them."

"Everything! About the truck. And about the plane. And the steel box."

"And did you describe me, as well?"

"Yes, yes. I told her everything – everything I could remember."

"Okay. Good, Hakim. The safety of a human is in the sweetness of his tongue." Hakim recognizes the proverb. But he has no response to this. *"Put our brother back on."*

Hakim hands the phone back, his eyes pleading.

"Hello," the big man says.

"Let him go."

Suddenly unhanded, Hakim takes a breath and rushes inside.

"Mama!" Hakim throws himself in his mother's lap, where she is tied to her chair. All the rest of his family members are tied up and gagged, sitting in various postures around the main room. But they appear unhurt. Both he and his mother are sobbing, the latter nearly silently.

It is just as the American warned him. Including the bundles of explosives tied to their chairs. But he's done what he was told to. It's all going to be okay now. He begins pulling at the knots of his mother's bonds.

He looks into his mother's eyes, and pauses just to put his hand on hers.

* * *

"He's inside the house?" Tucker asks, from 1,200 miles away in Tehran.

"Na'am, Sayyid."

"Okay. Blow the house."

Ezzat's eyebrows go north. "Blow it up?"

"'The tongue of the ignorant is the key to his death'," says Tucker, seamlessly switching Arab proverbs as suits him. *"Blow the house. Do it now. Though you might want to be on the other side of the street."*

Ezzat startles and looks around him. He fails to imagine that Tucker is actually watching him on video from a small Iranian *Ababil* ("Swallow") UAV circling overhead. The line goes dead in his ear. Ezzat removes the radio detonator from his jacket pocket.

His partner gives him a look. In response, he shrugs and says, *"Yallah,"* gesturing sharply. They both trot across the street, and then fifty meters down it.

With a last look around, he shrugs again.

Then he presses the button.

When Prime Minister Tzipi Livni strides into Sayeret Matkal's
Ops Center, the first person she greets is not the commander,
but Chaya Akhilov. The two are acquainted, having met during a ceremony honoring Natasha Akhilov after her death.
They are also, it turns out, slightly related. Small country. She
grips Chaya's hand in both of hers.

"Major Akhilov. How are you? How are your parents?"

"All very well, ma'am. Thank you."

"Good. Excuse me." She nods at Eshel and leads him
into his own office.

Twenty minutes later, she comes back out, salutes the
room, and climbs back in her helo.

"Chaya." It is Colonel Eshel, standing in the open door of
his office, hands on hips, looking at the floor. "You're with me."

* * *

"The Third Temple," Colonel Eshel says over his desk, "will
not fall on our watch."

"No, sir," Chaya says, sitting still and erect in a straight-
backed chair opposite.

The Jewish First and Second Temples, both located on the
same site on the Temple Mount in Jerusalem, were destroyed
by the ancient Babylonians, and the Romans, respectively.
"The Third Temple" is a very freighted and resonant way of

referring to the modern state of Israel – the nation reborn as home to a people who had been wandering without one for 2,000 years.

"The PM, and the cabinet, do not believe that Iran will launch a nuclear first strike."

Chaya nods. But internally she is calling to mind the infamous public statement made by former Iranian president Ali Akbar Hashemi-Rafsanjani: "The use of even one nuclear bomb inside Israel will destroy everything. However, it will only harm the Islamic world. It is not irrational to contemplate such an eventuality."

Not surprisingly, Eshel reads her mind.

"Rafsanjani's comments notwithstanding. And, yes, the current president's messianism also notwithstanding. Iran knows that a nuclear strike will bring a crushing retaliation. No matter how successful their attack, they will be destroyed in our second strike. However bad the damage here, our nuclear submarines will always be able to respond."

"A dead man's trigger," Chaya says. But she thinks to herself: *the problem with a dead man's trigger is that you're dead.*

"So Iran knows that to kill us would be to kill themselves. Nonetheless…" He flicks his eyes at his computer screen. Then he turns it off. "Nonetheless, a nuclear Iran is too grave an existential threat to be lived with."

Chaya exhales.

"The PM is unwilling to be the leader who gambles with the lives of another six million Jews. Is 'Never again' merely a slogan for a bumper sticker? If we do not act on our own behalf to prevent the next Holocaust… then what have we learned?"

Chaya is both relieved and terrified to hear her commander talking this way. Relieved because she feels the same. Terrified because she knows as well as him the costs this may entail.

"And even if we could rule out a first strike, the specter of an Iranian nuclear umbrella would itself be a nightmare. Imagine what Quds Force might do, with a nuclear threat backing them up. Think of Hamas and Hizbullah emboldened, operating against us virtually at will. Increasing rocket attacks on our borders both north and south, able to hit virtually all of Israel."

Eshel takes a look at his steepled fingers now.

"Between these escalating attacks from without, and the plague of terrorism within... plus a constant threat of nuclear annihilation... Israel could actually be destroyed in a very undramatic way." He looks up to face her again.

"Everyone will leave," Chaya says.

"Exactly. Out-migration exceeded immigration for the first time ever in 2007. People can only take so much. And if no one dares live in Israel..."

"...then there is no more Israel."

Eshel nods. "And the mullahs know this. All our enemies know this."

"Why don't our friends?"

"What friends?" Eshel says with a weary smile.

The Jews have never lost their gallows humor.

Often, it's been all they had.

* * *

"Now, listen. The PM was here because she wanted to know about our covert or commando options for stopping Iranian weaponization. In the final minutes."

"And?"

"I told her there are no such options."

"Too risky?"

"Damn the risk, or the cost. I'd send everyone here to their deaths, if it could succeed. The problem is that the chances of success are too low." Eshel sighs. "So that leaves war. A full bombing campaign – after first destroying Iranian air defenses so that the bombers can get in. Aerial dogfights. Bracing for retaliatory attacks on all our borders. Probably medium-range conventional missile strikes on our cities."

"But we could win."

"Win – yes. But can we degrade their weaponization program enough? That is a coin toss. Not to mention that anyone could be drawn into such a war. Anyone, or everyone – all the Arab states. The whole region could be in flames within days. And us in another war for survival."

Eshel doesn't need to underscore that the IDF can never afford to lose a war. When the Arabs lose, they go home. If the Israelis lose, they go into the sea – all of them. This has always been the case. And every Israeli soldier has always known it. Which might be one reason why they've always fought so superbly.

They share a silence, before Chaya speaks. "But you know for whom there probably *is* a viable commando option…"

"The Americans. What does your man there say?"

"When we spoke, thirty minutes ago, they were already scrambling. I'll get an update." She pulls out her phone and dials where she sits.

Maps, charts, binders, laptops, tablet computers, loose papers, and little plastic unit designators lie scattered across the boat-shaped table. Also sprawled across the table are Rheinhardt, Johnson, and Javier. They are leaning in, gesturing, pushing units around the map. They are arguing, brainstorming, troubleshooting, sharp-shooting, strategizing, hypothesizing, conjecturing, tabletop gaming.

"The real cocksuck of this is," BJ says, pushing his massive bulk up and away from the table, "is that we not only have to come up with a workable assault plan... plus make sure we're four steps ahead of the IRG with every move we make, in a non-permissive environment..."

Rheinhardt finishes for him. "But we also have to make sure fucking Rod Tucker doesn't know our own moves before we even make them."

"Exactly." BJ stops and gives Rheinhardt a skewed look. "Hey, man."

"Yeah?" Both Rheinhardt and Javier lock onto him.

"Did you know there's a shelved assault plan in here for *decapitating* the Iranian regime?"

Rheinhardt holds his gaze. "Yeah. I do know. I worked on it."

"I know we prepare for some seriously unlikely contingencies, but this..."

"What's the deal?" Javier asks.

Rheinhardt turns toward him. "Basically, it's a plan to go in with an extremely light force, take down critical Iranian military and government nodes, and take out the mullahs and the IRG leadership in a decapitating strike. Regime change in a bottle."

"No shit? Could that be done?" Javier asks.

Rheinhardt shrugs. "Maybe. There's an operational precedent for it: Operation Just Cause, when we took out Noriega in Panama. Really light footprint – us, a few SEALs, the 82nd Airborne, and some Rangers and Marines. It was in a heavily populated urban area in Panama City, lots of Americans living in the canal zone, plus the canal itself, so heavy armor and air strikes were out. It all played out as precision takedowns of military and government facilities. And all over in less than a week."

BJ says, "When did the idea of trying that on with Iran come up?"

"In 2009. Havering put together an ad hoc team to explore options, during the Green Revolution protests after the bullshit election. The idea was, All right, what can we do to support the Iranian people, who are out dying on the streets for their freedom? What if democratic revolution in Iran comes up to the tipping point – but needs a shove over the top?"

"Like Libya two years later. Except we got to do something in that one."

"How far did the Iran planning go?" Javier asks.

"All the way to practice assaults against large-scale mockups built by Unit engineers."

"And what happened in the end?"

"Nothing, of course. The administration didn't even give the protesters lip service. Never mind air support."

At that moment, Havering pushes in through the door. "Give us the room," he says.

"No," Rheinhardt says. "I need them working on this. I'll go to you."

"Fine." The two duck around the corner to Havering's office.

* * *

"Here's where we are. The president's not going to authorize a full strike package."

"So the flyboys and swabbies get the day off."

"Ask me," Havering says, "which nobody's asking me, but I think he simply doesn't have the political capital for it. It's a lot of wars – Iraq, Afghanistan, Libya, Horn of Africa, drone war in Pakistan. You almost can't blame the guy."

"You might if you're Israel," Rheinhardt says.

Havering looks pained, but lets this pass. "You talking to your friend?"

"Half-hourly. Sayeret and the rest of IDF are scrambling. But they don't yet know what for."

"There's comms at the top, too – American president to Israeli PM. Plus other allies in the region." Havering pauses. "Word is, the president is open to considering DA options. If they're small enough, and deniable."

"Direct action. That means us, then."

"That means us. Get me a draft five-paragraph version of an ops order, based on your current mission profile. Whatever state it's in. I've got to brief General Votel. Then we're both going to brief the Joint Chiefs. The Chairman will brief POTUS."

"So not too many middle men, then."

"Nobody likes a wise-ass, Sergeant Major." Havering tries not to crack a smile, but fails. "Don't worry, you'll want the extra planning time. Ten minutes for that ops order. Then you and your team load up that whole table of shit into the G6. And get your asses across the ocean."

"Roger that." Rheinhardt smiles himself as he rises. "Can I also take Mi—"

"Take whoever the fuck you want. Take anybody."

Havering is already back out his own door, and moving fast.

Eric Rheinhardt and Chaya Akhilov hold each other's eyes in fraught silence over the video link. They seem paralyzed, for just one second, by the danger, both physical and emotional. There's plenty of both to go around. And then sound and motion spool back up for both of them.

Behind Rheinhardt, in the cabin of the jet, three men remonstrate with each other over a tiny table – arguing about realistic response times for Iranian air assets. All around them, outside the cabin, the sky over the North Atlantic blasts by at 800mph.

Chaya only spins along at the usual rate of the globe she sits on, in the Sirkin telepresence room. But behind her, in the Ops Center, and across the base, IDF officers and enlisted personnel are moving at a million miles an hour.

"My head of state," Rheinhardt says, "will not launch another air war today."

Chaya nods once. "But mine is demanding some response. Or she will launch her own."

"Our analysts are advising that, in any case, only a nuclear strike could be guaranteed to penetrate and destroy the weaponization complex. It's buried too deep in those mountains. And of course the president is totally unprepared to go nuclear."

"Eh," Chaya shrugs, resorting to time-tested Jewish fatal-ism. "What are you gonna do?"

Eric startles, then laughs out loud. "Oh, hell…" He calls to mind an old Delta squadron commander's adage that victory depends on the ability to out-think and out-imagine the enemy – and that humor is inextricably linked to imagination. His shoulders shake and he wipes a tear from the corner of his eye. It's definitely one of those laugh-or-cry situations.

"With no air war, and definitely no nukes, that leaves only DA – men fighting their way in on the ground."

"Which is beyond our capabilities," Chaya says. Pride is an indulgence they can't afford.

Rheinhardt nods. "This has all gone up and down our NCA. Everyone's open to us trying a takedown of the facility. We have shelved assault plans for that contingency – developed, war-gamed, and even briefly rehearsed last year. But they need some critical updating. We're ETA five hours to Baghdad, where we'll be a few hours behind our B Squadron. Those guys will be making the assault. If there is one."

"That sounds hopeful," Chaya says.

"But far from definite. The first barrier to this is that we just breached the same facility only days ago. That was the raid to extract Sultan, and insert our exploits."

"So," says Chaya, "you're not going to catch them napping a second time."

"No, we will not. Sucker punches work once. Now everything will be six times harder. The new plan is necessarily elaborate. Plus risky. But our much more dangerous problem is Tucker. It is difficult in the extreme to know what of our tactics and tech he's going to be able to anticipate and counter. It's like trying to box with yourself."

On Chaya's screen, Rheinhardt's eyes dart up and right. A smaller video window has appeared on his, with Colonel Havering's face in it.

"Can you hold?" he says to Chaya.

"No. But you can ring me at my station when you're done."

Her face disappears.

* * *

Havering's face springs up to the full size of the screen. "Our lottery number's come up," he says. "We ID'd Tucker on biometrics from satellite. He's in Chalus. Down in the underground."

"You're certain?"

"Ninety-two percent. Excellent gait and visual match."

"What about IR/heat signature?"

"No match. But no mismatch, either. Analysts think he was doing something to mask his heat sig. But even a Nomex flight suit will do that."

Rheinhardt weighs this. Havering continues.

"Gets better. We've got your shipment of HEU going in there, too. Had a room full of intel guys playing back the last few hours of sat and drone coverage of the area. They spot the plane landing in Tehran, then cross-loading to a truck, which we then tracked straight back to Chalus."

"So both the uranium and Tucker are down there right now?"

"Almost definitely. Both bottled up in the one place. But for how long, we have no idea."

"Bottled up in the one place that happens to be our target site. A little tidy."

"Sometimes you just get lucky. God knows it happens seldom enough. And according to Sultan, we might have as little as forty-eight hours until they complete weaponization work."

"Forty-eight hours until Iran is a nuclear power."

"Yeah. But, listen – Major Garner and B Squadron are feet dry over Iraq now. They'll be landing and unloading in a matter of minutes. They've also been doing their own mission planning in the air – based on your original packet, but optimized for their people and profiles."

Rheinhardt's look darkens. "Is it optimized for the fact the Iranians have got a Delta cadre member who's going to be defending against them?"

"Garner knows about Tucker."

"Because it's not reality unless it's shared, Colonel."

"B Squadron is aware of the threat."

"What about Sultan? Are they using him? He worked in that site for years."

"We've got an enormous amount of intel on the site. Intercepts. Persistent eye-in-the-sky. Hell, we've got a dozen drones and sats just staring at that one spot right now."

"Aerial surveillance and intercepts are one-dimensional. They don't provide any context."

"Noted. Now where's your plan at?"

"Far evolved – and rapidly evolving."

"Send what you got to me here. All of it, whatever state it's in. I'll send it on to Garner, so they can have the benefit. Listen, everyone in B, plus the ops staff at Balad, are leaning forward on this one. And we've got a limited window. They may step off very quickly, if we get White House approval."

"As in before we get there?"

"We'll keep you posted. Anything else for me?"

"Negative."

"You fly safe." Havering rings off.

When Rheinhardt looks up again, BJ is staring at him. Both their looks say the same thing: *I've got a bad feeling about this*.

"The volume's starting to get turned way up," is all Rheinhardt says, as he rejoins them at the planning table. He takes a seat between Mike Brown… and Dr. Azad Sultan.

Havering did say to take anybody he wanted.

Sergeant First Class Aaliyah Khamsi is sitting directly beside Major John Garner, Commander, B Squadron, 1ˢᵗ SFOD-D. And she has been sitting there, more or less, for the entire flight. He's instructed her to stay right on him, at least through the planning of the mission.

The upper-level troop compartment of the transport plane is crammed to bursting with operators and support staff, and their personal gear and planning materials. They have been working non-stop as they crossed the Atlantic.

Now the enormous C5-M Super Galaxy screams into Sather Air Base, on the west side of Baghdad International. Since the 2003 invasion, the airport has been ringed by U.S. military bases, out of which the war and occupation was run. These have been disappearing since the drawdown of American forces began in 2010. And now the country is run by Iraqis, out of the Green Zone (the walled and heavily guarded international zone) in Baghdad.

But Sather remains the major transport gateway into Iraq of U.S. equipment, supplies, and personnel. These influxes, regular and mammoth, will likely continue as long as American SOF base out of Iraq in the war on terror, and as a counterweight to regional threats.

"Regional threats" being pretty much a shorthand for "Iran."

The gargantuan plane taxis a few hundred meters, then slows and stops. The entire tail section flips up, over, and back, to disgorge the plane's contents. The interior is so big, and the plane so powerful, that it is used to transport things like main battle tanks, and smaller aircraft – Chinook helicopters, the Space Shuttle – around the world. When the ramp slides out and hits the tarmac with a screech, Ali has already got all her kit packed up and ready to hump.

Like most everyone else on board, she's dressed in a mix of nondescript fatigues, casual civilian clothes, and high-quality technical garments – upscale outdoors store type stuff. Her side arm, personal hand-loaded ammunition, and various other pieces of operational gear, are all jammed into her enormous black rucksack.

However, before she can exit, the vehicles and cargo have to unload. Only then can the squadron members descend the steel ladder down to the cargo deck and walk out of the giant, globe-straddling machine.

Delta's Bowstring equipment load includes every sort of weaponry, ammo, explosives, electronics, computers, tools, breaching equipment, and other gear that a Delta squadron might need to operate in any environment on any conceivable hostage-rescue, counter-terrorism, or direct action mission. And all of that materiel goes on its own fleet of six-wheeled, all-terrain, 7.5-ton MTVR transport trucks.

The engines of these now roar to life, and the vehicles drive length-wise down the plane and off the ramp. Finally, the rest of the squadron streams down the ladder, balancing their rifles and rucks, then out of the plane and onto the trucks – some in the cabins, some in the beds, an unlucky few hanging off the sides.

Ali takes a spot on one, squatting down amongst a team of operators she knows and likes well enough, but with whom she's hardly ever worked. Of course, it won't affect her performance – only her feelings, which in importance rank about a thousand spots down below mission accomplishment.

Amid belches of black diesel smoke, the convoy chugs off base and begins the drive around the outskirts of Baghdad and north to Balad. The base there is the site of the largest and most capable American SOF footprint outside of the continental U.S. Former home to McChrystal and the fabled Task Force 121, which decimated al Qaeda and the rest of the Iraq insurgency, it is now site of the Joint Special Operations Task Force (JSOTF) – ground zero for U.S. and allied SOF operations across the Middle East and central Asia.

The drive through Baghdad is a hell of a lot safer than it used to be. But the convoy still moves at high speed, both as a standard defensive maneuver, and because they're on a clock. They arrive at Balad without incident.

The trucks jerk to a halt halfway between the Joint Operations Center (JOC) and a nearly empty and otherwise-disused hangar, which is maintained precisely for staging and basing detached or supplemental units. Major Garner and the rest of the B command element leap off the trucks and bounce into the JOC.

The trucks jerk into motion again and lurch straight into the hangar, lining up against the right-hand wall. Even as they're stopping, the 75 operators and 15 support staff dismount and begin carrying off equipment, or using mobile powered loading platforms to bring it down. They then sort it into piles in various zones around the hangar.

Their home world for this new mission begins to take shape.

* * *

At the same time, the command element – Garner, his 2IC, the squadron ops and intel officers, the squadron sergeant major, plus Ali – swipe their IDs for a third time and are admitted into the sanctum. The JOC, a basketball-court-sized room commonly called "the Death Star," is dominated by three massive screens on the far wall. When drones and gun-cams show live ops there, it is often referred to as "Kill TV."

There are separate desks for ops, comms, intel, aviation, and medical, all with their own banks of workstations and large, common display screens. A Judge Advocate General is constantly present, to provide immediate rulings on the legality of operations, even while they are playing out in real time. Along with the Task Force Commander, the NSA and CIA also have private offices off the JOC itself.

Garner motions for his leaders to get with their opposite numbers on the TF, and pulls Ali into the commander's office. They both salute.

"General Stamis," Garner says.

"Major Garner. Sergeant." He nods at Ali. They sit.

* * *

Major Jim Garner, age 37, is a former Army Special Forces ("Green Beret") officer, with nine years in the Unit. Like every other Delta officer, he had to pass the same Selection course as the non-com operators. He's built like a light heavy-weight, and looks like a cross between a boxer and a Calvin Klein underwear model, with his razor-edged and perpetually stubbled jaw. His mind is also razor sharp – he's precise in his thinking and speech, and not particularly known for his sense of humor. (Perhaps because he reserves it for special occasions, and then catches people off guard with it.)

"Thanks for having us," he says to Stamis.

"That's what we're here for."

General Stamis, 63, is a legend in counter-insurgency – not least for the critical part he played in both Battles of Falujah in the Iraq insurgency. Unusually for his current assignment, he's also a Marine. But he's held commands ranging from heading a naval task force to running CENTCOM, so commanding JSOTF is only the weirdest job he's had by a little bit. He popularized the slogan, used by marines in Iraq, "No better friend, no worse enemy." He pretty much embodies that himself. He also told his men, "Every time you wave at an Iraqi civilian, al Qaeda rolls over in its grave."

Stamis takes a look over Garner's shoulder out into the JOC. "Why don't you get your ground commander in here so we can get everything plugged into everything else?"

"I am the ground commander on this one."

Stamis nods. "Leading from the front, huh?"

Garner's expression remains even. "This may be the Unit's most important tasking – ever."

"Well, we better make it a good one, then. Good news to start. We've had eyes on the complex at Chalus for almost twenty-four hours now. Other than a handful of men with

Tucker, and the shipment of the presumed nuclear materials, nothing's gone in. There's been no particular movement or mobilization in the area. And nothing more than usual flying. If they know we're coming, they're being pretty damned slack about getting ready for it."

"Good to know."

"I've also gotten your transport, signals, and support in motion. Particularly transport. Our 160th guys are on the tarmac on the other side of the building right now."

"Outstanding."

"Gets better." Garner picks up a sheet of paper from his desk. "Since you landed, the president's issued a finding. Your op is go."

"That means tonight, then."

"That means tonight. Oh-dark-thirty. You're going to have eleven hours, sixteen minutes, and five seconds of darkness to work with. Make it count."

"Time's wasting."

Tucker walks straight into Suleimani's office this time, pushing past the aide with a single iron-like forearm. He's been a busy boy, is tired and grimy, and looks it.

"I'll call you back." Suleimani puts down his phone. "Mr. Tucker. I thought you would be in Chalus by now."

"That's pretty much what Rheinhardt and his people think."

"And how have you effected that sleight of hand?"

"By knowing their own technology better than they do. And using it against them. In this case, Rheinhardt will have painstakingly gathered up biometric data on me and plugged it into their satellites and drones."

"And they can find you from that? Just pick you out from the sky?" The general looks concerned. This was not a capability his intel people had alerted him to.

"They can. But only when and where I want them to. In this case, they think I walked into Chalus two hours ago."

"How?" Suleimani cocks his head. "And, more interestingly, why?"

Tucker sits down in one of the elaborately carved chairs and crosses his legs at the ankle. "The why is so that when they think they have me boxed in there, and are closing the noose... in fact I will be on the outside, closing a noose on them."

"And the how?"

"Sometimes fifty dollars of radio scanner can defeat four million dollars of UAV."

"I don't understand."

"The U.S. still has drones flying with unencrypted or lightly encrypted comms to their ground stations. They still act like they're fighting guys in caves. My Chinese techs were able to hack into their transmission and run a man-in-the-middle attack. Earlier, I filmed myself walking, from directly above. We then replaced the drone's live video feed with that one. And of course it hit on my biometrics."

"That is very clever."

"The clever part was knowing how they would be looking for me. Once you understand the patterns that inform your enemy's behavior, you can adapt to them. And then you own him."

Suleimani pauses and regards his mercurial, and probably dangerous, asset. He's convinced the man is a threat. But, so far, he has proved dangerous only to the Revolution's enemies. The general figures he needs to pay close attention for when this changes – which it almost certainly will. "And you are sure Delta will send their on-call squadron to Chalus?"

"They've already landed in Iraq."

"How do you know that? Our intel section has told me nothing of this."

"I have much better intel assets than you do, General. And I don't automatically share them."

Suleimani squints slightly at the other man. Dangerous, definitely. But controllable? And for how much longer? It is hard to say. But, then, the universe is forever out of control.

"And after tonight," Tucker says, speaking slowly and deliberately, "Delta will be spent as a flexible, reactive force.

They will have squandered their reserve strength, with the rest of the Unit committed elsewhere around the globe. Moreover, they will be discredited. Their own command will stand them down after a very public debacle. And the only force that might have stopped us will be out of the game. And then the other dominoes can fall."

Suleimani is starting to get his hopes up here.

Tucker stands. "And now I really do have to get to Chalus. I've got a complicated counter-assault to stand up. And not many hours left to do it in."

A Gulfstream 650 needs only half the runway to land as a C5 Super Galaxy. So Rheinhardt and his team are able to fly directly into Balad. When the plane's stairs go down, the team and their gear are out and on the deck in seconds. After another five minutes of Humvee ride, they are inside of the fenced and heavily guarded JSOTF area.

Swinging his legs onto solid ground, the first thing Rheinhardt sees is an entire company of Rangers camped out against the eastern wall of the hangar. Seating his ballistic Oakleys and squinting against the glare, he spots a Ranger officer roaming the ranks. A very familiar one.

"Take my gear in," he says, handing a bag to Javier. "Meet you inside in ten."

He trots off while the others unload the vehicle.

The hundred or so Rangers are sitting in small groups, partially in the shade of the structure, cleaning weapons and checking gear. A group of soldiers doing weapons maintenance is strangely like a ladies' sewing circle. There's the intricate finger-work, the manipulation of tiny tools, and the passing around of supplies. And particularly the bitching and gossiping.

Gossip aside, the Rangers have a unit history going back to the seventeenth century and have fought like panthers on speed in every one of America's wars. To wear the Ranger tab, a solider has to survive Ranger School, which accepts only outstanding infantry soldiers to start with, and still has a pass rate of only about 50%. Rangers generally do everything the hardest possible way, meaning life in a Ranger battalion is somewhere between austere and brutal.

Ever since Delta's very first mission, the Rangers have supported them – serving as a blocking force, to keep others out when Delta goes in; or as a quick reaction force (QRF), to come blasting in if Delta needs help getting out. It is totally uncoincidental that more Delta operators come from the Rangers than from any other home unit.

The strapping officer that Rheinhardt has spotted now spots him back, and drops what he is doing to pull Rheinhardt into a bear hug. He's wearing full desert "battle rattle" and tries to crush the other man against it. Smiling enormously, he says, "And where the blazes did you come from, my brother?"

"From going to and fro over the face of the earth, and walking back and forth upon it."

The officer is Captain John Miller, commander, Company E, 75th Ranger Regiment. He and Rheinhardt were platoonmates, as enlisted soldiers, many years ago. Rheinhardt went on to Delta Selection. Miller, as a consolation prize, went to Officer Candidate School. The two men step back and regard each other.

"What are you masochists doing sitting out in the hot sun?" Rheinhardt asks.

"Normally," Miller says, "we'd be in that nice shady hangar there. But your B Squadron buddies got there first, and now they won't let us in. RHIP."

"What kind of rat bastards operate that way?" Rheinhardt squints into the hangar from behind his shades. "You guys the QRF on this one?"

"We absolutely would be. But word is this one is QRF-free. Tonight B fights alone."

Rheinhardt frowns. Miller claps him on the shoulder. "Come. Much to tell you, brother."

* * *

When Rheinhardt finally makes it into the JOC, the rest of Alpha is just exiting.

"Kicked to the curb," Johnson says, leading the retreat. "Garner's in there with Stamis. But they're shoving us out to the hangar."

"What's your assignment?"

"Right now? Whole lotta sitting on our asses."

"Go see if you can find us a rat-free corner," Rheinhardt says. "I'll meet you out there."

When he enters Stamis's office, the general and the major are poring over live satellite imagery. In typical Delta fashion, Rheinhardt gets right to the point, taking little account of rank.

"What's this I hear about the ROE?" he says.

"President's issued a finding, so we're go," Garner says. "But terms and conditions apply."

"So I'm told. No QRF?"

Garner's expression remains neutral, while Stamis carefully eyes the other two. Garner says, "That's right. And no advance recce team. Only B goes in. And no one comes in after us."

"What about a Little Bird gun escort? In case of armor, or hardened sites on the ground?"

"We're working on approval for that. But we currently see no armor there, and we're prepared to go without if we have to."

"And if you get into trouble?"

"Getting in trouble is off the menu on this one."

Rheinhardt sighs, not quite heavily. "Anything else? Left wrists tied to right ankles maybe?"

Garner doesn't laugh at this, nor seem to appreciate it. "A few other parameters. Stealth drones only, a pair of RQ-130s. And no other air – no Spectres or fast movers. Nothing else crosses the border. This comes down the NCA – from the top bit. This is how the universe is shaped today, and how it has to happen. It's the only way we get our oar in the water."

Rheinhardt takes all of that on board. "Did you get my mission profile and briefs?"

"We've got them. We're working your stuff in when and as."

Rheinhardt pulls around a chair, uninvited. "Have you had a long, serious, careful think about what Rod Tucker's attachment to the enemy means? Have you evaluated every single mission component with a view toward how Tucker might compromise it?"

Garner exhales. "Yes, we have. He's clearly an unusual hazard. But at the same time, the guy hasn't been in the Unit for over six years. Most of our tech is new since then. And we've been force-innovating all of that time."

"And you assume he's stopped? Plus, tech is a force multiplier until it stops working – or starts working against you. And it's not so much his specific knowledge of tech or tactics

I'm worried about. It's concepts. Our high-level behaviors, how we operationalize our decisions, the things in our DNA. He's going to have a good idea of how you'll be coming. If you're not *extremely* careful, he's going to be there waiting for you."

"He's one man."

"One man can change everything. Ask Churchill."

Stamis visibly grows tired of this. "Thanks, Sergeant Major. That's all."

Rheinhardt stands, but says, "My commander sent me here to C2 this thing."

"With respect to the colonel," Garner says, "my guy has it. I appreciate your insights into Tucker, I really do. But if you're right about the danger, that's even more reason to have the mission commander I've had for years, and who knows what I need before I even do."

Rheinhardt sighs. He can't argue with that.

Garner brings it to a close. "We've got full operational authority here, Sergeant. But we'd like you to sit in the JOC and observe and advise."

Even Rheinhardt can tell when he's used up his rope. He salutes and exits.

* * *

In the hangar, he walks into a scene he's encountered a hundred times, going back to Mogadishu. B Squadron has spread out, setting up sleeping and briefing areas, arranged by troop and team. Cots, rucks, planning tables, laptops, cabling, weapons, and pallets of equipment form the landscape. Operators stand or sit in small groups, doing weapons and ordnance prep, and various stages of planning and check-off on logistics, comms, and the air mission.

With just a quick scan, Rheinhardt spots two dozen faces he knows well. Most are well into the process of "jocking up" for combat. Outside, the sun is getting low. Rheinhardt can feel it. Everyone is leaning forward.

He spots his Alpha guys in the back right corner, camped out beside the first truck. But amongst the 74 men kitting up, he also spies a single woman, at the very back of the hangar. He strides over to her through the improvised aisles.

"Your stock seems to have gone up lately."

Aaliyah looks up where she sits on her cot, pushing her hand-loads into seven-round box magazines for the CheyTac.

"You're late," she says. "But it looks like being a hell of a party." She lays the mag onto a pile of them on the cot, then pushes the pile aside so Rheinhardt can sit. "I read your briefs and mission profile."

"I hope so. I could get fired for sending them to you. Oh, wait, I already quit. How are you feeling?"

"Not sure. This is definitely a sketchy one... But I think the mission objective may be worth the stretch. There's nothing between the mullahs and nukes now but us."

Rheinhardt pauses, then speaks quietly. "Do you think they'd actually press the button?"

She pauses in turn. "I think I know how profoundly religion can warp people. And I think Ahmadinejad and Khamenei may really believe in an End of Days, which will bring back an 1,100-year-old imam. And that they can help make it happen. By setting the world on fire."

Rheinhardt frowns, but then softens. "And why'd you join the Unit, if not to save the world."

"Indeed," Ali says. "*Deo volente.*"

"Yeah. God willing." Rheinhardt looks across at her. "Let me tell you something."

"Go ahead."

"Two things. One is be careful."

"And the other?"

"I will come and get you if you need me to."

In spec-ops culture it is never acceptable to leave a man behind. It is one of the key things that makes it possible to do the job. You might be cut off, surrounded, wounded, captured, or dead. But someone will be coming to get you. Worst case, you'll be buried on home soil.

Ali makes light of this. "I hope so. It's just over the damned border."

Rheinhardt laughs and stands. "Seriously. Be careful, Ali."

"Roger that, top. Now won't your team be missing you? Skedaddle, I've got mission prep."

Cliff "Waz" Wasdun, Chief Warrant Officer, Four (CW4) and air mission commander, sits with his co-pilot, CW3 Donovan "Dono" Brill, in the blacked-out cockpit of their MH-47G Special Operations Aviation Chinook. The MH-47G is the latest and most high-tech version of the venerable twin-rotor transport and air assault helicopter. Tonight, they are call sign "Chuckles One," the lead element in a flight of four such helos. The first three will carry the 75 operators of B Squadron, with the fourth flying along as backup.

For the moment, the two pilots sit in the dark, with their NVGs flipped up. Their helos were long ago upgraded to accommodate night-vision kit – everything in the cockpit is visible and operable through it. It's no coincidence that members of the 160th Special Operations Aviation Regiment (160th SOAR) refer to themselves as the Night Stalkers. They're the guys who provide the rides for the Tier-1 operators.

And those guys almost only ever go out to play at night.

The 160th was formed in the aftermath of the debacle of Operation Eagle Claw, when inadequate (and quickly crashing and burning) helos and pilots caused the failure of the mission to rescue the American hostages in Tehran. The lesson was learned: an elite counter-terrorism force can't counter a shithouse if it can't get to where the terrorists are. Hence the 160th.

The Night Stalkers are the Delta of aviators. They fly over the most unforgiving terrain in the pitch black and terrifying weather conditions, close to the deck, in non-permissive environments, and under fire. They've been known to do things like hold a hover while large-caliber bullets tear through the airframe and air-burst RPGs explode all around, so guys fast-roping out can make it safely to the ground. They guarantee delivery of their "customers" to their target at the planned insertion time plus or minus 30 seconds. On time, every time.

Because they are so unbelievably good at all this, it makes one less thing Unit guys have to worry about.

* * *

"What's the command frequency, again?" Waz asks.

"Still four. Just like last time. All the freqs and encryption codes are keyed in."

Even consummate professionals get edgy sitting in a cockpit long enough. They're already completed and double-checked every possible bit of pre-flight, plus a custom pre-mission checklist and protocols review. They were put on a 30-minute standby in the afternoon. Then a cockpit standby an hour ago. A rotors-turning standby seems inevitable. They can feel it coming in on them, like a weather front.

"Sorry, man," Waz says. "This flying unescorted into the Islamic fucking Republic of Iran has me a little wound up."

Dono nods in the dark. "Not just you. But it's not exactly our first time. They seem to be able to turn on blind spots in their air defenses like flipping a switch."

"Yeah, and it's never failed – yet. Nothing ever fails until it does."

"Heh. Personally, I prefer being over denied airspace to being over the Hindu Kush."

"Yeah. At least *someone*'s in charge here."

Dono takes a bite of a half-unrolled hunk of beef jerky, offers it across. "I'm starting to feel like this command is getting a serious case of HPS." He's referring to helicopter-centric planning syndrome, the phenomenon, noted mainly by special operators, of making a helo insertion the hammer for every nail. In fact, even with the best birds and the most skilled pilots, helo insertions are invariably both noisy and dangerous. Sometimes you're simply better off in a ground vehicle, or on foot.

"That's because we're so damned good," Waz says. "Victims of our own success."

Without warning, the door of the complex bangs open and black-clad figures spill out onto the helipad. They don't stop coming until there are 75 of them, splitting like an amoeba into three masses, each group slithering up the low-ered ramp of one of the first three birds.

The pilots take this as their signal to start the engines.

"Guess we're go," Waz says, fingers poking at the illumi-nated touch-screen.

"Nice of them to let us in on it."

The unmistakable whine of four sets of twin turboshaft engines rips into the night.

Ali has barely gotten settled on the bench that runs the length of the blacked-out cabin, when the bird rocks from its four wheels, lifts, pedal turns, and soars smoothly into the inky night. Ali has the advantages of small size and legs that point together, which are helpful when crammed in with 24 men, every single one of whom is carrying at least one very large gun.

A Delta squadron is generally composed of three troops, two assault and one sniper/reconnaissance. Because they will be emplacing first in hides around the edges of the target site, the snipers are in the lead bird tonight. Feeling a change in the tremble of the airframe, Ali twists to look out the window. She can just make out a flight of four AH-6 Little Bird attack helicopters, literally buzzing in to join the formation.

Well, she thinks. *That's something.*

Little Birds are small, fast, incredibly maneuverable, and these ones mount forward-facing 7.62mm miniguns, as well as twin rocket launchers with anti-armor and anti-personnel rockets. These will be very helpful if they encounter anything armored. Or any people they just don't like.

They massively up the offensive punch of the mission group.

Ali takes a deep breath, settles into the confinement, then jockeys for a little extra room for herself and her stuff. All Delta operators have complete leeway in their choice of personal weapons. Delta snipers favor rifles from Accuracy International, Barrett or McMillan – and of course Ali's beloved CheyTac, which she's closer to than most of her family members.

The Cheyenne Tactical M-400 Intervention sniper rifle system is probably the best such weapon ever made, holding the world record for tightest grouping of shots at a distance: three bullets within 16⅝ inches at 2,321 yards – *nearly a mile and a half*. Ali has personally beaten that. Just not with official observers around.

In addition to high-power spotting scopes with laser range finders, the spotters (the other half of a spotter/sniper pair) generally carry assault rifles for team protection. Standard for Delta, if there is any such thing, is the Heckler & Koch 416. Developed in a partnership between HK and Delta, this was specially designed to solve the reliability problems of the Army standard M16/M4. The HK416 looks a lot like a sleek and well cared for M4 – except that it will shoot for ever, in any conditions, every time, with unchanging accuracy. The HK417, the same gun chambered for the heavier 7.62mm round, is also popular.

All sniper teams also now carry the advanced ballistics computers needed to make adjustments for shooting at extreme distances. These are either hand-held or, increasingly, integrated with their rifles and scopes.

All of the assaulters wear the same four-barrel Enhanced NVGs that Johnson wore when he was last here. They provide 120-degree viewing (versus 40 on two-barrel NVGs), have thermal imaging enhancement to make threats pop out of the background, provide awesome situational awareness, and cost $65,000 apiece. All of the sniping and spotting scopes have night vision built in, though, so most of the snipers and many of the spotters choose small night-vision monocles to save on weight.

Delta snipers specialize in long-distance shooting, stalking in extreme terrain and conditions, site intelligence gathering, and long-range recon. But, like everyone else in the Unit, they also cross-train heavily and can perform many military tasks to an exacting level of precision. Like everyone else in the organization, down to the armorers and cooks, they are the best in the world at what they do.

* * *

Like the others, Ali has now got nearly two hours in the air to bull through. Since operating on the razor edge of performance is primarily a mental game, they are trained to use this time for psychological preparation and other mental tasks. Nonetheless, Ali finds herself getting into her own head in a way that might not be helpful. She's thinking back to her talk with Eric in Virginia.

One of two things is true. Either they are going into a very sketchy situation. Or else Eric is spooked for no reason. And she's never seen him spooked for no reason. But then again, everything has been topsy-turvy lately – his departure, his return, and particularly all this Rod Tucker bullshit. Not to mention all the very heavy and unresolved history between those two.

She figures she's got three plausible theories for Eric being so unsettled. One, he's scared of Tucker. That one's a stretch. It would certainly be the first enemy she's ever seen him scared of. Two, maybe he's scared of getting another woman killed, after that IDF girl. Better, but still thin. Amongst the variety of things no one really gives a shit about at the Tier-1 level, just as long as you do your job with utter competence and fearlessness, is whether or not you have a penis.

Finally, she figures maybe he's scared of compromising his honor again in some way. Making the wrong call in backing Tucker has been a weight on him all this time. And it's perhaps the only thing that's really made him doubt himself. That one's got a little traction.

What she is only just beginning to sense, and maybe only at the edge of consciousness, is that what Rheinhardt is really struggling with is whether anything he does, or anything any of them do, can make any real difference in this world. He's struggling against nihilism.

And they are all up against a man, Tucker, who struggled with his nihilism… and lost. There is very little so dangerous as a man who has jettisoned the very categories of good and evil. He has also jettisoned all the constraints of conscience, honor, and civilized behavior.

He is horribly free.

But this line of thinking isn't getting her anywhere. She slips her palm-top out of a nylon thigh pouch and pulls up the region topo maps. Among other functions, the device runs her ballistic calculation software. She's already keyed in elevation, wind speed, temperature, air pressure, relative humidity, wind chill, dew point, latitude, and direction of fire off true north – everything her rifle needs to know to make absurdly long shots – based on map, almanac, and weather sat data. She double-checks it all again. Then she commits the figures to memory. She'll take readings of them all again at the site.

After that, she memorizes the interior layout of the target structure, also from floor-plan diagrams on the hand-held – diagrams which she herself helped to produce. She won't be going inside. But rule number one is: you never know.

Finally, she chamber-checks her side arm, an HK USP Tactical, a compact .45 with an eight-round mag, and which nicely fits her smaller hand. She drops out the mag and checks that. None of this double-checking is needed.

Just as she reseats the mag and holsters the weapon, they get the ten-minute warning.

* * *

After Garner had picked her brain clean, he decided he'd rather have the best sniper in the Unit (and thus, though this goes unsaid, probably the best sniper in the world) out on the ground shooting for him. Since she is emplacing furthest from the target, Ali's are literally the very first boots on the ground. The Chinook flares into a low hover over a steep bit of mountainside scree, nearly a mile from the compound. Ali fast-ropes out with her rifle on her back, hits the ground, flattens out, and waits for the storm of the twin rotors to blow away.

She stays in that spot for four minutes, tuning in to the mountainside and the night. It's not as long as she'd like, but it's as long as she's got. She then sets up in her overwatch position (OP), selected from topographic and satellite imagery, laying out her weapons and electronics just so.

Because she's the odd man out, and so far from the target site, and possibly because she's so damned good, Ali is working without a spotter tonight. It's just her and the mountain and the black veil of the night. And, finally, an unobstructed line of sight 1,583 yards straight to the front door of the complex. She quickly lases the door with her rangefinder, to tell her what she already knows. With current winds, about 4mph from her 10 o'clock, this is a dauntingly long shot for mortal snipers. But merely a modestly tough one for her.

From radio chatter and the sounds of the engines, she follows along as the bird drops off the other sniper teams around the mountain ridges that ring the target. Before that's even done, she sees the flashes of rockets impacting as the Little Birds start making gun runs on the compound. The crashing sound of the explosions follows nearly five seconds later.

Guess there was some armor down there after all, she thinks emotionlessly.

She then dials in and starts scanning for targets.

The JOC is seated past capacity, standing room only. It has the atmosphere of a blockbuster premier. All eyes are on the enormous wall-mounted screens at the front. The middle of the three shows a night-optic aerial view of the Chalus facility, spinning lazily counter-clockwise. It is delivered live from an RQ-170 Sentinel stealth UAV, one of two orbiting the area. These are single-engine tail-less flying wing drones which are basically invisible to radar.

Staff officers and enlisted guys sit at stations in three rows of desks. Field grade officers hold up the back wall. Agency, NSA, and assorted OGA-types ("other government agency") lean around glass partitions and corners. DEVGRU (aka SEAL Team Six), CIA Special Activities Division (SAD), and Delta's C Squadron, the operators on regular deployment at Balad, have all snuck team leaders in to observe. No one wants to miss the show.

Rheinhardt scored an actual station, which he shares with Mike Brown, their two chairs pulled in tight.

The JOC-side mission commander is Garner's ops officer, Lt. Buddy Su, known as "Mr. Clean." With his trademark bald head and dramatic features, Su's hallmark is his ability to immerse himself in a tactical situation and quickly identify, distill, and communicate the most mission-critical information to men on the ground. He is speaking now through an open channel to the ground commander, Garner, using his usual calming tones. The voice traffic also plays through wall-mounted speakers. He hails Garner's call sign for tonight, using his own.

"Boomslang Six, this is Joyrider X."

"Joyrider, go," Garner's voice comes back, clear and cold as ice.

"Little Birds are RTB. Chinooks are clear and feet wet over the Caspian. They will refuel, orbit, and wait for your extraction call."

"Copy that." The open channel now squelches and over-loads with the sound of thick gunfire. *"Joyrider, I'm in a gunfight right now. Wait out."*

The center screen still shows the aerial view, now sparkling peacefully with tiny firefly-like muzzle flashes. Mr. Clean clicks an icon and the right screen flips from an empty Chinook interior to on-the-ground helmet-cam footage from Garner's 2IC, Cpt. Mariusz Szewczyk, aka "Shrek." In his mid-thirties, with the wiry muscled build of a runner, and piercing Eastern European blue eyes, Shrek is the ideal Unit 2IC: calm and unflappable, super-fit, commonsense smart, and a superb organizer.

The video from his helmet-cam is of a green-and-black night-vision view over the top of his rifle's holographic diffraction sight (HDS) – and beyond that, straight down a gun barrel and into a whirling melee. Shrek's rifle is firing non-stop in searing muzzle flash, filling the JOC with its shuddering full-auto roar. The world beyond the rifle pivots from left to right and back again. Human figures run and sprawl out in all directions. Other weapons flash, blossoming and collapsing like fireworks, appearing in split-second strobe-like tableaux.

And everything in the background is either exploding or already on fire.

* * *

Mr. Clean flips camera views again and the screen switches to the roof of the building, near where it merges with the rock of the sheer mountainside. B Squadron's Two Troop has roped in there, and already set breaching charges on the roof. They're waiting for the signal to blow them, and then drop in from above, simultaneously entering with One Troop, who will go in via the front door. It was supposed to be a simultaneous hard entry, when they'd all go noisy together.

But everything has gone noisy right from the first second.

This second camera is mounted on the helmet of the squadron's most senior NCO, "Sergeant Major Bullethead." It's his job to blow the shaped frame charge, and he is staying put about ten meters away from the spot, detonator in hand.

But all around him, Two Troop assaulters have fanned out to the building edges. Most crouch, with their rifle barrels depressed at varying angles. They are putting out a heavy volume of fire in support of One Troop on the ground. Their IR laser designators, appearing in night-vision video as spectral green lines, point out in orthogonal directions, though mostly down, and outward in a 270-degree arc. They seek and destroy.

At the same time, the invisible barrels of the snipers on the surrounding ridges point in from the outside, endlessly sweeping the bowl of the compound – pausing to fire deadly single shots, and then sweeping on.

When the mission package flew in, the first surprise was the presence of a half-dozen BTRs, armored personnel carriers of Soviet design, as well as dismounted infantry in battalion strength. That's over 300 men on the ground. While that would normally be a pretty fair stand-up fight for 75 Delta guys, nobody with a brain fights fair. Or they don't fight long.

Instead, the Little Birds came blitzing in with anti-armor rockets for the BTRs, and flechette loads for the dismounts. The flechette rockets, containing 2,200 one-inch steel darts per warhead, tore through the infantry like a wheat scythe. This cleared the field enough for Garner's Chinook to set down in the open area in the center of the complex, and for the other to flare over the main building's roof, where Two Troop roped in.

Mr. Clean proceeds to flip through helmet-cam views from the half-dozen operators, two in each troop, wired up with them. He pauses at a sniper view, which effectively takes everyone watching in the JOC nearly a half mile away from the battle. In the distance of the complex, muzzles flash like cameras, and grenades and RPGs ripple like lightning. The sounds of firing and explosions drift in after a two-second delay.

The wearer of this guncam is First Sergeant Gordon "Gordy" Harris. Famous for pushing even the relaxed grooming standards of the Unit, Gordy proudly wears a Fu Manchu moustache that gives him the look of a 70s porn star. But this belies an extraordinary intellect and such steady nerves and hands that he makes other snipers look like ADD kids.

Beside him, invisible but just audible, his spotter, Sergeant Tom "Skippy" Wilkins, is calling out targets. Skippy is a lanky, handsome man with a sly sense of humor and a palpable joy in being in the Unit and doing what he does. This is good, because liking your work is what keeps you in the game, on your toes — and alive.

All that's visible of these two in the helmet-cam view in the JOC is that Gordy has his head down to his scope. About once a second, the camera jerks as he fires. After ten shots, he reloads for two seconds, then starts again.

He is firing absolutely ceaselessly.

* * *

When the view flips back to Shrek, on the ground out front, the chaos and carnage have almost wound down. When he swivels his head to scan behind him, it is over a carpet of bodies, all of them in Iranian Revolutionary Guard uniform. When he swivels back again, charges are finally being set on the front door.

Garner's voice returns to the JOC: "All enemy pax and victors suppressed. I have four WIA. All walking, none litter urgent. Stacking up and assaulting in now."

A low murmur floods the room. A Delta squadron has just killed 300-plus IRG, taking only four casualties, all of whom are still on their feet. The day you get ambushed by an entire mechanized battalion and everyone walks away is a pretty good day. It's a reminder that Tier-1 operators are not just clever infiltrators and technicians. Their specialized skills all rest on a base of superior conventional soldiering.

Still, there's a general feeling in the JOC of having dodged a bullet.

With only another few seconds' delay, the charges blow and python-quick figures pour into the building. Four-man teams remain out front and up top to hold the exits. And the snipers maintain a vigil on the compound, their sights and muzzles scanning tirelessly and mercilessly, putting finishing shots into anyone who moves on the ground.

* * *

Now two of the JOC screens show live helmet cam feeds, one from each assault troop. A team of Delta operators free-flowing through a target in close quarters battle (CQB) is one of the most breathtaking displays of precision pandemonium in modern warfare.

The assault teams train for this for thousands of hours in the Delta Shooting House. They do it in teams of two, four, eight, and more; with pistols, sub-machine guns, assault rifles, grenades, and bigger explosives; against unknown numbers and disposition of enemy; with and without hostages and bystanders; in rooms, in offices, in airplane cabins, and train carriages.

By the time a Delta assault troop goes operational, they have the ability to blast their way into any enclosed structure, spill into it in force with perfect synchronization, and flood through every square foot of space, making instant shoot/no-shoot decisions, killing every single hostile, and only hostiles, in less time than it takes to describe it.

Which is a good thing, because the weaponization facility turns out to be about six times as heavily defended as intel projections indicated.

"All sides heavy," Garner reports flatly, speaking to his team, but also audible in the JOC.

Both screens now fill with non-stop firing as the operators broadside straight into the scores of IRG who throng the halls, strongpoint the intersections, lurk in the stairwells, hide beneath desks. Bodies hit the floor over and again. More rise to take their place.

Occasionally operators jerk from hits on their Kevlar assault suits. Magazines are seated, drained in seconds, dropped out again, and replaced, all in a blur. Charging rods slam home and the assault rifles continue pouring out perfectly accurate and insanely lethal fire. And the two teams work forward, and down, and forward again, like a storm scouring the rocks.

As they take ground, two operators stay behind to hold each floor. Another, with a hand-held fingerprint scanner, goes from body to body, rolling anybody who could pass for Rod Tucker, and pressing dead thumbs onto the glass, in hope of a positive ID. So far, no news is bad news.

All the while, the storm blows on and down.

Their final destination: the secure and clean weaponization labs at the very basement level. Deep under the mountain, where the sinister project is safe from American and Israeli air strikes.

But not from these guys.

* * *

"Has anybody got *any* idea where those goddamned BTRs came from?"

A dozen heads swivel around, eyes wide and lips parted, a bit as if their movie has been interrupted by a loud talker.

Behind them they see General Stamis, standing against the back wall, chomping a cigar and looking pissed off.

This does underscore something they should probably be worried about: the appearance of an entire mechanized battalion nobody knew anything about.

"Tracing it back now," the intel desk duty officer says.

He slaps one of his guys on the back of the head.

Garner puts the enemy soldier's throat behind the red aiming dot of his HDS and squeezes the trigger. The man convulses and drops to the floor. Behind him, the door to the labs is revealed. Their target.

"Hall clear," Garner says over the squad net.

Breach-resistant and airtight, the door is more like a bank vault. But the demo guys are familiar with its specs and are already dotting it with pre-prepared shape charges that will drop it off its hinges. Everyone ducks around one of two corners, the charges go, and the door rattles on the ground like God's own manhole cover.

Garner leads them in to their final destination. It's unguarded, and they enter unopposed.

Within seconds, someone has gotten the lights on, and NVGs flip up onto helmets all around. Operators don't chatter on ops, and very little talking is required here. Every role is understood by the man responsible for it, as well as those of the men on either side. Garner's tech guys are already scouring the lab, while shooters take up a protective posture inside and out, and at strongpoints on the five floors between them and the world.

Six minutes later, Staff Sergeant Russell Lawson, call sign Bleep, trots up.

Bleep is 28 years old, but has a boyish enthusiasm that makes him seem closer to 12. Tall and lean with short blond hair, he has an incredible energy level and a sense of humor that helps keep things in perspective in a fight. He holds two different advanced engineering degrees (electrical and mechanical), and is an inveterate tinkerer on a never-ending quest to know how everything works. Most new tactical or technical kit gets run through his skunkworks first.

He puts his gloved hand on Garner's arm. "Dry hole, boss."

"You are shitting me."

"Nope. Those spheres and cylinders in the vises there? The ones that look like warheads and components? They're dummies. Totally non-functional. Just metal shells."

"What about fissile material?"

Bleep flashes a hand-held Gamma-Scout radiation detector. The digital read-out shows 0.0.

"We're reading traces on the tables. I think weaponization work has been done here. But whatever they were building, or whatever they built, they've taken it someplace else."

"Do a second sweep," Garner says. "Check everything again. Then accelerated SSE." Sensitive Site Exploitation: the art of collecting actionable intel from a taken-down target.

"Roger. Give me ten minutes." He turns and trots back to his team.

Garner flips to the command net. "Joyrider X, Boomslang Six. We've got a dry hole here. No weapons, no materials. And, so far, no Tucker."

"Copy that, Boomslang. Interrogative: what's your intent?"

"We're gonna pack up and exfil. How's my air?"

The room lights go out.

Garner flips down his NVGs – but the exit signs and floor-level LEDs, which previously provided the ambient light the night-vision needs to work, have gone out, too. Deep underground, in complete and utter darkness, there's nothing to amplify. Within seconds, though, IR illuminators, from rifle-mounted AN/PEQ-15 units, flip on all around. These are basically infrared flashlights, and provide what the NVGs need when the environment doesn't.

"Joyrider X, we'v—" a piercing, high-pitched shriek fills Garner's earpiece.

He yanks it out by its curly wire.

Shrek trots in from the hallway, his earpiece also flopping on his assault vest.

"Squad net's being jammed," he says.

"Command, too," Garner says.

"Gettin' a sudden bad feeling about this, Jim."

"Okay. We're going to audible away from the briefed plan. And make like the shepherd in the thunderstorm—"

"And get the flock out of here?"

"Exactly." Garner always does wait until some inappropriate moment to start being funny.

Shrek raises his voice. "Alright, gentlemen. We're Oscar Mike. Exfil now! Move, move!"

Ali shoots a guy making a run for it. He's one of the few IRG who survived the strafing of the Little Birds and the clean-up ground battle, probably by playing dead. Now, with the assault teams inside, he sensed his chance and is trying a runner. Ali doesn't feel great about topping him. But the law of land warfare is clear: if he's still armed and not surrendering, he's not running away, but merely emplacing to the rear – where he will have another opportunity to engage friendly forces, i.e. kill Ali's brother operators. So down he goes.

She changes out mags, absently noting that she's fired 20 rounds and scored 17 kills. Two needed two shots each. Another she missed totally, a show-offy headshot on a running dude. It doesn't matter to her. She's just benchmarking, to make sure she's up to spec, and as an aid to future performance.

But she has definitely been up here shooting people like it's cool.

With the field empty of targets for the moment, she flips down her LCD monocle from her helmet, and flips the channel switch of the receiver on her vest. This brings in video, four centimeters from her eyeball, direct from one of the Sentinel UAVs overhead. This gives her a real-time aerial view from directly over the battle. It also leaves her other eye free to maintain situational awareness.

There's nothing moving on the ground, in either view.

Unexpectedly, the scene jerks, then spins, as the UAV makes a sharp change in flight path.

That's weird, she thinks. Almost always the unarmed surveillance drones just do wide circles over whatever they're tasked to look at. But, sometimes they do get re-tasked. This one seems to be possessed, diving and accelerating. So she stays with it, intrigued.

It goes screaming down toward one of the surrounding ridges. As it descends, she can actually hear it coming in, off to her left. She swivels her rifle and scope around in that direction. Suddenly she can make out something through the monocle video. It's one of their sniper/spotter pairs, laid out prone behind some rocks, peering through their scopes. From the view of the drone, nearly directly above, their shapes are distinct.

In the fraction of a second that remains, the two both look up… toward the incoming noise… and then directly into the drone-mounted camera… and, via that, directly into Ali's eye.

Oh my God. It's Gordy and Skippy. The two figures rush in on her and then the monocle video goes black. A fraction of a second later, the explosion blossoms on the ridge off to her left.

"No!" She actually speaks aloud, albeit in an agonized whisper. There can be no doubt about what she's just seen. One of their sniper teams just got counter-sniped.

By a fucking unmanned aerial vehicle.

Their own UAV.

Ali flips to the command channel and breaks radio discipline.

* * *

In the JOC, a low murmur of horror has been supplanted by crisp voices trying to figure out what the hell has just happened. Ali's voice breaks through on the mission command channel.

"Joyrider X, this is Boomslang Three-One-Three, how copy?"

Mr. Clean clenches his jaw, but answers. "Boomslang Three-One-Three, Joyrider X, go ahead."

"I've got a Boomslang Three call sign DOWN. It's Three-Six, I think. Repeat, Three-Six is down."

"Yeah, all received, over."

"One of our Sentinel drones just crashed into their OP. Interrogative: what the fuck is up with that? Over."

"Three-One-Three, stand by." He clears the channel to field some of the frantic demands on his attention from the ground, and from there in the JOC. Plus he's got twelve things to tell Garner and the assault teams, ideally several minutes in the past.

* * *

Ali flips the monocle back up and away, and puts her eye back to her scope, scanning the spot where Gordy and Skip used to be. But then she pulls back again almost immediately. The unmistakable sound of helo blades whumps up over the horizon, from the peaks behind the target building. And they're not Chinooks.

She dials the magnification of her scope back a few notches and pans around until she spots them. They're Mil Mi-26 Halos – Soviet-era heavy transport helicopters, even bigger and heavier than Chinooks. There are at least a dozen of them.

And they are inbound.

"Can *anyone* get that sumbitch shut down?" General Stamis is shouting about the second UAV, after the organism that is the JOC took several beats to internalize that the first one had been seized and used against them.

"We've lost telemetry and control," says the officer at the aviation desk. "We're totally locked out."

And that's when satellite imagery, plus rapid but unflustered reports from the sniper teams, tells them of the arrival of an entire heliborne counter-assault – the flight of a dozen Halos.

"I've got the BTRs," Mike Brown announces. He has been spooling back cached drone and sat footage, trying to figure out where the initial surprise armored personnel carriers came from. But all of the desk staff in the room, and many of the bystanders, are frantically performing a thousand other tasks now. He's at least got Rheinhardt's attention. "Here, eight clicks south."

Rheinhardt gives it a hard look. "Isolated spot in the mountains, under camo netting. Our aerial sweeps missed them." He leans across the next console, grabs somebody else's mouse, and puts it up onscreen.

Screen One changes to a historical replay of the netting coming off the BTRs, then the vehicles roaring off. The room goes silent, all eyes watching their first setback take shape. Mike fast-forwards, and pans out and to the right. Now they can see the netting coming off the Halos, and their rotors spinning up. This is only a few minutes in the past.

They have been played. Bushwhacked.

Then General Stamis shouts from the back. "Over and done with!" he bellows. "Now manage this fucking battle!" Everyone and everything jolts back into motion.

But the entire JSOTF is in danger of task-saturation: experiencing one more simultaneous catastrophe than it can manage at the same time.

If they lose control of events here, the men on the ground are in serious trouble.

* * *

Ali watches in horror as the huge helo flight smoothly splits into three groups. One goes wide left over the surrounding ridges; one wide right; and a third, the largest, flares down, over and before the building and compound.

She sights in on the center group of birds as they wheel.

She hesitates.

* * *

Sergeant Major Bullethead and his security team on the roof are the first to hear the Halos roar in. They press back against the wall of the mountain. But there is nowhere to take cover from above on this rooftop.

Bullethead starts to press his transmitter button, to call it in and get a tasking.

No, screw that, he thinks. Instead he pulls his rifle to his shoulder, flips his selector switch to full-auto, and opens up on the nearest helo. His rounds spark off the skin of the wheeling bird. This was the right thought at the right time, and without hesitation. But it's not enough.

The center group of Halos swings broadside to them. Miniguns mounted in the side ports open up. Bullethead and his team are chewed through and cut down in seconds. Hundreds of 7.62mm rounds rip through their Kevlar and their bodies, and then pulverize rooftop and mountainside behind them.

The four-man security team on the ground by the front door meets the same fate seconds later.

* * *

Ali, laid out prone in her perch behind her rifle, swallows dryly. Then she chokes it all back.

And she shoots the pilot, and a half-second later, the co-pilot, through the first chin-bubble she gets a look into. Both are headshots. The helo's tail boom swings around, out of control, and smashes into the side of the bird beside it. Both explode together and drop out of the sky and into the compound. The other four birds in the center flight tilt radically, and bounce away to avoid the fireball and debris.

That leaves ten, she thinks. And she's got an awful lot of bullets left.

But now her earpiece is going hectic with traffic from the sniper net. Looking around, she realizes the two flanking flights of helos are flying over the sniper OPs on the ridges, miniguns blasting away. Guys on the sniper teams are calling in, shouting updates – and running like hell.

A voice from the command net cuts in. It takes Ali a second to realize it's Rheinhardt.

"All Boomslang Three call signs! Kill radio traffic and power down your receivers! The helos are triangulating in on your radio signals. Sign off and displace! Displace!"

Ali rips out her earpiece, tears open the Velcro pouch cover from her radio, and starts to fling it off the ridge – but reconsiders and just turns it off instead. She can't use it now, but she may need it again soon. Powered down, it's inert and untraceable.

She starts to heft her CheyTac to move out, when she has a sudden, horrifying thought.

She flips her monocle back down, and thumbs the receiver on her vest to the view from the second stealth drone. Just as she feared: she's immediately looking at *her own* position from above – and her image is expanding rapidly to fill the screen. She only hears the approach of the drone in the last second, as it's moving just under the speed of sound.

She pulls her CheyTac off its bipod and close in to her body, then rolls sideways three times and straight off the precipice of the ridge and into open air.

The heat and explosion of the crashing UAV singe her all the way down.

* * *

"Well-spotted," Rheinhardt says to Mike, hand over mouthpiece.

Mike is looking at broad-spectrum electromagnetic imagery of the battlespace from satellite, which he's managed to overlay with a radar view. The helos were vectoring straight down radio transmissions from the snipers. "You think Ali's okay…?" Mike asks. He gets about one second of looking worried, before Rheinhardt hits him, on the shoulder.

"Back in the game. Get me more."

Mike straightens up and snaps to.

All around them, the JOC staff are coming to grips with the impossible fact that they've lost both their outside security teams. And with both UAVs down, they've had to work this out from long-range satellite imagery. It's not the highest resolution. But what they can make out is definitely not guys still on their feet.

"This is fucked," someone nearby to Mike and Rheinhardt can be heard to mutter.

But now everyone is talking at once again. And trying to regain control of events.

Rod "The God" Tucker takes stock as his black boot hits the rocky ground of the Chalus compound. The two Delta outside security teams have been suppressed. The sniper teams on the surrounding ridges are dead or scattered. He lost two birds coming in, but that's within tolerances. The area is still slightly lit by the flames from the wreckage. He flips up his NVGs and keeps his rifle in the low ready position for the moment.

He scans the area and sees his jihadi teams exiting the helos. These are the 250 super-skilled fighters that he has personally selected from Hamas and Hizbullah and personally trained for months. They are the elite force that allows him to do the work that needs doing for the Iranians. And they are the ones who will finish this job tonight.

At the core of his jihadis is a sort of handpicked Praetorian Guard, the very most capable 22 shooters of all – tough, loyal, unflappable, and totally deadly. Their senior enlisted man, a spooky Gazan named Musa Harb, steps up and reports in. Medium size with a muscular build, spiky black hair, and a Gibraltar-like forehead, Musa is both an outstanding killer and an efficient organizer. He and Tucker understand each other.

"Team One is disembarked," Musa says, padding up in full tactical kit, assault rifle also at low ready. "Ground force is inbound. Two minutes."

Tucker nods. He can hear the groan of a fleet of transport trucks straining up the mountain. This is the additional IRG infantry brigade, almost a thousand men, that will be his blunt instrument. He will pour them into the underground structure and into the battle, and drown Delta's B Squadron in bodies.

And then his jihadi army will pick apart anyone who manages to claw to the surface.

"Boss, look at this." This time it's Bob Li, his half-Chinese/half-Californian hacker, whom he's tasked with hijacking the American drones. The young man steps up and shows him a portable control unit with a joystick and 4-inch display. Digital video from the UAV's camera rolls back at high speed, stops, then plays forward in slo-mo.

The view is of a sniper hide, coming up fast. The sniper is laid out alongside a rifle – but at the last possible instant looks up and directly into the camera. Li freezes it there.

"Yo, it's a girl," he says.

And it is a girl, Tucker thinks. *Delta's famous Somali girl sniper.*

He jabs the play button again. The girl starts to roll away, out toward the bottom of the frame. The rock surface lunges at the camera, then goes black.

"Did she survive?" Tucker asks.

"Doubt it."

Tucker taps his rifle's receiver. "I think she survived."

He gives Musa Harb final instructions for the counter-assault. Then he hoists himself back in the nearest empty Halo and gives the pilot a new insertion point. It lifts off into the night, as platoon after platoon of IRG infantry begin pouring off the backs of the two-and-a-half ton trucks that now stream into the compound and form up in rows.

Garner has lost comms not only with the JOC, but also with his holding teams on higher floors. At this point, though, they can hear firing from above. And it's getting closer. So everybody knows they're in for a fight.

"On me," Major Garner says to Shrek. "We're going to roll it straight back up and out."

Shrek makes a series of hand signs to the assaulters, who are now stacked up and ready to roll. NVGs down, illuminators on, rifles to shoulders – cocked, locked and ready to rock.

When they hit the first stairwell, for the climb up to subbasement four, his security team there is already in a grenade-throwing contest with opponents above. And guys with the higher elevation have a compelling advantage in grenade-throwing contests.

Garner pours people into the breach, moving in bounding overwatch. They quickly gain traction, and make headway, one landing at a time. After that, there's heavy opposition on every level. Through the eerie green-and-white view of the enhanced NVGs, picked out in the sweeping cones of the IR illuminators, it's like a kind of demon-green otherworld. Enemy fighters look like whited-out negatives of themselves, outlined in thick strokes, their barrels glowing as they heat up. With every muzzle flash, fields of vision white out for a split second. With every grenade blast, everyone is briefly blinded.

Thousands of empty shell casings clatter to the tile floor. Guys behind put their hands on the shoulders of those in front. When those in front go down, they are pulled to safety by those in the rear, who take their place. The bodies of the enemy tumble down the stairwells and have to be shoved aside.

The resistance now, the sheer volume of combatants pressing down on them, makes the earlier phase, when they fought their way in, seem in retrospect like a token resistance. Plus the reversal of direction, upward now, makes it all feel uncannily like trying to fight their way out of their own tomb.

Between levels three and two, the stairwell is so grenade-damaged and clogged by debris and bodies that they have to set breaching charges on the ceiling and blast through the floor above. They then hoist themselves up and fight their way through the hole. Then it's another fight back to the stairwell.

Floor by painstaking floor, they claw their way toward the surface, taking casualties the whole way. Garner is one of them. Shrek is another. Combat medics, which means every Delta operator, slap pressure bandages on them, and on the others. They also take their first KIAs – two guys felled by headshots, then two by multiple waves of grenade blasts.

And the survivors fight on. And up.

Never once does a single one of them falter, or panic, or lose hope, or lose his cool. They just keep operating, on the razor edge of performance, fighting like demons themselves, snake-strike fast and machine-tool accurate, workmanlike and remorseless, all in the direst extremity imaginable.

When they've shouldered through the last ambushers between them and open air, they burst into the courtyard, Garner and Shrek in the van. And everyone instantly goes blind.

It takes them a quarter-second to realize they've been hit by high-powered IR lights, mounted in an arc around the building. These massively overload their night-vision systems and temporarily, but badly, blind the assault team leaders.

Behind the arc of lights is another arc, one of Tucker-trained jihadis, who open fire.

Both Garner and Shrek are hit again, and retreat back into the building.

* * *

"This is Boomslang Actual, to all Chuckles call signs. Ground element in heavy contact, requesting immediate support and extraction. How copy?" Wounded, winded, and leading a dwindling band, Garner's voice is still calm and business-like. He's fallen back on an emergency short-range rescue radio, which he hopes will reach the helo flight offshore.

"Boomslang, Chuckles One copies all. We are inbound, ETA eight mikes."

Garner blinks heavily in the darkness of the building's ground floor, where his guys are hunkered down. He rubs his eyes, which physically ache. But, just conceivably, they may yet get out of this alive. "Chuckles One, be advised: Lima Zulu is hot – repeat, Lima Zulu hot. We have heavy SAFIRE from northwest, west, and southwest. You will have to try and suppress on approach with miniguns. We will synchronize and lead a break-out here. How copy?"

"Roger that, Boomslang. Solid copy. We'll give you a two-mike warning when we're on approach. Let's coordinate fires and see if we can't clear that LZ."

It occurs to Garner that the strength and disposition of the new counter-assaulting forces is unknown. Except that it's fucking big. Waz and his guys may be flying into certain death. *And he sounds like he's planning a meeting of his book club*, Garner thinks. Then again, he didn't just fight his way up five flights of stairs in 65 pounds of assault kit.

"Roger that. Thanks, Waz. Our guys would sure like to get out of here. Good luck to you."

"Roger that. Hang tight, Jim."

Ali struggles up toward consciousness through the darkness. The first thing she's aware of is the sound of spinning rotor blades. These could be real, or a memory running by as echoes, or a wholesale auditory hallucination. But it fades away as mysteriously as it faded in.

She realizes she's lying on something hard and uneven. It's definitely not her rack.

And now it all comes back to her. Iran, the mission, the counter-assault – and her tumble over a sheer precipice, and down a rocky mountainside, chased by a rabid UAV.

When drones attack, she thinks, amusing herself.

She's lying where she landed. That she's aware of this means she both came to a stop, and survived. So that's good. She tries to move her left arm, which is twisted and trapped underneath her. *Wow!* she screams internally, *that'll wake you up in the morning.*

Her whole body has gone tense with electric, crashing pain. From that alone, she knows her humerus, the long bone in her upper arm, is broken. Keeping it as immobilized as she can, she does a combat casualty self-assessment, basically feeling herself up. Other than being stunned and slightly singed, everything else seems to be in working order.

She freezes again. Not voices… but that was definitely a pebble spill, which means one or more people walking, and trying to do so silently. She swivels her eyeballs around, looking for resources. She can't see much. Her NVG has snapped off her helmet mount. Wherever her CheyTac is, she can't see or feel it.

And whoever is stalking her, she knows they are only a few meters behind her now.

* * *

Tucker knows better than to fall for this. Or, anyway, he knows better than to assume he's gotten that lucky. Delta guys don't give their opponents a lot of easy breaks. So he lets the two crew chiefs from the Halo take the lead.

The first has just touched the sniper's shoulder to roll her over... when she rolls over herself in a snake-strike blur and double-taps him point-blank in the head. The other crew chief barely has time to startle before getting the same treatment, two more close-range headshots in a precision double tattoo.

Both hit the ground, falling to either side.

Five meters behind, Tucker throws his forearms up before his head – as two heavy .45 rounds from Ali's weapon thwack in on them, only stopped by the gelling liquid Kevlar in his assault suit. The force of it nearly breaks his arms, and he shouts in pain and rage while throwing himself sideways. Three more rounds wallop him in the chest and abdomen before his dive is stopped by a crash into the sheer cliff side.

He hears the distinctive metal scrape of a magazine dropping out of a pistol.

It doesn't fall far – Ali is prone on the ground, pointing her side arm up one-handed – and Tucker heaves his entire weight forward, and straight down on top of her.

They both grunt from the impact, but Ali instantly wriggles away like an electric eel that's going to fucking electrocute your ass. She's already let the .45 go in mid-air, and her Gerber Mark II fighting knife comes out of nowhere for a wicked back-hand slash, which opens Tucker's glove and the top of his left hand, all the way to the bone. She comes right back with a straight stab at his throat.

He brings both forearms together in an X, trapping and deflecting the blade down into his chest, where it's stopped by the suit. He grabs her knife hand, yanks her violently toward him, and aims a forehead smash at her nose.

It's an old bar brawl trick and she sees it coming a mile away, spinning her body sidelong to him. As his head rockets at her, she takes hold of it with both hands to bring it hammer down into her knee, which is already racing upward. But her broken left arm fails her and she lets go. Tucker twists away.

He clocks the location of her injury instantly and in the same motion brings a vicious right roundhouse kick into her upper arm. This stuns her long enough for him to again bring his full body mass, and greater upper body strength, crashing into her, and up against the sheer stone wall behind.

Ali's arm is screaming, and the wind gone from her lungs, but she's not out of the fight. She aims a decoy four-finger jab at Tucker's throat, which he deflects, but she's already swinging her knee up with the full force of her hip behind it, for a one-shot-one-kill stroke at his groin.

But she's badly hurt now, and a beat too slow, and Tucker's thigh has twisted to where his junk used to be, by the time Ali's would-be killing stroke lands. It's so brutal it actually does significant tissue damage to his thigh. But it also leaves her off balance, and Tucker's next two precision strikes go home.

There are 108 pressure points on the human body that when struck can cause paralysis, unconsciousness, organ damage, or death – and Tucker personally knows about 40 of them. With middle knuckle protruding, he pops Ali in a nerve nexus in the side of her neck. This causes her vision to dilate and dim, and her chest and leg muscles to give out. Before she falls, he resets and strikes a nerve bundle on the side of her abdomen, at the eleventh rib.

Ali collapses, faints, and sinks back down into the blackness.

* * *

When she comes to again, her vision foggy and spinning, extremities numb and buzzing, she's been flex-cuffed at the wrists and ankles. She's also in a fireman's carry over someone's back, and after a few strides gets thrown through the cargo door of one of the Halos, which has set down in a flat spot somewhere behind her OP.

She doesn't let on that she's conscious as someone ropes her ankle ties to a strut. By the time the aircraft lifts off, she's worm-crawled to where an Inter-crew Communication System (ICS) headset lies on the deck, and pressed her throbbing head up against it.

Tucker and the pilot are speaking Arabic, which Ali can follow well enough.

"—ack down to the compound, Boss?"

"No. This fight is over. Straight back to Tehran. Kazemi Garrison."

Ali's training and experience have conditioned her never to jump to conclusions. So, while that doesn't sound good, neither does she despair. Also – the fight is *never* over. Not until you're under the ground, and they've shoveled at least a few feet of earth on top of you.

It's what you do at precisely such moments as these that defines you.

THE PHYSICAL AND VIRTUAL BATTLESPACE
AROUND THE CHALUS TAKEDOWN
04:23:44 AST 06 APR

"Boomslang, Chuckles flight is inbound. ETA TWO MIKES. How copy?"

"Chuckles, Boomslang copies your last. Inbound, two mikes."

Garner has lost some blood, so he's feeling light-headed. But he's still running this fight, nor is his squadron out of it. They have lost all contact with the JOC, though, so they're going to have to fight their way out of this one on their own.

Shrek hands him a collapsible periscope, which he sticks around the edge of the doorway. Out and to the right is north, where he should be able to spot the helos coming in.

"Uh, Boomslang, be advised. We're getting painted up here."

"Ohh, shit…" Garner says aloud.

"Yeah, we've got active and passive radar all over us like a cheap suit. Whatever air defense blind spot we were in has closed up."

Garner doesn't know what to say to this. It's like listening to a man calmly read his own death warrant. He drops the periscope and prairie-dogs his actual head around the edge of the door. Out behind the cordon of troops, he sees four IR laser designators light up and point off into the sky, in the direction of the approaching rotor noise.

"Oh, no…" Garner says, stabbing at his transmit button.

* * *

"Yeah," Bob Li says into his hand mic, sitting on the hatch lip of one of the Halos on the deck. He's speaking to Tucker, who is in the air and already 60 clicks south, halfway back to Tehran. "The counter-hack's initiated. We've bumped their intrusion and locked them out. All the anti-air systems are back online."

"Are the Chinooks in sight?"

"Just coming over the saddle now."

"Well for fuck's sake take them. Right now their ECM pods are going batshit from the radar."

Li waves at the semi-circle of eight Hamas guys manning four RBS 70 man-portable laser-guided/beam-riding surface-to-air missiles. "Go, go! Fire." Li's English is perfect, but some of the jihadis' leaves a little to be desired. "Shoot! Shoot!" That gets the message across.

As per their training and mission prep, the pairs divide up the inbound helos, put their laser pointers on their nose cones, and launch, with a dramatic whoosh and smoky back-wash. As long as they keep their laser dots on their targets, the missiles will follow them in, immune to all conventional countermeasures. And Chinooks are big, fat, and slow to maneuver, especially when flaring to land.

At the last second, their electronic counter-measure (ECM) systems shrieking, the four birds break to the left and right, spitting flares and chaff, and go evasive. But it's too late. And keeping the lasers on them proves easier than in some video games.

Just like Half-Life, actually, Li thinks to himself, whistling admiringly as the missiles fly unerringly home.

* * *

Garner sees all four birds simultaneously disintegrate into bloating fireballs and begin raining metal shards and flaming fluids across the side of the mountain.

He pulls his head back in and takes one second, and one breath, to recalibrate.

"Okay," he says, turning and walking back into the interior. "Huddle up." The remaining 34 operators, most of them wounded in some way, circle around.

"No air extraction," he says. "Waz and Dono are gone. And all their guys."

No one says anything to this. People are still checking weapons and tightening up bandages, not to mention catching their breath.

"We can't hunker down, because it's a non-permissive environment, and there are never going to be fewer Iranians outside than there are right now. And no other friendlies will be coming – the ROE are clear: we're on our own. Now. Who's got the S-raws?"

Two guys turn away and the men closest to them unruck their FGM-172 Short Range Assault Weapon (SRAW) missiles. These are lightweight, close-range missile systems built to replace the old AT-4 anti-tank infantry weapon. The SRAW is lighter, inertially guided, and more lethal.

Garner steals a glance at the topo map on his palm-top.

"We've lost commo, drones, and the outside security teams. So we don't know what we're facing out there. But it looks like a lot of guys. And they've got the only exit totally ringed in." He exhales quietly into the silence. "Our main chance is north. That means turning right out the front door, for you guys who can't orient without GPS." This gets a couple of grim laughs.

Garner briefly considers asking for the two volunteers he needs. But this would be pointless and a waste of time, as everyone would instantly raise a hand. Instead he picks basically the two most fearsome and bulletproof guys still standing.

"Thing and Dogface. You're on me and Shrek."

Two huge and imposing men step forward.

Thing, an enormous ex-football player with short sandy hair, a square head, and deltoids that actually look like shoulder pads, is considered one of the best men to be beside in combat, fearless and deadly in a fight. Utterly courageous (except for parachuting, which terrifies him), he's absolutely unflappable no matter how bad things get. But he's also friendly with a dry sense of humor – a powerful man, but also a big kid.

Dogface, a brown-eyed Kentuckian with a thick dark beard and cannonball biceps, looks like an eight-year-old's drawing of a superhero. He has a general disdain for the chain of command, which probably would have badly hampered his career in regular Army units. When not working out or shooting, he is usually playing his Fender Stratocaster in a room at home he had sound-insulated for the sake of his hot but famously neurotic Swedish girlfriend.

The pair also came into Unit from the same Selection class, and have slung a lot of brass downrange together. They are, if not inseparable, then possessed of some unbreakable private connection. They stand side by side now like a matched set of giant temple-guarding statues.

"The four of us," Garner says, "are going to drop smoke into the courtyard, then fire both S-raws into the enemy emplacements at the far right. Then we're going to go out, jog left, emplace, and provide a base of fire. Right behind us, everyone else goes right and hauls ass north. You break through the cordon around the missile impact point." He steals another look at his device.

"From there, it's an easy scrabble up into the foothills. Once you're over the first rise, you disperse into the mountains and escape and evade. You know your E&E corridors. Land, sea, or air, just get back over the friendly border of your choice. And stay alive. Your significant others are going to give me shit for months if you come back dead."

He casts his eye over the extraordinary group of men before him.

"Questions?" Nothing. "Push-back?" Virtually every Delta planning session ends up being a "Chinese parliament," a spirited multilateral negotiation. But not this one. This is a simple, terrible plan of assaulting straight through an ambush. And it's all they've got.

Thing and Dogface sling their rifles, shoulder the missiles, and step forward.

The others lines up in the starting blocks.

Garner and Shrek pull the pins on four smoke grenades and take a last breath.

* * *

Shock and near silence have reigned in the JOC since the four helicopters went down. People haven't ceased functioning. But they have started talking in hushed voices, like at a funeral. Everyone's more or less having a Mogadishu moment. The bottom's fallen out, and what has happened is much worse than anything they could have imagined.

Rheinhardt goes to the back of the room and gets in General Stamis's face.

"You've got to send the Little Birds back. The men need their guns."

"Negative. That is specifically disallowed by the presidential finding. There can be no additional assets in theater after infil." The general sinks down into a chair, looking as if he's aging years every minute. "Anyway, they're almost to the border already. They'd be an hour getting back." Left unsaid is that this is all likely to be over much sooner than that.

Much of the activity in the JOC has been around frantic efforts to get comms back up. If they can't talk to their guys on the ground, they can't do much to help them. Thinking laterally, as usual, Mike is the first to accomplish something.

"I've got video from one of the helmet cams," he says, as Rheinhardt comes back. "Their overloading of our comms channels is optimized for voice. It's basically a loud squelch. If I disentangle the audio and video streams from the helmet cam, the video's intact."

Rheinhardt leans aggressively across desks again, and puts this too up on the big screen. With the UAVs down, it's the only close-up view they've got into any part of the battlespace.

And for the moment all it shows is a patch of shoulder, and some sort of tubular object.

* * *

This picture is in night-vision green, grainy and flickering, with no sound.

A hand goes up in the frame, showing all five fingers. The view lurches as his shoulder heaves in a throwing motion. Five beats pass, while thickening smoke can just be seen piling up outside. And then the wearer of the camera, whom they know to be Shrek, rushes forward and out the door. And he immediately hits the deck. Even through the smoke, the black-and-green darkness lights up with muzzle flashes, dozens of them.

And then hundreds.

Shrek, on the ground, looks to his right – following the smoke trail of a missile, which is immediately followed by a second. The two projectiles streak into a dense line of men, maybe 75 meters away, their ranks standing before a foothill. They're all firing small arms when the missiles hit. The huge dual explosion whites out the night-vision video for a full second.

None of it makes any sound. Just a silent movie version of a raging, desperate battle.

By the time the explosions and their afterglow settle, Shrek, still prone, now faces forward, and begins firing at full tilt. He empties his rifle magazine, then all three 40mm grenades from his underslung Metal Storm grenade launcher, then reloads both in a blur.

While doing so, he steals a look to his right. A staggered double line of operators now run flat out, away, north, toward the foothills, heads ducked down, firing their weapons from the hip, mostly off to the left, a few to the front. Many of them jerk as they run, taking hits from the withering incoming fire.

Whichever way Shrek pans there are galaxies of silent muzzle flashes, visible through the billowing clouds from the smoke grenades, on all sides of them but one. Men in the sprinting lines begin to sprawl and go down. Others help the fallen, and are hit themselves. The headlong sprint continues, an endless 75 meters.

No one in the JOC so much as breathes.

* * *

Beside Shrek, Major Garner shakes his head to clear it. The sound of the full-auto firing, from hundreds of weapons, is beyond deafening. It's hellish. So are the smoke, the cries of wounded men, and the backlighting of flames from the destroyed helicopters.

Garner hears Dogface say, conversationally, but loud enough to be heard, "Damn, I'm hit."

"We're all hit, brother!" Thing says, blazing away from the shoulder, down on one knee.

Garner sees Dogface being knocked backward by the force of the rounds. His assault suit will keep the bullets from penetrating, for a little while. Meanwhile, his monstrous physical strength, and insuperable mental resolve, keep him upright and fighting.

Looking past him, Garner can see Thing's chin covered in blood. He must have internal bleeding. But he's still upright and blazing away. Garner leans forward into his weapon and continues firing. He feels a terrible, hot pain in his ear. He thinks it may be gone, but he doesn't have time to check.

On the ground before him, Shrek has stopped firing now, collapsed over his weapon.

Thing is slumping down, closer and closer to the ground, but still firing and reloading all the way down. His motions are slowing, winding down. Dogface takes a round to the face and pitches over backward. Bullets are hitting everywhere – ground, building, men.

Garner goes empty again. He looks to the right. He can just make out the backs of a handful of running figures. They are disappearing into the crags of the mountains.

He smiles. They'll be safe there.

His right arm has gone totally numb. He tucks the rifle in the crook of his arm, and tries to reload with one hand. He can taste blood himself now, backing up in his throat.

* * *

On the screen in the JOC, the view from Shrek's camera has stopped moving. The scene it shows is static, flat on the ground, turned 90 degrees on its side, with pebbles and grass in the foreground. Everything is peacefully still, and still deathly silent. A few feet away, beyond the pebbles, a man slumps forward into the frame. He turns his face toward the camera.

It's Major Garner.

His NVGs have fallen off, or been shot off. His gaze is long and wistful, eyes cloudy and going out of focus. But a smile plays at the edges of his lips.

He mouths a word. Everyone can make it out: *Shrek*.

Several people in the JOC are crying now. These stoke one another, and a few sobs break out. Guys who go six-two and 220, with fifteen years in spec-ops, equally hard and smart, are breaking down.

"Someone get that off the goddamned screen," Stamis mutters.

But before anyone does, the camera view twists and pans, up toward the sky. The view now is up along a black sleeve, terminating in a curious, bearded face. The hand pulls the camera off and up. Other figures can be seen now, rifles lowered, walking amongst and checking the bodies.

The screen goes black.

Rheinhardt's cell phone goes off.

It's way too loud in the horror-show silence and muffled sobbing of the ops center. He pulls himself woodenly to his feet and stumbles out the door at the back of the room. He looks at the phone screen. Unrecognized number. That is very rare on a secure, encrypted cell.

"Go for Rheinhardt," he says.

"Hey, man."

Rheinhardt freezes dead.

* * *

Uncle BJ rounds the corner and comes charging down the hall. He sees Rheinhardt.

"Is it true? They're sa—"

But then he too freezes when he sees the look on Rheinhardt's face, holding his phone to his ear, not speaking. The two stand facing each other in the empty hall. Then Johnson leans in and puts the side of his head against Rheinhardt's, their ears side-by-side, cheeks pressing together.

"I knew you'd come," Tucker drawls.

"You evil son of a bitch," Rheinhardt says. He's grinding his jaw so hard it looks like he's trying to eat his own teeth.

"Hey, it had to be this way, bro." There's a pause and a slight change of tone. *"Though none of it would ever have happened if you hadn't sold me out. After Anbar."*

Rheinhardt twists at the neck, bonking Johnson and pissing him off. "You unbelievable bastard. I didn't sell you out. I fucking covered for you. Biggest mistake of my goddamned life."

"That so? Then why am I out here, alone, instead of in there with you? I wasn't surprised the government sided with the Israelis against me. But how'd they find out what happened in the first place? It could only have been you."

Rheinhardt is scowling. "They find everything out. That's what they do." He only realizes that Johnson's entire face is red and trembling when the big man grabs the phone out of his hand.

"Now you listen to me, you cocksucker." BJ struggles to hold the phone still in his quaking hand. "When we find you, you cockroach, I am personally going to kill you *all kinds* of dead. I'm gonna cut your head off, and I'm gonna make you eat it. I'm gonna blow your face straight through your hat—"

Rheinhardt retrieves the phone, not least because he's afraid BJ's actually going to crush it. He takes a deep breath. "Okay, I'll bite. What in God's name are you doing?"

Tucker seems to leer at him through the phone. *"You've been sold a bill of goods, Bo. You're out there fighting and dying for the Zionists. The Gulf Wars? Defense of Israel. Nine-eleven? All because of our troops in the Holy Land, protecting a tiny outpost of Jews. And then a few of them happen to get killed on an op, and America betrays one of its own best soldiers."*

"You're unhinged."

"No, man. I just see the underlying patterns. Ever take a look at the people who really run things in the U.S. Government? Wolfowitz, on the national security teams of both Clinton and Bush, and who planned the Iraq War – a Jew. Elena Kagan on the Supreme Court. Ari Fleischer, Bush's Press Secretary. Madeleine Albright at State. Cohen at Defense under Clinton, and Janet Reno as Attorney General. Rubin at Treasury. ALL Jews."

Rheinhardt looks incredulous. "Why do you give a shit who the Treasury Secretary is?"

"Because I'm sick of our brothers dying in the desert to prop up international Jewish financial interests."

Rheinhardt draws a breath to steady himself. "The main thing about conspiracy theories, you nutjob, is that they're never true. And the less evidence, the more sinister the cover-up is said to be."

Tucker snorts. *"When those CIA pussies came to kill me, they found some books they didn't like. Patriot literature. They only had two minutes to look at it, before the room went up. But you ought to read some of it for yourself. Might open your eyes."*

"Great, nutjob pamphlets. Have you ever actually seen any evidence of any of this Jewish conspiracy yourself? Firsthand? No, nobody has."

There's a heavy pause on the other end. *"Nobody's seen anything firsthand, huh? Well, I saw those CIA paras in my bedroom, guns drawn, ready to take me out, a revenge killing for the Israelis. And you can walk yourself down to the memorial room at the Ranch and look at the names on the wall. So many of our fallen brothers, killed in Lebanon… and Iraq… and Libya… and Yemen… fighting all of Israel's goddamned dirty proxy wars…"*

For a second, Tucker seems to be steaming into his axe murderer persona. But then he climbs back down to cool surfer dude. *"A thousand stories like that one in the big city, brother. It's all there if you've got eyes to see."*

Rheinhardt is seized with the urge to put his full weight into a punch through Tucker's face. For calling him brother, after everything, after today. But of course Tucker isn't there to be punched. Rheinhardt speaks through clenched teeth.

"You talk about our brothers dying. Can you even understand what you did today? You murdered an entire squadron of our brother operators. You're so full of shit."

Tucker pauses. *"A few have always had to be sacrificed to save the many. With 5,000 dead in Iraq alone, and 32,000 wounded, B Squadron's just a rounding error. And, you'll forgive me, but Delta is no longer my personal favorite unit in the U.S. Army."*

"Fuck you."

"But don't worry about a thing, brother. I'm going to make it right. When there's no more Israel, there'll be no more American soldiers dying to defend it. And after all this is over, I'll be on my way, made whole again, and America can go hers. She can once again hide between the wide oceans, and avoid, as Washington put it in his farewell address, 'foreign alliances, attachments, and intrigues'."

His magma-core anger slowly subsiding, Rheinhardt begins trying to figure out whether Tucker is simply insane. Or if he's trying, masterfully, to manipulate them into something again.

"It's good to hear your voice, little brother – despite everything. But I've got a few more moves to make before all this is over. I don't expect you and I will be talking again. Stay cool."

The line goes dead.

* * *

As Rheinhardt stands there regarding the phone, and Johnson regards him, Mike Brown fast-walks into the hallway from the direction of the JOC, laptop under arm. He stops when he sees the other two. An instant later, Javier comes in from the other direction, from the hangar.

Everyone's looking at Rheinhardt, like *Now, what?*

He shakes his head. The look on his face is somewhere between complete helplessness and unendurable frustration. In fact, it's the former causing the latter, and the sense of helplessness is nearly killing him. He's never been good with it. And it's never been this bad. Finally, he speaks.

"I'm sorry, I don't even know what to tell you. I don't know what happens now." He swallows heavily and looks around, for nothing in particular. "I don't honestly know that anything we're doing is helping. Maybe Tucker's right. Maybe all we're doing is getting more good people killed."

No one has any response to this.

"I've got to report to Chaya, and IDF. That we've failed." He walks away in a daze, thumbing at his phone, utterly alone.

The others watch him go in silence.

"I've never seen him like that," BJ finally says. "Never."

"So it's war, then." Chaya's voice is calm over the line. Rheinhardt has just broken for her the news of the debacle at Chalus. And this is her verdict.

Rheinhardt sits half-slumped on one of the unused cots in the hangar. They're all unused now. The racks, rucks, and personal effects of the 75 operators and officers of B Squadron sit laid out in orderly and empty rows, in a deathly silence. It's like the frozen remnants of the dead. It's like Pompeii. The few survivors, B support and signals guys, wander in and out, to smoke and to grieve. They are like ghosts. Haunting their own house.

"I don't know," Rheinhardt says quietly into his phone. He knows he is speaking to a woman who may be in the next Pompeii. "I don't think the U.S. has anything left to offer. The president's ruled out air strikes. And Delta's done after this. I'm sorry. What's the IDF plan?"

Chaya pauses. *"I know this is a secure line. Nevertheless."*

Rheinhardt gets it. Israel is on her own again. And when they can only rely on themselves, they can't take the risk of trusting anyone else.

"I've got to go," she says.

"Okay," he says, consciousness already slipping away from him. He's been awake for 56 hours in a row, and his brain has been pummeled. He manages to terminate the call, curls up on the cot, and descends into the blessed blackness of knowing nothing anymore…

***

*But it isn't knowing nothing – any more than it is not being responsible
for anything. From out of the blackness, which had promised him solace,
he can now hear the shrieking of the 105 rounds, coming in remorselessly, and faster than their own sound, churning the earth. Once again
he sees the field below him turned into a glowing green hell. And this
time there is no rolling into a ball and covering up his head. He is naked
before it all.*

*Once again, the flayed, roasted, glowing bodies crawl out of the
green flames toward him, their fingerless hands clawing at his feet. He
tries to jerk his legs away, looks around for somewhere to flee to. But
there is a black, lightless wall surrounding him. When he pushes against
it, his muscles turn to jelly and he moves in a kind of tar, digging
himself in deeper with every attempt to break free.*

And when he looks down toward his feet again…

*The faces on the dying bodies are now those of his brothers in B
Squadron.*

*Garner… Shrek… Sergeant Major Bullethead… Thing…
Dogface… Gordy… Skip… Murph… Jester… Too many to
make out, but all of them damningly familiar. And all calling out
to Rheinhardt to save them. He shakes with sobs, trying to shut his
ears to their cries.*

*But they are now drowned out by another voice, this one behind
him. He whirls and sees her behind him, up on the mountainside, nearly
a mile away. But he can hear her voice perfectly. She's calling out to him
to save her, too, and he calls back:*

"Ali. Hold tight! I'm coming!"

*He looks down, trying to free his legs from the tangle of grasping
arms… and when he looks up again, it is not Ali before him… but
Sergeant Major Rod "The God" Tucker. Heat Rash.*

239

Rheinhardt feels his .45 in his right hand. But he can't raise the arm. It's gone numb, completely without feeling, from the shoulder all the way down. Tucker is laughing at him, and now the man's right foot is on Ali's back, pinning her to the ground.

Rheinhardt manages to get the .45 into his left hand. With terrible effort, he raises it and fires. The bullet hits Tucker square, and makes him jerk. But he quickly stands upright again, and laughs aloud.

Rheinhardt fires again and again. With each shot, the rounds lose power, until they are falling out of the barrel. And it's hopeless anyway, because more Tuckers are coming now, from behind the first, spreading out in ranks beside and behind him, Tucker after Tucker, bad guy upon bad guy, in legions inexhaustible.

"Ali..." he calls out, in despair and terror of what's going to happen to her.

"Come and see her," the first Tucker says, grinning. "Our girl's on TV. Come and see..."

Rheinhardt is utterly confused. "She's where...? On TV...?"

But now someone has grabbed his shoulder from behind, and shakes him violently...

* * *

"Wake up, buddy. Come on."

Rheinhardt jerks violently, nearly falling off the cot. Leaning over him, blotting out most of the light, is the hulking form of Uncle BJ. Behind, leaning around him, are Mike and Javier.

"You need to get in the JOC," BJ says. "Now."

"Trust us here," Javier adds.

Mike, remaining silent, just looks badly distraught.

When they reach the JOC, it's nearly as full as during the mission the night before. Ops and intel staff generally keep vampire hours, working to support nighttime missions, then racking out between 4am and noon. But with the frantic efforts to locate and extract survivors from B Squadron, virtually all of the stations are occupied. And more bodies are piling in now, as word spreads around the base.

All eyes are on the center screen, which is showing CNN. A correspondent talks into the camera, with early-morning Tehran as her backdrop.

"…*Iran State Television is broadcasting footage of an American special forces soldier allegedly captured in a raid on Iran's nuclear research facilities. Images of the woman, who was wearing a headscarf, show that she appears to be in good health. Iranian military sources claim that she was captured in an illegal attack on Iranian territory early this morning…*"

There's a slight but distinctly uneasy murmur through the JOC at the headscarf bit. And now the camera cuts away from the reporter, to jerkier and grainier footage. All eyes are glued to the screen. And up above them all, larger than life, sits First Sergeant Aaliyah Khamsi.

Live and on TV.

* * *

The room has now gone totally silent. Footage plays of Ali sitting in a chair, being walked around between two buildings, into a courtyard, and then back inside. She's being put on parade.

Her left arm is in a sling, with the upper arm in a splint. She wears a loose, nondescript, light gray jumpsuit. And covering all of her hair, and framing her face, which is devoid of expression, is a darker gray headscarf.

"Goddamned sons of bitches," BJ mutters.

Javier says, "I wouldn't want to be one of the first three guys who tried to get that on her."

The reporter continues in voiceover, while the footage rolls.

"The Iranian embassy in Washington has released a letter they claim was written by the captured soldier. It calls for American forces to withdraw from Iraq and Afghanistan, and condemns the quote-illegal attack on the Islamic Republic of Iran by the United States…"

Rheinhardt squints more deeply up at the screen. "Look at her face. It's been covered with makeup, but she's definitely banged up. You can see the swelling and bruising beneath the tint."

No one wants to follow this thought anywhere it leads.

But now, improbably, it gets more surreal – as Ahmadinejad himself appears, sat at a table in front of a microphone. The reporter provides translation.

"The Iranian president has also spoken from Tehran, declaring that the failed attack will have no effect on Iran's march toward peaceful nuclear power – and that the captured soldier will be held indefinitely, while Iranian officials investigate whether she will be tried as a spy."

Blood goes cold throughout the room. But as the out-door footage of Ali plays over again, Rheinhardt cranes his neck toward the screen, obviously trying to make something out. And then his face goes through several fascinating shades of emotion.

"Well, that's good, then," he says finally. The others look at him like he's got four heads. He returns their gazes, seeming both calm and sane. "Now we know where she is."

"What?" the others say in unison.

"Everyone on me," he says quietly. The four of them file out, keeping their heads down.

* * *

They stand now back in the same stretch of hallway where Rheinhardt so recently voiced near total despair. Where he told them he didn't know what to do anymore. That nothing they were doing was helping. And as they stand in silence, the team look at him expectantly again.

BJ says, "Okay, I'll bite. Where is she?"

Rheinhardt doesn't answer right away. He seems occupied with waking from his torpor, shouldering his way up from his despair. Finally he pins the others with his gaze, each in turn. And when he speaks, it's in his old voice. The doubt and helplessness have gone.

"Brown. Find a corner and get back in your Matrix. Whoever Tucker's got counter-hacking us, it isn't him and it isn't the Iranians. Find out how they turned their air defenses back on, and how he hijacked our drones. We just got hit, and it's time to get up and fight harder. Get offensive. Counter-hack back."

Mike nods briskly.

"Javier. You're in the JOC. *Don't let anyone kick you out.* Lethal force is authorized."

"Roger, boss. What's my tasking?"

"There's going to be a massive operation to locate survivors from B Squadron – to exfil anyone who lived long enough to get into their E&E. But B Squadron is not our responsibility right now. *Our job is to get our girl back.* Task whatever ISR assets you can from here. Ride asses. Stay in the loop on the overall effort. After that, get on the horn to the Intel Shack at the Ranch. By then, I'll have made sure Havering understands the new regime. Everything we do, have, and are is now in service of this."

"Got it."

"BJ, you're with me, in the hangar. We're going to open up the shelved Iranian missions again – one in particular. And we're going to get deep into it. This shit isn't over." He's already marching away when BJ's powerful hand grabs him by the shoulder.

"Wait a minute. Where is she, man? Where's Ali?"

Rheinhardt almost smiles. "What – you didn't recognize it?"

"From what? What the hell would I recognize it from?"

"From the assault plans for Operation Eagle Claw."

BJ's face goes through a couple of dramatic little motions, Javier following suit.

"She's in Kazemi Garrison," Rheinhardt says. "Quds Force Headquarters. Which is also the former U.S. Embassy compound in Tehran."

"Holy shit," BJ says, his arm going slack and letting Rheinhardt go.

"C'mon," Rheinhardt says. "We've got a hostage rescue to execute. And we're thirty-three years late."

Don't give up the whole store, just the sale items.

This was one of the rules drilled into Ali at SERE School at Bragg (Survival Evasion Resistance Escape). SERE teaches military aviators how to survive a shootdown, evade pursuers on the ground, resist if captured, then escape if possible. The infamous 21-day course is made so brutally realistic that, in more than one instance, the newly freed "prisoners" have turned on and tried to kill their "camp guards."

But this still sucks harder, Ali thinks, pushing her back up against the cold stone wall with bare feet. There's a wooden bench, but she's decided the splinters are worse than the hard rock. There's a wooden bucket in the corner for a bathroom. And that's the extent of the amenities.

So far on her stay here at the Hotel Shithole, she has been subject to one interrogation session. That was when she began to give up useless, false, or misleading information, in exchange for things like food, medical treatment, and a cessation of the beatings.

The medical treatment, it turned out, was hardly worth having. They set her arm, but she's pretty sure they didn't set it right. And re-breaking and resetting it later is going to be deeply unpleasant. As for the beatings, well, the interrogators they had on the job were pussies – certainly as compared to Tucker, and the pummeling he gave her back on the mountain. That man can hit. She has to give him that.

But she plans to give him a whole lot more, just as soon as the moment for it comes. She has an entire plan for the hurting she's going to put on that son of a bitch…

* * *

She's interrupted in these mordant thoughts when the locks on the door start turning. The door bangs open loudly – and Rod Tucker himself stands silhouetted behind it. He enters and plops himself down on the wooden bench, across from Ali's spot on the floor. He rubs the top of his right hand, which is wrapped in a thick bandage. Ali recognizes her own knife work.

"I've heard about you," Tucker drawls, his voice deep and smooth. "Rheinhardt's pet."

The man kind of radiates menace, and Ali hesitates before mouthing off. She'd rather work out what his game is, before inviting another unnecessary beatdown.

"Must be very convenient," he goes on, looking thoughtful. "Having a hot girl right in the team with him. I can see why he keeps you around."

Ali sees absolutely no point in rising to this bullshit. Instead, she silently entertains herself by weighing various options for killing Tucker bare-handed. With the door locked and half of Iran between her and the world, there'd be no point. But it would damned pleasant.

"Rheinhardt," he says again, snorting slightly. "Fucking Little Bo Peep." He squints at her and inclines his head. "He ever tell you how he got that call sign? No, I bet he didn't." Tucker seems to settle himself onto the bench for his story.

"It was from his Selection course. I was cadre then, I saw it all. During the overland navigation tests, as you'll remember, none of the candidates is allowed to follow anybody else. Each has to blaze his own path. But Rheinhardt…"

He pauses, drawing his boot up onto the bench, and his knee in toward him.

"Fucking Rheinhardt had this thing about not letting other people quit. Hardly mattered whether he even knew 'em or not. I mean, along the way, on some of these marches, including the fifty-miler at the end of Stress Phase, he personally talked like a dozen guys into not quitting. These ruined, dead-on-their-feet guys – none of whom, incidentally, were ever going to complete Selection, or get in if they did – he talked them into carrying on, just for another few miles.

"And so Rheinhardt would rock up to the final checkpoint, and there'd always be this little train of people, like three or four, twenty or thirty minutes behind him. All of 'em saying they only gritted it out to the end because of something Rheinhardt said to them."

Ali actually never has heard this story. The origin of Rheinhardt's call sign has always been a minor mystery. Tucker leans over her now, practically dripping menace *on* her.

"You know the nursery rhyme, don't you? *Little Bo-Peep has lost her sheep, And can't tell where to find them; Leave them alone, And they'll come home, Wagging their tails behind them.*"

And then he laughs, in a profoundly disturbing way.

"Everybody always followed that guy." He leaves the last bit unsaid, about where that got them last night. Instead he just looks at her, then finally gets up and walks toward the exit. He knocks twice and the door opens. But he pauses and turns back to her again.

"You know why your little op last night went to hell? It's like what General Pickett said about why his famous charge at Gettysburg failed. He said, 'I've always thought the Yankees had something to do with it.' The enemy always gets a vote."

The heavy door whumps closed, leaving Ali in darkness.

"So Operation Eagle Claw is back," BJ says, still sounding amazed. "And this time we're going to do it properly. Starting with, I hope, some decent fucking helicopters. And pilots."

"Precisely," Rheinhardt says.

The two of them have just finished transforming their area of the hangar, by the trucks. First they scavenged furniture and whiteboards, and set up their laptops, tablets, and binders. The scavenging was both grim and horribly easy in the depopulated hangar. But no one was too precious about pilfering from the dead, if it could still help the living. Finally, Mike got them credentials to get them onto the local secure wireless network.

"Okay," Rheinhardt says, typing and peering intently into his hardened laptop. "I've got high-res imagery of the compound in Tehran, from about five seconds ago." BJ leans in. "Here it is side-by-side with the diagrams in the Eagle Claw assault plan, circa 1980."

BJ whistles. "Looks like not a hell of a lot has changed, building or layout wise."

Rheinhardt nods. "Not a lot – except, as you said, our rides. Hand me my phone." He speed dials with one hand while tabbing through screens with the other. "Richie, Eric. Yeah. I'm sorry, too. Really sorry. Those were your brothers who died flying. Yeah, mine, too."

There's a longish pause.

"Yes. I am. You want in?"

* * *

Rheinhardt and BJ have been working at their table, without rest, for four hours now. They're slugging coffee, popping pills, and flipping map charts, when Rheinhardt's phone rings. When he answers, it's audible out in the room.

"RHEINHARDT. Havering."

"Thank God," Rheinhardt says. "I've been trying like hell to get hold of you."

"Yeah, I've heard that. I need to talk to you, too."

"She's alive," Rheinhardt says. "And we know where she's being held."

"Yeah, I know. Sergeant, you just secure that shit right there. There's not going to be another American operation on Iranian soil – probably EVER. This has been an international diplomatic catastrophe. State and the Pentagon are both in full retreat, putting down FPF and covering asses in bounding overwatch. There are flaming bags of shit flying in all directions, but mostly down toward us. The president is cursing our very name. You, me, all of us – we are under extremely unambiguous orders to STAND DOWN."

Rheinhardt exhales as he considers this. He may only have a few words to work with here. "You know they may hang her? And that a kangaroo trial might start and finish in an hour?"

"Yeah." Havering sighs audibly. *"I know all that."*

"I've got all the resources I need to go and get her. I can make it happen."

There's a heavy pause. *"…Transport?"*

"Richie's putting together the entire flight we need from helos and pilots on training and maintenance rotations."

"What, so you can get your asses all shot down again?"

"I've got Mike working on getting the AA network back down. And even if he can't, Rick's got stealth helos."

"Jesus Christ, the whole world knows about those since one went down in bin Laden's back garden."

"Knowing they exist isn't the same as being able to counter or detect them."

Havering sighs audibly. *"Okay. Now you listen to me very carefully, Sergeant Major. You are hereby ordered to stand down from planning or executing any hostage rescue, or operation of any sort, against the Islamic Republic of Iran."*

"Bu—"

"You are further hereby personally ordered into a mandatory training cycle."

Rheinhardt clenches his teeth. BJ watches him with concern.

"Now. As for the disposition of your training… where, what, and for how long is entirely at your discretion. Moreover, if some of your colleagues there in Balad want to participate in your training op, that's up to their local unit commanders."

Rheinhardt's mouth goes from clenching teeth to broad grin. BJ raises his eyebrows.

"So I don't think we'll see you back here at the Ranch for a while. Do we understand each other, Sergeant Major?"

"Yes, sir. Zero distortion." Rheinhardt shuts the phone and looks at BJ.

"Well?"

"We're in business."

* * *

Two hours later, Rheinhardt and BJ are still neck-deep in planning, with Mike and Javier periodically darting in to coordinate. However, late in the morning, a newcomer lurches in.

"I heard you were planning some very interesting training op."

The voice is recognizably feminine, but deep, with a heavy Slavic-sounding accent. Its owner is Staff Sergeant Egle Markunas of C Squadron. She's six-foot-five, Lithuanian, former Olympic basketball player, a super athlete, and totally physically imposing. One of her specialties is languages – six of them, including Russian and Urdu. Another is close-in combat – a devotee of the Close Quarters Defense method, she can grapple you to the ground, knock you out with her gun barrel, or shoot you in the face with equal facility. She's also the Unit's only woman assaulter – *ever.*

"Yeah, we might be doing something," Rheinhardt says noncommittally.

"I think maybe the C Squadron here would be interested in this sort of training."

Before Rheinhardt can answer, four men, of average height and build, but somehow displaying the walk and demeanor of complete and total badasses, come in through the same door. Rheinhardt clocks them as guys from DEVGRU – the Naval Special Warfare Development Group, previously known as SEAL Team 6. And, ounce for ounce, the only spec-ops team *in the world* that can rival Delta.

Their leader, whom Rheinhardt knows as Homer, steps to the fore. A quiet, careful, and compact man in his mid-thirties, Homer has an unassuming manner, but also an inner power that can be felt from a distance. Fearless and out front, he's well known to be willing to risk everything for his fellows – an unhealthy but common trait amongst SEALS. In his free time, he likes carpentry, horses, single-malt Scotch, redheads, and his church.

"Heard you're on a training cycle," Homer says.

"Word gets around," Rheinhardt says.

"We're due some field exercises ourselves. Thought we might do some cross-training."

But before Rheinhardt can respond, four CIA SAD paras, also complete and utter asskickers, that fact obvious even in casual clothes and absent their tactical kit, are already queuing up behind the SEALs. Their leader is a man the Delta guys know only as Spider.

Six-one and wiry with an angular and stubbly face, Spider is known to be one of the best combat leaders in the Agency, or anywhere. He's also a master climber, spending most of his personal time mountaineering, usually above 12,000 feet. As he hasn't had personal time since 9/11, he's also occasionally seen scurrying up the sides of unclimb-able-looking structures in theater, using a combination of world-class climbing techniques and total disregard for his own well-being. He's also rumored to have killed more people than heart disease.

He leans in and says, "Yeah, we're on a training cycle, too. Funny with the timing there."

Rheinhardt and BJ are both smiling now – plus present-ing with an air of masculine sentimentality usually only por-trayed in Jerry Bruckheimer movies. All of these guys arrayed before them are monumentally seasoned veterans of many battlefields, over many years. And as there are few if any shortcuts to combat wisdom, this experience makes them *human gold.*

"Gentlemen," Rheinhardt says, nodding respectfully. "And lady. You are most welcome."

One of the founding members of Delta once wrote: "Don't quit. Never quit no matter what. Keep going until someone tells you to sit down. Keep going as long as you're able to move, no matter how poorly you think you may be doing. Just don't quit."

He was talking specifically about Delta Selection, which all operators understand tests only one thing: *resolve*. Does a man have the resolve to do what is necessary? No matter the obstacles, no matter the difficulty, and no matter the sacrifice? According to local myth, there was once a Delta Selection where they took *no one*. Not one man in the hundred-plus group of the Army's very top soldiers had the necessary resolve.

Rheinhardt and BJ are walking back toward the hangar, with two large boxes of sandwiches, survival rations for their team's mission-planning death march. But something is visibly bugging Rheinhardt. He stops and puts his box on the deck.

"What now?" BJ asks.

"Israel," he says. "Just say we pull this off, and get Ali back. It doesn't change anything. Israel, Sayeret, Chaya... they still have to deal with a nuclear Iran. They're still looking at all-out 360-degree war at best. And nuclear annihilation at worst. It just goes on and on."

"Hey, man," BJ says. "Israel, and the military of this United States of America, will just have to deal with the nukes issue. I mean, we learned to live with a nuclear Pakistan. And they're definitely a bunch of whackjobs. Maybe this will be okay, too."

BJ puts his box on his knee and claps Rheinhardt on the back. "Anyway, we can only do what we can do. Come on. Let's just get over there and kill some people."

* * *

"Where are we?" Rheinhardt asks, putting the grub down on the piles of maps and charts.

"Combat loads," Egle says. "Whoever the machine gunner is to hold the southern sector, we think will need 2,000 rounds of 7.62. And I think it's going to be me, because none of you shrimps can hump that much weight."

"What I can't figure out," says Spider, "is what this Tucker dude was thinking when he kidnapped a Delta shooter. Rescuing hostages is basically your number one job. Is this guy really as stupid as a box of rocks?"

The group laughs. But Rheinhardt looks unamused.

"He's not stupid at all," he says. "He's fucking lethal. He out-maneuvered an entire Delta Squadron into early graves." From his tone of voice, the whole group stops laughing and pays attention. Rheinhardt goes on.

"Our primary tasking is the rescue. But I can tell you it's also extremely likely that Tucker is going to be in the same complex." He puts his palms on the table and looks at each person in turn. "And we're going to kill him. He was our mistake. And, as we just learned, he's too dangerous to have running around. It ends here."

* * *

Mike threads his way through the hangar, looking for Rheinhardt. "Word with you, Sarge?" The two step away to a dim corner.

"What have you got?" Rheinhardt asks. "Good news, I hope."

"Some. On the air defense issue, I think I've figured out how they kicked us out."

"Can you get us back in?"

"Not sure yet. It may require getting physical access to a node of their air defense network."

"Okay. Looks like we're getting the stealth helos, so it may be academic."

"Speaking of that," Mike says. "I've, um, 'cut' orders for Richie's fliers to report to Balad for training. The papers are now at the duty officer's station here, as well as with airbase flight control."

"Nice. How'd you do that?"

"I sent mail from the JSOC ops desk at Bragg."

"Sounds like a nice hack."

"No hacking involved. I've already got access to every JSOC system. I can send mail as anybody I want. The only thing stopping me is scruples."

"Remind me not to piss you off. Or introduce you to my ex-wife."

"There's another thing," Mike says. His tone says this might be a big deal. "While I've been tunneling around

Iranian military systems, I find I've now got root access to a machine that I'm pretty sure is *their* primary mail server."

"What does that mean?"

"It means I can read the mail of anyone with a dot-mil-dot-ir address. And I also have the master list of all those addresses. So I can also write to them."

"So you're saying—"

"I can now spam the entire Iranian officer corps. Or specific units, or combinations of units."

"Interesting. When I need to sell them Viagra, I'll come to you. For now, can you get in there and see if anyone at the general staff level has said anything in the last seventy-two hours about uranium or nuking Israel?"

"You got it."

* * *

On his way back to the planning table, Rheinhardt's phone goes.

"Eric, it's Richie. You want the good news first, or the good news?"

"Good news."

"I've got the good stuff. Two Ghost Hawks, the gen-three stealth birds. They're like mist."

"Awesome."

"Yeah. And they're both in top flying shape, but with two days left on their maintenance cycle. I've even got guys to fly them. Of course, I'm going to get my ass court-martialed for joyriding in two hundred million dollar top-secret helos. But I'll worry about that if we come back alive."

Rheinhardt smiles out loud. "You might actually be okay there. We cut you orders for you to fly to down for a training op."

"Funny I haven't seen those orders."

"But flight control at Balad has. When can you be here?"

"When do you need us?"

"Right now we're thinking we launch tonight. Oh-dark-thirty."

"We'll be there. Let's call it zero-hundred hours, just for a little shared reality for once."

"You are an excellent friend."

"Ha. It's just that I haven't gotten payback yet for you getting my ass shot down in Baluchistan. I've been sitting around waiting for an opportunity to fuck you up."

* * *

Two hours later, at the planning table, there's a long-ish silence.

"What else?" Rheinhardt asks.

"Nothing," says BJ. "This plan's as good as it's gonna get. Better than the day we wrote it."

"Fucking 1980," one of the SEALs quips. "Such a shame you didn't get to run it then."

"We were delayed at your mom's house," BJ advises, indulging the habit of inter-service rivalry.

"Okay," Rheinhardt says. "We launch at zero-hundred. Birds will be on the deck out back. I expect you're all perfectly able to kit yourselves out. But, for anything else you need, heavy weapons, etc., you can go through B's load-out pallets." His voice drops, before trailing off. "There's a lot of good stuff lying around…"

"And it'll be our honor," says Spider, "to fire all of it up Tucker's asshole. Point blank."

Mike sits in a corner of the NSA guys' office, typing intently into his hardened laptop.

Ali once told him that the job of the snipers is to tip the odds as much as possible in favor of the assaulters, so when they kick down the door they have the best possible information about the tactical situation inside, and face the fewest enemies with the most degraded capabilities.

Now, with some really long-range weapons – sniffers, spoofers, OS fingerprinters, rootkits, port scanners, decrypters, and keystroke loggers – Mike is trying to give his team the best odds of success and survival when they go through the door at Kazemi. Because their opponents there are no joke. Quds Force has killed a lot of good American soldiers, mostly through lethal bombings in Iraq. And this one is unlikely to be a walkover.

But if Mike can break in and fuck with their comms and security, he can make things a lot safer for his friends when they go in. And, mainly, he can help them get Ali back out again.

Mike is in total awe of nearly everyone in Delta he's worked with. But Ali has a special place. It was she who taught him to shoot long guns; she who drove him through the mountains of Baluchistan on a tricked-out ATV; and she who kept him alive, from afar, with her unstoppable sniper skills, while he sat at a computer in a safehouse – operating in virtual space, while real bullets and shrapnel whistled all around him.

Tim McDonough, Alpha's former tech guru, had a PhD in computer science and was most like Mike in temperament and outlook. When he was killed, Mike felt for a while like he might die from it himself. But he's not too sure he could survive losing Ali. It would just be too cruel, unfair, and basically ugly.

But that's where Mike is still a very "boot" recruit in the spec-ops world. He hasn't internalized that even the God-like operators of Delta are mortal. And he hasn't reconciled himself to the reality that, here, he could lose anybody, at pretty much anytime.

Right now he's working hard to make sure it just isn't today.

* * *

Mike's so engrossed in his exploits that he doesn't see his new mail icon – until his secure cell rings and rouses him. He takes the call and reads the mail simultaneously.

"Go for Brown."

The call is from the Ranch. And the mail is from the alert he set up for intel reports from around Sebastopol or the Russian or Ukrainian navies.

"Are you serious?" he says, cradling the phone with his shoulder, while typing. "You're sure of that? Can you do me a 3-D scan of the chipset and send it to me—*oh, shit.*"

While the man on the other end is telling him about a circuit board they've discovered, in a very unexpected place, the intel summary on his screen is telling him about a missing warship.

It's two pieces of game-changing information, literally all at once.

"Gotta run," he says, pushing himself up out of his chair. "But keep talking…"

Back in the hangar, operators are checking weapons, loading gear, testing comms, and running through actions-on. Nineteen new C Squadron guys are now in the corner with Egle, getting briefed on their role in the assault. Rheinhardt and BJ are going from group to group giving supplementary orders and fielding questions. With less than two hours to launch, everything and everyone is abuzz. This is when Mike runs in shouting for Rheinhardt.

"Ukraine," he says, breathless. "You remember how Tucker was in Sebastopol?"

"Yeah. And?"

"I just got a CIA spot report from there. The Ukrainian navy lost a frigate. Disappeared on the Black Sea. Five weeks ago. Just… gone. Believed hijacked. No trace of wreckage. And guess what kind of frigate it was?"

Rheinhardt holds his gaze.

"*ASW – anti-submarine warfare.* The *Tuman.* It's a sub killer."

Rheinhardt absorbs this, thinking it through.

"Israel's nuclear deterrent," Mike says, emphatically. "Their roving subs."

"I know," Rheinhardt says, pulling his phone from his belt and thumbing it on. Mike physically grabs his arm.

"Lemme go," Rheinhardt says. "I've got to warn Chaya."

Mike steps in closer. "Not with that phone, you don't."

Rheinhardt thinks for one beat. His trust in Mike Brown, he now realizes, is total. "Give me yours, then."

Mike slaps his own phone into the outstretched hand – but hangs on to it. "I need ninety seconds first. You have to hear this."

Rheinhardt decides again. "Go."

"I also just got a call from the armory at the Ranch. This morning they took possession of that SR25 sniper rifle the Iranians used to try and top you in DC. The District police had it, finally finished their forensics, and handed it over. So today our armorers took it apart screw by screw. And they found something embedded in the stock."

"Oh, hell," Rheinhardt says, grasping at memory. He mentally flashes back to the odd balance of the rifle, and the stripped screws on the butt-plate.

"They found a circuit board inside. It's got a GSM transponder on it – and a high-power, short-range receiver. Plus a hardware encryption chip." Mike pauses. "You've been carrying a DoD phone, right?"

"Yes."

"Okay, so it's most likely got their old bullshit 56-bit encryption. *Did you use it anywhere near the sniper?*"

Rheinhardt tenses. "Standing right over his body."

"Give it to me," Mike says. He's already totally torn about whether to melt it down into smoking plastic to mitigate risk, or take it apart for forensics.

"It's definitely compromised?" Rheinhardt asks.

"Not definitely. But there's no other explanation or use for that circuit board. It was born to hack a GSM phone from short range. And it's actually worse than that. If they infected your phone… they could theoretically have piggy-backed malicious code on top of the signal to anyone else you talked to on it."

"Chaya," Rheinhardt says. "And from her phone…"

"Yes. If Sayeret's set-up is like ours, with a secure internal GSM network… then in theory any of their internal systems could be compromised. Or all of them."

"Motherfucker," Rheinhardt says.

"Tucker," Mike says.

Rheinhardt stabs at the buttons on Mike's phone – while Mike pulls the battery out of his.

Rod Tucker leans over Bob Li's shoulder, monitoring the screen.

He set the young man up in this computer room two days ago, to do his dirty work online. Li's exploits and preparation of the ground have been excellent. But now it is Tucker who delivers the lethal grace note.

"I told you," he says, a leer in his voice, "that I'd get you in when the time came."

"Sweet," says Li, typing blazingly, and flipping amongst command line windows. "This is it – the whole IDF spec-ops directorate internal network. How'd you do it?"

"Let's just say I abused the trust of someone there. And then phoned it in."

Li doesn't know what that means, but seems not to care. He's off to the races. "Muahahaha… down go mail servers, down go wireless and cell networks, down go tactical systems…"

Tucker almost smiles. "Good. Now just keep them down. For twenty-four hours. And keep all the other systems disrupted for the same period of time. After that… well, they won't have any systems left to hack."

* * *

Tucker shoulders his way out the door, exits the building, and pulls his phone. While walking back toward Suleimani's office, he makes a call to a certain ASW frigate at sea – the *Tuman*.

"It's me," he says. "What's your status?"

"Our helo picked up the Israeli sub an hour ago, right where you said. It's continuing on the circular pattern you predicted. Never closer than a hundred kilometers to shore. And no other vessels nearby. We've fallen in behind, trailing at forty kilometers."

"Okay, good. Be careful you don't close the distance. You have to stay far enough off its stern that it won't pick you up on sonar."

"And our ship's helo?"

"Unless you fly nearly directly over it, they can't detect you from depth. How many sonar buoys did you drop?"

"Just a four-buoy localization pattern."

"Okay. Maintain distance until I give you the word. Then you start herding them. Timing's critical. Everyone knows the drill? No fuck-ups?"

"With these weapons locked on, it's like a video game. We can do it, inshallah."

Tucker hates it when they say that. "Inshallah" is basically giving yourself permission to fail in advance. "We failed, but it was God's will." *Bullshit.* You simply failed. Men determine outcomes, and it's our choices that determine success or failure.

He puts away the phone and shoulders his way into Suleimani's office.

* * *

"*Salam, Agha-ye Tucker*," says Suleimani. He doesn't bother to rise, as Tucker didn't bother to knock.

"General," Tucker says, nodding and taking a seat. "Your officers are in place in Baghdad and Kabul?"

Suleimani smiles slightly. "It is your men they will be leading. And your men will have already informed you that they are ready."

"Just wanted to hear it from you."

"They are in place. And your sub killer? And the rockets for the port at Haifa?"

"All good to go. But the timing is the main thing. Once we put things in motion, we're going to have a very limited window to finish it. Which is why I wish you had just let me load up the warheads and missiles on the frigate in advance. Having to rendezvous on the water takes time, and adds risk."

Suleimani steeples his fingers. "Yes, that would have been nice. But these are the only two nuclear warheads we've got. And we can't afford to lose them if things go badly – if your sub killer is killed by the sub, for instance. Sometimes, in these types of contests, the prey comes out on top. We'll embark the warheads when you take out the sub. Then I can be confident all this is really happening."

"It's happening, believe me," Tucker says tightly. "And our prey will be doing nothing but going straight to the bottom. Once we located it in the Red Sea, its doom was sealed. It's totally overmatched by the frigate. And the two Mcd-based subs, when they are in port together for the change of duty, are sitting ducks." He leans back in his chair. "But it would all be moot if you'd just launch from one of your damned ground-based missile silos."

Suleimani puts his hands palm-down on his desk. "Out of the question. Deniability, Mr. Tucker. When the launch comes from a frigate off the coast, it could plausibly have been the act of any group of jihadis. But if the launch came from Iranian soil... well, we do not want to hand the cowboys in Washington an excuse to attack their third Islamic country in row."

"Literally in a row," Tucker says. "Iraq and Afghanistan to either side."

"Well... after tomorrow, I think we are all going to have a little more breathing room."

"Inshallah," Tucker can't resist saying.

He knows that Suleimani is secular, and it will piss him off.

All around Rheinhardt, the teams are finishing their final prep. They are basically jocked up and ready to rock. But Rheinhardt has been sidelined, trying to get a call through to Israel.

"Chaya. Do you copy? Chaya?"

"Yes, yes, I've got you. I saw all the dropped calls. Comms are a wreck here."

"Listen carefully. We have very good intel that Tucker and the Iranians have hijacked a *Neustrashimy*-class ASW frigate. A sub killer. From the Ukrainians. Present location unknown."

"How certain are you?"

"Moderately. We're very sure the Ukrainians lost one. And we know Tucker was nearby when it happened. And nobody knows where it is now. Can you alert your roving subs?"

"They only rise to radio depth once a day." Another pause. *"They missed their last check-in. But ALL of our comms are in a bad way. We're losing contact with bases, with patrols, with aircraft. And all of our systems suddenly seem to be crashing or locking up. We think our network's been compromised. And we're also getting scattered and broken reports of troops massing on our borders – Hamas in Gaza, Hizbullah in Lebanon. And the Syrian army, at the Golan Heights. But right now we can't confirm anything. With our systems blinking*

271

out… we're losing our ability to affect outcomes. Or even to know what's happening."

"Listen, Chaya. There's something else. Tucker may have breached your systems by piggybacking from my phone onto your internal network. You need to scour your systems for intrusion. I want to put you in touch with our tech guy here, who – Chaya? How copy?"

The line's dead.

* * *

Rheinhardt is still holding the phone, trying to work out how all of this impacts their assault plan, when a phone goes off on somebody in the hangar, then a pager, then several more, a whole electronic choir, beeping in chorus. As people grab for their devices, Javier explodes into the room from the direction of the JOC. He's wearing his assault suit and carrying a rifle.

"The world's blowing up," he says – telling them what they're all reading on their screens. "Insurgents have just overrun the American Embassy in Kabul. They've taken the entire staff hostage. And the Green Zone in Baghdad is under siege – insurgents attacking in brigade strength. They're at the walls. Stamis wants anyone who can fog a mirror to truck down there and get their guns in the fight. RFN."

"Looks like Tehran is on hold," Homer says, as his guys begin gathering up their stuff.

BJ looks gobsmacked. "Who the hell could have marshaled attacks that big at this point?"

"It's Tucker," Rheinhardt says. "Tucker and IRG, leading the militia remnants. It has to be."

"How do you know?"

"It's a fucking diversion," Rheinhardt says. "They're trying to draw our last reserves off."

"But a diversion from what?"

"I don't know exactly. But it's Iran doing it, and it's about Israel. And right now every shooter left in CENTCOM is racing to either Baghdad or Kabul. And away from Iran." He looks around him, at his whole mission team evaporating before his eyes.

"Sorry, man," Spider says, hefting his ruck and weapon. "You know those order things you're always hearing about in the military…"

"It's a feint," Rheinhardt says. "The real attack's coming elsewhere."

The door kicks open again. This time General Stamis himself storms in, followed by a dozen staff officers, all trying to remember which end the body armor goes on. Stamis takes in Rheinhardt's ad hoc planning area in one wide sweep of his fierce eyes.

"What kind of fucking sausage festival have you got going on in here?" he bellows, looking balefully around. "Never you mind. Get your asses on these trucks. This everybody?"

Homer answers quietly. "Affirmative, all our shooters are here."

"Sorry, man," Egle says, trotting with the C guys over to one of the trucks.

Javier gives Rheinhardt a pained and questioning look. But then Stamis slaps him on the ass, physically pushing him toward the nearest vehicle. Javier changes his expression to one of apology, charges his rifle, hops aboard – and then pulls his phone and waggles it at Rheinhardt.

"Keys in ignitions!" one of the B support guys shouts. Trucks start roaring to life.

"Goddammit," Rheinhardt says.

"Are you going?" BJ asks.

Rheinhardt looks around. Stamis has already climbed onto a truck, along with his staff.

"No. I've got to stay here and figure out what the hell's really going on. But you should go. No point in both of us getting court-martialed."

BJ crosses his mammoth arms in front of his bigger chest. "You stay, I stay. Anyway, we're way too valuable to waste on bullshit like military justice."

Mike Brown comes dashing in, wearing an assault suit and carrying a rifle, not looking very comfortable with either. He looks around, then heads toward one of the trucks. Rheinhardt whistles, catches his eye, and points at the tarmac at his feet. Mike gets the message and stops. He looks around wide-eyed, pulled in two directions, both dangerous.

As the trucks start beeping and backing out, a Humvee cuts across their path and squeals into the hangar. Out climb two guys from the 10th Mountain Division, a unit Rheinhardt and BJ know to be tasked with patrolling the Iranian border on the Iraqi side. They open the back door and pull out a third man. He's festooned with empty magazine and grenade pouches and so stained with mud and blood that he's hardly recognizable as an American soldier.

"Hey, guys," he croaks. He looks up at the trucks. "Wherever you're goin', take me. Just need to re-arm, and I'm good to go…" He begins pawing at a crate of 5.56 magazines.

"Jesus Christ," BJ says, walking up to the shambling wreck of an operator. "Bleep? That you? Jesus, you look like Joe Shit the RagMan." Sure enough, it's Garner's young tech sergeant, the one who scoured the weaponization lab, under there somewhere.

"At your service," he says. His lips are cracked and the whites of his eyes mostly blood red.

"How the hell…?"

"Walked over the mountains to Chalus city. Stole a car, drove it to within five clicks of the border. Walked across. Then these assholes nearly shot me. Most dangerous part of my day."

"Jesus Christ, brother…"

One of the 10th Mountain guys says, "We also got word the Navy's picked up two more of your guys. In the Caspian Sea – four miles offshore. They swam out."

"Jesus Christ…"

ON BOARD THE INS *LUBETKIN*
150 METERS BENEATH THE RED SEA
23:58:00 AST 06 APR

Captain Gabi Telem paces his deck in a slow circle around the conn, threading amongst the stations for fire control, quartermaster, and helm. None of the thirty souls aboard are making a sound. Silence on the boat isn't unusual – it's pretty common on any submarine. But the silence tonight has got a definite spooked quality to it.

"Sonar," Captain Telem says. "Update."

"Buoys still receding in our wake, Captain. No new contacts."

Telem turns on his heel and paces back in the other direction. Pacing options in his job are somewhat limited. He stops and rubs his chin instead. Where would four sonar buoys come from? Out here in the dead middle of the Red Sea? It's more or less inexplicable.

But, still, Telem thinks, *a little early to start worrying.*

* * *

On one level, worry is not a major theme on the *Lubetkin*.

She is an SSK *Dolphin*-class attack submarine, and one of the most sophisticated non-nuclear submarines in the world. Her onboard systems, developed by a consortium of Israeli high-tech and defense firms, are computer-integrated, with automatic sensor management, fire and weapon control, and electronic counter-measures. She mounts ten bow torpedo tubes, and can carry 16 torpedoes or surface-to-surface missiles, plus sea mines. She can also launch underwater swimmer delivery vehicles, which makes the *Lubetkin* very popular with Israeli and allied spec-ops forces.

On another level, though, worry is built into the very fabric of her existence. Because four of those onboard missiles are actually nuclear-tipped Popeye AGM/142 cruise missiles. Each has a 200kg warhead with 6kg of plutonium, and an explosive yield of 100 kilotons, which can be delivered at a stand-off range of 1,500 kilometers, with extremely high accuracy.

Ever since Iran moved a significant number of ballistic missiles from Syrian territory even closer, into Lebanon, one of the three *Dolphin*-class subs has been deployed to the Red Sea, as part of Israel's nuclear deterrent.

The other two alternate prowling the Med.

Except for a tiny handover window once a month, two of the *Dolphins* are at sea at any given time. The goal is to ensure that even a devastating nuclear attack on Israel, one which wiped out all of its ground-based missiles, would still not totally destroy Israel's second-strike capability. And by this means, it is hoped, a nuclear first strike on Israel can be prevented.

The horrifying logic of mutually assured destruction.

But when your enemies really are bent on destroying you, sometimes it's all you've got.

* * *

The *Lubetkin* was christened in 2001, in honor of Zivia Lubetkin, one of the leaders of the Jewish Resistance in the Warsaw Ghetto Uprising of 1943. After 90% of the Jewish population had been sent to the Treblinka extermination camp, the survivors banded together to fight. They knew they were going to die. But they chose to die on their feet.

They were mostly young people, badly underfed, armed only with pistols and homemade Molotov cocktails. Three times the Germans came against them with machine guns, artillery, and armored vehicles. And three times the Jewish fighters drove them from the ghetto. In the end, the Germans had to nearly burn the ghetto to the ground to dislodge them.

One of the few to survive was Zivia Lubetkin. After commanding a fighting group in the battle, she led a small group of survivors out through the sewers. She immediately joined the resistance outside the ghetto, taking part in the Polish Warsaw Uprising in 1944. After the war, she helped smuggle Holocaust survivors out of Europe and into the Palestine Mandate.

In 1946, she emigrated to Israel and helped found Kibbutz Lohamei HaGeta'ot ("the Ghetto Fighters Kibbutz") in the western Galilee. In 1961, she testified at the trial of captured Nazi war criminal Adolf Eichmann. She died in 1976. But her granddaughter went on to become the Israeli Air Force's first female fighter pilot, in 2001. The same year the *Lubetkin* was christened.

Every member of the crew knows by heart the story of their boat's namesake.

Never again.

* * *

The Captain hovers now over the station for sonar, forward of the conn. Multiple digital displays bathe both him and the sonar officer in blue. "What's this?" he asks, pointing.

"Most likely surface clutter, sir." But immediately the display resolves and the sonar officer corrects himself, his speech crisp and loud. "Close contact! Submerged, bearing zero-nine-seven. Descending. Probably water entry of a small object."

The Captain squints at the screen, disbelieving. "…You're telling me something just fell out of the sky over the Red Sea?"

A single concussion rocks the sub. Sailors grab on to their stations. The lights flicker once.

"Depth charge," says the XO, the words tasting strange on his tongue.

"Aye, sir," the sonar officer says. "And I've got more – two new contacts… four of them… six. Similar relative bearings."

The Captain straightens up. "Helm! Come right thirty degrees rudder! Ahead flank speed!"

"Aye, sir." The boat swivels and accelerates, moving perceptibly beneath them. As they zip away, another concussion, milder, rocks the boat – then several more, each quieter than the last.

Peering into a monitor while scribbling an emendation on the status board, the XO asks, "Shall we rise to radio depth, sir?"

The Captain swivels his head to look at him. His calm seems to roll back in. "In a depth charge attack? No. That's some sort of ASW aircraft up there, and I don't think we'll give it any better a look at us for the moment." He walks back to the conn. "Navigator, make your new course one-eight-zero."

"Coming to one-eight-zero."

Captain Telem puts his palms on the navigator table. "No, we'll just lead them back toward the Gulf of Aqaba. And our air patrols. We can dodge depth charges until then. Planesman, make our depth two-fifty meters."

"Aye, sir. Descending to two-fifty." The nose of the boat dips. Everyone leans slightly.

* * *

A few tense minutes have passed at the new depth, heading, and speed.

"Conn, sonar! New contacts. Several short transients close aboard."

"More depth charges," says the XO.

"Bearing zero-nine-four. It's a whole row of them."

Telem stands straight again. "Helm, ten degrees left rudder."

Again, explosions jar the sub, again growing fainter as she angles away.

"What are they playing at?" Telem wonders out loud.

As if in answer, the sonar officer shouts, "New contact! Surface vessel, zero angle on the bow, closing fast. Thirty knots at forty kilometers. She's cutting big holes in the water, sir."

"Thirty knots?" The Captain looks to his XO. "What the hell? And coming straight for us."

The XO shrugs. "Radioman. Any transponder signal?"

"Nothing, sir."

With a look like he doesn't quite believe what he's doing, Telem grabs a phone handset. "Torpedo room, conn. Flood tubes four through eight. Arm DM2s. Stand ready."

The atmosphere on the deck now goes from bemused to deadly serious. This is for real.

Sonar sings out again. "Multiple contacts, coming in extremely fast! Eight of them, deployed in a thirty-degree arc… High-speed screws! Torpedoes in the water!"

The XO moves to the sonar station himself. "Not torpedoes. It's a spread of guided ASW missiles." He looks to the Captain.

"They've been herding us," Telem says, holding his gaze.

"Captain! Missiles have locked onto us and are homing!"

Telem spends two seconds working out everything he's pretty sure is going to happen now.

"Weaps – fire the counter-measures."

"Aye, sir… counter-measures away."

"Get me a firing solution on the surface vessel."

"Aye, sir… Solution figured and keyed."

"Match bearing and fire all tubes."

"Aye, sir!… Torpedoes away."

"Captain. Four of the missiles are going for the counter-measures. The rest are still incoming: ETI, fifteen seconds."

"Planesman, dive the ship. Blow all tanks."

"Diving!"

As the floor beneath them dips to a 45-degree angle, the XO whispers to the Captain, "There's no way we can jig that many at this range…"

Telem gives him a look that says he knows this.

"Our torpedoes are in acquisition! Locked onto surface target!"

Captain Telem exhales. "Send up the distress buoy."

"Aye, sir… Buoy away."

The Captain reaches for the tannoy hand mic. "All hands, brace for—"

A series of wrenching concussions rocks the sub, knocking the Captain and XO to the deck. A saltwater relief valve overhead bursts open, then two more. The fire control panel explodes, the lights go out – and the sailors' narrow world buckles, twists, and collapses in on them.

Billowing pockets of gas heave and warp in the deep.

On the surface, a white mountain of displaced water and air explodes into the starlit night.

Israeli Navy Lieutenant Adisu Sami replaces the phone in its cradle on his control station. Temporarily speechless, he looks out over the harbor and docks of Haifa. The whole port is lit like daylight by hundreds of high-powered LED streetlights. The glinting black of the sea forms the limit of their world and seems to wrap them on each side with infinite arms.

Sami was only a small boy when his entire extended family was airlifted out of Ethiopia in what was called Operation Solomon. The Ethiopian regime, which had made it difficult for Ethiopian Jews to leave, was in danger of falling to Eritrean rebels. Civil war and famine loomed. Fearing for the safety of Ethiopia's large Jewish community, Israel offered to take them in. In 36 hours, non-stop flights of Israeli aircraft transported 14,000 Ethiopian Jews to Israel.

Today nearly all Ethiopian Jews reside in Israel, where they are integrated into society and enjoy full rights – including serving in the military, a right which Lieutenant Sami has availed himself of. There have been better days, and worse days. But he has no doubt his opportunities and quality of life here have been far superior to what they would have been in his homeland.

Today, though is not shaping up to be one of his better days.

He has just gotten a call from Eilat naval base, which controls the Red Sea theater. They have reported that the INS *Lubetkin* has sent up its distress buoy. Attempts to contact the sub have failed. And search planes have been scrambled.

* * *

As unthinkable as the loss of one of their nuclear-deterrent subs would be at any time, the timing couldn't have been worse. At any given moment, two of the three subs are underway – underwater, moving fast, and location known by only a handful of officers.

Any time, that is, except for one tiny window in each month, when the two Mediterranean-based subs switch places, one taking over the patrol, the other going into port, at Haifa. The two subs sit in port together for a maximum of two hours. This is done primarily to conduct the physical exchange of the nuclear launch authorization codes. They are literally passed over by hand, because no network is deemed secure enough to transmit them.

Looking out and down, the Lieutenant can see both the INS *Leviathan* and the INS *Tekuma* docked on opposite sides of the sub pier, lit by rows of LED lights. Supplies and ordnance are being moved on and off the two boats on rolling pallets and by forklift.

For a few seconds after hanging up, he stares wide-eyed at the pier, willing the *Tekuma* to cast off and get underway. Because, if the unthinkable has happened and the *Lubetkin* has gone down... that means that as of this moment, Israel has *no* nuclear-armed sub at sea.

* * *

After he's briefed the radio operators on each sub, he wonders if he should order the whole base to go firm, into a defensive lockdown. To ask the question, he decides, is to answer it. However, he needs higher authorization to make it happen.

Before he can grab the red phone, he's stopped by the sound of the air-raid siren starting up, a continuous droning, which rises and falls. All across Israel, this sound means the same thing: an incoming rocket attack. In Haifa, they have approximately one minute before the rockets arrive from Gaza. Luckily, Hamas's weapons are very inaccurate – a pure terror weapon, like Hitler's V2 attacks on London.

Still, everyone will need to get under cover. The Lieutenant casts his eye over the docks. Sailors, loaders, harbormasters, and dockworkers are running for nearby buildings, most of which have reinforced basement shelters. Everyone is clearing out smartly.

Everyone except for a single man.

Sami snatches his binoculars off the desk and dials in. It's one of the loading crew, not in uniform – a civilian employee. The man not only doesn't flee… but he is walking toward one of the abandoned loading pallets. Shifting his view up and over, the lieutenant can see that it's a pallet of ordnance. Sea mines. The man's walk toward the pallet is neither fast nor slow – and very ominous. Sami's hand moves toward an alert button for the port security teams.

By the time it gets there, it's too late.

Yousef Amr was born in the camps. As were his parents before him.

His great grandparents were driven from their ancestral home in Palestine, in the *Naqbah*, "the catastrophe," – in which the Zionist crusaders stole the historical land of his family and his people. The Amrs came to rest in Gaza, in the squalid "refugee" camps which the U.N. set up. Half a century later, three generations of Palestinians have grown up there.

Yousef was raised to believe that regaining their land, and their national dignity, was the highest duty of a loyal Palestinian and good Muslim. In his schools, in his summer camps, the message was the same: Jews have stolen our land and our national honor. We have been shamed. And somehow, some day, that shame must be erased.

* * *

But life has a funny way of going on. By the time Yousef finished school, his parents had become small business owners, and moved out of the camps and into a humble but respectable home in Gaza City. As they prospered, their views on the conflict changed. Fighting was bad for business. And the Amrs had come to believe that business was good for people. And good for their family.

But Yousef grew to despise them for this. Nothing could be more important than their land and their national honor. Certainly not mere money. At age 15, Yousef attended a Hamas summer camp. By 17, he had become active in the movement.

His Hamas handlers used his respectable background, the fact that his parents were moderates who traded with Israeli businesses, to get him a work permit in Israel. He started as a dockworker, backbreaking labor, in the Port of Ashdod, one of Israel's two main cargo ports.

For four years, he worked, waited, and kept the faith alive in his heart. All while pretending to be moderate, to be developing loyalty to the hated oppressor nation. And all while watching for openings at the military port of Haifa. This was the core of his assignment.

Now, he is 23. And everything he has done has led him to this day.

A week ago he got the call. Yesterday, he traveled to a safehouse near the border. An upstairs room had been done up as a crude surgery. They put him under with anesthetic, then surgically implanted the device. When he woke, he had an angry, stitched-up wound, very bad pain, and a tight pressure in his abdomen. They gave him pills for the pain. And a "detonator" for the device.

It was simply a phone number.

* * *

When he passed through the security station for his night shift, he had to explain his sweating and paleness. He told the security officers he had been ill. They nearly sent him home.

But he convinced them to let him work. And he passed through the full-body scanners without a hitch. The air raid siren was his signal. As the others sprinted toward the buildings, he ducked behind his forklift. After they were gone, he emerged and walked toward the pallet of mines.

He looks around him now. The siren aside, he's never known the port so peaceful, serene, or empty. The majesty of the sea out beyond the pier affects him. It is the glory of God's creation.

He pulls his phone from his pocket. He exhales a lungful of sweet night air, then drapes his body across the crates of mines. *Ma'shallah*, he thinks to himself, smiling drowsily. Then, with one thumb, he makes the call to the device in his belly.

And Yousef Amr goes out of the light, through the darkness, and on to his reward.

Commander Mohammed Deif slings himself out of the truck cab and up on to its running board for an elevated view. Ahead of him, only a few hundred meters away, is the security wall with Israel. Behind him, a line of vehicles and men stretches back into the darkness of the town.

This is his army – of jihad, and of liberation.

Dief is commander of the Izz ad-Din al-Qassam Brigades, the military wing of Hamas, a position which he has held since Israel killed his predecessor ten years ago. But he started out as a bomb-maker, and Israel holds him responsible for the deaths of hundreds of civilians in suicide bombings. He has been at the top of their most-wanted list for years.

They are not wrong, and Dief wears both the accusation and the target on his back with honor. So far, he has survived five Israeli air strikes, including one that killed his second-in-command. Despite that the cowards attack from the air, with weapons given them by the Americans, they have been unable to stop him.

He has begun to feel unkillable. Like God's chosen instrument.

His phone chirps from his pocket. It is an advanced smart phone, but he still has to change it every two weeks, to keep it from becoming a homing beacon for an IDF missile.

Luckily, the European aid money never stops flowing. God provides what the faithful need.

He clicks through to a new text message. It is from the hidden observer in Haifa. The martyrdom operation has succeeded. The Israeli docks are in flames.

A fighter appears beside the truck to report in. "We are on track, God willing. All units are in place in the column. Some fighters are still trickling in from the south. But it is the biggest force we have ever mustered."

"Twenty thousand fighters?"

"Yes, commander. God willing."

"Go to the front and check on the armored trucks and breaching charges. When the time comes to break through the wall, all must be ready. Report back to me here."

"*Na'am, Sayyid.*"

Soon it will be time for his final check-in with the American – the American traitor, who has helped to take Hamas' best fighters to the next level of skill and ferocity. All of which will soon be loosed on what is left of the Zionists. But the American is merely another instrument of God, giving the righteous the power they need to strike the final blow.

Lieutenant Sami has stayed on station through the attack –
or, rather, attacks. First, the suicide bombing on the sub pier.
And then, seconds later, the rain of rockets around the station. Sami can see the wreckage and debris in 20-meter wide
circles, the blast radius of the rockets. So far, no casualties
have been reported from these.

The same cannot be said of the bombing on the pier.
Twenty sailors were aboard the two boats when the sirens
went off. Most decided to stay put rather than risk trying to
outrun incoming rockets. They had no way to know about
the simultaneous suicide bomber.

And now their status is unknown. Comms with both
subs have been knocked out.

Worse, the fire on the sub pier, and the enormous secondary explosions, are making the area a no-go for rescue
and recovery personnel. Mines, torpedoes, and other ordnance are cooking off in the heat of the fire, like a Bastille
Day celebration in hell.

But Israelis are very good, and very experienced, at recovering from suicide attacks – from anything that goes bang,
really. In this case, first the fire control unit will go in, then
Explosive Ordnance Disposal (EOD) teams, to make the area
safe. Then emergency medical personnel. Finally, engineers will
assess the damage and begin the recovery and repair operation.

In most cases, after suicide or rocket attacks, the area is cleaned up and in use again the next day. Doing this is important to the Israelis. To demonstrate that they are not defeated. To show that they are not afraid. And also to remember that they have endured much worse.

The lieutenant continues to direct the crisis response from his control station. This is a lot of emergencies to manage at once. And very serious ones. But they are of a sort the Israelis have faced many times before.

And these too will be overcome, Sami thinks to himself.

And that's when the radiological alarms go off, flashing the room a dangerous and frightening red.

* * *

Within minutes, a team of high-risk operators in white CBRN suits is out on the ground with radiation detectors. They verify the verdict of the radiological alarms: there is radioactive material present. Soon after, they confirm that all of the rocket hits were dirty bomb strikes – explosives cased in with some kind of crude radiological material.

There are many ways Hamas could have acquired such material. There are literally millions of radioactive sources used worldwide in industry, medicine, and academic research. Israeli intelligence has mainly been surprised that it has never happened before.

As the lieutenant gets off the phone with another alarmed senior officer, he sees the fire truck roar onto the docks. It is manned with CBRN-suited fire control technicians. They get to work spraying the pier with a thick white foam.

As the fire goes out, the secondary explosions slow, then stop.

Now EOD guys – doubly suited up, with CBRN kit pulled over their bomb suits – rush onto the pier to begin making the ordnance safe. Behind them, white-suited medics wait for their turn, to begin pulling wounded men from the subs.

In the couple of free seconds he has before his next critical task, the lieutenant considers that perhaps no other military in the world would have a prayer of coping with this triple attack as well as the IDF is doing now. But he also knows a little something about dirty bombs.

A radiological bomb is a crude weapon. It's unlikely to cause mass casualties, or massive destruction. What it is good for is making a whole area very unhealthy for human beings to be in, for a very long time. And this, the lieutenant knows, is not going to be a 24-hour clean-up operation. This is going to take weeks, before they are operational again.

And there's absolutely no telling when they might be able to get one of the Dolphins back in the water. Until that time, every single second, Israel is naked.

"You dumb motherfuckers."

Motherfucker translates very well into the Arabic. Tucker is staring daggers into his phone, talking to his sailors, standing in an alley between two of the garrison buildings. He takes a breath and masters himself.

"How did you let them get a torpedo off?"

There's a bit of spluttering on the other end. *"No one wanted to risk missing. We sailed in as close as possible before firing."* A pause. *"It was the bravery of the men. They were not afraid."*

Tucker stalks around the corner, through a doorway, and back into the computer lab. He leans over a machine, grabs a mouse, and flips through video windows. He finds the drone he's looking for, tweaks its flight path, and zooms in.

"Not afraid? They weren't fucking smart, is what they were. And you didn't follow fucking orders." He starts to think maybe he was kidding himself. That he could turn these fucking ragheads into proper soldiers, never mind elite operators.

But he doesn't have the time to revisit that now. His mind's already racing ahead. Right now he's got to acquire another waterborne missile launch platform. And he's got to do it in the next 16 hours. Because that's how long he has before all the carefully sowed mayhem he has laid in and around Israel will die down.

"We will not sink!" his phone says at him. *"We can bail the ship."*

"Bull-*shit*. I'm looking at you on aerial video right now. You're hit dead amidships below the waterline. You dipshits are going to be kicking it with Davy Jones in a matter of minutes." He uses the English for dipshit. No known Arabic translation.

"You're already dead, you just don't know it yet. Like the song says: 'Learn to swim'."

He snaps the phone away from his head violently. And recalls another line from the same song:

The only way to fix it is to flush it all away.

* * *

Suleimani's door flies in, actually kicked open this time. The general, seated behind his desk, eases his .45 from his belt holster and slides it underneath his right thigh. This probably isn't the bit where Tucker, the previously loyal dog, goes rabid. But you can't be too careful in a game like this one.

"You were right," Tucker says, crossing the room in three strides. "We lost the frigate."

Suleimani takes his hand off the gun. "And the submarine?"

"Sunk. They killed each other."

"Well that, as they say, is something."

Tucker exhales loudly again and plops himself down. "And the two subs in port at Haifa are toast as well, ticking hot for the duration. The Israelis are naked now."

"That's an amazing achievement, Sergeant Major."

"I need another frigate, Brigadier General." Tucker sweeps his hair away from his forehead with his hand and leans forward. "Something big and solid enough to launch Shahab-3s from."

The general steeples his fingers. "I am, as they say, way ahead of you."

"Iranian Navy?"

"Impossible. Deniability."

"What then?"

"The *Mavi Marmara*."

"The Gazan aid ship?"

"Not anymore. As of two nights ago, she's in the hands of my operatives."

"Well, points for thinking ahead. Plus, it'll point to Hamas, not Tehran. But will it work?"

Suleimani nods. "She displaces over four thousand tons, so she's stable enough. And she has the square footage for the launchers on the top deck."

"Where is she now?"

"She transited Suez last night. Heading for the Gulf of Aden as we speak."

"So she can rendezvous with your tub with the missiles?"

"Only about twelve hours behind your original schedule. I take it that is within tolerances."

"Just. Glad I left some."

"Yes. Nothing ever quite goes to schedule in war."

Tucker thinks through the follow-on effects. "I've got the Gazans and the Lebanese holding their positions near the Israeli borders. The Syrians?"

"The same. Now – what else is there?"

"The hacks. I'm pretty sure there's no way the Israelis will get their systems in any kind of working order in that time. My guy will see to that. But there's also the diversionary attacks for the regional coalition forces, in Kabul and Baghdad…"

"I don't suppose we can keep that up for very long."

"No. Those guys will all be dead, or scattered, within hours. But it doesn't matter. I don't think the Americans could mount anything serious regionally anyway. And if they were able, I don't think they'd be willing."

"I expect you're right there."

Suleimani slips his side arm back into leather as Tucker exits.

Johnson keeps his huge arm around Bleep's shoulders until the trucks have safely roared off. The two 10th Mountain guys also saddle up and roll out, right behind the convoy, leaving Rheinhardt, BJ, Mike, and Bleep alone in the enormous hangar.

"C'mon, man," BJ says to Bleep, gently steering him toward the door. "Let's get you down to the med shack and get you checked out. There'll be plenty more battles later, believe me."

Bleep is still pretty clearly disoriented, or maybe delirious. "Wait, hang on," he says, shrugging BJ off, and twitching slightly. He pulls a nylon duty bag off his belt and starts digging through it. He comes up with two stacked metallic objects, and holds them up: a pair of printed circuit boards. "These are from the weaponization lab."

No one responds to this.

"Who can get me on an electronics test bench?" Bleep looks around somewhat wildly. "Multimeters. RF probes. I need a spectrum analyzer…"

"I can," Mike says quietly. "There's an engineering and electronics workshop a couple buildings over."

"They got something with a GBIP interface…?"

"I don't know, probably."

But Bleep is already pulling on Mike's arm and pushing him out the open hangar doors.

Rheinhardt and BJ look at each other a little sadly.

Stepping out into the base's bright sodium streetlights, Bleep shields his already badly traumatized eyes. With his other hand, he slaps absently at his chest webbing. As they disappear around the corner, he can be heard to mutter, "Damn Iranians got my Oakleys…"

* * *

BJ exhales heavily, sinking back into his chair. "Okay," he says. "What now?"

"I suppose we could launch a two-man suicide rescue mission. Go out blazing."

BJ swivels his head to look at him. "You mean a three-man suicide mission."

"What, Bleep? Guy can barely stand up."

"I meant Mike, actually." Rheinhardt looks at him skeptically. "Mike can shoot. I damn well taught him."

"Fair enough. So all three of us can go get dead." Rheinhardt shakes his head and sits up straight. "Whatever we're going to do next, we need intel. The shit's coming down all around the region. And with an eighty-billion dollar intelligence budget, somebody better have worked out where the hell it's coming from. And why."

He flips open a laptop and starts mushing keys, willing the thing to wake up.

BJ sits up and grabs a phone. "Try this," he says. "It still works better."

Rheinhardt takes the device. "You call the Ranch. I'll get Langley. And the Pentagon. I do still work there, last time I checked…"

Sooner than expected, Mike and Bleep come tripping back into the hangar.

Rheinhardt throws up a halt gesture with his left hand. With his right he holds a sat phone. "Yeah. E-mail's great. The full report. Thank you." He rings off and looks up. "Speak."

Sounding steadier now, Bleep says, "It's a programmable chip for controlling a warhead."

"How do you know?"

"Because I've designed them myself," he answers, without any apparent pride. "Well, one of them is a warhead controller. This is just junk, a testbed." He tosses one of the boards roughly on the table. He then produces the other and lays it down reverently. "This is what I was hoping it was when we found it. But it doesn't do remotely what I thought it would."

He puts his finger on a small black protrusion. "See this? It's a barometric sensing switch. This whole thing is essentially a barometric fuzing system."

Rheinhardt squints at it. "So it detonates the warhead at a given altitude, right?"

"Precisely. But what's bizarre is the altitude this one is set to detonate at. An airburst at *thirty kilometers* above sea level." He looks around the group. "Fat Man and Little Boy were airburst detonations, too. But they went off at eighteen hundred *feet*. At thirty kilometers, there would be no blast damage on the ground. And precious little fallout."

Rheinhardt's lips part slightly. "No fallout…"

"I mean, you probably wouldn't want to take your beach vacation downwind of there."

Rheinhardt stands, looking slightly dazed.

"There's only one reason for a nuclear detonation at that altitude," Bleep says.

Rheinhardt paces a couple of steps, muttering, as if to himself. "The troops massing on Israel's borders – Gaza, Lebanon, and the Golan. It didn't make sense before."

"And now it does?" BJ asks.

"Is all that actually happening?" Mike asks.

"Yeah," BJ says. "We got triple confirmation from U.S. intel, mainly sats and drones. Hamas, Hizbullah, and the Syrian Army. All lined up on three sides of Israel like a line of scrimmage."

Rheinhardt's expression changes from dazed to admiring. "Oh, man," he says. "They're not launching a nuclear war and triggering the arrival of the Twelfth Mahdi. That was just a dodge."

"What the hell are they doing, then?" asks BJ.

"It's an EMP strike," Bleep says, with finality. "An electromagnetic pulse, caused by a high-altitude nuclear detonation. Set off in the right place, it will turn every single electrical or electronic system in Israel into burnt toast. *Everything* will go down. Everything will stop. Comms. Computers. Sensors. Drones. Ground and aerial vehicles. Weapons systems. Not just down. *Out*. Fried and dead. Stone age time."

BJ's expression goes severe. "And with every defense system down… the bastards can just walk right in like they own the place."

Rheinhardt looks up from his reverie. He's got it now.

"They're not nuking Israel," he says quietly. "They're taking back Palestine."

Sergeant Major Eric Rheinhardt, Alpha Team leader, 1st SFOD-D... former adviser and observer to the catastrophic Chalus takedown op... semi-retired operator on a mandatory training rotation... briefly commander of a daring and totally unauthorized rescue mission inside of Iran... now leader of no one and nothing... and faced with imminent global catastrophe, and the likely execution of one of his people, yet powerless to impact anything... sits literally in the dark, on the ground, his back pressed up against the rear of the staging hangar.

Who you are in the dark.

That phrase got into his head from somewhere. Now it's coming back to him, flashing before his eyes in the gloom. Who you are in the dark. When no one's there to see your actions or to judge you. The person you *really* are. All the way down at bottom.

He's already savaged by guilt over the destruction of B Squadron, which he somehow failed to prevent. And he may now be looking at the imminent fall of Israel. And after it is overrun and conquered, the banishment, enslavement, or death of another six million Jews. In his mind's eye, he sees Chaya dying bravely and hopelessly in the defense of her tiny homeland...

And it may all be his fault.

Because of his relationship with Chaya, where he let his feelings rule him, and didn't use good judgment. And because of his sordid history with Rod Tucker, where he stood by and let evil triumph. Those two things have come together to result in the compromise of the IDF systems, and the disarming of Israel. All by his own hand – or the phone he held in it.

He has brought the wolf right inside their door.

* * *

"Hey, man." A voice rumbles out of the night.

It is followed by a very large man, approaching and resolving from out of the darkness. He comes to stand over where Rheinhardt sits on the ground, forearms resting on bent knees, head hanging between them.

"Well," says BJ, sitting down in the dirt beside him. "What's it gonna be?"

Rheinhardt takes a very deep breath, then exhales it.

"It's got to end."

"Too true."

"I'm serious. I've had enough of this piecemeal shit. I'm sick of fighting Iranian-controlled Shia militias in Iraq… and Iranian-trained Hamas in Gaza… and Iran's proxies Hizbullah in Beirut. It's all just shoveling seaweed against the tide. And it never ends. Even getting Ali back, as important as that is, would only be one more holding action."

"So what, then?"

"So the Iranian regime. It is literally behind half of the evil in the world right now. And it's got to go down."

BJ looks over at him in the dimness. "You serious?"

"Totally. Our problem's not eighty million Persians. They're just more victims. Our problem, everyone's problem, is a few hundred theocratic nutjobs, the mullahs. And maybe a few thousand hard-core loyalists in the Revolutionary Guard."

BJ pauses to take that on board. "I see your point. It's only ever just a few assholes who make all the trouble these days. Bin Laden and al-Zawahiri. Saddam and his sons. Hell, a bullet in Hitler's head might have saved fifty million lives. Maybe Ahmadinejad needs one."

"Not even him. Iranian presidents come and go. It's Khamenei, the Supreme Leader, who has all the power. He's the top of the food chain. But, anyway, the point is that if we're going to change anything," Rheinhardt says, looking across at his friend, "…we're actually going to have to change something. We've got to fix it. Before it's too late."

"I don't know. Maybe you're right."

"Plus… no one else is going to do it now. Israel's crippled. Our NCA, the whole U.S. government, is back-pedaling at high speed." He exhales again. "There's only us."

BJ grunts. "Well… if we're going all the way to Tehran anyway, I suppose we may as well do the job properly."

"And we're already off the reservation."

"True. May as well be hung for a sheep as for a lamb. In for a penny, in it to pound your mom. All that good stuff. You're talking about executing the Iranian regime takedown, aren't you? The decapitating strike."

"Yeah."

"Well, okay… but we're going to need a lot more guys."

"Yeah."

"And I expect you know where to get them."

"Yeah, maybe."

Now BJ exhales. "Well… it's not gonna suck itself. C'mon, let's get moving."

***

Back in the hangar, Mike and Bleep are running nuclear blast simulations on a laptop, while Bleep lectures excitedly. "Okay, when it goes off, gamma rays will hammer into the atmosphere, electrons will blast out along the Earth's magnetic field lines, and electrical and magnetic fields will fluctuate massively. The fluctuations will couple with electric devices and electronics to produce catastrophic current and voltage surges in exposed conductors and boards. The result will be like the biggest lightning strike in history. Commercial computer equipment will be destroyed. Industrial control applications, road and rail signaling – all fried. Flight control systems will short out, so planes will fall out of the sky…"

They both look up when Rheinhardt and BJ march back in, like men on a mission.

"What's going on?" Mike asks.

"We're going to unfuck Iran," BJ says, sitting and rifling through binders of assault plans.

"Awesome," says Bleep. He sits up, looking both impressed and more alert.

"What are you even talking about?" Mike asks.

"Regime change," Rheinhardt says, pulling up a laptop.

"You're kidding."

"With a name like Little Bo Peep, would he kid you?" says BJ, while opening a very thick binder and laying it flat. "This is the one."

"Okay," says Rheinhardt. "This is where the superhero stuff starts…"

After Tucker's disturbing visit, Ali has had only long hours alone in her cell. The only diversions were one delivery of bad food and warm water, and one emptying of her charming bucket. SERE school instilled various techniques for dealing with extended time in captivity. Much like being a special operator, surviving as a prisoner of war is largely a mental challenge.

On arriving, she immediately performed an assessment of the security in and around her cell – with an eye to vulnerabilities, and how she could exploit them. But she also knows there's no point in doing anything for the time being. She has no doubt she could kill the guards and get out of the cell, virtually anytime they open the door to bring her something. But then where would she go? She's at the heart of some military complex, and she's empty-handed. It would be a hell of a long walk from there to freedom.

Also, at this point, the most likely outcome to her capture is some diplomatic arrangement, conducted at a high level. Then she will be repatriated – either very quietly, or else very publicly.

She ardently hopes it's the former.

Ali remembers too well the capture of fifteen British sailors by Iran, during the Iraq War. They had almost without question been in Iraqi territorial waters at the time – the whole thing was basically a high-seas kidnapping, state piracy. And Ali winces to remember the British politicians falling over themselves, groveling and apologizing, begging to get their people back.

Jesus Christ, she thinks. *A hundred years earlier, half of Her Majesty's fleet would have sailed for the Gulf, and their only apologies would have been in the form of cannonballs and grapeshot.*

So, Ali's not entirely sure she *wants* to go back, if it's as a gracious "gift" to the American people from fucking Ahmadinejad. She'd almost rather just do her time like a man.

* * *

A short while later, the door knocks. *They knock?* she thinks. *Who knocks?* The locks turn and a man sticks his head in. "Sergeant Khamsi?" he asks. He speaks in elegantly accented English, and wears a moustache and a starched collar. "May I come in?"

Ali waves vaguely, and the man enters. He wears the uniform of the IRG, with insignia indicating the rank of brigadier general.

"I am Qassem Suleimani," he says. "I just wanted to make sure you have everything you need." He pauses. "Is there anything?"

"Well," she says, looking up at him. "I wouldn't say no to a business-class ticket to JFK. One-way is fine."

He smiles, somewhat winningly. "I'm afraid New York is off the menu for the moment. But you've had enough food? And your injuries have been cared for?"

"The food was adequate, thank you," she says. "However, due to the lumpiness of the bed, I'm afraid I'm only going to be able to give you two stars in my review on TripAdviser.com."

"I will see if we can't dig you up some more blankets." He pauses and cocks his head at her. "I'm told you are Somali?"

"I am American. Of Somali origin."

Suleimani continues to regard her, intrigued. "Is it true that you are really a... Delta Force operator?"

"Nope. Food service specialist, 501st Sustainment Brigade. Khamsi, Aaliyah, First Sergeant, one-nine-six-three-eight-six-five-three."

The general smiles at her, with a look of amused and kindly admiration.

And, unless Suleimani is totally mistaken, he'd swear she's having to work pretty hard not to crack a smile back at him.

Rheinhardt may be off the reservation. But that doesn't mean he can keep most-critical and urgent intel to himself. As soon as he worked out his conclusion that Tucker and the mullahs were planning to disable Israel with an EMP burst, then over-run them from three directions, he wrote it up and logged it with the Intel desk at the Ranch. He then put it in e-mail to Havering, Victor Michaels at the Pentagon, and Chaya, and placed follow-up calls to all three. The first two went through to voice-mail.

Chaya's number just rang and rang.

But at least one message did get through. This comes clear when Mike's phone goes off. It's Havering, frantically looking for Rheinhardt (who now has no phone). Rheinhardt takes Mike's and steps outside.

"Your report," the colonel says tightly, from six time zones over. *"You still standing by that? Including your conclusions? An EMP attack on Israel?"*

"That's affirmative."

"Where's that warhead guidance chip?"

"Right here. Sitting on a folding table."

"Jesus. Dammit," Havering says. *"We need to get that under proper analysis. I'm going to have a courier pick it up and fly it to Langley."*

"Fine," Rheinhardt says. "But all this will be over before they get it."

Havering just breathes heavily, and audibly, on the other end.

Finally, Rheinhardt speaks. His voice is level, and obviously dead serious. "Are we going to act to prevent this?" No answer. "Is this Unit, or this U.S. Army, or the United States of America, going to act on this intel? To prevent the destruction of our ally?" From his tone, he's obviously not expecting much.

Havering's voice is flat in reply. *"For starters, no one's seen your intel. Our conclusions may not be your conclusions. And even if we agree... you know I don't have the authority to say what's going to be done about it."*

The two sit on the line in silence for most of a minute. Finally Havering speaks: *"Sergeant Major. You remember from before, when I told you to stand down?"*

"Yeah."

"Well listen to me very carefully. Because now I'm telling you to stand down – and this time I mean it."

"Yes, sir."

"No, seriously, Eric – STAND DOWN."

Rheinhardt sighs out loud. It's all so tiring.

"The incident in Anbar," Havering says. *"With Tucker. And the dead Israelis."*

Rheinhardt stiffens at this.

"I know what happened. There was a record of all your voice traffic, on your squad net, and also with your air support. It all got recorded, back at the Balad ops desk. I managed to bury the recording at the time. I'd hoped it would stay buried."

Rheinhardt has no response to this. It's his breathing that's heavy and audible now.

"The Pentagon, and State. With the disaster of that goddamned raid, and with Ali getting herself captured and put on CNN, they're

all in super-power ass-covering mode now. And somebody up there has dug up this audio recording. Maybe they had it all along. It ties you to Tucker, and not in a good way. And those same somebodies are trying to make you a scapegoat for this whole thing."

All Rheinhardt can think is how mind-wrenchingly trivial all this is, with everything else that's going on.

"Do you get me? They're tying you to Tucker – and they're on the verge of saying out loud that you were in on the destruction of B Squadron. That you were a co-conspirator."

"Roger that," Rheinhardt says. "Goodbye, Colonel."

He hangs up. He's *really* off the reservation now.

* * *

While he's outside anyway, he calls Javier to give him a heads-up, as well as the short-form summary of their new plan. Despite the gunfire and explosions in the background, Javier's disbelief comes through loud and clear.

"Are you seriously talking about overthrowing a U.N. member state? With no military or political authorization?"

"They won't listen to me anymore," Rheinhardt says.

Now even Javier's sigh is audible over the battle.

"Okay. We've broken the back of the assault here, and I think we'll RTB in no more than a couple of hours."

"And you'll talk to the guys en route?"

"Yeah. I'll do what I can to brace them for this… idea. But, I've got to tell you, I can't say I'm more than fifty percent on board with it myself."

"Just get back here, alive. We'll all make our individual decisions then."

"Roger that, Top. Gotta roll. Out."

Rheinhardt puts the phone down. Next stop, he suddenly remembers, is around back, to the helipad, to talk to Richie and his aviators. As with everyone else, selling them on an unauthorized rescue op into a denied area to get a team member back was one thing.

But this is just a whole other one…

In a better stroke of luck than anyone hoped for, Stamis and his staffers stay in the Green Zone to take meetings with the Ambassador and Embassy staff – mainly about diplomatic security, and the use of JSOC operators for same.

So Rheinhardt's ad hoc regime-overthrow SMU (special mission unit) continues to enjoy the untroubled use of the staging hangar. For now.

Homer and his SEALs, Spider and his CIA paras, and Egle and her C Squadron brothers, have all rolled back in on the same trucks they rolled out on. They're all sporting dirty and disheveled clothes and hair, zombie-like eyes – but with their weapons and equipment perfectly maintained and form-fitted to their bodies. It's the timeless look of the Tier-1 operator returning from a night of combat black ops.

Now they stand and sit in groups of three or four, at various points spiraling out from Alpha's table. They're poring over intel summaries, interrogation reports, NRC data, live drone and sat video – plus the enormous shelved assault plan for taking down the Iranian regime. They're also debating loudly, pushing back, generating enthusiasm, calling bullshit. None of them have signed on the dotted line yet. But none of them have said no yet, either.

They're not so much trying to figure out if what Rheinhardt has in mind is batshit crazy.

What they're trying to figure out is if it's batshit crazy *enough.*

* * *

Mike's got Javier buttonholed in a corner. He looks concerned and a little out of his depth, intently whispering questions. "Can we seriously put together something like this, that quickly?"

Javier nods. He's used to briefing Mike, as he was his mentor and handler during his first hours and days with Alpha. This was back when Mike was very on edge and unseasoned and in particular not used to being shot at or blown up.

"Our planning, briefing, and rehearsing windows have been shrinking pretty much since the morning of 9/11. And these shelved assault plans are incredibly detailed. In many cases, we've actually rehearsed them on full-scale mock-ups of target structures, built by Unit engineers. When the plans go on the shelf, the idea is that they can come back out again in an emergency and get executed almost immediately."

Mike nods. "But all these new guys? Non-Unit guys?"

Javier smiles. "They're only new to you. JSOC has been teaming up disparate SOF elements for years. We work hand-in-glove. And it's only Tier-1 guys here. The CIA paras are the best operators working out of uniform anywhere. Half of them are ex-Delta or DEVGRU. This is their idea of a relaxing retirement activity. The Team-6 SEALs can share any battlespace on Earth with us. It's a bit like if you got swarmed by Makos, Tiger sharks, and Great Whites – and pinned your hopes on them not working well together. Everyone here knows exactly what to expect from everyone else in a fast-moving or ambiguous situation."

"But all working together on something this complex?"

"This mission profile is very modular, actually. It's basically a series of simultaneous building takedowns – one for every critical government and military node in Tehran. We just need enough teams to slot into each of them." He casts a look around the hangar. "Which we don't remotely have yet… Come on, I know Eric wants to have you online preparing the battlespace, not shooting the shit with me…"

* * *

Rheinhardt is huddled up with the leaders from each team: Spider for the Agency paras, Homer for the SEALs – and, in true Delta fashion, since she was first in and has the best knowledge, SSG Egle Markunas for C Squadron.

Rheinhardt says, "Okay. You know the old chestnut about how you eat an elephant?"

Homer smiles. "Yeah. One bite at a time, Sarge. One bite at a time."

Rheinhardt nods. "Right. But not on this one. On this one, we're pretty much going to have to eat the whole elephant in one huge bite. You remember the Panama takedown – very low footprint, dense civilian population, precision takedown of key gov and mil facilities."

"Yes," says Spider. "But that was a population of three million, versus *eighty* million in Iran. And a military of about fifteen thousand, not half a million."

"But think about the technology force multipliers we've developed since then. We toppled the entire Taleban with about two hundred guys, plus air."

"You sound like you think you're Cortés. Like with a few guys on horseback with guns, and some impressive technology, you can go in and take down a whole mighty empire."

"Lesser known fact," says Rheinhardt, who like most of them is a student of military history. "It wasn't really the technology that did it. The Conquistadors only had a few crappy arquebuses that hardly fired, and not that many horses. What they *did* have was a force small enough to slip in quietly, and to continuously improvise, where a larger one would have bogged down. They had total self-assurance and faith in their fellows. And they had imagination and audacity."

He leaves out that the Spaniards also had the will of an iron leader, who made them believe that they could do the impossible.

Such a feeling can be highly contagious.

* * *

Rheinhardt leans over a large touch-screen tablet and starts calling up map overlays.

"Here's our complete target package." He starts pointing out red triangles. "This IRG Garrison here. These ministries – including state TV, radio, and online. This building, home of MOIS, the Ministry of Information and Security – basically, the Iranian secret police. Major part of the internal security apparatus."

"Those guys," says Spider, "are like the fucking Middle Eastern SS."

"Yeah," says Rheinhardt. "But they're only tough guys when murdering dissidents and intellectuals. I have us taking them down with two four-man teams. On the other hand… here – the Ansar-ol-Mahdi Corps. An elite force, they protect the Supreme Leader. They'll be a little tougher. But, conveniently, they sit right next door to Khamenei. And he's the crown jewel."

He flips quickly through building schematics. "As you can see, we've got blueprints for all the target structures." He flips back. "In addition to Khamenei, we also need the Assembly of Experts – eighty-six Islamic scholars who oversee the Army and in theory elect the Supreme Leader. They meet in the Palais du Senat, the Senate House." He scrolls the map a bit more.

"Then, very close by, the Guardian Council, that's twelve mullahs. And here – the Expediency Discernment Council of the System, twenty-eight advisers to the Supreme Leader."

"It's gonna be like a mullah rodeo," Homer says.

"Yes. But we've got to be careful with this last one, because one of the men who sits on it is Mir-Hossein Mousavi – the guy who actually won the 2009 election, and now the main opposition figure in the Green Revolution. We're going to need him to step up."

"And will he?"

"If the regime appears to be falling, then it's likely. I think if we bag Khamenei and the Assembly and Guardian Council, and neuter the IRG, the whole house of cards goes down."

Spider smiles. "The moment when Cortés really took down the Aztec empire was when he waltzed into

Tenochtitlan with his big nutsack hanging out and simply kidnapped Montezuma."

"Yeah, everything old is new again." Rheinhardt takes a breath and taps his laptop screen. "Okay, then. Here are your individual team assignments…"

* * *

BJ has got the nineteen-man C Squadron detachment in conference.

An assaulter known as the Grinch is shaking his head. Tall and broad-shouldered, with dark hair and penetrating brown eyes, he sports a thick goatee he's known to shave off only once a year, for his required Department of the Army photo. Fond of doing 15-mile runs in the North Carolina heat wearing full body armor and a gas mask, he's also known for his famously low tolerance for bullshit. He's willing to play by the rules – after they've passed some basic no-crack-smoking tests.

"Kind of a big fucking country for the thirty of us?" he says.

BJ shoves him in the shoulder. "What, have you turned into a bunch of pussies over here since the Iraq War ended? It's not so big."

"It's the size of the fucking Western U.S.," the Grinch says.

"Okay, maybe it's big. But it's also a totalitarian state – which means everything is controlled from the center. And most of the main government and military facilities are tightly clustered around Meidan Sepah, a central square in the government district. And few of them, including where the mullahs sit, are well defended. They're expecting an attack on their capital about like they're expecting an outbreak of the galloping pneumonic chlamydia."

The Grinch shakes his head. "Okay, I know the Unit places a premium on personal initiative and independent thinking. But this might finally be taking that too far…"

"You, shut up," BJ says. He spins around a laptop with a map of Tehran displayed. "The rest of you, pay attention. I'm going to take you in and out again. With a little luck, your total time-on-target will be inside of twenty minutes."

A sniper known as Bishop leans back and raises his hand. Mid-thirties, quiet, unassuming, average height, with brown hair and regular features, he is the archetypal gray man. But he also has a dry sense of humor under the surface, perhaps due to being born and bred in "the Republic of Texas," as he insists on calling it. He's also shrugged off no fewer than three helicopter crashes in his time in Delta.

"TOT for what target?" he asks.

BJ eyes him and says flatly, "C's primary assignment remains just what it was in the original hostage rescue plan. And it's still the tough one: Quds Force HQ, at Kazemi Garrison."

Bishop shakes his head. "The former U.S. Embassy Compound. So you mean the *original* original hostage rescue plan."

"Yeah. Unfinished business. Anyway, now we've got not quite as many shooters as before, and they've got just as many, so we're going to have to tweak things a little."

"Well, maybe less is more on this one," Bishop says.

"No," BJ says, sounding annoyed, "*more* is more. That's why they call it 'more.' Nonetheless, you ladies are going to have to make do with what you've got. And make it up in balls and sheer firepower…"

* * *

Mike and Bleep are now huddled up at the table with the computers.

Mike says, "Rheinhardt and I have gone over it. And, basically, there's no way this is going to succeed without cyberwar dominance. It's our number one force multiplier. First thing, we have to take out military comms."

Bleep nods. "So they can't start trucking in reinforcements from around the country."

"Exactly. First we isolate the head. Then they can't reinforce, mobilize local forces, or direct the defense in any kind of coherent way."

"Can we do that?"

"Yep. We've been preparing the ground, that is laying exploits, in Iranian systems for *years*. It's all ready to kick off."

"And you can kick it off yourself?"

"Yeah, I can. Cyberwar is so new that they don't really have the controls and authorizations in place, like with, for instance, nukes. I'll probably spend the rest of my term of service in Leavenworth, and never be allowed to touch a computer again…"

"You and me both. Now, what about power? How do we bring down all the generator stations?"

"It's simpler than that, really. You take control of a *single* generator station, then surge power across the network. All the others blow up. No place can store power for any length of time, so it's lights out until replacement generators get trucked in. And these things are building-sized. Sometimes replacement generators don't exist, so it's a custom engineering job…"

"Kick-ass."

"The best part is this will also put the nail in the comms coffin. All the phones will go out."

"I thought landline exchanges, and most cell towers, have generator or battery backup?"

"Sure, in the U.S. But in Iran? Not so much. Telecoms is state owned. It's unreliable even when not under attack. Knock out the power and virtually all of the cell towers, and most of the landlines, will go down. And of course Tehran sits in a basin, surrounded by mountains, so radio for them has its own entire set of problems…"

* * *

Rheinhardt's on the move again, but Homer intercepts him.

"Hey, Bo. I hear you're planning to run this during daylight hours. Not exactly ideal, is it?"

Rheinhardt turns. "No. But so little in life is. Anyway, daylight wouldn't bother you if you were going in under the water, would it, frogman?"

"No. And if my grandmother had balls she'd be my grandfather."

Rheinhardt laughs. "Two factors militate for daytime. The first is that the mullahs will all be packed together in a handful of central government buildings – instead of asleep in houses all over the city, which we don't have the manpower to hit. We need to seize the control levers of state. But we also need the leadership rounded up."

Homer nods. "So we can hand them over to the Iranian people."

"Right. But the big reason is, we're simply out of time. We can't launch tonight, and tomorrow night will almost certainly be too late…"

With that, Spider comes piling into them, waving a fat copy of the assault plan.

"Hey, D-boy," he says to Rheinhardt. "This whole regime takedown plan was written during the 2009 protests. And it's all predicated on thousands of Iranian dissidents taking to the streets and occupying government buildings. That still your big idea?"

Rheinhardt nods.

"Okay. You got some pipeline to the Green Revolution the Agency doesn't? Some way to get half the population of Tehran out in the streets?" Spider sees that Rheinhardt isn't looking at him, but around him, and gets annoyed. "Talking to you, pal. Something interesting out—"

Rheinhardt is smiling big now, as his old friend Captain Miller of the Rangers strides into the hangar, with a man on his arm. Though wearing tan military ACUs, the second man is small, middle-aged, and Middle Eastern.

"Yeah, I do, actually," Rheinhardt says. "My secret weapon for actuating the Iranian people: Dr. Azad Sultan. Thanks for keeping him squirreled away for us, John."

"Happy to do it, brother," Miller says. "And I've got the men outside. They're jocked up and panting for a real mission."

Rheinhardt points through the miasma of planning activity toward the geek table. "Dr. Sultan. You remember

Mike Brown? I need you to get with him now. He'll brief you on what we need from you. Okay?" Sultan nods and leaves.

"You and me," Rheinhardt says to Miller. "Outside."

As they disappear, Homer and Spider regard each other with bemused expressions.

"This guy," says Spider, "is a fucking wild man."

Homer nods serenely. "Yeah. I'm not saying there's any chance of pulling this off. But if I were picking someone to try it, I'd pick him."

Spider claps the other man on the shoulder, turning him back inside. "Come on. You got a more interesting way to get yourself and your team killed this week? I didn't think so…"

Rheinhardt finds Company E, 75th Rangers, right where he saw them last – holding up the outside wall of the hangar. Only now they're doing it in the dark and cool of the very early morning. And this time their weapons are already cleaned and squared away, and held as if ready for use on very short notice.

They are a cocked gun.

Rheinhardt and Miller stand a few meters away and talk through it.

"Everyone on this one," Rheinhardt says, "is making his own decision. Out or in."

"C'mon, Eric. You know I'd follow you straight to hell."

"Not on this one, John. On this one, you're on your own."

"Okay," Miller says. "Listen. My *standing orders* are to accept any tasking from any Unit operator working out of Balad. Right? And I naturally assume you have higher authorization for any show you're putting on. So my ass is covered. Plus, you got another elite infantry company sitting around that's previously rehearsed this assault?"

Rheinhardt doesn't. And it was in fact the 75th Rangers that rehearsed with Delta back in 2009, when they first developed the plan.

"Also," Miller says, lightening his tone, "I assume you're not going to get my whole company killed. And if you do, it will be in some truly spectacular way – something every last one of them will be happy to die doing."

Rheinhardt swallows and doesn't speak for a second.

Where, he wonders, *does this nation find such men?*

* * *

Finally he speaks. "Well… you may regret this before it's all over."

Miller pulls himself up to his full height and breadth. "Regrets are for the Air Force. I am an Army Ranger. Anyway, you think I'm going to miss out on being part of this Coalition of the Retarded you're putting together?"

"Ha," Rheinhardt laughs out loud. "That's got a hell of a ring to it."

"Yeah, I thought so."

Rheinhardt straightens up. "Captain. Please have your company report for formation on the parade ground at the north side of this complex. There you'll find men taping down the floor plans of your target structures. You'll have a little time to rehearse your assaults, with full-speed walk-throughs. No live fire, please."

Miller turns his back and raises his voice to his men. "Okay, girls, anyone who wants to kill somebody today, get your ass around to the other end of this majestic army base…"

"Gee, Cap," says a young specialist, "I was kind of hoping to sleep in this morning…"

Miller chases after him, hissing in his ear: "Genius does what it must, talent does what it can, but you'd better do what you're fucking well told…"

The whole company disappears into the almost breaking dawn.

But the dawn never does quite break, through dark clouds on the horizon.

There's a storm brewing out of the East.

"Good to see you again, Doc," Mike says. "Dr. Sultan, this is Bleep. He's going to take you through it all." Mike swivels a laptop, then turns to face the Iranian. "You are the linchpin here. This won't come off without you. You think you're ready to lead Iran to its day of freedom?"

"I was born ready, motherfucker," Azad says. Mike and Bleep stare open-mouthed. "Sorry, line from a movie. I love American movies."

"O-*kay*…" Bleep says, as Mike scoots off around the table, "First is the military. I'm told you don't believe they'll fight."

"I do not believe that the regular army will support the government in the pinch. If it looks like the mullahs will fall, the soldiers will switch sides. They have all seen the events in Egypt and Libya. They would side with the people against the regime."

"What about IRG?"

"The IRG, not so much. And especially Quds Force. They may fight to the last man."

"But they'd be outnumbered by a liberated regular army in revolt."

"Not outgunned, but certainly outnumbered."

Bleep shows a trace of a smile. "What if I told you we could speak to every officer, at every level, in every unit of the regular Iranian armed forces?"

Sultan's eyebrows go north. "I would say that we would have a lot to say to them."

Bleep slides a laptop toward him. "That message you see onscreen will go to everyone from commanding generals down to second lieutenant platoon leaders. I need you to help me word it."

"You need me to translate it into Farsi!"

"Yeah, that too. But we have to make sure and say it right. Rheinhardt drafted this text. Can you take a look and tell me what you would change? It has to be right, and it has to go out at the right time. Because when it does, there will be no turning back."

* * *

Twenty minutes later, the message has been drafted and approved.

Bleep puts it on a timer to go out two hours before the planned assault. Too early, and word will get out, and surprise will be lost. Too late, and it's too late.

"Okay," Bleep says to Sultan. "Second thing is the people. There was a revolution in 2009. You didn't win that time. But now we need you to re-stage it. Can you make it happen?"

"I think so. The networks are there, everyone's been waiting – but afraid to begin. So many have been killed, imprisoned, tortured. But I know the Facebook groups, the Twitter hashtags – and I know who the dissident leaders are. If I can convince *them*… everyone else will believe."

Bleep pauses to think. "Suppose the power went off in the capital, at a predetermined hour. And military, police, and state security buildings started blowing up. Would that be enough of a sign to convince them?"

"Yes, I think it would."

He pushes the laptop at him again. "Tell them. Tell them all." He points at a hand-written scribble on a loose piece of paper. "At this exact day and time."

Sultan nods and starts typing.

While he does so, Bleep looks thoughtful and says, "You know, if we do this right… when it's all over, we may be able to slip out quietly and it will look like it *was* a popular uprising."

Sultan responds while he types. "If it's a popular uprising we want, Mr. Bleep… Do you know that there are five million Kurds in Iran?"

"Vaguely."

"And do you know that half of them are Sunni, and that they are no friends of the regime? Maybe a quarter million in the capital alone." He finishes typing, pushes his glasses up, and looks seriously at the soldier beside him.

"And?" Bleep says.

"And… I have a couple of names. And a phone number."

Bleep regards him, intrigued.

"Got an e-mail address?"

Hajji Ahmadi rises from his prayer rug, after completing the sunrise prayer.

He says an additional prayer of thanks for being back on home soil, in the Kurdish city of Mahabad in the northwest of Iran – otherwise known as Iranian Kurdistan. For most of the last decade, Ahmadi has been in exile in Germany. This is because he is the political and spiritual leader of the Party of Free Life of Kurdistan (Partiya Jiyana Azad a Kurdistanê or PJAK).

The Kurds have long been the world's largest stateless people, numbering 30 million, and living in territory spread across Iran, Iraq, Syria, and Turkey. For long years, they've been badly oppressed by the Sunni Ba'athists, the secular Turks, and the Shi'ite mullahs.

However, Hajji Ahmadi watched while their brothers in Iraq rose up against Saddam again and again, finally succeeding in the liberation with America and the Coalition in 2003. Soon after, they had control of their own semi-autonomous region in the north. Commerce flourished, infrastructure grew, and tourists came.

The Kurds in the Iraqi government are also famously capable and incorruptible, happily sharing power and oil revenues with their Shia and Sunni brothers – despite the murder and genocide perpetrated on them by the old regime. The Iraqi Kurds have not only survived and prevailed.

But they have forgiven as well.

Hajji Ahmadi takes inspiration from all this – it is in part why he has taken the risk of returning to Iran. To work for the freedom of the Kurdish people there. His party, PJAK, aims to replace the Iranian theocracy with a democratic and federal government – one where all ethnic minorities, not just Kurds but also Arabs and Azeris, are respected and protected. As well, half the members of PJAK are women, and the organization is strongly supportive of women's rights.

These are all reasons why the mullahs in Iran have ruthlessly oppressed the Kurds whenever possible. PJAK's armed wing, the Eastern Kurdistan Forces, have clashed with IRG frequently. And, as many American military personnel will tell you, Kurds make stalwart and totally fearless fighters and allies.

* * *

Hajji Ahmadi rises now from his prayer rug, and takes himself to the low desk where his laptop is plugged in. He checks messages, as well as his schedule for the day.

A knock sounds at the door. That should be his tea.

Should be, but is not. It is in fact Leyla Elahi, who is one of the leaders of the local party, and who has taken on the job of protecting and chauffeuring Ahmed, since his return to the country.

"Excuse me, Hajji. But there is something you need to see."

"Yes?" He twists at the waist and motions her in.

"It is in e-mail. I've forwarded it to you."

Ahmed turns back to his screen. He finds the message and opens it. He reads it. Then he reads it a second time.

He gives Leyla a wide-eyed and enquiring look.

She shrugs. "I believe it's really from Azad Sultan. Unless he's been tortured into giving up the code words."

"But is this possible? An American attack against the regime?"

She leans against the wall and releases the air from her lungs slowly. "God does not forget anyone. All things are possible. Either this will happen, or it will not. That is in God's hands."

Hajji Ahmed nods respectfully. "But for now, it is men and women who must prepare. Can you get hold of Karim for me, please?"

He means Karim Fallah – military commander of the Eastern Kurdish Forces.

Leyla nods and turns to exit. But she cannot conceal from the old man that she is trembling slightly. Could it be possible? Could today be the day of their emancipation?

Indeed, the Hajj thinks to himself. *God does not forget anyone. Even in the mullahs' Iran.*

Mike types rapid fire, assaulting the keyboard. He sees nothing outside of the narrow cone of the command line in his terminal window. The pressure is on. Unless he can get back inside Iran's air defense systems, and bring them back down, the whole assault force, every man and machine, will be blown out of the sky within minutes of crossing the border.

It's all down to him now. Mike is very, very good at what he does. But he's also smart enough to make a tactical retreat when he has to. He calls Rheinhardt over.

"It's not happening. Not in the timeframe we've got. Not from here."

Rheinhardt pauses. "What's your recommendation?"

"I can do it. But I've got to get access to a *physical* node of their air defense network."

"That's the only way?"

"That's it. Can you get me over the border? Look, they have air defense stations close to the frontier, one here at…" and he flips to a map, "…Kerend Gharb, less than fifty clicks in."

"In theory, yes. We could insert you with one of the stealth birds, and enough shooters to take down the facility."

"Perfect." Mike's already thinking about another one of those missions where he'll be shot at while typing.

"The problem is the bird. And the shooters. We don't have enough of either. And none to spare."

"Who else is there, then? What about the Israelis? They're close. And presumably incentivized."

"Good thought. But we have no comms with them. I haven't been able to get through in hours. They're totally shut down."

"It's Chaya Akhilov, in Sirkin Ops Center, right?"

"Yeah."

"Give me twenty minutes, free from other taskings. This I can make happen."

* * *

Seventeen minutes later, he calls Rheinhardt back. He hands him a hard-line handset.

Rheinhardt looks incredulous. "It's secure?"

"As secure as anything. It's encrypted VOIP on a low-level VPN I just set up. Unless Tucker and the Iranians are sitting nearby with tin cans and string attached to the actual cables..."

Rheinhardt takes the phone. "Go for Rheinhardt," he says.

"Eric." It's Chaya's voice. *"Thank God. We've been cut off here."*

"Listen, I don't have time to brief you. But I've got a mission for you. Listen carefully. Do you have access to the Stealth Hawks we sold IDF last year?"

"Access is a fuzzy term. I know where they're parked. And I know the pilots."

"Can you put together an assault team? Maybe a heavy platoon?"

"No problem."

"Great. Now. Can you fly across Jordan and Iraq, and over the border into Iran?"

"*Jesus... Okay, why not? If it's going to be that kind of day. What do you need us to do?*"

Uncle BJ is out on the parade ground, running through the Kazemi takedown with C Squadron. The twenty operators are free-flowing through an imaginary compound of buildings, demarcated by taped lines on the blacktop. They hold imaginary assault rifles at their shoulders and move in a complex choreography between, amongst, and through the buildings. They call out their actions as they execute them.

"Left side heavy. Going left."

"Firing. Firing. Firing. Room clear. Building clear."

"Bounding… set."

"Base of fire."

BJ's phone goes off. "Go for Johnson… Kick-ass. Put down on the western end of the runway. I'm on my way."

As BJ jogs off, he's already shooting a text off to Rheinhardt: "*ISOF inbound.*"

* * *

The Iraqi Special Operations Forces (ISOF) were stood up in 2005 after two years of intensive training. They now consist of a two brigades: one stationed in Baghdad, and another dispersed to regional counter-terrorism centers around the country.

One of these is home to the ISOF Diyala Reconnaissance Detachment (DRD), an elite-within-the-elite unit. ISOF

DRD was provided with advanced training by an American joint special mission unit that was never formally named. But it was headed up by a really big man with an impressive moustache and a funny call sign.

ISOF moves around in Russian Mil Mi-17 helos, flown by top Iraqi pilots and aircrew who have received training in NVG flying and CT aviation. It is four of these birds, known by the NATO designator as "Hips," that land now in the thin dawn light of Balad. And it is the Recon detachment commander who hops off the first bird and takes a look around for the moustache.

* * *

"*Salaam aleikum, akhii*," says Major Ali al-Samarrai, using the Arabic term for "my brother." He wears Iraqi battle fatigues and his own bushy black moustache, still popular with Iraqi soldiers even in the post-Saddam era.

"*Waleikum salaam*," BJ responds, gripping the man's right hand then touching his breast above his heart.

Armed, armored, and kitted-out men begin pouring off the helos and forming into ranks. It's the entire recon detachment, one hundred men. And they look loaded for bear and ready to work.

"Good of you to come," BJ says over the whumping of the rotors.

"For you?" al-Samarrai says. "Always. The men still speak of you with awe."

"How'd you get away? Not too busy?"

The Iraqi smiles and shrugs. "A good horse never lacks a saddle. But the new Iraqi Army is a bit like the old one – very flexible furlough policies. Suddenly, all of my men had to go home for a few days. Where are we going, by the way, old friend?"

"You fought in the Iran–Iraq War, right?"

"Sure. Why?"

"Uh, never mind just now. For the moment, what we need is to get your men running through their assault drills out on the parade ground, while we brief you and your officers inside."

"Just as you say, *Amm*," he says, switching family terms again, to the Arabic for "uncle." He speaks a terse series of commands to his company first sergeant, who puts the men in a marching column and herds them toward the rehearsal area.

The grizzled and resolute special operators of free Iraq have just joined the Coalition.

Rheinhardt comes trotting around back onto the helipad in response to a terse text from Richie. As he rounds the corner, he sees the original flight of Little Birds, from the Chalus raid, buzzing back in for a landing, their engines burbling like oversized lawn mowers.

Richie trots up in his flight suit. He is a seasoned CW4 who's been flying with the Night Stalkers for twelve years. At 38, his hair is starting to go gray and he can no longer run as fast as the new guys. But what he lacks in wind he more than makes up for in experience and dirty tricks. Moreover, in a community of hotshot aviators who swagger big and claim to enjoy dicing with death, Richie is not afraid to admit that combat scares the crap out of him.

"Okay, you insane son of a bitch," he says. "By some miracle, not only are my two Ghost Hawks and crews still here. But we've got the whole flight of AH6es back – *plus* four Little Bird lifts." He's referring to the version configured with pods on both sides to carry operators for insertion, as opposed to the ones bristling with rocket pods and miniguns.

"Outstanding. Thank you," is all Rheinhardt can say.

Richie nods. "But you're not done owing me yet. Luckily for you, I've still got friends in the Air Force. As did Waz and Dono. Ones who want in, if it's going to be payback for Chalus."

"It'll be payback," Rheinhardt says. "And it will be a game changer."

"It had better be. I've got an MC-130 inbound, fully crewed and fueled. Two jumpmasters on board – and a hundred static line rigs. So whichever group of maniacs of yours it is you have in mind can do a combat parachute jump into downtown fucking Tehran."

Rheinhardt nods. "I've got one company more shooters than I can infil on helos."

"Shut up. I'm not done. Also on board is a complete FARP-on-a-pallet, with a team to jump in and run it." A FARP is a Forward Re-arming/Re-fueling Point – a huge bladder of aviation fuel, pumps, and boxes of rockets and minigun ammo, all palletized and slung under three enormous parachutes. It's followed out of the plane by a small team of very brave 160th support personnel, who float down under fire and set it all up in some hopefully safe corner of the battlefield. There the Little Birds can return again and again for fuel and ammo.

And thus stay in the fight as long as it takes to win it.

"But wait. There's more. I've also got a fully armed and fueled Spectre inbound. With two CCTs aboard." The AC-130 Spectre is the aerial gun platform that covered Rheinhardt and Tucker's team in al-Anbar. Despite that tragedy, AC-130s and their super-skilled crews have saved more American troops in contact than God. The CCTs are Air Force combat controllers, elite special tactics guys who get up to their necks in ground combat, in order to direct precision air support from above.

"You're really going to appreciate those guys," Richie says, "when you get in the shit."

Rheinhardt nods. "Yeah. You may have just pulled our bacon out of the fire in advance."

"Wouldn't be the first goddamned time."

Rheinhardt bites his lip. "Got a bit of bad news. It's going to be a daylight op."

"Jesus Christ! Which part of 'Night Stalkers' don't you understand? No, belay that. It's obviously the 'Night' part."

"It's the only way on this one. A whole pile of mission parameters dictate it. But the good news is they're calling for a big thunderstorm. Low cloud cover, pelting rain. You can see it in the distance now. It's an enormous front."

Richie shakes his head. "That's the *good* news?"

"I figured you'd rather fly in heavy weather, if you have to fly in the daytime."

"Well, it's better than a poke in the eye with a frozen turd, I guess. Cloud cover's something we can hide in. Okay, man. Just one last thing. You think you can have that Ferris Bueller hacker dude of yours cut orders for the AF guys and Little Bird jocks? Nobody minds risking their lives and careers. As long as we have at least an outside shot of coming back with one or the other."

"No problem."

Uncle BJ and the eight Iraqi officers are huddled up in the center of the hangar. Iraqis understand English at various levels, from "attended the Royal Military Academy at Sandhurst" to "once watched all the Rambo movies back to back," so BJ is taking it slow. He has just briefed them on the Iranians' plans for an EMP attack.

When he finishes, Major Ali Al-Samarrai politely raises his hand.

"You know, I hate to bring this up, but… Iraq is a Muslim and Arab country. Perhaps only so many tears would be shed by us were Israel to be… knocked back this way."

BJ clamps his hand on Al-Samarrai's shoulder. "Oh, come on, man. You know you guys are *this close* to normalizing relations with Israel. You've got MPs visiting Jerusalem and calling for military intelligence sharing!"

Al-Samarrai shrugs elaborately. "Well… perhaps if they would stop their attacks on Gaza…"

"Okay," BJ says, changing tack. "How about this? If the Iranians pull this off, the Israelis may nuke them back, and then all your Shia brothers and sisters in Iran are going to be *dead*."

Al-Samarrai arches his eyebrows. "Yes, I suppose that is compelling."

* * *

Fifteen minutes into BJ's briefing on ISOF's target package, Bleep trots up with an open cardboard box.

"Come and get 'em," he says. "Green armbands for everyone."

BJ pulls out a handful. "What's this?"

"That, my friend, is the color of the Iranian Green Revolution. What do you think it's going to look like when a bunch of Americans and Iraqis land in downtown Tehran? These will at least identify us to the people and dissidents. Dr. Sultan's idea."

He plops the box down and turns to go.

BJ calls after him. "…Hey, where'd you find all this green fabric?"

Over his shoulder, Bleep says, "It's the goddamned Army, you bozo."

BJ looks down at his armband, befuddled. "Not really that shade of green…"

* * *

Thirty minutes later into the briefing, Bleep trots up again with a clipboard.

"Hey, I've got your call signs for the ISOF assault teams."

"Yeah? Hit me."

"It's Retard Four-One, Four-Two, Four-Three, and Four-Four."

"Retard?! What! Why?"

"Because sometimes the NATO phonetic alphabet just gets *old*." He winks at BJ before dashing off. "Welcome to the Coalition of the Retarded…"

As Chaya's station in the TOC is the only one with a comms channel to anywhere, she has staffed it with an attentive private. Whenever her screen flashes with a call from Rheinhardt, his job is to sprint to wherever Chaya is and grab her. In this case, she is in a dirt lot behind the building, rehearsing a takedown with Master Sergeant Dov Levy's squad of twelve shooters. Virtually everyone else operational has already been scrambled out to the borders, to man the walls against whatever is coming.

While she dashes back inside to take the call, Dov continues leading the drills, based on their limited intel on the Iranian target site. When Chaya returns, she's got a laptop and satellite modem jammed under her arm. Breathless, she pulls Dov aside.

"I've got an update," she says. "We're out of time. We've got to get in the air – now."

Their team has everything they need to fight loaded up in their rucks. They shoulder them now and jog for the hangar, where the Stealth Hawk sits on the deck. It's also where its four-man crew is hiding out, wondering A) what the hell they're getting themselves into; and B) what their chain of command is going to think about it when they find out.

Chaya grabs her own ruck, rifle, and load-bearing vest.

At the last second, she turns on her heel and dashes back inside. "Meet you there!" she calls over her shoulder, then heads for Colonel Eshel's office. Inside, Eshel is with an IT guy, having a furious debate about pulling the whole camp's network out of the walls and starting over.

When Chaya gets his attention, she says, "I've got a mission, boss. And I need to take Dov's team with me to do it."

"What? Where?"

"I can't tell you. If I do, you'll forbid it. You'll probably arrest me. But I have a chance to help fix all this."

He looks up at her with exhausted eyes, but not without humor behind them.

"Go with God," he says, waving a hand tiredly, meaning: *Do what you want.* She generally does anyway.

She salutes, turns, and dashes back outside.

* * *

"Extra fuel?" she asks one of the helo crew chiefs, over the noise of the engines and rotors.

"You're sitting on it," he says, stabbing a finger down toward the enormous fuel bladder underfoot.

Chaya was unaware that's where it went. She hopes, more ardently now, that this stealth thing really works. Because if they take significant ground fire or AA, Chaya and her team will basically be sitting inside a very large Molotov cocktail.

But this stealth version of the MH-60 Black Hawk, with its rivetless skin, smooth control surfaces, swept stabilizers, covered tail rotor, and silver-loaded infrared suppression paint finish, is nearly invisible to radar. You can't make a helo as stealthy as a fixed-wing airplane because of all its moving parts. But on the other hand, a helo is generally operating at low altitude in ground clutter, and is not an easy target to start with.

The flight plan Chaya put together with the pilots has them staying within 100 feet of the deck when they cross the Iranian border. The problem with this plan is that it's not actually a deck – it's the surface of the earth, and it rises and falls and has things like trees and power lines jutting out of it.

The helo taxis out of the hangar on its four wheels, increases power, and lifts off while accelerating quickly. Even fully loaded, with the stealth skin and extra electronics, she is a fast, lean, powerful bird of prey.

Chaya plugs in the laptop to onboard power, fires up the sat modem, and checks comms. Rheinhardt's tech guy assured her they could still use the VPN in the air. And from what she gathers, the D-boys will be bringing a whole cyberwar operation on board one of their birds… And, sure enough, not long after she gets it online, the laptop flashes an alert at her.

It's Rheinhardt. He's reporting that the rules of the game have changed. Again.

Now that he has a couple of non-task-saturated minutes to
rub together, Mike is trying to fulfill a tasking that Rheinhardt
gave him last night: find out who is counter-hacking them.

It isn't Tucker, who is a shooter, albeit a supremely versa-
tile and dangerous one. And it isn't the Iranians themselves,
who Mike feels certain aren't nearly that good.

So the question is: who's the talent?

The more he can learn about his shadowy adversary,
the better his chances of taking him down when it counts.
Real pros won't leave a lot of loose ends. But real pros
also generally have tell-tales and trademarks. And Mike
knows what to look for, based on the things he does himself. It's like a sniper duel: you squint very hard, looking
for the guy who looks like you, is trying not to be seen,
and is trying to spot you, too.

Mike swats away sweat droplets to keep them off the
keyboard, as he types frenziedly. He's in the zone. He doesn't
even notice when Bleep sits down next to him.

"I'm mission complete with Sultan," Bleep says. "What's
all this?"

"A snipe hunt," Mike says. During the entire conversation that follows he never once looks away from his screen,
nor pauses typing for more than a second or two.

"Target?"

"Whoever the hacking talent is that Tucker brought in. *That's* the guy who killed B Squadron. The one who made it possible. I'm gonna find and fix him."

Bleep has so far displayed no grief over what happened to his teammates. Other than getting the names of the other two known survivors, and an update on the rest (nothing yet), he's not addressed it at all. If it turns out that most of his brothers are dead, he'll deal with that down the road. Today he's still operational. And he has to remain effective. But he does tense up when Mike names the target hacker as the one responsible for it.

"How do I help?" he says.

* * *

Forty minutes of team hacking later, Mike whoops. "Gotcha, motherfucker."

"Where?" Bleep says, leaning in.

"Here," Mike says, tabbing through the output of his scan. "A secure VPN – low down to the network, an off-the-grid comms channel. Just like the one I did for Rheinhardt and Chaya. I knew it. There's always a symmetry to this shit. Watchers watching watchers."

Bleep follows his finger. "Comms for their command element maybe? Tucker?"

Mike nods. "If I were a betting man, I'd say so."

"Encrypted, of course. What grade, though?"

"Hang on… Wow. Blowfish, at 224-bits."

Bleep whistles. "No known effective cryptanalysis. Never been cracked."

Mike smiles. "*Understood* to be uncrackable. But only if you don't happen to have access to the largest concentration of computing power on Earth…"

"NSA," Bleep says, wide-eyed, watching him flip to a remote shell.

"Yep. And I can use not only their supercomputer array, but also their secret fast factoring algorithm. With the two together, I can use a second-order differential analysis to crack Blowfish. Which I am… doing… now…"

"Man. I see why you get paid the big bucks."

"I get paid what a WO1 with about five seconds of service time does."

"Figure of speech. Obviously you're doing it for the chicks."

Within another two minutes they've decrypted five messages. Four are of no immediate or obvious value. But the fifth has Mike and Bleep *sprinting* out the hangar doors into the early-morning light.

* * *

They find Rheinhardt on the parade ground, supervising the taping down of floor plans, finished bits of which the Iraqis are already assaulting through.

"Priority highest," Mike says, all but side-tackling him. "Signal intercept from Iranian systems." He shoves a tablet in Rheinhardt's face. Rheinhardt reads a single paragraph of text.

```
Updated details for rendezvous. New loca-
tion: 430 nautical miles NNW of original
```

```
grid coords. New time: approx 1230hrs
AST. Wait on station. Rendezvous now not
with the Tuman but with MV Mavi Marmara.
Cross-load the Meteors as per instruc-
tion. Proceed to launch point as per.
End.
```

Rheinhardt meets Mike's eyes, then Bleep's, his eyes slitted. Working it out.

"Meteors?" Mike asks.

"Yeah. You'd say *shahab* in Arabic."

"As in Shahab-3?"

"As in the missile. Medium-range ballistic. Operational range of about two thousand kilometers." Rheinhardt speaks quietly and calmly now. "It all makes sense. Not ground-based. It's going to be a sea launch. And we've got four and a half hours, plus an unknown amount of time for them to maneuver into launch range. And then it's all over."

"A sea launch," says Bleep. "What? For deniability?"

"Exactly. It's probably a bunch of Hamas guys on a frigate. Israel won't be able to just nuke Gaza in response, even if they still could. And if they can't prove Iran was behind it, they can't nuke them either." Rheinhardt shifts his gaze to Mike. "Go back inside and make me a map that shows every inch of blue water within two thousand clicks of Tel Aviv."

"Roger that."

As Mike leaves, Bleep says to Rheinhardt, "Your guy's good."

"Yeah."

"But so's his opponent. I wouldn't count on too many more breaks like that one."

"Understood," Rheinhardt says. He then turns to face Bleep. "Hey. You said you know something about programming warhead guidance chips."

"Yeah, a bit."

"Walk with me."

As the two Delta men step away, the already thin light dims further. Both men look up to the horizon. That storm front, which Rheinhardt promised the aviators, is definitely moving in now. The sky is a gunmetal haze of engorged clouds. The wind picks up and sweeps the parade ground behind them, chilling the sweat of the nearly 200 men now rehearsing upon it.

Rheinhardt makes their walk in the direction of the hangar, because after this conversation, he's got a thousand things to do there, starting with updating Chaya. They hit Mike's station to get back on the jerry-rigged comms channel. When they get there, Mike has got that map.

"Two thousand kilometers in every direction from Tel Aviv," Mike says, "is a lot of water."

Rheinhardt leans in. "But it's all in the Med, the Red Sea, or the Persian Gulf. Hey, can you get me Chaya on the line?"

Rheinhardt studies the map. "The message intercept indicated a new rendezvous '430 nautical miles north-northwest of original coords,' right? That's about 800 kilometers. And the Med's only 650km from top to bottom at its eastern edge. There's almost no such thing as 800km NNW of anywhere in the Med. Ditto the Gulf."

Bleep leans in and squints. "So that leaves the Red Sea. It's angled the right way."

Rheinhardt takes the phone from Mike.

"Chaya. Eric. You're airborne? Listen carefully, because we've got new intel – a possible partial fix on the launch site. It's going to be from a sea-borne platform. We think in the Red Sea. And we think from a passenger ship called the *Mavi Marmara*... No, actually I'm not."

Rheinhardt's expression betrays little as he listens.

"No. Give us the frequency. We can find and fix it. You have to trust me. And you *have* to take the Iranian AA station, or we're all gonna be meat confetti. Stand by for now. Out."

He puts the phone down on the desk. Mike and Bleep look at him expectantly.

"The *Mavi Marmara* was the ship that tried to run the Gaza blockade in 2010. Israeli commandos boarded it, got attacked with pipes and hoses, and had to shoot some guys."

"Yeah, I remember," Bleep says.

"Chaya says, and I quote, 'You don't think we risked boarding that boat just to get our asses stomped?' They put a tracker on it. GPS, with satellite comms. It's been there all this time."

"Holy shit."

"Yeah. But with all their mil-com systems scrambled, she can't track it. It's supposed to be talking to their Ofek-9 mil-sats. But she can't even talk to Jerusalem down the road."

"We've got satellites," Mike says.

"I've heard that. Can you task something over the Red Sea?"

"I think so. What frequency is the transmitter on?"

"X-band, 11.725 gigahertz."

"But what do we do when we find it?"

Rheinhardt exhales. "I think we're going to have to go get it. Chaya's already in the air – and Sayeret is still struggling to bring up comms with anyone in their chain of command. They're making unencrypted calls direct to the personal cell phones of guys across the country. And even those are getting dropped. They've been sending out runners. Basically, they're massively degraded."

Mike says, "Okay. So can't we just task some air, off a carrier strike group or something, to go blow the shit out of this boat?"

"Not really. First of all, if you blow the shit out of a nuclear weapon of this design, there's a chance it'll go boom." He leans in to the map display. "And if it goes boom in the Red Sea, we could irradiate the Straits of Tiran – Israel's only southern shipping route. Or if it's further south, we'd nuke Mecca. Which would probably mean global holy war."

"Yeah. I suppose that would be a pretty huge Kilo Mike Alpha to the Muslim world."

"Secondly, even if they don't go off, they go to the bottom… and we won't know for sure we got them. The thing about nuclear weapons is that they have to be secured. And, finally, I'm not sure I'm in a position to task a shithouse, never mind a carrier strike group. If I call Havering to ask, he's going to tell me to eat a dick. Being as that's what I last told him."

Bleep nods. "It's a toss-up when you leave the beaten path. Many are called, few chosen."

"No, we're going to have to go get them ourselves." Rheinhardt puts his hand on Mike's shoulder. "That boat should be putting out a quarter-hourly signal, clean and strong. Get me at least an eight-digit grid reference. Bleep, you're on me…"

* * *

The two of them find Homer and his SEALs out on the parade ground, rehearsing their takedown of the Palais du Senat.

"New tasking," Rheinhardt says, pulling Homer aside. "How would you feel about jumping from 20,000 feet over the Red Sea with one of your SDVs – then motoring in underwater and taking down a 90-meter passenger ship with nukes on it. In broad daylight."

"Sounds good," Homer says. "We've got an SDV all packed up and with a cargo canopy practically already attached. Ten-minute prep. Enemy strength on the ship?"

"No idea."

"And my team for the job?"

"Just your team. The four of you. I can also give you Bleep. And a pilot."

"What are we flying?"

"Thought you might take our Gulfstream 650."

"Beautiful."

"So hit it. Wheels up as soon as you've got your gear on board. Oh, and we're going to have to get you exact target coords in the air."

"No problem." Homer nods and he and his guys head for the hangar at a trot. You've just got to love the *we'll-make-it-happen* SOF mindset.

Bleep gives Rheinhardt a bloodshot look.

"Well, go help them load out," Rheinhardt shoots back. "And try not to get killed in the takedown."

Bleep nods. "Okay, Bo. Good luck in Tehran. And I'll see you on the other side."

* * *

As Bleep trots off, Javier trots up, phone to his ear.

"Bad news, top," he says, slipping the phone into his vest. "General Stamis is inbound. ETA sixty mikes. And he's gonna shit anvils if he gets here and sees all of this. He'll lock everything down. We won't be launching so much as a weather balloon."

Rheinhardt exhales mournfully, then almost smiles. "Jesus, what's going to happen first – we all get busted down to private and RTU'd... or Iran and its proxies conquer the Middle East?"

Javier smiles in return. "Both of the 130s are on the ground and fueled up. Ditto the helos. We could use more rehearsal time. But that's always true."

"Yeah," Rheinhardt says. "I suppose there's no time like the present."

"Especially when it's now or never."

"Okay. Get everyone loaded up and moving out."

The sky, now a bruising gray and seemingly about 60 feet above their heads, opens up and the first few fat warm drops hit the tarmac. No lightning yet.

But there's an ominous rumbling on the horizon.

Uncle BJ walks up with Rheinhardt's rifle in one hand, and assault suit and tactical vest in the other. The suit has already got a green armband tied around the sleeve.

"You might be needing these."

"Almost forgot. What, you mean I have to go on the ground and trade lead with people?"

"It's your party."

"Yeah. And I've got to confess it's starting to feel like a one-way mission."

BJ half-sits on the edge of the table. "Life's kind of a one-way mission. Anyway, you got somewhere else to be?"

Operators swarm all around them, carrying or rolling crates of ammo and gear out of the hangar and to the helipad out back, or the runway down the road. Others are filling any empty pouches with mags and grenades, pulling straps tight, and heading out to the aircraft themselves.

Captain Miller trots up. He's in full battle rattle, plus a static-line parachute rig on his back and an additional leg bag full of combat load.

BJ says, "You look like you're ready to jump out of a perfectly good airplane."

Miller smiles. "Only two things fall from the sky. Manna from heaven and airborne Rangers. My men are ready to jump in and fight."

"Rangers lead the way," Rheinhardt says, standing and saluting. "Good luck, Captain."

Miller returns the salute, turns on his heel, and heads out. He moves pretty smartly for a guy who currently weighs a hundred pounds more than his body weight. He'll be the last of his men to board the MC-130. And the first one out into the sky over Tehran.

Rheinhardt suddenly seems slightly amused by this whole thing. "You know," he says to BJ, "if we do this, and fail, our careers are over. That's if we survive."

"And *you* know that if we do it and *succeed*, our careers are also probably over."

"I was retiring, anyway." He looks up at his friend. "Why, do you think we might survive?"

"Ha! Are you kidding? The only difference between this and the Alamo is that Davy Crockett didn't have to fight his way in first."

The two look up as Spider gives them a wave from the entrance. He and his team are kitted up and heading out into the rain.

Now it's only the two of them left.

"C'mon," Rheinhardt says. "Too much reflection is no good for unstoppable badasses like you. The reason you can't be killed is it never occurs to you that it's possible."

* * *

As the two brothers leave the safety of the hangar and the base behind them, Rheinhardt reflects that they've had plenty of hard losses, many of them very recent, and still raw. But it doesn't make any sense to dwell on them.

In their line of work, violent death is only a matter of fate and chance. Maybe today would be their day. And maybe it wouldn't. But until their last breath left them, they would focus on two things. Achieving the mission. And not letting down their brother warriors.

On shuddering transport planes, wheeling helicopters, and one executive jet, 230 very skilled and extraordinarily audacious men get in the air. Only some of whom would be coming back.

If any.

"What?!" Chaya hopes she's misheard Rheinhardt, with the rotor and wind noise.

But she hasn't misheard. She signs off, unplugs her headset from the laptop and back into ICS, and motions to Dov to listen in while she talks to the pilots up front.

"Tactical update," she half-shouts. "The Americans are having to launch early. We now have exactly twenty-six minutes and… ten seconds to get to the Iranian AA station, take it down, and get their code uploaded."

"Say again," says the pilot, a seasoned IDF aviator who's been flying spec-ops missions for 13 years. *"Was that twenty-six minutes?"*

"Affirmative! At that time, the American planes and helos will cross into Iranian airspace. And if the AA net is still up and running, they will be blasted out of the sky. So, basically, our slush time is gone."

Dov is smiling at her across the dim cabin. Dov is always smiling.

This is funny? Chaya thinks.

Dov and the other eleven commandos sit up against their rucks around the inside edges of the airframe, weapons jutting up between their legs. The whole bird is already shaking and rattling, from their very high airspeed and from the dark and menacing weather front they are flying straight into.

Somebody flips on one of the red overhead combat lights, as the ambient daylight in the cabin drops to nearly nothing.

"Be advised," the pilot says. *"I am already using that slush time. I've burnt most of it to plot the safest course across Iraqi and Iranian airspace. We've been dodging AA, military, and civilian air control sites."*

Shit. "Why didn't you tell me this?"

"SOP, Major. You tell us where and when. I decide how."

"Can you meet this new deadline? Belay that. You've got to beat this new deadline."

She almost fancies she can hear the pilot sigh out loud. *"I'm going to open it up and put it on the deck. Hang on to your privates back there."*

With this last sentence, he switches to English to make his pun work.

* * *

The other problem with air infiltration, and indeed with stealth technology, is that air defense radar and missiles are not the only things that can fix and destroy an aircraft. Anybody on the ground with a rifle, an RPG, or (God save them) a Stinger missile can take a potshot. And, on any given day, anybody can get lucky. The best way to mitigate the threat of ground fire is to fly *even lower*. The closer to the deck, the more you come out of nowhere and the faster you zip over enemies' heads. But, the lower you fly, the faster the trees and power lines comes out of nowhere at *you*.

It sort of comes down to which form of violent death you find scarier.

The IDF Stealth Hawk is just crossing the Iranian frontier, when the pilot puts the nose down and twists the throttle close to its extreme limit. They drop to fifty feet as pelting rain starts slashing the windshield and airframe. Winds buffet the bird, causing it to ascend and drop in increments that are way too big a fraction of their total altitude.

Both crew chiefs have epoxied themselves to their side windows, fingers on minigun triggers, necks on swivels, spotting for ground obstructions and enemy emplacements. They're not far inside Iran before they encounter both.

Chaya listens to the crew's chatter on ICS.

"I've got vehicles hunkered down, ten o'clock!"

"Shifting right."

The bird lurches, along with stomachs, and loose equipment.

"Tracers!" both crew chiefs shout simultaneously.

But the pilots can see perfectly well the angry green hornets snapping up at them, from a heavy machine gun down below. They bank again, hard enough to knock over *sitting* people in the back – then drop another twenty feet closer to the trees and ground features that could transform them at any instant into a tumbling fireball.

Chaya checks her GPS, then her watch. "You need to fly faster," she says.

But she can tell they're already twisting the guts out of the engine, doing over 160 knots.

Chaya switches her headphone jack again and gets an update from Mike. She switches back and says, "The Americans say, 'If we can't be there in ten minutes, don't bother showing up. Because they'll all be dead.'"

What the pilots hadn't told Chaya is that they have continued following their zig-zaggy waypoints, mainly to dodge a full armored division Iran has deployed near the border.

Now the two men look at each other across the cockpit.

"Fuck the waypoints," they both say in unison.

* * *

They set the nose straight for their final grid coordinates.

Then drop to *twenty* feet off the deck.

And they charge.

They can see tracers coming at them through the dark air of the storm. But what they can't see are the 4 to 14 regular rounds between each of the tracers. They also can't hear the firing over the engine and the storm. But soon, the rounds plunking into the helo's skin are perfectly audible.

And that's when the great sea of the Iranian armored division spreads out beneath them. They are so low and hot, they come on it in a single second – a sprawling expanse of main battle tanks, APCs, trucks, and artillery. There are also hundreds of Iranian soldiers standing around, huddling out of the rain – then looking up, ducking their heads and, finally, firing their weapons into the sky.

The helo's non-retractable landing wheels are nearly shearing off tank antennas.

The small-arms fire ramps up – but they are blasting over so quickly, and are so unexpected, that none of the Iranians can track.

And just like that they are past it.

They blast over a small river, scattering a flock of some kind of waterfowl. The pilots bite their lips, praying that they don't suck the birds into their engines, causing a flameout and crash. They then blast up over the opposite shore, nearly decapitating a donkey.

In the back, the twelve men and one woman grip the walls and straps with bloodless knuckles. Chaya keeps re-swallowing her stomach. Dov is still smiling – but in sheer terror now. His knees grip his assault rifle and both hands are up over his head clinging to nylon webbing.

It's been like a barrel ride over the falls – in a shooting gallery. And nor is it over. The white dish of the AA facility looms in the distance through the wet and dark. And a second later, so do 100-foot-high power lines between them and it, directly ahead.

"I'm going under!" the pilot shouts.

"Negative!" the co-pilot shouts back, pointing to lower levels of line strung beneath.

The bird groans and stretches as the pilot yanks the cyclic into his groin, while frantically pulling pitch, desperately climbing. Everyone is pressed into the back of the cabin. The crew chief on Chaya's side hangs on to his minigun while his feet lift off the deck and point toward the back. The other tumbles ass over teakettle, halted only by his safety harness. The whole airframe lurches to a 45-degree angle as it clears the lines with inches to spare.

At the apex, they all briefly become weightless, and ICS goes hectic again.

"Missile! Missile!"

It's from the air defense station itself. Someone there has got a visual on them.

The pilots go evasive, rolling the bird hard to left and diving, while firing all of its counter-measures, flares and chaff. Gripped by madness and genius, out of time, out of luck, the pilot tries to combine missile evasion with his approach. Spotting the insertion site, he hauls the screaming helo around in a hard bank, then kicks the left rudder pedal, making the tail rotor spin like a weather vane.

The top of the building centers directly below them, as they come to a dead stop, the tips of the blades spinning inches above the radar dish.

And the laser-guided anti-air missile has almost completed its desperate bank, centripetal forces ripping at it, shrieking around toward them, coming in nearly head-on now.

Riding in the lead bird for the whole air armada are Rheinhardt and Mike, Spider and his para team, four C Squadron guys including Bishop, and one of the Air Force CCTs. The helo behind them holds two more four-man C Squadron teams, led by Javier and Bishop. Both birds are Ghost Hawks, the third generation stealth aircraft, and *not* available for export, even to Israel. Behind them are the four Iraqi SOF helos, the MC-130 turbo-prop plane with the Rangers aboard, and then the AC-130 Spectre.

Mike has brought along a whole mobile computing and comms infrastructure, with multiple satellite uplinks. He's set up in front, behind the pilots, and near the navigator's jump seat. After they land and the shooters leap into the fight, the helo will climb again and follow a wide track around the battlespace, through the skies over Tehran.

From there, Mike will manage comms, tech, and cyber-war, and try to tip the murderous odds against them in a favorable direction.

But as it turns out, things get murderous before they've even crossed the border.

* * *

Rheinhardt is in the front of the cabin, leaning over Mike and his IT center, shouting at him both through ICS and straight to his face.

"What do you mean, the Israelis burnt their slush time?!"

Mike adjusts his headset. "They've been flying evasively, avoiding ground fire."

"It's a fucking stealth bird. They should be able to fly where they like."

"They're making up the time. They can make it!"

"Chaya says they can make it?"

"I'm telling you, they'll make it."

"Because I either have to turn all these aircraft around right now and re-stage everything… or else fly across a defended frontier, hoping they take their target in time to save our asses."

"They'll make it!"

Rheinhardt gives Mike a look, then stalks back to the rear of the cabin.

He checks his watch and GPS.

"Hey, man," says Spider, who is kicking back on the bench with his legs sprawled out, and smacking gum. "What's going on?"

"Nothing," Rheinhardt says. "We're all going to die."

"So business as usual then."

Rheinhardt's anger breaks and he fights a smile. "I lied to the pilots. I told them the AA network was already down."

Spider says, "That wasn't very nice."

"They'll live."

Spider nods solemnly. "Maybe they will. And maybe they won't."

They both laugh and shake their heads as Rheinhardt sits and tries to relax.

* * *

It's only a few minutes later when Richie pops up in Rheinhardt's ear. He is not happy.

"We're getting painted, you son of a bitch."

Rheinhardt doesn't say anything.

"They shouldn't get a reading on US, but they'll damn well see the Hips and 130s… Hang on, the Spectre reports getting painted, too… Oh, FUCK. Now they report missile lock…"

Rheinhardt unbelts and rushes to the window on the port side. He's just in time to see the AC-130 Spectre, lumbering though the dark gray cloud of the storm, fire off a brilliant set of a dozen flares, six from each flank, a glorious fireworks display. It then goes evasive, lurching to the left and diving heavily out of the sky – a much less soothing sight.

Rheinhardt scrambles the rest of the length of the cabin, back to Mike's station.

Mike is frantically typing in a terminal window. He puts his hand up over his shoulder at Rheinhardt. Message received: *Shut the fuck up and leave me alone for a second.*

Seconds are literally all they have now.

Chaya actually uses her body, and body armor, to cover the computer on the desk before her. Rounds are coming through the windows, the open doorway, and the wall itself. She raises her head just enough to verify that the memory stick is still seated in the USB port.

Most of the Sayeret shooters in the room are prone, or taking cover behind desks. Dov however, is standing like David, firing directly over Chaya's head, first one direction, then the other. They're kind of surrounded. This is because they didn't have time to actually take down the facility – only to punch a hole straight to the heart of it.

They have taken the air defense control room.

If they can keep it, and keep from being overrun, the dozen of them can then push out and sweep clear the rest of this building, and the barracks next door. That's unless they're not already too late, and the Americans are all dead. In which case there won't be any point.

* * *

When the pilot spun the Stealth Hawk around on its tail, the incoming missile couldn't turn quickly enough. It blasted inches by them and smashed into the radar dish only a few meters beyond. The resulting explosion, though, nearly knocked them out of the sky.

The bird and everyone on it lurched forward, the nose angling groundward. The pilot battled the controls and leveled them out after the front edge of the whirling rotors actually clipped the rooftop.

Dropping it straight into a four-point landing on the gravel of the roof, he motioned at the co-pilot to take the controls. He then unbuckled himself and waded back into the cabin, bellowing at the stunned squad of soldiers to *"Get the fuck out of my helicopter! Fuck off! Go, go, go, go, go!"* while windmilling one arm toward the outside, sliding open the side door with the other.

Soldiers obey, and so out they spilled, sprawling, recovering, through the roof access door, tumbling down the stairs, Chaya second from the front, yelling, *"Get to the control room!"* and clutching the memory stick against the foregrip of her rifle.

The four duty officers of the Iranian Air Defense Command were too startled to need killing, so were just flex-cuffed and piled in the corner. But the rest of the 30-man garrison pretty quickly worked out that they were under attack, and responded.

Most of them are now riddling the control room with gunfire, oblivious to their guys inside.

And the ones who ran up to the roof only got off a handful of potshots at the Stealth Hawk, which was making for the horizon on one axis, and outer space on the other.

* * *

The fire is slacking off in the control room now, as Dov and his team push security out.

Chaya picks up her rifle from where she dropped it, and tries to develop some situational awareness. Until now, she's been focused on her one mission, which was getting that memory stick in that machine.

As it's been explained to her by the Delta techie, all of Iran's radar sites transmit their local data, via a nationwide microwave packet network, directly to their air defense mainframe at a hardened command post buried in the mountains. The executable file that Mike sent her would open up a hole for him to get into and shut down the whole network.

And he can keep it shut down – for just as long as no one comes back and kills the executable. So now all she and her team have to do is hold the place.

"You, Corporal!" she yells to a man holding the doorway. "You see this station? Kill anyone who approaches it. Die defending it. While you live, this memory stick stays in this USB port."

"Yes, ma'am," he says, and takes a knee in front of it, facing the door.

Chaya heads out to look for Dov. And to begin the work of barricading themselves in. Coordinating a fixed defense is not really something they spend a lot of their training time on. But, like all special operators, Chaya knows it's all about mindset – about figuring out how to be effective, regardless of circumstances. Sometimes you pick your missions.

And sometimes they come out of nowhere and pick you.

Mike lowers his hand and resumes typing in the near dark, Rheinhardt hunched over him. For four seconds there is only the sound of the rotors, engines and wind – and the keyboard.

Mike hits return.

Richie comes back on ICS. *"We're clean again. No radar, no missile lock. Nothing."*

Rheinhardt rushes back to the porthole. He actually sees the surface-to-air missile fly past where the Spectre was seconds ago. With no guidance, it blasts off into space.

"I've got it," Mike says. "Their whole AA net is down again. I own it."

Before Rheinhardt can respond, his headset speaks.

"Sergeant Major," Richie hisses through it. *"A goddamned word with you up front."*

Rheinhardt claps Mike on the back and heads off for his dressing-down.

However bad, it will be a lot better than being dead.

It's a small and austere room, the one where the trial is held. Only a dozen people attend. Then again, as Ali herself knows, only one of them really matters – the lone judge, robed and bearded, who now reads the verdict in quiet and menacing tones.

The Iranian Revolutionary Court is a special arm of the judiciary designed to try those suspected of blaspheming or trying to overthrow the government. Both of which categories Ali figures she falls comfortably into.

Trials here tend only to go on a few hours, or minutes, and the concept of the defense attorney is unknown. The kinds of offenses people get charged with include "spreading corruption on Earth," "insulting Islam and the mullahs," and "opposing the Islamic Revolution."

In Ali's case, the charges were "illegally entering Iran," "spying for the U.S.," and "bearing arms against the Islamic Revolution." For the first two, she might have gotten off with ten or twenty years of imprisonment. But the last one seals her fate.

The verdict and sentencing are rendered in Farsi, as was the entire trial. Ali understands enough to get the gist. When the factotum beside her leans over and explains in English that she is to be hanged at sundown, Ali's silent response is:

Yeah… that's not gonna happen.

***

On the long manacled walk back to her cell, she continues to clock the security procedures used in moving her around, and works out her tactical plan of action in pretty short order.

She figures her main chance will come either when they take her from her cell, or on the walk to the execution. That's when she will make her move. Worst case, she'll have to go for it up on the gallows. Maybe they'll even be filming it. Maybe it will even be broadcast live.

She's never forgotten the Italian security contractor Fabrizio Quattrocchi. Taken hostage by Islamist terrorists in Iraq, he was forced to dig his own grave, then kneel hooded beside it, waiting to be beheaded, the whole thing being captured on video.

But he didn't wait to be beheaded. Instead he yanked off his hood and shouted, "I'll show you how an Italian dies!" They were forced to shoot him in the back. What was supposed to be an Islamist propaganda film became its opposite – an eternal symbol of defiance to the Salafist head hackers.

But, whether it's in the cell, in the hallway, or at the gallows, Ali intends with deadly seriousness to take as many of these bastards with her as super-humanly possible. There's going to be a very nasty fight in very close quarters. She is definitely going to enable a whole bunch of these guys to live a lifetime in an instant – their last.

And she absolutely will go down not mewling, but fighting.

ON BOARD DELTA GULFSTREAM 650
20,000 FEET OVER NORTHERN SAUDI ARABIA
10:52:33 AST 07 APR

The life of a Navy SEAL, beginning with their initial training and selection, with its infamous "Hell Week" and 80% attrition rate, is one long epic of training, deployment, austerity, and brutally hard work. That's why SEALs are the most devastatingly capable maritime commando force in history.

It's also probably why Homer and his guys can't help luxuriating a little on the Gulfstream.

Delta owns and operates the executive jet to move small teams around fast. But they didn't exactly rip out all the luxury appointments. Suddenly these naval special warfare combatant swimmers are wondering if they joined the wrong branch of service. But when somebody starts making a cappuccino, Homer decides enough is enough.

"Hey, Starbucks. If the Iranians get these fucking missiles off... *Israel goes down.*"

The guy frothing milk is Rip, a relatively young, good-natured, and new operator in DEVGRU's Red Squadron. He puts down his pitcher and heads back toward the planning table.

"And be advised that we are the only five guys on the planet tasked with stopping this." He knew this would get their attention. Most guys who make it as SEALs secretly want to be caped superheroes and save the world.

Virtually the entire back half of the plane is filled to the roof with weapons, explosives, ammo, scuba suits, air tanks, rebreathers, parachute rigs, and not to mention the giant and bulky Seal Delivery Vehicle (SDV). After clambering around all of this, Rip rejoins Homer, Bleep and the two other SEALs, Tiger and Murph. These are also Team Six SEALS, both with Senior Chief Petty Officer ratings, and both extremely veteran, grizzled, and absurdly skilled and deadly.

Tiger is large for a SEAL, six-two and 210 pounds. (Even more than D-Boys, SEALs tend to be average size. Pulling yourself through sand and surf is another activity that does not favor huge men.) He's got bulging muscles, a square head and jaw, and a sandy crewcut. He grew up in a scary neighborhood in Pittsburgh, then enlisted in the Navy about five seconds after high school. He has seven operational deployments with SEAL Team Eight, including years of fighting in the mountains of Afghanistan, before joining DEVGRU.

Murph is smaller, with curly dark hair, soft brown eyes, and an easy grin. He's from an Irish family in Boston, with a ribald sense of humor not to everyone's exact taste. Before getting the call from Team Six, he served as senior training chief at a Special Boat Team. He's also a fully trained hospital corpsman, able to deal with anything that combat can do to a human body.

Homer pauses and pins each man with his gaze. "We've also got…" and he checks his Seiko Automatic Divers watch, "…three hours and thirty-six minutes before they get the nuclear weapons on board. After that, they could be within range to launch at *any time*." He looks to Bleep, who is still wearing what he went to war in Iran in, and sitting slightly to the side. "Update on our target coords?"

"They're coming," Bleep says. "Mike says they're coming, they're coming." Bleep hasn't slept in several days, and not since his last major battle and overland exfiltration. So far it's not impairing his performance. But it is making him a little weird.

"Okay." Homer nods and looks back to the tabletop. "Okay, obviously, this is gonna be an underway. We've got blueprints for the target vessel, courtesy of our friends in the Israeli Navy." He smoothes them out, as they spill over the edge of the table. "The *Mavi Marmara* is a twin-motor-driven, 93-meter passenger ship. She maxes out at only 10 knots – which is excellent because our SDV can do 18. She has three decks above the bow, crews 25 in normal operation, with capacity for 1000 passengers."

"And how many on board today?" Tiger asks. This is of keen interest due to there being only four of them, plus Bleep. The four SEALs of the famous Operation Red Wings in Afghanistan took on about 100 Taleban. So there would certainly be bragging rights in going up against 1,000. Then again, only one of the Red Wings guys survived.

"Unknown," Homer says. "I've got a request in for sat or drone surveillance. But as I think you know, today's op is a little bit… deniable."

Murph chimes in. "I also seem to recall that Shayetet 13 kind of got their asses kicked when they boarded this boat." Shayetet 13 is the premier Israeli naval commando unit, which was enforcing the Gaza blockade.

Homer nods seriously. "The world was watching that time – and so they went in with paintball guns and pepper spray. Gentlemen, we have no paintball equipment on this op. And we will be shooting to kill."

An hour into their assault planning, Bleep claps his hands. He's been monitoring his laptop non-stop, and reads from it now. "They've sent us an eight-digit grid reference for the boat." Eight digits means it's accurate within 100 meters. He pauses while he plays with maps. "Southern part of the Red Sea. Off the Eritrean coast. And a vector: still heading SW, making 10 knots."

Bleep pauses to run some calculations. "Okay... the good news is that when they hit their rendezvous, they will be outside of range to fire the missile at Israel. They'll have to sail north first. That means we can let them make the transfer before we take them down."

"Good news, gentlemen," Homer says. "We don't have to fight the Iranian Navy."

"The bad news is... at their top speed, they'll be only 45 minutes sailing from launch range. That's a tiny window. Not much time to jump, swim in, and take them down."

"No problem," Homer says. "Tiny windows are our specialty."

That's when the pilot comes on over the cabin loudspeaker.

"Uh," he says, then just clicks off.

Before he can elaborate, Homer and Bleep head up to the flight deck. "What's up?" Homer says.

"That was JSOC on the horn," he says. "I've been ordered back to Bragg. Under pain of not just court martial, but firing squad."

"Are they serious?" Homer says.

"Completely."

"We got our target coords for you," Bleep says, holding up his laptop.

The pilot gives him his best, and most unmistakable, *Are-you-a-fucking-idiot?* look.

"So what now?" Homer says.

The pilot glances over at the senior SEAL's chest combat rigging. When Homer doesn't respond, he arches both eyebrows and sort of jerks his head. A look of comprehension washes over Homer. He draws his side arm and levels it at the pilot.

"Captain," he says. "Kindly fly the plane to these grid coordinates."

"You're all crazy," the pilot deadpans, his tone completely flat. "Maniacs. Don't shoot. Don't shoot. Okay, okay. I'll do it."

He swivels back to his console and begins calculating their new heading.

Still facing away, waving his hand over his shoulder, he mutters, "Well, don't just stand there, you dipshits, go get ready to jump."

This time, Mike goes to the back of the cabin to roust Rheinhardt. "They've sentenced Ali." He swallows dryly. "She's going to be executed."

Rheinhardt doesn't visibly react. "When?"

"Sunset. That's 19:36."

"Okay. Doesn't matter, Mike. We'll either have her out, or all be dead ourselves, long before sundown. Are you ready up front?"

"I think so."

On Rheinhardt's signal, just before insertion, Mike is going to cut off all electrical grid power across Tehran. Little Bird gunships are going to attack, and hopefully destroy, backup generators at most of their target sites. Mike will also take down virtually all military communications across the entire country – he hopes.

The red interior lights flash. Rheinhardt looks to the nearest crew chief, who flashes five fingers at him. Five-minute warning. The nose of the bird dips into the storm, everyone's ears popping as they shed altitude. And then the shooting starts.

All of it seemingly aimed at them.

* * *

"Big sky, little bullet," Rheinhardt says to Richie. He's leaning into the cockpit, articulating an old expression that pilots use to give themselves courage when flying through fire.

"No," Richie says, wrestling the controls. "Those look like pretty big fucking bullets."

They're taking a startling amount of ground fire on approach, much more than anticipated. Kazemi Garrison seems like it's loaded for bear. Moreover, it seems very much as if the defenders were just waiting for them. The question quickly becomes whether continuing the insertion as planned is suicidal.

Out through the cockpit glass, in the storm's slashing winds and heavy sheets of rain, and the additional storm of small arms and AA fire, Rheinhardt can see the Little Birds beginning their gun runs. Their mission here is to suppress enemy personnel and gun emplacements around the landing zone.

The Little Birds are attacking in pairs, the muzzles of their miniguns flashing red and blue, rockets streaking out of the pods on opposite sides in slashes of flame and fat pillows of smoke. After zooming in suicidally close to their targets, blasting away the whole time, they break left and right, looping back around in a butterfly pattern, then joining up again for another attack run.

But whatever's shooting at the Ghost Hawk has definitely not been suppressed. From where they are sitting, the LZ looks *magma* hot. And they've still got some seriously deadly air to descend through to get to it.

"*Facilis descensus Averno*," Rheinhardt says, clapping Richie on the shoulder.

"Huh?"

"Virgil. 'It is easy to go down into Hell.'"

"Wonderful! Fucking wonderful. You overeducated asshole."

Rheinhardt slaps him again, then heads back to the rear.

* * *

Thirty seconds later, lights begin flashing above the cockpit. The Missile Warning Receiver (MRW) begins an implacable, zombie-like wailing. The decoy flares blast out of the fuselage like Roman candles.

At this point, Rheinhardt's starting to wonder what the goddamn point of stealth is. He also knows that by now the MWR will have detected the incoming missile's thermal signature and shown the pilots the direction it's coming from. They'll be going into a scripted series of evasion tactics, but they'll have to perform them fast, because the missile's probably moving about Mach 2.

No sooner has Rheinhardt thought this, than the big aircraft twists into a near vertical corkscrew dive. All the shooters in back are suddenly lying on their sides, first one then the other, as the helo spirals in, the men only kept from flying across the cabin by their safety harnesses.

As the cabin flips over, Rheinhardt briefly shares a G-force-pancaked look with Spider. It says, unmistakably, *Okay, now we're all REALLY going to die.*

Within a few rotations, no one knows which way is up and their brains are trying to make a getaway from their skulls. The shrieking of the engines and the MWR only increase the Seventh-Circle-of-Hell effect. Most of the shooters have been in this boat, or one like it, before. Mike Brown hasn't. He feels like he's participating in some horrifying and lethal roller coaster accident. Also, bullets are flecking through the thin fuselage now. Though that seems strangely like the least of their problems.

The world continues spinning, the buildings of downtown Tehran flipping past the porthole glass, as Richie struggles to keep the 12-ton aircraft in the air, while basically dropping it out of the sky. He pushes the cyclic forward and drops the collective, steepening their nosedive. Then, without warning, the missile lights and siren cut out completely.

And the helo levels off, inflicting even more severe G-forces on the people inside. And then it settles, two seconds later, inexplicably gently, onto solid ground.

The side door rattles open. Beyond it is a majestic gray stone gate.

And soldiers with AKs are running out of it, through the rain, and straight toward them, firing from their shoulders and hips, some of the rounds flecking off the fuselage – and others coming straight into the cabin and pinging off the walls.

Captain Miller stands up, squat-pressing his overloaded frame up off the bench. The MC-130 turbo-prop aircraft is shaking like a runaway subway car, partly from the fury of the storm. This is nothing new for the Rangers.

For them there's not yet any flak or other ground fire from downtown. As promised, the nationwide AA network is out of action, and the Iranians seem to have no idea the MC-130 is inbound. And when they bank in over the city, no one on the ground can see them through the extremely heavy and low cloud cover.

They'll be jumping from 500 feet. This means no reserve chutes. If your primary doesn't open at that altitude, you'll only have 5.6 seconds to worry about it anyway.

The red light flashes the five-minute warning.

Facing down the four ranks of men, using hand signals, Miller stands 'em up, has them check out the man in front, then clip onto the static lines that run down the center of the cabin. He then hauls open one jump door, while his Company First Sergeant does the same on the other side.

Stinging rain and shearing wind zip inside on the slipstream.

When the light goes from red to green, Miller turns and hurls himself out the door. The First Sergeant does the same on the other side. The men follow, their shrinking columns like depleting magazines of ammunition, feeding into the breach of an Airborne Ranger gun.

Two ranks of opening canopies trail across the sky, but in cloud so heavy virtually none are visible to the others nor, until it is too late, to the defenders on the ground below. When they do finally appear, like angels out of the whirlwind, above the downtown garrison of the Iranian Revolutionary Guard, coming in fast and mean, no one is even looking up for them.

They begin to land, as close to the parade ground as they can manage with their steering lines in this wind. Hitting the ground and rolling, they release their risers, the soaked chutes rolling over and blowing around, charge their weapons, and head to their initial rally points.

For 1st and 2nd Platoons, this will be the north and south edges of the central parade ground, from whence they will move out and overrun the garrison. For 3rd Platoon, who drew the less tough but more exposed assignment, they will rally outside the front gates. From there, they will dash down the road to take down the Ministry of Intelligence and Security (MOIS), the regime's secret police.

As Rangers splash through the rain in multiple directions, not a shot has yet been fired.

* * *

The four Iraqi spec-ops Mi-17 "Hips" also stay above the cloud cover on their way into the sky over Tehran. The four birds fly in a wedge formation until they hit downtown, then split off at curving tangents, the pilots flying by instrument and GPS to their four closely situated but separate target sites. It's a testament to the training and skills of the Iraqi pilots that their wheels touch pavement within seconds of one another.

The first is in the front courtyard of the Palais du Senat, home of the Assembly of Experts.

The second is down the block, in the middle of the road that runs in front of the hulking government office building that holds the Guardian Council.

The third is around the corner, in the back courtyard of the government ministry that is home to state television, radio, and online.

And the fourth, landing a few seconds after the others, comes to rest smack in the middle of Meidan Sepah – the open and central square anchoring the whole government district.

First off this last helo is Uncle BJ Johnson.

In his black assault suit, festooned with ammo, pistols, and grenades, holding his big 7.62mm SOF Combat Assault Rifle (SCAR) with one huge hand, cheek bulging with chewing tobacco, blue eyes scanning all angles and corners, he looks like some Phoenician or Macedonian Emperor Warlord, coming in at the head of his legions, first and worst of the destroyers in the train of destruction he brings.

The 25 ISOF operators who spill off behind him, and who push out a security perimeter to the edges of the park, will act as a QRF and flexible reserve. This operation doesn't have a lot of manpower to spare. But flexibility is life. And BJ's team will go where things are worst – and where a quick injection of sharp force might tip disaster into survival.

Or maybe even success.

* * *

Egle Markunas is also scanning the angles and corners of Tehran's streets from above. She is sitting on the outside of a helicopter, the Little Bird MH-6, which hardly has any inside to it. Two daredevil 160th pilots sit hunched over the controls behind the bird's insect-eye-like chin bubble. And along two benches on the outside, with nothing between them and the ground but a nylon harness, sit four Delta operators.

There are three of these Little Bird "Lifts," each ferrying a four-man C-Squadron team, darting and buzzing into downtown Tehran like a miniature swarm. The complete exposure of the passengers to a hostile environment says something about the confidence of the guys who go in this way – and about the devastating effects of speed, surprise, and violence of action.

The twelve veteran operators straddling the three birds are completely exposed to the storm. But they have all done this routine many times before. As they infil, descending and streaking over the city blocks, they coldly survey the streets, tabulating targets, noting enemy firing positions both actual and potential. They decide on rally points, strong points, and exfiltration routes as they go. They miss nothing.

Within thirty seconds of breaking through the cloud cover, they are on target.

The first two birds set down lightly, twenty meters apart, on adjacent rooftops. The first building is the urban barracks of the Ansar-ol-Mahdi Corps – the elite, secretive force within the IRG tasked with protection of the Supreme Leader.

The second rooftop is the Office of the Supreme Leader himself.

Egle hops off the second bird with her three comrades and jogs toward the rooftop stairwell door, her assault rifle in one hand and an enormous set of bolt cutters in the other. The four of them are going to dive straight into the belly of the Islamic Revolution in Iran.

And they are going to try and seize its beating heart.

* * *

The third Little Bird, which breaks away as the first two descend, skims four blocks to the east, until it reaches the building that houses the Expediency Discernment Council of the System. After they set down, they too will swarm down inside and suppress the onsite security force, ideally in the first minute of the fight.

They will then try to locate and detain the 28 mullahs who make up the council.

And, if they're really lucky, one of them will be Mir-Hossein Moussavi – the artist, architect, and reformist politician who had the 2009 election stolen from him, sparking massive protests against the regime. He's also been a wearer of the revolutionary green banner, and with luck can be convinced to loft it again.

For the convincing, there is a fifth passenger on this Little Bird, strapped down behind the operators, wearing an ill-fitting Delta assault suit, clinging for dear life, wondering what in good God's name he's gotten himself into. It is Dr. Azad Sultan, nuclear physicist, American spy, short-term expatriate – and, with a bit more luck, once-and-future dissident leader. He's coming back to home soil in a way he never quite imagined, but one which might perhaps prove triumphant.

It will probably either be that, or fatal.

* * *

Throughout all this, the AH-6 Little Bird "Guns" have been raining rockets and minigun fire on fixed military emplacements in the government area – mainly .50-cal machine gun nests, with the odd Russian S-300 surface-to-air missile battery. Virtually every one of these has been reduced to ragged dances of flame, smoke, and debris within minutes of the initial assault.

The Little Bird pilots chatter tersely and professionally on their squadron net.

"Inbound hot."

"Copy that."

"Moving to next target in package two-one."

"Roger that."

"Engage, engage."

"Roger, engaging."

"Break off! Break! Tracer fire on your nine."

As hoped for and advertised, the AA network failed to alert the Iranians to the threat until it was happening to them good and hard. And the Iranians were expecting a full-spectrum special forces raid on their capital about as much as they expected to wake up to find Godzilla rampaging through downtown.

Which perhaps wouldn't have been a whole hell of a lot more destructive.

Certainly the Iranian officer corps would have expected to be alerted by some communiqué from the top, if the Islamic Revolution were under attack. But there's been nothing. There's only the buzz and rumble of the unfamiliar aircraft, the occasional explosion and shriek of rockets and whine of minigun fire. And radio silence.

There have been a few streams of tracers, return fire, rising up through the billowing black smoke like lightning through a thunderhead. These make an odd mirror image with the actual thunderheads above, as the storm picks up and begins to flash.

But minutes after the beginning of the Little Bird assault, there also appeared spewing strings of answering tracer fire, from the AC-130's Vulcans, auto-cannon, and howitzer. An AC-130 Spectre is like its own private artillery company, but poised looking down on the head of all possible targets. It's truly like having the gods on Olympus fighting for you.

Also, it doesn't take a whole lot of air to achieve air dominance, when you're the only ones up there. As of H-hour plus eight minutes, the stacked up Coalition aircraft have little to worry about short of running into one another.

* * *

Finally, in the very last insertion of the day, out on the edge of the city, the MC-130 the Rangers leapt out of loops back around in a wide arc. It zooms over Sorkheh Hesar National Park, a 9,000-hectare urban wild space flush with the eastern edge of Tehran. At 2,000 feet, the plane's tail ramp opens to the storm.

At the top of the ramp sits the hulking, 12-foot-high, plastic-wrapped FARP-on-a-pallet. As the ramp passes the horizontal, a crew chief throws out a pilot chute, which catches the wind and drags the pallet backward and out into the open air. As it hits open air, free-falls, and picks up speed, its three enormous canopy chutes deploy with raucous pops.

No sooner is it clear than three rifle-clutching and jump-suited figures, badass and totally insane 160th Airborne Platoon members, hurl themselves out behind it, spread-eagled, bellies flat to the earth, goggles set against the rain, but mouths open to the air.

They holler joyfully as they go out, raging against the storm.

"*Yeeee-HAAHHHH!!!*"

When they hit the ground, they'll have at most twenty minutes to build out their refueling and re-arming station. Because by then the first thirsty and depleted Little Birds will be inbound.

And there will still be plenty of shit that needs blowing up.

The Seal Delivery Vehicle (SDV) is a manned wet submersible craft used to insert SEAL teams under the water into denied target areas. With electric propulsion, nav and comms gear, plus extra air tanks, it's essentially a big submarine engine that wetsuited SEALS hang on to while it blasts along under water at high speed.

It's also pretty damned big and bulky out of the water. All four SEALs, plus Bleep, are manhandling it across rollers on the floor of the Gulfstream cabin. The weather over the Red Sea is not the raging storm they've got in Tehran. But it is gray and windy, as the air blasting around the cabin through the open cargo door attests.

Finally, the palletized and parachuted SDV passes its center of gravity and tumbles out into the churning sky. And without a backward glance, the four sailors and one soldier, all wearing full SCUBA gear, plus HALO parachute rigs, launch themselves out after it.

* * *

Homer is first to reach the SDV, which floated down to the surface under its canopy and now floats on the surface, totally stable in the water, via its ballast and buoyancy system. He releases the parachute, runs up the onboard systems and engine, and puts himself in the pilot position.

By the time he gets all that done, the other four have swum up and taken their spots.

Their planned intercept vector with the *Mavi Marmara*, if everything goes to schedule, will only leave them 14 minutes to take down the ship and disarm the missiles, before it sails into launch range of Tel Aviv.

And they have no idea whatsoever how many armed hostiles they will face on board.

Regulators already in mouths, the operators exchange hand-gestures to indicate that they're good to go. Homer ramps up the throttle and releases compressed air from the trim tanks to submerse them. As soon as they're ten meters below the surface, he checks the color screen of the moving map GPS, into which has been programmed the waypoints to their target, based on its observed course and speed. The SDV blasts up power and accelerates quickly to its top speed of 18 knots, forcing the swimmers, Bleep in particular, to hang on for their lives.

As they get closer to the target they should pick it up on onboard sonar. That's if it doesn't pull some kind of a crazy Ivan and radically change direction on them before that. But within a few minutes, Homer spots its glowing dot on their screen.

Now they just have to hope it doesn't spot them back.

Deep within the interior of Kazemi, Rod Tucker wakes to the sounds of explosions and shouted Arabic.

Springing to the door, he finds his number-one jihadi lieutenant, Musa Harb, looking calm and mean. He's been quartered one building over, along with his 22 all-star shooters. Tucker has kept them close, for the end game, however that plays out. Because Tucker knows he can trust Suleimani just as far as the general has a use for him. And because Tucker is a survivor. And because flexibility is life to evil operators, too.

Standing in the doorway, Musa is carrying his rifle and wearing his tactical vest. "American commandos, in platoon strength. They set down in two weird-looking Black Hawks and came right through the front gate. They're rapidly rolling up the garrison buildings."

"Delta?"

"I'd say so. Somebody who knows what they're doing."

The ferocious buzz of a minigun tears the air, startlingly close, followed by the clatter of *buckets* of empty 7.62mm casings splashing and rattling upon the tin roof. Tucker darts to the window in time to see a Little Bird blast by through the gap in the buildings.

As he pulls on his assault suit and chamber checks his weapons, he gives Musa a series of terse instructions. "Put your men in a tight defensive perimeter, back by the helipad.

Do not get engaged with this assault force – and definitely do not get bogged down. Got it?"

"Got it, boss. Where will you be?"

"Conducting our regular business. After I find the general. And after I kill this assault team."

* * *

When Tucker kicks in Suleimani's door this time, the general is not behind it.

Tucker guesses he is out there somewhere directing the defense. The two of them have their differences. But the general is a stand-up, lead-from-the-front kind of officer. And Tucker figures the defense will hold for the moment. Not least because he put most of it in place himself.

He guessed the D-boys might be coming. Flying in to rescue their princess. Working out their endlessly rehearsed hostage rescue mission templates. He knows the failure of their 1980 Tehran mission still haunts them. And that maybe they wouldn't be able to resist another run at the ole Embassy Compound.

And Tucker also has a pretty good idea of how they're going to try and go about it.

When he does find Suleimani, after following the sound of the guns, the man is on the front lines, pistol drawn. But the front lines are nearly everywhere now.

Black-clad American commandos can *almost* be glimpsed, moving and firing, half-spectral ghosts flitting through the mists of the splashing rain, dropping defenders like pop-up targets, and enveloping the complex by sectors. Rounds seem to come in from everywhere and nowhere. And periodic explosions are going off in very unexpected places.

On the other hand, increasing numbers of Iranians from the garrison are now reinforcing. The 50% watch that Tucker ordered, after news of the girl's sentencing hit CNN, has held long enough for the rest of the garrison to get into the fight. And if Musa's assessment of enemy troop strength is right, and there are only 20-some invaders, they'll be outnumbered 20 to 1.

* * *

When Tucker turns back from his peek around the corner to assess the tactical situation, Suleimani is briefing one of his lieutenants. The junior officer turns and takes off at a run.

"Where's he going?"

"To the garrison at Kahrizak. For reinforcements."

"Reinforcements? What are you talking about? We can repulse this raid."

"It's not a raid, you idiot. The whole city's under attack."

"*What?*"

"I've got people coming in on foot muttering about paratroopers and helicopter assaults across the government district, supported by air strikes. The secure comms network is down, and you might have also noticed that power's out. And not only here – all across Tehran. We need the infantry division at Kahrizak to defend the capital."

Tucker leans back under cover and squints off into the rain.

Could Rheinhardt...? No, it ain't possible...

Well, whether this is just a hostage rescue, or more than that, Tucker is first going to make sure there's no hostage to rescue. He dashes down the alley to the rear, straight to the detention facility. He's greeted with multiple gun barrels in his face. The whole place is locking down in response to the attack.

"Execute the American girl. In her cell. Do it now. General Suleimani's orders."

The lead Ghost Hawk just *soaked* up assault rifle and machine gun fire, from the second it touched down outside the
front door of Kazemi. Rheinhardt, Spider, and the rest of
the shooters went sprinting out before the door even locked
back.

The blood of Mike Brown went ice cold as all the men
and equipment between him and the enemy evaporated. He
sat in the front of the cabin, literally covering up his head, and
hunching over his computers, as dozens of rounds pinged
angrily around him. After a long age, the door slid shut and
the bird rocked off its wheels and into the sky.

Now Mike continues to sit and stare in horror as dozens
of rounds still come in and score the airframe. He tries to
make himself small, while feeling like the mouse in the Swiss
cheese – while they're *making* the Swiss cheese. But he knows
he needs to suck it up and "Charlie Mike" – continue mission. He turns back to his bank of computers and radios and
gets on with it.

Both crew chiefs stand at their window miniguns, pouring out whining, devastating fire, at every point where they
can see a muzzle flash or an armed Iranian. When one of
them looks back and sees rounds flecking off things very
close to Brown, he releases his gun, grabs up a couple of the

Kevlar ballistic panels on the floor, and tries to stack them around him.

"The laptop!" Mike shouted over his shoulder, still typing. "Protect the laptops!"

The crew chief gives him a look of mixed horror and admiration.

Then rushes back to his station.

* * *

On the ground, Rheinhardt, Spider, Javier, and Bishop each lead their four-man teams into the deadly choreography that is the live assault and takedown of Kazemi. In an ideal universe where everything goes to plan, time on target would be 20 minutes. Aside from the unfriendly welcome at the gate, the first seven minutes go as planned.

And that's when they start running into groups of two and three Quds fighters, then tens and dozens. And they are not in their racks, or checking e-mail, or peeling potatoes, as expected. Most of them are kitted up, buttoned down, and shooting back with authority.

The defending force has reacted *much* more quickly than anticipated.

And Rheinhardt simply doesn't have enough shooters to out-maneuver them all. By the time his four teams have cleared halfway through the complex, the defenders are dug in, rallying, and getting reinforced. Their famous free-flow is clogging up, snagged in thick ranks of defenders. The assault is being slowed, stopped – and bottled up.

And in that static posture lurks defeat, and death.

Rheinhardt pulls a grenade with a 1.5-second fuse, chucks it through the glass of the window beside him, then follows it through the door. Smoke and debris wash over him as he barrels in, firing his weapon from out of the cloud, dropping four guys who look like clerks, but who are all carrying AKs and hunkering behind desks.

He charges straight through the building and intends to go right out the back again, letting his number two man deal with any survivors in his wake. He kicks open the back door then ducks to the side, as withering fire blankets the side of the building.

He pulls the door shut, finds solid cover, changes out mags, and calls for his CCT.

The Air Force Tech Sergeant, call sign Chef, moves from his cover to Rheinhardt's and squats down. He's a medium-skinned black man with startlingly leonine amber eyes and a thick but neatly groomed full beard that he picked up during four tours of Helmand Province.

As is obvious from Chef's body armor, rifle, ammo, grenades, and side arm, Air Force combat control teams (CCTs) fight. Among the most highly trained military operators in the world, their commando and pathfinder skills match up against anyone's. But they're also FAA-qualified air traffic controllers who are masters of calling down devastating fires from fast-moving jets, attack helicopters, and gunships.

So, as heavily armed as CCTs are, their personal weapons are basically peashooters. More deadly by far are their secure SATCOM radios, GPS units, and laser target designators.

Your average veteran CCT has killed more bad guys than an entire Army infantry brigade.

"How we doin'?" Chef shouts over the noise of the battle.

"Looking at twenty to thirty enemy pax dug in across the courtyard. Range two-five."

"Roger that," Chef says. He flips down his augmented reality monocle, with integrated head tracker. The device overlays digital symbols on top of his field of view, showing him the location of all friendly aircraft in theater, including distance, altitude, and remaining armaments.

He pans his head around, virtually peering into the air battle, then reports. "The Spectre's still busy across town, so it's gonna be Little Bird city here for a while. And it's gettin' a little tight for unguided rockets. But I'll see what I can do."

* * *

While Chef gets on the CAS net, Rheinhardt rings up the other team leaders. "Retard One-Two, this is One-One, send sitrep."

"*Copy, Bo, wait one.*" It's Bishop, leading the next team over.

A massive volume of small-arms fire and explosions ramps up from across the complex to the west. After five seconds, it settles back to the normal level of chaos, and Bishop comes back on. His tone of voice is more relaxed than the content of his report. The unflappable sharpshooter is also still firing while speaking, his rifle's receiver a few inches from his mic.

"We've lost momentum. A little bit boxed up, if I'm honest. And multiple casualties."

"Anything serious?"

"Not yet."

"Two-Three, go."

Javier comes on. *"On schedule plus or minus ninety. Stiff resistance. But still rolling up. Zero casualties."*

"Two-Four." Spider's team.

"Yeah, we're busier than a one-legged puppy with two-tails in an ass-kicking contest. Hit a wall of tangoes – and starting to get hemmed in. More in sorrow than in anger, Bo…"

Rheinhardt realizes he now has to start thinking about a contingency plan. If they withdraw, where to? He supposes they could execute a fighting retreat and try to break contact long enough for Richie to land and extract them. If that fails, they could try to fight their way to their other forces in the government district.

But that's pretty much a half-completed screenplay for *Black Hawk Down 2 – Even Worse This Time*. And even if they do make it, they might find themselves boxed up in besieged buildings, depending on how badly things are going there. Alamo time.

Rheinhardt makes the call.

"Okay, I want all teams to consolidate on my position, south side of the central courtyard. It's a lateral displacement, so I'll look for you in five mikes. Then we'll see if we can't mass enough force to break out, roll over their main opposition here, and take it home. And if we can't, then we'll just… do something else."

The team leaders acknowledge, but Rheinhardt is already switching freqs to the mission command net and hailing Mike.

"Okay, I'll bite," says BJ. "Where are those goddamned thousands of protesters we were promised?" The streets are completely empty, as perhaps befits a war zone. A steady rain pelts the pretty square.

BJ walks the lines with Major al-Samarrai, the ISOF Commander. "Perhaps the Green Revolution has been oversold?" he says.

This ISOF detachment, which is composed of only 25 men from their 1st platoon, has been holding firm. They've been taking sporadic fire, coming from seemingly random directions.

But now the incoming seems to pick up. The volume of their outgoing fire rises in response. The two leaders can now spot small groups of shooters, two or three at a time, darting across intersections, shooting haphazardly.

"Who do you suppose these gentlemen are?" the major asks, as he and BJ take cover behind a stone gate on the north edge of the square.

BJ pulls his rifle into his shoulder in a blur and triggers off four rounds. Two sprinting figures in an alley, off in the distance, and only just visible through the mist of the rain, sprawl out, hit the ground, and stay there.

BJ grunts in approval. He then spits into the grass, viscous brown tobacco juice.

"Hell, they could be anybody. We were only able to account for so much in the sixteen hours we had to plan this caper. A billion things could have gone wrong. Welcome to one of them."

"It's a good point," al Samarrai says. He hasn't yet raised his rifle, nor fired. There's still more of the aristocracy about the Iraqi officer corps. "Perhaps it was optimistic to think we'd identify every military installation and security service in Tehran."

"It's a fucking police state." BJ snaps his rifle to his shoulder again, but his targets have slunk off too quickly this time. "Half of *them* probably don't know half of what they've got here."

* * *

The two combat leaders have moved to the center of the square now, partially covered by a heroic war statue. BJ is on the radio, taking reports, via Mike, from the other teams. The ISOF men, hunkered down in all-around defense on the edges of the square, fire steadily. The noise of the battle is ramping up. And the sounds of explosions and strafing still echo from all directions.

Al-Samarrai stands erect beside where BJ kneels in the soaking grass, still too refined to fire his weapon – but also utterly fearless and oblivious to incoming fire. He raises his rifle sight to take a magnified look down one of the streets that runs off the square.

"You recognize these uniforms?" he asks, lowering his weapon and pointing.

405

BJ unpouches a monocular optic and follows his friend's finger. About ten blocks away, but rolling in quickly, bounding figures fill the street. In high magnification, BJ can see that they are young, pumped-looking guys, carrying black folding-stock AKs. Some are in civvies, but many wear identical woodland camouflage, with red headbands and bright white scarves.

"Basij," BJ says. "The Supreme Leader's paramilitary goon squad."

"They're not very good," Al-Samarrai allows. "But they are many."

In addition to the foot mobiles, BJ can also make out a dozen aging Mercedes buses rolling toward them in a column. They are overflowing with Basij.

"Your recommendation?" the major asks politely.

"Swing half the force to strong-point that intersection," BJ says. He then keys his mic and says, "Gimli, get up here."

Gimli is the other Air Force CCT. Slightly vertically challenged, but very muscular, Gimli still wears the half-Afghan, half-commando mufti he picked up with Chef in Afghanistan. He's known for his jovial disposition and dedication to the men on the ground. He's also developed a good feel for cultures in which honor, hospitality, and revenge are paramount.

"You rang?" he says, trotting up.

"Two words," BJ says, pointing toward the vehicles in the distance. "Carpet bombing."

"I'm on it," Gimli says, switching radio frequencies as he turns away.

BJ raises his rifle again, and rhythmically puts rounds downrange, methodically emptying his magazine. In the far distance, in the haze, improvidently exposed figures drop.

Some of the ISOF guys look back at BJ in awe. The column of Basij is still well out of effective range of their AKs.

"We can hold for a while," BJ says, dropping out his empty mag, pulling a fresh one from a chest pouch, and slamming it home, all by touch. "But pretty soon we're going to have to get off the street." Rain has soaked BJ's moustache, and he blows some of the droplets off. "And once we're forced to hunker down inside buildings… it really is going to be Alamo time."

Al-Samarrai shrugs, philosophically. Then, even he slowly raises his rifle to his shoulder and takes a couple of measured shots.

There are about to be plenty of targets for everyone.

Tucker is moving fast, M14 up and ready, neck on a swivel. With Delta guys still free-flowing, it will only take about a one-eighth-second lapse of attention to do him in. He's been doing this long enough to know that, at this level, nobody gets a pass.

As he moves laterally across Kazemi, somewhat to the rear of the line, he notes that the battle seems to be forming up around the central courtyard. Quds guys are massing in and around the buildings on the north side. But they're strong on the flanks as well. And holding firm.

Rheinhardt and his guys will be running low on options.

Low, but not out. This he realizes as a Little Bird comes screaming into a gun run on the north side of the courtyard, minigun chattering bloody murder. Wood and dirt and flesh churn up into a sawdust-and-meat mulch. Three thousand rounds a minute of 7.62 will chew through a lot of reinforcements. And that's another thing Tucker has to keep from catching him back-footed. Particularly those hellish rockets.

Dashing through another alley, covering both sides, then the front again, Tucker does wonder if this country doesn't have a fucking air force. But it must be the comms thing.

Which he intends to get fixed right now.

* * *

408

Bob Li spins so hard in his chair that he falls out of it. Tucker advances, sweeping the room with his barrel, the door banging behind him, and chortling at the Chinese kid's terror. *I often have this effect on people*, he thinks. Though he does have to give the kid some credit for staying on station through the assault.

"We've got a nationwide military comms outage," Tucker says. "The packet microwave network. Can you fix it?"

Li blinks hard. "Yeah. I'm looking at it now. While I've been in the IDF systems, someone's been in ours, fucking shit up left and right. I think it's the Delta tech guy we talked about. They've also snuck back into the air defense network and put that out again."

Tucker squints over his rifle at Li's screen, as rattling machine gun fire and explosions gently rock the building. "Wait a minute – how do you have power?"

"They blew up the main backup generators outside. But not mine." He points to a small gasoline-powered portable model, visible through an open closet door, chugging away.

"Nice," Tucker allows.

"They're not backups unless they're redundant."

"Can you fix the commo thing?"

"Yeah, man. I just need a little time."

"How about the power?"

"Doubt it. They almost certainly just surged the local generators. Damage done."

Tucker nods, then wrinkles his brow. "Hey. You once told me you can crack their radio encryption protocols. Can you pick up their local squad or command net here?"

"I could. But which job do you want me working on?"

"Okay, fuck it. Stay on the comms. But… you still have their tech guy's cell?"

"That I've got."

Now that the command bird is back up at 2,000 feet, they are above small arms and shoulder-fired missile range. As long as the Iranian AA net stays black, they're golden. Richie and his co-pilot keep the bird on a long banking track around Tehran, while Mike receives and relays individual unit reports, and keeps one eye on the cyberwar.

The early news is good. At most of their targets in the government district, the Iranian soldiers or security personnel ran out outside when they heard the helicopters – and immediately got cut down by door gunners on the Hips, strafing from the Little Birds, or the all-seeing Spectre. Those that remained were mopped up by the operators when they hit the ground. People inside the target buildings were too stunned to resist. It became more like a bank robbery than an air assault. Everybody down on the floor.

The Iraqi SOF at the Palais du Senat and the Guardian Council report that they are now arresting robed and bearded mullahs, and gleefully explaining, in poorly understood Arabic, what the Iranian people are going to do when they get hold of them. State TV, radio, and online, mostly producers and web developers, also folded fast.

Egle's two teams are having a serious punch-up with the Ansar-ol-Mahdi Corps. But they came in so hard and fast that the eight of them have killed, wounded, or driven off most of the 100-strong gang of "elite" enforcers. Egle reports no casualties so far.

But they also haven't yet located Khameini.

Mike learns that the Rangers, as usual, are having the toughest fight of the day. The downtown IRG garrison housed nearly 500 troops – and Captain Miller has just two platoons to take it down with. Even with surprise, speed, and superior toughness and training, they're having to battle toe-to-toe, machine guns, rifles, knives and bare hands. He reports casualties, including KIAs, though the numbers are not yet clear.

And then Mike learns that the shit has *really* hit the fan at Kazemi.

* * *

While Mike is fielding sitreps and relaying orders across the battlespace, Chaya rings for the second time. "Hi, Chaya. Listen, I don't have any new updates on the missile frigate. And, I'm sorry, but I'm not going to have time to give you tac updates from here."

"Roger that. Sorry."

"I know IDF needs to know what's happening. How about I just patch you into our command net? As long as you keep the channel clear you can listen and stay looped in."

"Excellent. Thanks, Mike."

As Mike is patching her in, his GSM/SATCOM phone rings.

"Go for Brown."

"Hey. I want you to put me through to Sergeant Major Rheinhardt."

With trembling fingers, Mike squelches the command net.

"Uh, Retard One-One, this is Retard X, over."

"This is Retard One Actual, send it," Rheinhardt responds, over gunfire and explosions.

"Uh..." Mike knows he's got to just spit this out. "I've got Rod Tucker on the line. He's asking for you... Do you want to take it?"

There's only the slightest hesitation on the other end.

"Yeah. Why the hell not."

With the Iranian AA station secure, the prisoners cuffed and guarded in a single room, and all-around defense in place, Chaya can almost relax. They haven't yet been counter-attacked. And the pilots and crew of the Stealth Hawk, keeping up their aerial recon circuit, haven't spotted any new enemy forces inbound.

Chaya has planted herself in the control room, in front of her laptop, and is now wired in to audio from the battle in Tehran. Obviously, the tension is enormous. If this thing succeeds, it will completely reshape the political landscape of the Middle East. Without Iran's support for Hamas and other terrorism, a Palestinian state may finally become possible. Without their support of Hizbullah, no more war on the northern border with Lebanon. Without Syria as an Iranian client state, a peace treaty with them as well.

But if it fails…

And there's also still one or more nuclear weapons out there, pointed straight at Chaya's homeland and everyone she loves.

So she is avidly listening in on the tactical updates that flow through Mike's orbiting command post. But when other traffic stops, making way for a conversation between the two great lions of this contest, Sergeant Major Eric Rheinhardt and former Sergeant Major Rod Tucker, her blood runs cold.

And when she hears what Tucker has to say, it freezes dead in her veins.

* * *

"Hey, man."

Tucker's voice is like aged wood and arsenic. Smooth, low, and menacing, slightly southern-accented, it chills Chaya down to the pads of her feet.

"I thought you might be dumb enough to come all the way out here for a rescue. But I didn't think you'd try something as insane as taking down fucking Tehran. Is that your big idea?"

When Rheinhardt's voice comes on, it initially reassures her. But it also sounds unfamiliar, in a way Chaya cannot quite work out.

"Hello, Tucker. Why don't you do us a favor and stick your head out into this courtyard? It's been too long since I've gotten a look at you."

"Heh. You just don't fucking quit, do you, Bo? And everyone still following behind you, like little sheep."

"We've all decided on our loyalties. You might have chosen yours more carefully."

Chaya gets the unmistakable feeling there is something between these two, some dark history, to which she is not party. Something perhaps she does not want to know.

"Oh, I feel fine," Tucker purrs. *"You fucking wannabe Captain Americas have been walking into my traps since the very first day of this campaign. And now here you are in another one. And Israel's in a worse one. It's all over but the crying now."*

Chaya's hand moves toward her transmit button. But she knows this battle is not hers to fight. And she is powerless to impact it.

Eric sounds almost amused when he comes back on. *"Always counting your chickens early, Rod. Some god you are. But guess what? You're still on the outside. And I'm still inside."*

Tucker's voice goes dark and knowing. *"No... No, man, I think maybe you're outside, too. Somehow I don't see Havering sending you off to Tehran on a sanctioned mission. Or JSOC authorizing any of this. I think you're off the reservation. Am I wrong, Bo? Tell me I'm wrong."*

Rheinhardt says nothing. Tucker continues.

"And you know what? You never WERE so different from me. You were just never as GOOD as me. You make out like you're better than everybody else, above it all. But I'm going to put the lie to that. I'm going to kill you dead, and all your fucking guys. Just like I killed B Squadron. And just like I killed those Sayeret Jew motherfuckers back in Anbar."

There's a long pause in the transmission.

Chaya, her breath magicked away, stares holes in the speaker through slitted eyes.

Finally, Rheinhardt speaks.

"You're going to hell for what you did back there, Heat Rash. And so am I, for letting it happen, and for lying to cover it up for you... Unless I can redeem myself somehow. Sending you off to hell personally ought to just about do it."

Tucker pauses, then audibly snorts.

"There's no redemption, man. All that courage, honor, faith bullshit. None of it's real."

Another pause. But this one has a strange calm to it.

"Maybe, maybe not. But last time I checked, incoming 105 rounds are as real as it gets. And you'd better keep your goddamned head down. Because the only Spectre up there today is flying for me." There's an angry click.

And the channel goes dead.

* * *

When the IDF Stealth Hawk flares back down onto the station rooftop, only one soldier is there to greet it. It's Chaya, with her helmet on, rifle in one hand, laptop in the other. Before she can climb aboard, she feels strong fingers gripping her arm, holding her to the earth.

"And where do you think *you* are going today, Sabra?"

It's Master Sergeant Dov Levy. And he's got his helmet on, too, and is also holding his rifle. Plus is smiling, devilishly. But then, uniquely, his smile melts away, as Chaya turns and he gets a look at her face. It's like he's never seen it before.

Her cheeks are tear-stained, eyes red-limned. But, mainly, her expression is one of ice-cold vengeance and murder. It's like the death mask of some homicidal Egyptian Pharaoh Queen.

Something has changed her nearly beyond recognition.

"Take your hand off me, Sergeant," she says. "You're to lead the defense here, and hold until relieved."

For a second or two, Dov tries to take her measure, staring at her quizzically. Then he decides. "No. Wherever you're going, I am to go, too."

"Master Sergeant…"

"The last time I left you alone for ten minutes, you had flaming Hamas fighters falling on your head."

"Mother of God. Fine, get in. But we go now."

The pair clamber on, the helo lifts off again – and Chaya not so much informs the pilot of their destination as gets into what feels like an argument with her grandmother over whether they're going there or not. In the end, the bird turns its nose to the east, and toward the interior of the country.

Toward Tehran.

The ISOF defenders are now heavily engaged on three sides of the rain-sodden and now bullet-pocked square. BJ and the major hunker down at their central statue, trying to run what's turning into a proper battle. If things heat up any more, they're going to have no choice but to get off the street.

And that's if they can get out of the square. The Basij have been flowing out and around, flanking them, using their numbers to envelop. And right now there is only one corner of the square that is still open and affords them egress.

"We've got to have aerial recon," BJ says. "Or we're going to get boxed in here."

He was counting on the Little Birds or the Spectre for eyes on from above. But they're all so heavily engaged, and over-tasked, they can't take on the job.

BJ rises to his full height and does a 360 over his sights, taking in the tactical situation. Then he breaks cover and runs powerfully toward their grounded helo.

"Back in a flash," he bellows over his shoulder.

* * *

While he's calmly jogging through heavy rain and what's becoming a murderous crossfire, BJ overhears radio traffic between Gimli, their CCT, and one of the Little Birds.

"Retard Four-One, this is Longbow Two-Two, inbound with ammo resupply. ETA two mikes."

"Longbow, this is Gimli with Four-One. Negative on resupply. Lima Zulu is too hot."

"Roger that, Gimli. We've got you in sight now. Yeah, looks like a real party. But we are advised that Four-One will be black on ammo in approx fifteen mikes. We're coming in."

"NEGATIVE, Longbow. Be advised, you will be shot down if you flare into this square."

"Yeah, well... as long as we're shot down in the right place, you'll still get your ammo. Longbow Two-Two out."

BJ, still running, laughs out loud. "God, I love those fucking guys!"

And then he takes a stray 7.62 round to the shoulder blade. Happily, he's wearing his ceramic inserts in his tactical vest. He shrugs off the shot, rolls his shoulder, and reaches the helo.

Climbing inside, he finds that both pilots have abandoned their ride and are now out on the ground, holding the line with their beleaguered customers. Heavy rifle rounds clunk into the helo's skin like a lead rainstorm, punctuating the sound of the regular rain pelting down. And this bird is increasingly looking too shot up ever to fly again.

BJ roots around the back until he finds what he's looking for: their RQ-11 Raven – a hand-launched, remote-controlled mini UAV, with a tiny electric motor and two onboard cameras.

He flips open the case and assembles the plane, to all of its 55-inch wingspan. He grabs the control terminal, hops back out, starts the plane's motor, and gives it a mighty heave into the stormy sky. The toy-like UAV takes off across the square, and BJ follows behind it at a run, rifle slung now, holding the controller and flying the plane with both hands.

* * *

By the time he regains the statue, the Raven has climbed to 300 feet. Peering through the camera down into the battle, BJ banks it around toward the one side of the square he hopes is still clear enough for them to retreat through.

The volume of fire, both incoming and outgoing, has been ramping up steadily. But now their most heavily-engaged point, on the northeast side of the park, goes manic with small-arms fire and grenade blasts, and their squad net goes hectic.

BJ looks up from the controller at the surge across the square.

"*Fuck*," says Gimli, looking around intently through his CAS monocle. "I've got the Spectre coming on station – but the bastards are already in our lines."

Chaos reigns as the Basij throw what looks like hundreds of bodies at the reinforced corner of their north and east picket lines. It seems inevitable now that they are going to be overrun – within minutes, if not seconds.

And when that happens, and their lines are breached, with the enemy swarming over them and in their rear… the whole unit will be enveloped and wiped out.

Sweeping around the starboard side of the bridge deck, Homer fires non-stop at rapidly shifting angles. There are not a thousand passengers on board the target vessel. But the *Mavi Marmara* has a hell of a lot more defenders than any but the most gung-ho and deranged SEALs would try to take on with a five-man team.

In his head, the veteran team leader figures: *maybe two platoons*. He'd probably want about two platoons of 16 enlisted SEALs and two officers each, one sweeping from the stern forward, the other from the bow back. And a third platoon, floating at standoff range, as a QRF.

But none of that matters now. Because Homer doesn't have three platoons. He has three SEALs, plus one very twitchy and sleep-deprived D-boy.

But, should any of them live, they are going to have one kick-ass set of bragging rights.

Homer slips his last four grenades out of their vest pouches and pulls the pins. Two of them he bowls smoothly down the deck's walkway. They hug the bulwark and curve out of sight around the front of the wheelhouse. The other two he sends with a gentle underhand lob, threading them between the overhang from the deck above and the forward gunwale, after which they clatter down the cowling and onto the foredeck.

The SEALs have been driving the defenders toward the front of the boat, putting them on their heels with the blunt force trauma of their initial assault. But the Quds Force sailors and shooters are now out of room to retreat. From here on out they will be fighting to the death.

Thudding explosions shake the 4000-ton ship as Homer's grenades go off, fire blossoming from the front of the bridge deck, and off the foredeck below. And then two new and unfamiliar grenades arc back over the gunwale, hit the deck, and skitter straight toward him.

Returning the compliment.

* * *

Eight minutes earlier, Homer brought the SDV up to a depth of two meters, then overtook to bring them up to the ship's stern. He matched speed and bearing while Tiger suction-latched onto the stern and climbed five meters up to the gunwale, using sheer bicep power. He then performed a one-handed chin-up, in order to lift his eyes over the edge, his silenced SIG pointing in his other hand.

There's a reason these guys stay in such unbelievable shape, and it's not just to kick ass at beach volleyball and pick up chicks.

Tiger then secured a coiled rope ladder, unslung his HK416, and covered the others as they climbed up. Murph was third, then Rip. After they shucked their SCUBA gear, Rip unslung a waterproof duffel with an M240L medium machine gun, with 600 rounds of 7.62mm linked ammunition. Rip got the duty because he's the new guy. And they have it with them at all because there's every reason to fear they're going to need the heavy-punch firepower.

Homer was the last out of the water. With one hand on the ladder, he let the SDV go and hauled himself up. Behind and below them, their submersible steed powered down, spun off in the wake, and then slowly sank from sight. The SEALs would either take down their target, or they'd be swimming home.

Or perhaps sleeping with the fishes tonight.

* * *

Homer clocks the speed of the two grenades tumbling toward him and dives over them, sprawling out flat on the deck, legs together and boot soles facing backward to absorb the blast. Nonetheless, when they go off he feels the burn. He's pretty sure he's taken some shrapnel and blast damage. But there's no time to check.

Rip has been fighting up the same deck on the opposite side. Homer keys his mic and says, "Rip, I need you in that wheelhouse with the MG *now*."

"Check. Thirty seconds."

If they can get the 240 emplaced there, it will cover the whole front of the ship. Moreover, they can use it to clear the foredeck, where most of the baddies now make their last stand.

From his prone position, Homer can hear the 240 firing non-stop as Rip drives his way forward. Underneath the noise of it, and through the decking below, he can hear stuttering rifle fire and grenade whumps as Tiger and Murph fight their way through the lower decks.

Now Bleep comes on the channel. *"Homer, Bleep. I'm on the upper deck. Definitely two big-ass missiles here, one vertical, one prone, over."*

"Copy that," Homer says, doing a tactical reload and sucking oxygen in the few seconds he has before they assault the wheelhouse.

"I'm also in a gunfight with about four pax across the deck. But I think their job was probably preparing the missiles, judging from the way they shoot."

Homer works up his best Sean Connery Scottish brogue: "Hey, Ryan, be careful what you shoot at. Most things up there don't react too well to bullets…"

"Jesus Christ. Out."

Homer takes a last lungful of air and tenses his arms to lever himself up and forward. But before he can move, the porthole glass of the wheelhouse, a few feet in front of and above his face, explodes outward in flame. Glass shards shower down around him.

And bits of charred wetsuit float down in the smoke.

* * *

Homer shakes his head to clear it. Trying to stay lower than the pummeling small-arms fire from the foredeck below, he rises and can just see Rip through the empty porthole. He is lying on his side, facing away in the cloud of smoke, badly burnt and bleeding. Maybe dead.

But the M240 looks intact. And they have still got to get it emplaced to have a fighting chance. There may be some other workable plan than this one. But Homer can't think of one, and he's out of time for tactical innovation.

The port-side hatch to the wheelhouse was rigged with a VIED (victim-operated IED, i.e. booby trap). The starboard-side will either be booby-trapped, or it won't. Homer sticks his head through the port and looks around. Nothing bomb-like jumps out at him.

He puts his gloved hand on the latch, and tightens his grip.

Captain Miller walks his lines.

Taking the IRG garrison wasn't the bloodiest fight of his career. But it was one of the ballsiest, taking down an entire supported battalion with two platoons. But with surprise, and the usual Ranger tactic of bare-knuckle brawling, they have killed, captured, or driven off the entire garrison. Though they paid a price for it. Their casualty collection point (CCP) in one of the main buildings is a busy and hellish scene.

Miller steps over one of his machine gunners, dug in near the front gate.

"How we doing, Brad?"

"Outstanding, sir. These guys want back in. But they're not coming in this way."

The significant portion of the IRG who legged it are now mounting half-hearted counter-attacks. Nothing life-threatening yet. The Rangers' hastily arranged defense of the captured base holds. Miller has called this all in on the command net. But he's not getting much news in response. Nothing seems to be happening.

And something had better happen soon. His men can't live here. But they could still die here.

His 3rd Platoon, up the street at the Ministry of Information, are in a similar boat, but indoors in a less conspicuous and more defensible building. As predicted, when the state security goons there met real soldiers, most of them headed for the hills.

At both locations, groups of Basij have started sniffing around and taking potshots. And Miller has no way of knowing how many are out there. But their ranks are growing.

And now the silence between probes is mainly ominous.

Miller keeps walking the lines.

* * *

The three other Iraqi teams have had an easier day of it.

At the Palais du Senat, where ISOF 2nd Platoon is committed, one squad guards a lecture hall where 80-some mullahs sit cooling their beards. The rest of the platoon stands in uneasy vigil around the doors, windows, and roof of the ornate building.

Down the block, in the Guardian Council, the small detachment from 1st Platoon holds their 12 mullahs and strongpoints the site. Since they overpowered the security detail, no one has taken too much interest in them.

Again, the silence is unnerving.

At state media, 3rd Platoon stands vigil, but also has work to do – updating government web sites, and putting out pre-prepared messages on TV and radio. By creating perception, they are perhaps doing more than anyone else to make the fall of the regime real.

But it's never over, as the saying truly has it, until it's over.

* * *

A few blocks from there, Egle and her team, having shocked the shit out the Supreme Leader's security detail, then had to search the building, nook and cranny, to locate the exalted man himself. They found him trembling in a food pantry in the basement kitchen.

Now they are sitting on him, all but literally, in a room on the top floor, just below the roof egress. Egle's not too surprised that the faithful of the Revolution haven't flocked to his rescue. Generally, when a bully goes down, no one on the playground rushes to his aid. Though she's sure she did hear something about a popular uprising.

And the growing groups of heavily armed Basij surging through the streets don't look like it.

For now, she's just enjoying Khamenei's shock and incomprehension at being captured by a woman. And waiting for the call. To get him, and themselves, the hell out of Dodge.

* * *

In a nearby building, a single Delta shooter guards twenty-some mullahs of the Expediency Discernment Council, all of whom came quietly, once their guards fled. The other three operators on this team strongpoint the building, albeit sparsely.

And in a closed office downstairs, Azad Sultan sits with Mir-Hossein Moussavi. The two talk seriously and intently about the post-mullah future of Iran and of the Iranian people. Smiling through his salt and pepper beard, beneath his trademark shock of white side-parted hair, Moussavi seems genuinely glad to see them. This is an excellent first sign.

The sounds of the crescendoing street battle outside, less so.

BJ shoves the Raven UAV console into Gimli's chest.

"Here. Fly this for me for a minute."

He brings his SCAR to his shoulder and takes off at a run toward their crumbling line.

Major al-Samarrai watches him race off, and says to Gimli, "Perhaps I should go and help…"

Gimli, who's now trying to call in fires as well as keep the Raven from crashing, says, "If I were you, I'd just stay out of his way for a minute."

* * *

BJ gallops at stallion speed toward the corner where the ISOF shooters are being overrun by the Basij. He runs slightly oblique to the main line of resistance, traversing it as he approaches it. With the angle, and his speed, he may be running too fast to realistically be tracked or hit. But not to make shots himself – and he is firing absolutely unceasingly.

Before he's within 50 meters of the line, the Basij start falling like leaves. In twos and fives, right in the skirmish, grappling with Iraqis, they start taking center of mass and headshots from range. BJ drops empty mags straight out and slaps new ones in, going through three of them, 60 rounds, all at a run. He never lowers his rifle for a second.

He is single-handedly plugging their collapsing line with a wall of precision lead.

He also lets fly, at intervals, with all three 40mm grenades from his underslung Metal Storm 3G semiautomatic grenade launcher. He doesn't arc them over the top. He shoots them flat, through the shifting gaps in the line. They hit Basij 20 or 30 meters back, explode on contact, ravage the militia, taking down a half-dozen at a time.

By the time he reaches the line, the Basij have abandoned it, in full retreat, panicked, whipped.

BJ takes a knee and empties his current mag into the rear of their jumbled column. Another half-dozen go down in the street. When he finally ceases firing, Johnson holds the line.

But he holds it nearly alone.

Only two or three of the ISOF operators in this sector are still on their feet and combat effective.

The others lie dead or badly wounded.

* * *

Al-Samarrai calls out cautiously as he approaches from the rear.

When BJ sees the major over his shoulder, he props his rifle against a tree, and begins trying to stem the bleeding of one of their badly wounded men.

"*Ma'shallah*, Uncle," al-Samarrai says breathily, lips parted. "I have never seen such a thing as what you just did."

"When next they come," BJ says, "they'll come right through."

"I don't think they will come this way – ever again."

BJ rips open an extra-large gauze pad with his teeth, and presses it down on the man's abdomen. "They're paramilitary volunteers. They've got no proper training, and their only combat experience has been against street protesters. But they'll be back."

He tears open a pill pack, a mix of painkillers and antibiotics, and tips it down the wounded man's throat. "*Kayf sihhatuk alyoum?*" he asks, looking down into the handsome, sweat-drenched face.

"Good enough…" the Iraqi answers falteringly, and in English, "to fuck your mother."

"Whoah hoah!" BJ's moustache flaps, and tobacco juice spurts down his chin, as he laughs uproariously. "The best medicine is fire superiority, right? You're gonna be fine, dude."

While he's still heaving with laughter, Gimli rocks up with the Raven controller.

"Remember that last avenue of retreat from the square?"

"Yeah?" BJ says, looking up.

Gimli reverses the console. On the 4-inch LCD, hundreds of Basij surge forward. "Well, it's not anymore."

BJ picks up his rifle again. "Last stand, gents." He seems strangely jovial.

A happy warrior.

When Mike sees a broadcast message on the command line of the Iranian server he's logged in to, *addressed to him*, he knows this has turned into a no-holds-barred hacker smackdown.

Back in Balad, when he had time to track his online opposition, Mike discovered not only the guy's handiwork. But he also discovered the man himself. *Ecce homo* – behold the man. Trying to profile the guy's patterns, he followed a trail all the way home to a server in the CS department at Cal Tech. After that, only a little more skilled digging was required to get a name.

Hello, Mr. Bob Fucking Li.

Chinese national. Former CS doctoral candidate at Cal Tech. And almost certainly also a student, somewhere along the line, at one of the People's Republic of China's lavishly funded cyberwar academies.

Mike had long thought that a cyberwar showdown between the Americans and the Chinese was inevitable. He just didn't figure it would be in the skies over Tehran, flying through flak and airburst rounds, in a battle royale over the future of the Islamic Republic of Iran, and the survival of the state of Israel.

Now, his attention perhaps more divided than it's ever been in a long career of multi-tasking, Mike monitors radio traffic, forwards updates, hangs on for dear life as the helo goes evasive in response to ground threats… and squares up for the fight of his life online.

* * *

Straight away he checks on his suppression of the AA network. Because if he gets beaten there, two things will happen very quickly. First, he will personally be killed, as their helo is blown out of the sky. And second, with their top cover gone, the Delta-led invasion of Iran will end in ignominy, defeat, and death for all involved.

Mike doesn't think Li can dig him out of the AA system – not as long as he, or rather the Israelis, maintain physical control of the machine that's his infection vector. But that's the last comforting thought he has for a while, because he then gets a call from the AC-130, via Richie on ICS.

"Hey, Brown. You're the guy charged with keeping Iranian military commo offline, right?"

"Affirmative. That's me."

"Well I just got a call from the Electronic Warfare Officer on board the Spectre. He reports military transmissions are spooling up all over the province. He's picking up chatter across the board. He says his Farsi ain't great, but the general theme seems to be 'What the fuck is going on?' and 'Where the fuck has everybody been?'"

"Fuck me. I mean, roger that."

On the command line before him, typing blazingly and squinting fiercely at the symbols and data, Mike is already deep into an exploit he desperately wants to leverage – and which he really needs to pull off in the next few minutes.

But should he break off from that to try and repair the hack on the comms systems? Because the restoration of Iranian military comms will also be a total disaster. Tehran will be swarming with hundreds of thousands of troops within hours.

It's a hell of a choice. But to live is to choose.

Mike carries on with what he's doing, firing up the pace and intensity into the red zone.

And that's when the son of a bitch starts taunting him.

* * *

```
[root@174.36.26.64 ~]#
Broadcast message from root (Sun Apr 7
13:08:22):
Hey, Mike Brown - CyB3rw4r N00b. I just
beat your comms h4X0r.
```

Mike grimaces, then just grits his teeth and bends his mind to the task at hand. He figures he can fix the comms hack in a minute – if he lives that long. *Just need another twenty seconds or so...*

He types at blinding pace now, not pausing to wipe away the sweat that drips across his face and forearms. When the helo banks or dives, he just leans with it, a dogged symbiont with the machine before him.

```
[root@174.36.26.64 ~]#
Broadcast message from root (Sun Apr 7
13:09:01):
```

```
And   now   1'M   going   to   take   the   AA   net
8acK,   g1mP.
Ur   K0unter-h4X0r   from   Kerend   Gharb   won't
last   long,   then   you   cr@$h   &   burN…
```

GodDAMNit…

Mike spares one hand for one half-second to wipe his eyes clear of sweat.

Then he makes his last digital lunge.

One way or another, this is going to be it…

BJ has done all the patching up of wounded he can make time for. Because he's also got to put this defense on some kind of a viable footing. Not to mention figure out how to get them the hell out of there. And he's got to do it now. He's got to juggle these priorities, and he's got to juggle them expertly. Or they're all dead.

He's already sent the pilots back to the helo, who verify that it is no longer flyable. Leaving it on the deck was obviously, in retrospect, a shit call. But they simply weren't expecting a couple thousand heavily armed thugs to encircle their position from out of nowhere.

BJ is now personally emplacing their remaining shooters around the perimeter, and lining up interlocking fields of fire, to have some prayer of withstanding the next rush – when Gimli runs up and buttonholes him. He's still got the Raven control unit, and their toy plane is still in the air.

"Hey, man," Gimli says. "Shit just got worse. Check this out." He tilts the screen. "Another force closing on our position. They're in the rear of the Basij, but coming up fast."

BJ looks down, exhaling tiredly, with a *Great-one-more-goddamned-thing* look on his face.

"Wait a second…" Gimli squints back at the screen. "This is weird…"

"What now?"

"Fuck me. The new force looks like it's *engaging* the Basij."
"What?"

BJ takes the console, loops the bird around for another pass, then zooms the camera tighter.

And now he can make out the newcomers: foot mobiles in wildly mixed camouflage, hundreds or maybe thousands of them, carrying AKs and PK machine guns, plus a few RPGs. Many are wearing checked keffiyahs around their heads. They've also got pick-up trucks with mounted weapons in the back, careening through the cross streets. And, from their size and shape, and the way they move, some of them look to be young women.

And they are just *tearing* into the Basij from their rear.

BJ shoves the console back into Gimli's arms, hefts his SCAR and heads out into the intersection at their bloodiest corner. There are still Basij snipers and sentries out there, and they take a few potshots at him. He returns fire, rather more effectively, dropping two.

But, more importantly, he can see Basij are starting to come off the line. The fight's moving to their rear. Looking past them, squinting deeply, and trying to focus on individuals, he can now see that at least some of the newcomers are wearing bright green armbands.

Turning and trotting back into the square, he bellows. "Everybody take cover! Hunker down! And who's got an American flag? Okay, a free Iraq flag? Good, give it here…"

* * *

Twenty minutes later, when the new force rolls up to their lines, BJ and al-Samarrai stand and go out to meet them, rifles held one-handed and out to the side. Behind them, the Iraqi flag flaps in the wind and the now-slackening rain, stuck to a tree with a commando dagger.

One of the leaders breaks with the group and trots up, two lieutenants in tow. The man is young and good-looking, confident and fierce. One of the lieutenants is a chick. And she's hot.

"*Asalaam alaikum*," the young man says in Arabic.

"*Walaikum salaam*," BJ and al-Samarrai answer together.

"I am Karim Fallah," the man says, extending his hand, "commander of the Eastern Kurdish Forces."

BJ takes the man's hand, then touches his chest over his heart.

"You are the American strike force," Fallah says. "We didn't really believe you were coming. But, Iraqis, as well…?" Looking confused, he gestures at the major's shoulder patch.

Major al-Samarrai steps forward, taking the Kurdish man's hand with one of his, and gripping his bicep with the other. "We are your brothers," he says. "Here to do what we can to help you on your liberation day."

The man nods sharply, once, and appears briefly speechless.

"You are welcome here, brother," he says, finally. "You are very, very welcome."

Lieutenant General Mohammad Husayn raises his left hand politely. The driver brings his staff car to a halt, and with it the convoy behind them.

They are now stopped dead in the middle of Highway 7, also known as the Persian Gulf Highway, which runs from Isfahan, in the center of the country, through Qom and up to the capital. More to the point, it runs by the Army base at Kahrizak, where Husayn is commanding general of a full infantry division, plus supporting units.

That division, men and equipment, is currently loaded up into half-ton trucks, which are all lined up behind his car, snaking out of sight back down the deserted and rain-buffeted highway. They sit at the junction of the Azadegan Expressway, otherwise known as the Tehran Ringway.

At the gates of the capital.

And they are there, Husayn recalls mournfully, because one of General Suleimani's staff officers raced down in a wild panic and demanded the deployment of Husayn's division to downtown Tehran, immediately.

And despite that Lieutenant General Husayn outranks Brigadier General Suleimani, Husayn is obliged to answer the junior man's summons. Because Suleimani's real superior is not in the military chain of command at all. Suleimani takes his orders from the Supreme Leader.

And so Husayn will take his orders from him.

* * *

Husayn's deputy, Colonel Mirza, who has been riding in the truck behind, taps on his window. Mirza's aide holds an umbrella over his head. Husayn rolls down the window.

"Your orders, sir?" Mirza asks.

Husayn sighs out loud.

His mind's eye ranges over the catalog of escalating horrors that has been life under the Islamic Revolution since 1979. He thinks of his wife, Nazila, whose family is of Jewish descent. Practically speaking, treatment of Jews in Iran is much superior to that in the rest of the Muslim Middle East. Nominally, Iranian Jews have similar rights to Muslims, as do adherents of other revealed religions.

But there's little question that his wife has been a weight around the neck of Husayn's career. He's had to work twice as hard every step of the way. And now to end up as the errand boy of a general officer junior to him, but favored by the mullahs and Khameini…

Also in Husayn's thoughts is the legacy of the Green Revolution in 2009. That movement was crushed in its cradle. But for a few minutes there, it had seemed that anything might be possible… It also left a feeling that: this can't go on forever. The regime can't last.

Finally, Husayn looks out and surveys the skies over Tehran. Mixed with the thick gray storm clouds are thicker columns of black and white smoke, billowing from destroyed and burning buildings and military emplacements. It is also worth remarking that the entire military command and control apparatus currently seems to be missing in action.

What exactly this represents, it is too early to say. But not too early to consider.

He pulls out his phone, and flips to the e-mail – the astounding one, only a few hours old, from the dissident scientist, about the Americans invading today. He regards it for a moment, then throws caution to the wind, holding it up for Colonel Mirza to see.

"Did you… happen to get a copy of this message?"

Mirza hesitates only fractionally. "Yes, sir. Yes, I did."

Husayn nods seriously at his deputy. "Well. I think… I think that we are having some mechanical problems."

"Mechanical problems, General?"

"Yes. And I think we will just wait here until the service vehicles and mechanics arrive."

The slightest curve tugs at the corner of Colonel Mirza's moustache. "And perhaps also to see how things play out in the capital?"

"Perhaps that too."

General Husayn rolls up his window and settles back into his seat.

And proceeds to serenely monitor the shifting patterns of rain on the windshield glass.

From her cell, Ali regards the muted sound of explosions and gunfire with detachment.

It's definitely not a general bombing campaign. Nothing like a 2,000-pound JDAM has gone off anywhere nearby. She does recognize the whump of 2.75-inch rockets, and the distinctive buzz of M134 miniguns. Those are AH-6 Little Birds overhead. Judging from that, and also from the small arms fire, she figures a hostage rescue is in play.

And given that she's the hostage, there's very little she needs to do but be ready to move.

Then again, whoever it is running this show, they've flubbed it. The fighting has dragged out too long. Something has gone wrong.

When the metal peephole of her door snaps open, and there are Persian features behind it, Ali realizes she has slightly miscalculated. If her captors come for her, to bundle her away elsewhere, or to execute her, then she's back on her own again.

Thanks, guys, Ali thinks. *Thanks for nothing.*

* * *

Having fixed the prisoner, sitting on the floor, the first of the four Iranian guards makes the critical tactical error of

444

shutting the peephole before opening the door. When the door swings open, the prisoner is no longer behind it.

His eyes go wide and then the soft tissues of his nose compress into his face as the heavy steel door bashes straight into it, shoved mightily from behind. Before he can react, an arm from around it grabs him and yanks him into the cell.

The door slams shut again.

* * *

When the second guard, pistol in hand, finger tensed on trigger, totally freaked out by whatever just happened, slides open the peephole again, he is instantly shot twice in the face, and drops like a bag of sand.

Two .45 ACP rounds from the first guard's Colt M1911A, the standard issue Iranian side arm.

Nice, Ali thinks. *Could hardly have asked for better.*

Neither of the last two guards, before backing away in horror, thinks to relock the cell door.

* * *

They retreat in opposite directions down the dim hallway, both pointing AKs with shaking hands, over the body of their now-faceless comrade lying in a large dark puddle before the door.

The cell door cracks open again.

The guard to the right, who can see into the crack, opens fire, emptying his 30-round magazine at the black sliver of negative space.

As he goes dry, a dark eye and gunsight appear from inside the slit, and he drops, also from two rounds in the head.

* * *

The fourth guard runs for it.

Ali steps into the hall and fires. He sprawls out, fifteen meters away.

She drops her mag out, reloads with a new one from a guard's belt, then presses herself against the wall and waits ten seconds.

No others come. There's too much ambient gunfire for her six shots to have drawn notice.

Okay then, thanks after all, guys, Ali mentally amends. *Sorry I gave you shit.*

Stepping back out into the hall, she yanks off the sling supporting her broken left arm, picks up an AK, reloads it, gathers ammo, and heads out.

Straight toward the sound of the guns.

Bob Li actually pauses to rub his hands together over his keyboard.

The shooting outside isn't getting any closer now, which makes him think the battle is turning. More importantly, it increases his sense of physical security. High-value, high-tech geniuses like him definitely do not belong anywhere near the firing line.

Particularly when he can pretty much win the war single-handedly, with his incomparable skills, all online. He shut down the Israelis. He drove the Americans out of the air network, dooming their assault at Chalus.

And now he's on the verge of pulling the plug on their invasion. Comms are back online. He's personally got power. And, in a few minutes more, he should have the AA net back up. At that point, he'll have driven his dipshit Delta adversary out of every system the guy got into.

In fact, Li's feeling so ebullient, he takes time to talk a little more shit.

```
[root@174.36.26.64 ~]#
Broadcast message from root (Sun Apr 7
13:17:25 2011):
Ive g0T commz, Ive got poWr & Ill soon
have AA b@ck.
```

```
R3@DY 2 take teh 8IG plunGe, @$$hat?
Im in ur base, killin ur d00dz!! LUlzz!
```

* * *

Mike says the quickest prayer of his life, then hits the return key.

And it comes back: all ten digits. Accurate to within one meter.

He pivots and inputs the grid reference into his Blue Force Tracker with trembling fingers. The location comes up on the theater map. It's inside Kazemi. But... and he checks the units for distance, then calculates... there are no friendly units within 200 meters. He switches over to the CAS net, calling it in personally.

"Longbow One, this is Retard X, priority fire mission, over."

"Retard X, Longbow One. Send it, over."

"Requesting 105, one round only, at following grid reference. Four Niner Sierra... Foxtrot Juliet... Two Niner... Zero Eight... Zero Four... Eight Four. Readback, over."

"Longbow copies your last, Retard. We have target grid reference four niner sierra, foxtrot juliet, two niner, zero eight, zero four, eight four. Confirm clear hot, over."

"Retard X confirms, cleared hot."

"Retard, we show friendly units within 250 meters. Re-confirm that, over."

Mike knows that with the Spectre's 105mm howitzer, "danger close" is inside of 200 meters. Two-fifty is probably too close for comfort. But it's close enough for rock and roll.

"Longbow, Retard confirms all. You are cleared hot, 105, one round only. Over."

"Roger that. We have target in view now, wait one... Round is away, ETI eight seconds."

Eight seconds.

Just time for a little shit talking.

* * *

```
[root@174.36.26.64 ~]#
Broadcast message from root (Sun Apr 7
13:19:09 2011):
So you've got power and comms?
Well I've got your fucking PHYSICAL
LOCATION.
Who's the cyberwar noob now? Welcome to
the WAR war.
Oh, and learn to fucking spell.
```

Li looks up from his screen, and over to the rain-spattered window.

Above the noise of the battle... or, rather, underneath it... he can just hear the beginning of a deep rumbling, like a train, or tires on pavement, coming down and toward him, coming in very, very fast through the storm.

"Fuck," he says to no one. "Pwned."

* * *

"Retard, Longbow. Fire mission complete. We show good effect on target. Send BDA, over."

Mike takes a deep breath.

Now he can get to work repairing his comms hack. And shoring up the AA one.

Not to mention attending to the hundred other critical claims on his attention.

With his back to the courtyard, and also to the thundering storm of incoming fire, Rheinhardt finds himself facing the Grinch and Bishop, both of whom are huddled up opposite him, sharing the same bit of solid cover. The Grinch looks across at his buddy and says, "Do you think it's time, Bishop?"

"I think it might be."

In tandem, they both reach into vest pouches and produce two identical red clown noses. They then mount them on their faces and begin squeezing away. *Honk, honk, honk!* The sound is just audible over the gunfire.

"Yep, this now a genu-ine three-ring ass-clown circus!" the Grinch says.

"Yee-hah," echoes Bishop, in his slight Texan twang.

Rheinhardt shakes his head. *Must be a C Squadron thing…*

* * *

All four of the four-man teams on the Kazemi assault have consolidated on Rheinhardt's position. They are strung out across several structures fronting the south side of the courtyard. They are strong-pointing windows and doors, defending their patch, and fighting off envelopment. And they are trying to formulate a breakout plan.

Basically, they are now in a totally static position – not unlike their B Squadron brothers of a generation ago, who got cut off and pinned down in the bloody streets of Mogadishu.

And this is the last place they ever want to be.

Surprise, speed, and violence of action have wound down and bled away. Flexibility is gone. And they have utterly lost the initiative. Rheinhardt knows something is going to have to change. Or they'll all soon be dead.

And he's just about to take that burden on himself, knowing it will mean his own death. But then he cocks his head toward the window. The sounds of the battle are shifting.

He raises his eye over the bottom edge of the window.

He can see that the enemy is still massed on the opposite side of the courtyard. They are only kept at bay by the deadly rain of the Little Bird gun runs. But they are building their strength. Inevitably, they will use it to press home their counter-assault. And to overrun the assaulters.

But now Rheinhardt sees that their aspect and disposition have changed.

There are fewer guns facing out. And the Iranian lines seem to be buckling. Quds guys are turning and heading toward the rear. Something has definitely upset their applecart.

And Rheinhardt knows this is almost certainly the best chance he's going to get.

"All Retard One call signs," he says across the net. "Grenade volley and FPF. *Now.*"

Within seconds, the opposite side of the courtyard erupts with rolling explosions, as the 16 operators hurl or launch all their remaining grenades nearly at once. Before these explosions settle, fully automatic rifle fire dials up to 100%, instantly.

It's a wall of death. But one that won't last long.

Rheinhardt hurls himself out the door and into the courtyard.

Alone.

Volley'd and thunder'd
Storm'd at with shot and shell

It occurs to Ali to do something about not getting accidentally shot by whatever rescue or assault force is rolling out there. But she quickly concludes her hair will have to do. With the vile headscarf gone, along with her hair band, her wild curls are probably visible at 400 yards.

She works her left arm around a little, to check its mobility without the sling. It hurts like hell, but has a pretty full range of movement, and the splint seems to be keeping the bone basically in the right place. So out she goes, into the compound and the melee. And with all hell already breaking loose, she's not making stealth a big priority.

This pretty much means killing anyone she meets.

Because she's moving fast and light, and because she's in their rear, and because she looks like nothing remotely familiar or expected, and mainly because she's *really fucking good*, she knocks down an awful lot of opponents in the first few minutes. She also senses they are moving to the south – toward the sound of heaviest contact.

Whatever's going down, she figures, *it's going down there.*

Rounding corners, traversing alleys, peeking into open doors – in almost every case, there's a new Quds Force guy, running at her, or away from her, or operating a radio, or trying to clear a weapon stoppage. Those that she doesn't completely get the drop on tend to give her half a beat, while they try to figure out what the hell she is.

And that's half a beat too long.

What the hell, Ali thinks, putting three-round bursts into each of two guys who round a corner ahead of her. *These assholes never did anything for me.* They did imprison her, kill her brother snipers, and put her on trial in a goddamned kangaroo religious court. And not to mention they put that fucking headscarf on her, and paraded her around on television like a devout monkey girl.

Fuck it, she thinks.

Normally, she'd think twice before going around killing everyone, if only on aesthetic grounds. But not today.

Today she's the Angel of Death.

* * *

One of the guys Ali kills is carrying a Soviet PKM 7.62mm light machine gun. It's got 250 rounds of belted ammo in a box magazine.

And it feels *good* in her hands.

She puts the stolen .45 in a holster on a stolen web belt.

She slings a pistol-grip AKM on her back, for possible future use.

And she hefts the PKM and starts rolling with impunity through Kazemi.

* * *

While still well in the rear, she's got a compelling edge, mostly in surprise, and angles.

But as she gets closer to the main line of resistance (MLM), she's going to have to worry more about her flanks – because Quds shooters are still flocking to the front. And as they all converge, well, they'll all be converging.

And the PKM doesn't exactly turn on a dime.

But what it lacks in maneuverability, it makes up for in horsepower. Ali holds it at waist level, bearing the weight with a shoulder strap, as she moves forward.

And she begins to feel as if she's mowing the grass of this joint.

Three guys in full tactical kit and body armor appear up ahead, Ali approaching them from their nine. About 30 rounds, at 850 rounds per minute cyclic, chew through them in seconds. The body armor might as well be cling film. They manage to turn to face her, but don't get a shot off amongst them.

Ali steps over the bodies, checks her corners, then turns right down another alley.

A shooter runs into the intersection ahead of her – but sprawls out the other side again, cut down by five rounds from the PKM. His buddy runs out to help him, but is instantly shot and merely goes down on top of him.

It pays to look behind you periodically in combat. Ali gets that feeling, spins, and sees four guys fall in behind her two blocks back. She drops straight forward and hits the dirt on her belly as AK rounds snap over her head. Now prone, an outstanding position for a machine gunner, she goes to work. The Quds guys are too surprised to go for cover, and instead try to shoot it out with her. Down they all go.

Ali's actually lost count by now.

And that's when she finally hits the front lines.

From the rear.

That's one big problem with a line: it faces a certain way. And when your opponents don't all happen to come from that direction, you're in big trouble. This is what it means to have enemy in your lines. And why it sucks to be overrun. But it sucks worse to be assaulted from the rear.

Ali just pours into them. She's afraid her barrel's going to overheat.

Fire from the other side of the Iranians, from their front, has also picked up, dramatically. Ali doesn't know why. On the one hand, it's great. It means the Iranians can't hear her machine gun. So she can go from position to position, rolling them up, like Sergeant York.

On the other hand, there's now a shitload of fire coming her way, through the Iranian lines.

The doors of the buildings on her side of the courtyard are mostly open, presumably to admit more defenders. Ali simply walks into one and, keeping low, kills a whole room full of them.

She goes to the next building over and does it again. This time, the defenders do turn to face her, but too late. They get a few shots off, one of which creases Ali's waist, a sharp hot pain, which she ignores.

And she figures that's probably all the walkover she's going to get.

When she pops out into the alley again, Quds fighters on the line are turning to the rear.

They now know that something is up.

And she sees she's about to be in a serious gunfight here.

But then, just as suddenly, most of them turn to the front again! Why? Who cares!

Ali moves to assault into the third structure – but sees that the Iranians in it are already being assaulted. There is a man in their midst. And he is on a kill-crazy rampage.

Storming through the middle of the room, firing at impossible angles, pirouetting as his rifle goes dry, he uses it to club and topple an Iranian. Then in the same motion he pulls two handguns and instantly resumes firing, point-blank into multiple opponents, in wildly different directions, all at the same time, bodies spinning and falling, blood droplets following graceful arcs. Spinning, dervish-like, shooting non-stop, seeing all sides of the room at once, clearing everything, finally he comes to rest, like a gymnast landing at the end of an impossibly complex move, facing the rear door, the one which Ali stands behind, holding her PKM at the waist.

The whirling man now points one gun at her, while with the other puts a no-look shot into a wounded guy behind him on the ground. And Ali can see the slide is locked back on the .45 pointing at her, which means the gun is empty, and thank fuck for that.

The man holding the two handguns is Eric Rheinhardt.

This time Tucker and Suleimani kick in the general's office door together.

They're both holding weapons, reeking of cordite and smoke, and both slightly blood splattered. Something has gone badly wrong.

"What the fuck was that?" Tucker says, locking the door behind them and propping his rifle.

Suleimani rounds his desk and drops into his chair. He also drops the magazine out of his pearl-handled .45 and inserts a new one. He then lays it on the desk before him. "I've never seen a line crumble so quickly," he says. "Or so completely."

The two of them were close enough to the front lines to see them dissolve. And when the entire battle turned on a dime, in mere seconds, they did what commanders have done during breakthroughs in battles since Marathon: they moved to the rear.

"That was *very* strange," Tucker says. "Like somebody let a tiger loose behind our lines. But it doesn't matter. I've already ordered the American girl killed. So Rheinhardt's rescue is DOA. And..." he checks his watch. "And, most importantly, the missiles will be on the wing by now."

The general nods. "So Israel is only a few minutes from destruction."

"Yes. But we verify that. Then we get the fuck out of Dodge."

"How do we verify? I have no comms. With anyone."

"Yes. But I don't believe for a second you'd put that team on the water without a sat phone. And whatever spooky shit Rheinhardt's pulled, I doubt it extends to civilian telecom sats." He pulls his civilian Globalstar GSP-2100 from his tactical rig and flashes it.

"Wow," Suleimani says. "That's really small."

"Thanks. Now give me the fucking number. Before we're overrun again."

* * *

The team of Navy SEALS is still hard at work upon the Red Sea. As usual.

Murph is searching flexcuffed prisoners, while Homer keeps them covered. Tiger, being physically strongest, has the duty of throwing bodies overboard. Bleep is up top, with a palm-top plugged in to the launch console for the missiles.

And Rip has been laid to rest in the wheelhouse. He lies beneath the American flag the team always brings along – either to raise in triumph over a patch of ground taken, or to honor one of their brothers before putting him in the ground. Or into the sea.

It had been a hell of a fight. But Homer was right that getting the M240 emplaced in the wheelhouse would bring them home. And Tiger and Murph came through their sweep of the lower decks, slightly wounded, but victorious. And the nukes up on the top deck are secure.

It was a righteous takedown.

Homer looks up from his reverie when one of the dazed Iranians starts ringing. The ringtone is the theme from *Mortal Kombat*. Murph steps over to him, reaches into the man's jacket, and comes out with a chunky sat phone.

"Hey, gimme that," Homer says.

"I got this," Murph says, folding out the antenna.

"Gimme it, Murph."

But Murph is already answering the call, in his inimitable way.

"*Surprise, cockfags!*"

"Goddammit, Murph…"

* * *

Suleimani can hear the voice of the SEAL leaking out of the speaker on Tucker's phone.

"*We got your boat, we got your missiles, and we got all your fuckin' guys. How about that?*"

Tucker's expression goes stony, and he jams the sat phone back into its pouch.

"Well," Suleimani says. "That didn't sound very good."

"The third missile," Tucker says icily. "We can still launch the third one on Tel Aviv."

Suleimani sighs. "What third missile?"

Tucker's expression darkens further, almost all the way down to serial killer. "The one with the third fucking warhead. The one you had enough extra HEU to manufacture. And that you've held out on me. And that you've now got secreted away at Doshan Tappeh Air Base, twelve clicks south of here."

Suleimani squints at the other man, chin on palm, fascinated. "How *do* you know these things?"

The sound of gunfire is approaching again, and more quickly now.

"Stop fucking around, General. We're out of time."

"Okay." Suleimani straightens up in his chair. "I did keep a third warhead, in case both of yours were captured or destroyed. Which is just what I gather has happened. But, obviously, we're not launching it from an Islamic Republic of Iran Air Force Base inside the city limits of Tehran. Israel has dozens or hundreds of nuclear missiles. And, cyber-crippled or not, there's a chance at least a few of them will eventually make their way here in response. If not from there, then from America. It would be national suicide."

But Tucker has turned his back and paced several steps away. "You make the mistake, General, of imagining I give a shit about the Islamic Republic of Iran."

When he spins to face Suleimani again, he is drawing his .45 at blinding speed.

"I told you I'd come and get you."

Ali and Eric embrace. Aside from the fact that they are standing in a room full of bodies and shell casings, on an Iranian special forces base, it seems natural enough.

"That was *if* I needed you to," Ali says, leaning back. "Do I look like I needed help?" She gestures at her PKM.

Firing close by causes them both to duck their heads. From the sounds, it quickly becomes apparent they are also standing at the center of an all-new assault, a resurging storm. This fight has been reborn.

When Ali came at the Iranian line from the rear, and Rheinhardt, sensing the buckling that she brought, came at it unstoppably from the front, the whole edifice crumbled. The two of them together chewed a gaping hole in the middle of the Iranian force. But the remainder of that force, reacting, losing the thread, losing the initiative, panicking, fell to pieces as well, all within seconds.

And also within seconds, Javier's team, and Bishop's, and Spider's, and the remainder of Rheinhardt's, also recognized the opportunity of that moment of chaos. And now they whirl like a wind of death through and around the central courtyard, rolling up, mopping up, sending the remaining enemy into headlong flight, or to their graves.

The whole assault has gotten unjammed. They are free-flowing again.

And they are unstoppable.

* * *

A voice calls out from the alley, "Friendlies! Comin' in…"

It's Javier, holding his smoking rifle at low ready.

"Jesus, Top," he says, looking around at all the bodies in wonder. "What the hell was that?"

The Grinch, coming in behind him, shakes his head and says, "Seriously. Goddamn, Sarge, that was just about as cool as a ninja on fire riding a motorcycle."

Javier spots Ali and moves in for a hug. She hugs him back with authority, albeit with only one arm. They've got their girl back.

Rheinhardt gives them half a moment, then speaks crisply. "Okay. This fight isn't over. And unless somebody's already seen him lying on the ground, Tucker is still out there somewhere."

Ali lets her machine gun fall to the ground. She kicks over a couple of bodies until she finds something to her liking – an AK-200. With Picatinny rails, an optical sight, and a vertical foregrip, it's practically a modern weapon.

"I'll find him for you," she says, charging the weapon. "He and I have business."

When a Delta operator quick-draws on you at close range, that's an excellent time to have your affairs in order. But three facts favor General Suleimani: one, his pistol is already out on the desk, inches from his hand, plus chambered and cocked. Two, he's a general officer – but also a combat veteran, one who still puts in the range time to keep his shooting skills up. And, three, he knew this was coming.

He knew it all along. He just didn't know when.

By the time Tucker turns and draws, Suleimani is already raising his gun and firing.

Both .45s trigger off together, wide sparking barrels facing each other across open air, fat balls of lead coming and going.

Suleimani's rounds hit first. Tucker, pummeled across the chest and shoulder, but unhurt due to his Kevlar assault suit, stays upright but is knocked to the side and back. This causes his shots to go wide.

They catch the Iranian through the left pectoral and upper arm, and he tumbles backward out of his chair. It's the tumbling that saves him from the rest of Tucker's volley. And it's the sound of the advancing assault force that saves him from Tucker simply walking around the desk and finishing him off.

Tucker roars with rage at the pain of the blunt force trauma – and again as he hears the sound of American weapons firing, just on the other side of the back wall.

465

He turns on his heel, scoops up his M14 by the door, and exits in a dark flash.

* * *

His last detour, in this crumbling place, is going to be by the microlab, to pick up Bob Li.

Because Tucker figures he's going to need his boy hacker again.

He rounds a corner, rifle up and out, but then skids to a stop. Because the microlab isn't there anymore. There's only a lot of smoking wood cinders, crumbled concrete, and twisted and burnt plastic. Three walls and the roof of the former structure are completely MIA.

And there's a deep crater where most of the floor once sat.

Tucker actually works out that the bottom of the crater is right at the spot where Li had his workstation set up. He shifts the rubble around a little with the toe of his boot. But it's pretty obvious Li isn't there. Li isn't anywhere anymore.

Al-righty, then, Tucker thinks, moving out. *Fuck him.*

* * *

Survivors of the garrison are fleeing toward the back of the complex. Tucker actually shoots one, mistaking him for an American, when they round a corner into each other. *Whoopsies.*

But within two minutes, he reaches the helipad.

It looks as if some of the Quds officers were a little too insistent on getting to the helicopters, to make their escape. It looks this way because several of them are lying dead around the perimeter. And that perimeter is being held, unbreakably, by Tucker's men.

The collapse of an elite military force is not pretty, he thinks, nodding to his guys, and moving through them to the big Mi-26 Halo on the deck. Luckily, the most unflappable operators are all loyal to him. He's also got his own pilot, namely himself. He takes the pilot's seat and begins running up the nav systems and APU.

The 22 picked men collapse their formation in overlapping segments until all are aboard. By then the rotors are spinning, and the rain has also nearly stopped, Tucker notices, looking up into the still stormy sky.

And then he and his team lift off into it, the disintegrating vortex of Kazemi falling away, and falling apart, beneath their arcing flight.

When Rheinhardt, Javier, and Ali crash into General Suleimani's office, they do it in the usual way: tactically meticulous, covering all sides, and moving a hundred miles an hour.

Rheinhardt, in the lead, rounds the side of the desk, his barrel depressed. On the ground is a well-turned-out but badly wounded brigadier general. Rheinhardt puts his boot on Suleimani's hand, which still holds his nickel-and-pearl .45.

"No need for that," Suleimani wheezes. "I'm done shooting today."

Rheinhardt leans over and takes the handgun.

Javier rounds the other side of the desk and looks a question at Rheinhardt.

"Do it. Treat him."

Suleimani nods his gratitude, as well as he can with his head on the floorboards. While Javier rips open the general's jacket to examine the chest wound, Rheinhardt squats and speaks.

"Rod Tucker," he says. "Where."

"You just missed him," Suleimani says, raspily. "Pardon me, but... would you happen to be Sergeant Major Rheinhardt?"

Rheinhardt nods.

Suleimani smiles, amusement jostling with pain on his face. "I am afraid Mr. Tucker has badly misjudged you. To hear him tell it, you'd be the one at our mercy right now."

"*Where is he?*"

"I believe him to be en route to Doshan Tappeh Air Base, twelve kilometers south of here."

Rheinhardt cocks his head. "And why would you so readily tell me that?"

Suleimani winces as Javier inserts a tube into his chest to drain fluid.

"I will readily tell you why. It is because there is a nuclear-tipped Shahab-3 missile at that location. And I'm very much afraid Tucker is going to launch it, and detonate it over Tel Aviv. And I needn't tell you what the response will be to Iran, should that happen."

"Can he launch it?"

"He shouldn't be able to. The missile is under heavy guard, at a secret location within the airbase. But I have learned, perhaps too late, not to underestimate that man's capabilities."

"You and me both."

"I would warn the missile's guard detail that he is coming. But I'm afraid you have… shit-canned all of my comms. There is, however, a helipad at the back of the complex. And it may still have aircraft on it, if you have a pilot."

Ali nods from across the room. "I saw it."

Rheinhardt stands up. "Good luck, General."

Javier finishes taping down a trauma pad across the wounds and drainage tube.

"Godspeed, Sergeant Major," Suleimani says.

* * *

When they step outside again, they run into Spider's team, who have just cleared an adjacent building. At the same time, a huge Soviet helicopter blasts by overhead.

Spider points as it disappears. "There goes Tucker with his chimp militia."

"Did you see him?" Rheinhardt asks.

"Yeah, just. He's flying it."

By the time the group reaches the helipad, there's only one bird left on it. It's an AH-1J SeaCobra.

"No," Ali says, circling it. "It's an Iranian overhaul of the export-version SeaCobra. It's got front and rear 20mm Gatling guns, and 70mm rockets."

"What it's got," Rheinhardt says, "is two fucking seats, pilot and gunner."

"Lesser known fact," Ali says, coming back around. "The door where the minigun ammo is loaded can be dropped down." She twists a latch and yanks open the port-side door, beneath the cockpit. It stays horizontal, seat-like. "And you can even snap onto the handles on the ammo crate."

"Is that safe?" Javier asks.

"About as safe as riding on the outside of a Little Bird. And it's been done with the Cobra in emergencies before." She pops the canopy and climbs in. "We can take five plus me. One in, four out. Who's coming?"

The other operators regard one another warily. This is definitely not the kind of stupidly dangerous shit that spec-ops guys are able to back down from.

Tucker flips up his helmet visor, then sticks his head out of the pilot-side window, just to get a bit of breeze. The air feels clean and cool after being scrubbed by the all-morning storm – and after the smoke, shoot-out haze, and death stench of Kazemi. He breathes it in, letting the wind dry the sweat from his face.

Today hasn't gone precisely to plan. The nuclear EMP launch hasn't happened, for one thing. Somehow Rheinhardt fucked him up there. *It hasn't happened YET*, Tucker mentally amends. *There's always another shot for those with resolve.* And for those who prepare for contingencies.

Also, there's the small matter that the Islamic Republic and the whole Iranian military seem to be going straight down the toilet.

Which is just fine as far as Tucker's concerned. It was only a temporary alliance anyway.

Tucker sees the airbase and the hangars coming into view up ahead.

Time to get the hell out of Dodge.

* * *

Still keeping one eye out for Little Birds or other hostile American aircraft, he banks it around and sets down between the hangar and the runways. He shuts everything down while the team piles off the back, led by Musa Harb, his shit-hot jihadi lieutenant.

Within two minutes they are all trotting into the south-ernmost hangar.

The hangar is far from empty, but largely disused. This whole airbase has been in the process of shutting down for several years. And, just as the hangar across the way met Suleimani's needs for secreting away a spare nuclear missile... this one has served Tucker very well as a cache for his getaway supplies. And its proximity to the last nuke is no accident.

The hangar also holds his getaway ride – an Embraer Lineage 1000 jet, parked beside the locked shed that has his cached gear in it.

The gear consists of weapons, ammo, explosives, cash (though most of the money he's made off the Iranians is in numbered Swiss and Grand Cayman accounts), fuel for the plane, travel clothes, and passports. And, by far most valuable, the shielded cask with the 7.5 kilograms of HEU Tucker skimmed off the top for himself.

That magic material is going to take him a long way. If he needs cash, it will fetch an awesome price on the black market. And if he wants entrée into any of the American patriot groups or militias... well, with this in hand, he can walk through any cabin door in Montana.

With that, plus his cash earnings, plus his cadre of 22 loyal and highly skilled shooters, he will be, as the Americans like so much to say: in business.

* * *

Tucker works the locks on the shed and gets most of the men busy loading the plane. Then, with the others, he's simply going to pop by next door and liberate the third nuclear weapon from its security detail. A quick bit of guidance programming on the launch console, a short drive of the launcher out onto the tarmac... and off it goes.

And bye, bye, Israel. It's only the one missile and warhead. But it will be enough.

So now he's got the money, he's got the HEU, he's fucked up Rheinhardt and Delta... And in a few minutes, he'll have fucked up Israel. Not a terrible outcome, all things considered.

But just as he's swinging open the jet's passenger door and stairway... the steel hangar doors they just came in, 50 meters behind them, blast back open again.

And two shooters come blasting right in after it.

Tucker swings back around from the shed and grabs his M14 in a blur.

The fucking Americans? Here already...?!

But, pretty quickly, he makes out that these are *not* the Americans...

"Hey, man!! Are we really flying straight into an Iranian military air base?!"

Bishop is having to shout at the top of his lungs, through his team radio, over the crushing wind, rotor, and jet engine noise. He is trying to be heard by the Grinch, who is bunched up next to him in the tiny space left on the improvised bench astride the hurtling SeaCobra.

The Grinch's eyes crinkle behind his goggles as he smiles into the crashing wind. *"We're in an Iranian military aircraft! What could be more perfect?!"*

Bishop shrugs. Amazingly, they are both still wearing their clown noses.

Spider and Chef (the CCT) cling to the bench on the opposite side. Rheinhardt sits inside, in the co-pilot/gunner's seat, behind and above Ali, trying to assist her with weapons and nav systems. They six of them are blasting over west Tehran, very close to the deck.

They are still taking sporadic ground fire. But assuming they don't get shot down, their flight time to the airbase will only be a couple of minutes. The rain has nearly stopped now, but the sky is still sodden, and the sun presents no threat of making an appearance.

While Ali flies low and evasive, Rheinhardt navigates from the rear.

"Okay," she says via ICS, "I've got visual on the base. But it's big. Where are we going?"

"There should be three hangars on the southeast edge. Our target is the middle one."

"Roger that. Coming into visual now."

Rheinhardt's personal radio chirps. Switching channels, hand to head, he says, "Go for Retard One Actual."

"Retard One, Retard X." It's Mike, calling from somewhere out there and overhead. *"Tactical update, most critical, over."*

"Send it."

"Okay. You remember how Tucker hacked your phone? Well, the dumb son of a bitch called me not thirty minutes ago, just to talk shit to you. On a CIVILIAN sat phone."

"Interrogative: are you telling me you've got a fix on Tucker?"

"That's a-ffirm. I've got a lock on his phone, and a nine-digit reference. Over."

Rheinhardt shakes his head. That cocky son of a bitch…

"Send grid reference, over."

Mike does, and Rheinhardt reads it back while keying it in. He can see on the GPS that the coords are in fact at the air base. But in the southernmost hangar, not the middle one. That means Tucker and the nukes are in different buildings. At least for the moment.

"Interrogative: how timely is this?"

"Totally. I've got a lock on his phone, and as of now he's RIGHT there, and he's static."

"You alert me if he moves. Out."

* * *

475

Rheinhardt switches channels again, and hails his CCT on the outside of the helo, a few inches away through the airframe. "Chef, Bo Peep, stand by for traffic."

"Roger Bo, send traffic!" Now Chef has to scream, the helo's jet engine running hot four feet from his head.

"MTO, fire mission for Longbow One," Rheinhardt says, using the AC-130 Spectre's call sign. "105, time in effect, five rounds, at following grid coords. Break." He then reads out the grid reference. Chef reads back and Rheinhardt confirms.

Twenty seconds later, Chef comes back on.

"Bo, fire mission is confirmed. Longbow turning to come on station, ETA four mikes. They will then fire for effect, five rounds 105, over."

Rheinhardt exhales. He switches to ICS.

"Ali. Bring us in. I want to watch this son of a bitch burn."

"You wanted to go to Tehran," the IDF pilot says, sounding very Jewish, "we're in Tehran."

But his tense posture and expression belie his flippancy. They are flying alone into the very heart of the evilest and most dangerous place on the planet, as considered by Israelis. So far they have taken no fire; but the silence is chilling.

"Kazemi is in the west," Chaya says, pointing to it on the moving map on the console.

She leans into the cockpit, half a headset on ICS, her other ear plugged in to the sat-connected laptop, following the battle in Tehran on the American command net. Below them, smoke billows from dozens of points around the city. The pilot puts them into a right-hand bank, placing the garrison at the top of the map display and dead ahead of them.

Chaya frowns and puts her hand to her earpiece. There's new traffic between Brown and Rheinhardt. She listens in.

"Retard One, Retard X. Tactical update, most critical... Okay. You remember how Tucker hacked your phone...?"

Chaya listens grimly for thirty seconds, then speaks.

"Change of target, Captain."

* * *

Chaya can practically hear the pilot slapping his own head as she leans in and inputs the grid location into the nav system herself. The GPS centers on the new objective.

"Brilliant," he says. "An airbase? That's even better."

"Turn the aircraft," Chaya says, so little humor in her voice she might be holding a gun to his head. "Do it now."

"ETA two minutes," he says tightly.

Chaya returns to the rear of the aircraft.

"Well?" says Dov, looking up.

"Button up," she says. "Two minutes."

Chaya pulls off her headset, unplugs from the laptop, and puts in her team radio earpiece.

While strapping on her helmet, she thinks about her sister. And she thinks about the impossible fact that the man who is trying to destroy their whole nation is also the one who killed Natasha. It's too much – far, far too much. No one could endure it. Tucker has got to die, and it has to happen now. Chaya feels she can't even breathe, until it is done.

She hauls on the straps of her tactical vest, tightening them to the point of pain.

She chambers both of her weapons, then unsafeties both.

And then she sits and stares sightlessly at the side door, her face still that regal death mask.

Waiting. But not for long.

* * *

Dov moves to the side door and hauls it open, so they can hit the ground at the same time the bird does. But just then, the helo lurches terrifyingly down and to the right, accompanied by the roar of something huge and loud passing by them very close in the air.

"What the fuck was that?" Dov says aloud.

But Chaya has no time to answer, even if she knew. Because they've arrived.

The Stealth Hawk rocks again as it touches solid ground. Dov takes a look around, then jumps out. Chaya doesn't look, but just follows straight behind. An enormous hangar, five stories high and two football fields long, sits hulking in front of them. Two more hangars stretch out to the left of it.

They run forward, weapons up. So far, no one is shooting at them.

Reaching the nearest hangar, the pair stack up on either side of a steel double door. Dov yanks it wide, and in they both go. Each covers the other, while also trying to cover the vertigo-inducing volume of space that opens up before them.

In the middle of it there are rusting aircraft sections and parts, pre-fab maintenance sheds and offices, and huge pallets of God-knows-what. In an open space ahead, better lit, sits an intact aircraft. Around it are human figures, dressed in black, hauling boxes – and carrying weapons.

And *now* someone is shooting at them.

Also, something explodes behind them, outside the door, followed by an even louder crash. But they haven't the time to turn around to spectate.

They are weapons up, shooting and moving.

And they are wading right into the middle of a highly-trained commando team, no fewer than 22 shooters. Plus, presumably, in amongst them somewhere, their ring-leader – the unfathomably evil one. The murderer of Natasha, and would-be destroyer of Chaya's world.

Rod "the God" Tucker.

The great expanse of the airbase opens up under the SeaCobra suddenly and dramatically. Ali brings them into a broad, banking turn, feeling out the contours of resistance below.

"Closer," Rheinhardt says. "I need to confirm the kill."

"Yeah, I know," Ali replies on ICS. "And I need to make sure we're not between that Spectre and its ordnance terminus…"

She's also taking care not to overfly the hangar, to avoid tipping off their prey. She brings the helo around, juking sharply and unpredictably, to throw off ground gunners, from whom they're now taking potshots. As they clear the edge of the hangar, they can see Tucker's bird sitting on the deck. And as they rocket through the turn, the Spectre comes into view on the horizon to their northwest.

Finally, as they straighten out suddenly and blast low over the runways on the far side of the hangars, the airborne collision avoidance system (ACAS) goes apeshit, howling and flashing like Judgment Day.

All four shooters sitting on the outside of the helo scream, high-pitched and in unison.

It is *right* fucking in front of them, sleek and bat-like, coming straight on, slightly below.

A Stealth Hawk.

Fucking stealth aircraft, Ali says to herself, lips pursed, climbing and turning for every ounce of maneuverability the Cobra is worth, battling to avoid a mid-air collision.

In the rear seat, Rheinhardt's head snaps like whiplash, trying to track the other bird.

Ali brings it around 90 degrees again, and now they can see the Stealth Hawk flare and land, 50 meters from the target hangar. The right-side door of the helo lurches open, and the instant it touches tarmac, two shooters jump down and run straight to the hangar.

Rheinhardt can see that one of them is small, thin, and narrow-waisted. And both of them have light-blue Star of David insignia on their tactical helmets. They pause for an instant on either side of the door to the hangar, backs to the sheet metal.

Then they fling it open and disappear inside, one and then the other.

* * *

Rheinhardt shouts into his radio. For all he knows, he can be heard right through the canopy.

"Chef, Bo! ABORT Longbow fire mission! Repeat, ABORT ABORT fires, how copy?"

"Roger, Bo, solid copy! Will relay, wait ou——"

The entire world explodes, turns sideways, and spins, a noise and force of impact like a train collision, flame and flash and violence. Everyone aboard the Cobra is instantly concussed, bones pummeling their flesh from the inside out, vision gone all white then blacked out, hearing overloaded into a single high pitch. The two men out on the left side of the helo are caught full and in the open by the blast and ripped into by expanding gases and casing shrapnel.

The port-side engine screams in failure, smoking, the other one whining to take up the slack. Then the transmission goes, and the bird begins to spin and fall out of the sky. Later, Ali will conclude they got hit by an airburst RPG, only inches from the engine cowling.

For now, she battles the shuddering and disintegrating aircraft, trying to auto-rotate it into some kind of a controlled crash on the runway below.

In the back seat, which was closer to the blast, Rheinhardt tries to speak into his mic to raise Chef, but his vocal cords won't operate. Head lolling, half-lidded, he turns and looks out onto the men on the left-side bench. They don't look good.

And the spinning black tarmac is racing toward them *way* too fast.

When Rheinhardt comes to, he is badly shaken, but not disoriented.

He knows right where he is, and he knows exactly what just happened – they got shot down. He also knows that, in some length of time that cannot exceed four minutes, that AC-130 Spectre is going to come on station and blow the ever-loving shit out of the southernmost hangar alongside the runway. And, finally, he knows that two Israelis just ran into that hangar.

And one of them was almost certainly Chaya Akhilov.

How the hell she got to Tehran, he has no idea.

Well, okay, he actually knows that, too. She pretty clearly flew here from the AA station at Kherend Garb in a stealth Black Hawk.

Why she did so, he has no idea.

But it doesn't matter. What does matter is that if he doesn't do something very compelling, and do it fast, then Chaya is going to die exactly the same way her sister did.

In a super-heated inferno of 105mm howitzer fire.

* * *

As he unbuckles himself and shoves upward on the shattered canopy, Rheinhardt can see Ali's helmet in front of him through the smoke, lolling from side to side. She's alive.

But he doesn't have time to check on her. Or anyone else.

Levering the canopy up enough to squeeze himself under, he rolls out and over the lip of the cockpit, and falls all the way to the black tarmac below, landing face down.

He doesn't feel any pain from the fall. His nervous system is still shorted out. But when he tries to stand, the world does a loop around him. He goes straight down onto the deck again.

This time he's lying on his back. And in the still dark, but slowly lightening, northwestern sky, he can see the ungainly shadow of the Spectre heading into a lazy, banking right-hand loop around them, putting its weapon systems in position to engage its target, the hangar below.

Rheinhardt rolls over onto his stomach, and struggles to push himself up on his elbows.

He crawls painfully back up to the ravaged airframe.

Chef and Spider are still clipped onto their bench. Both are either unconscious or dead. Rheinhardt unstraps Chef's helmet and removes the earpiece and chin mic. He coughs and tries to make his voice work. "Longbow One... This is Retard One Actual... How copy?"

Nothing comes back. And he doesn't trust his buzzing hearing, but he also thinks nothing went out. Still half lying in the man's lap, he pulls Chef's radio from his tactical rig. It's in three pieces, savaged by shrapnel from the blast that took down the Cobra.

He remembers that Mike also has comms with the Spectre, and tries to reach him on his team radio. "Retard X, Retard One Actual. How copy? Acknowledge. Any Retard call signs..."

Nothing.

He can't tell whether his own radio is damaged, or if they're in a radio skip zone – sitting in the depression of the airbase, mountains all around, the storm pressing the ionosphere down.

Whatever the explanation… Rheinhardt is on his own.

Still half on top of the two men, he can now see that both Chef and Spider are breathing.

Mustering his strength, he unclips Spider and lays him on the tarmac, then goes back for Chef. Something on the man's vest jumps out at him. The shape of it, long and thin.

He flips up the pouch cover. Flares. One visible spectrum, one infrared.

He looks up. The Spectre has just finished lining up for its attack run.

He pulls the caps off the flares. He strikes one, then the other.

And he levers himself to his feet with a Herculean effort of will.

* * *

Once he gets vertical, his own tipping momentum seems to drive him forward. He runs now, not very straight, weaving like a drunk actually, toward the north side of the hangar. That will put him, should he make it that far, between the Spectre and its assigned target.

He waves the two flares, one showering him with red burning sparks, the other with invisibly burning ash, over his head, crossing them and then out to either side, like a half-stoned teenager at a rave. With that, plus his wobbly running, he probably looks like the biggest retard in an entire invasion of retards.

Oh, well.

When he reaches the corner of the hangar, he wills himself to stay upright, and just keeps on waving. He can see the gun ports on the side of the Spectre dead ahead, and up above. But he can't make out the barrel of the howitzer. This is because it's pointed directly at him.

In the next few seconds, he'll either be dead, or he won't. *I don't even care at this point*, he thinks. *I just want to lie down.*

The Spectre flashes its landing lights three times in the dark gray sky and breaks off.

"Thank fuck," Rheinhardt says aloud, dropping the flares.

He sinks down onto his ass, back propped up by the steel wall behind him.

And now he can both hear and feel heavy small arms fire, through the wall at his back, inside the hangar.

Guess this day's not over yet, he thinks, staring blankly ahead.

Pushing himself woodenly back to his feet, he tries to remember where his rifle is right now…

When Rheinhardt staggers back to the helo, Bishop and the Grinch have set up a two-man security perimeter around the crash site. They're bloody and banged up, but look basically good to go. Bishop even waves at Rheinhardt. "Fourth helo crash, man! I'm now the all-time record-holder!" Rheinhardt waves wearily in response.

On the other side of the airframe, Spider is awake now, and also still in the fight. The same cannot be said of Chef. He's flat on his back, Ali working on him with a med kit from the cockpit. Spider is half helping, half patching himself up, pressing a seeping bandage to his own neck. Ali looks up to clock Rheinhardt's arrival.

"Well, looks like you saved your Israeli friend."

Rheinhardt leans on the side of the helo with his forearm, forehead resting upon it. "Yeah. I also saved Tucker."

While Ali jabs an IV drip into Chef's arm, Rheinhardt climbs back up to the cockpit and recovers both his rifle and Ali's. He takes a second to survey the scene.

Directly in front of them is the south hangar. As far as he knows, Tucker and his men are still in it. And so is Chaya. He can still hear faint firing from within. To the northeast is the center hangar. To the best of their available intel, that's where the nuke is.

Rheinhardt ponders which one he should go after with his tiny, banged up team.

Save all of Israel? Or save the one Israeli he personally cares for?

But, then again, today has been all about doing the impossible with the totally insufficient. *What the hell*, he thinks. Hopping back down to the tarmac, he parcels out assignments.

"Bishop and Grinch. Take down the middle hangar. Secure the nuclear weapon."

They both give him slightly disbelieving looks, like, *What? Only a single 100,000-square-foot hangar? For all two of us?*

But then they merely nod, stand up unsteadily, and take off at a jog.

Just before they go, Rheinhardt notices that their clown noses didn't survive the crash.

"Spider. You're between the two hangars. If there's a door to the south hangar, go through it. If not, blow one. Then sweep southeast to join up with us. Whatever happens, don't let Tucker get past you. You're between him and the nuke."

Spider nods, ties off his neck bandage, hefts his rifle, and limps off at a trot.

"That leaves us, then," Ali says, standing up over Chef's prone form.

"Yeah. Straight up the middle. He gonna make it?" Rheinhardt says, nodding at the unconscious airman on the ground.

"I don't know. I've done all I can for him. He's stable, I think."

She takes her AK-200 from him, then drops and checks the magazine.

"C'mon," she says. "I'm sick of Rod Tucker monopolizing my day. Let's finish this."

Tucker holds his .45 to the wounded Israeli woman's head.

Her buddy is dead, sprawled out on the hangar floor, a few meters away.

And so are *four* of Tucker's guys, scattered around the space between the door and the jet. And that *really* pisses him off. Those were good men, skilled and loyal.

There were only two assaulters. But they came in fast and hard, and they had surprise. The girl in particular seemed highly motivated. She fought like a hell-cat on meth.

And she gave me a hell of a scratch, Tucker thinks darkly, holding his left hand to the bullet wound on his upper right arm. He also notes that they had to kill the other one, the big man, before they could get to her. He obviously died protecting her.

As usual, there were good and loyal men on both sides. Bleeding and dying.

"Okay," Tucker says. "I'll bite. Who the hell are you?"

The woman kneels before him, hands now cable-tied behind her back. She's also bleeding from a shoulder wound, which Tucker gave her as she was giving him his. She doesn't answer, but only gives him a look so full of hatred that it actually draws him up short.

"Wait a minute," he says, stepping around to face her full on. He flicks his eyes to her helmet, which lies on the ground. "Does this have something to do with that dead Sayeret team? In Anbar?"

Chaya's expression changes slightly, giving it away.

"It *is* about that! Wow. Let me guess. I got your brother killed. Am I warm?"

Chaya spits blood onto his boot, then answers in Hebrew. "*Achoti, ya ben shel kah-ba.*"

Tucker listens politely, then responds in English. "You didn't know my mother. And perhaps it was your sister who was the whore." He squints off into his memory, and remembers now that the Sayeret team leader was in fact a woman. And he *almost* imagines he can see the resemblance to this one. But that was a long time ago.

He pulls the hammer back on his .45. He takes a deep breath, building up a head of steam.

"Don't you try and imagine," he says, looking down at Chaya, working up that famous black-ice temper, his voice even deeper and more menacing in person. "Don't you imagine that you can understand what went down in a combat op. Not when you weren't there. And definitely not if you're getting your information from fucking Eric Rheinhardt."

They hold each other's gazes long, her warm deep-green eyes meeting his of ice-pale blue.

Tucker's lip and moustache twitch. He adjusts his grip on the .45. "And not until your own fucking hands are clean. You think you've got nothing to answer for? You and Israel? You think there's no blood on your hands? *Do you?*"

Chaya purses her lips even tighter. She doesn't look away.

The double steel doors blast open again.

Tucker looks up. *Speak of the devil... it's goddamned fucking Rheinhardt.*

At the back of the enormous room, Tucker holsters his .45 in a blur, hauls Chaya up by her hair, and brings his M14 to bear over her shoulder.

And at the front, just inside the entrance, Rheinhardt goes right, and Ali goes left, both firing non-stop while dispersing into the nearest cover, which is the rows of stacked crates to either side of the entrance.

On their way there, moving fast and diagonally, they fire rapid single shots, dropping four of Tucker's remaining shooters, two apiece, out in the middle distance by the plane. They never had a chance to react. Now under cover, Rheinhardt and Ali begin working forward.

Tucker backs away, toward the aircraft, pulling Chaya along by a fistful of hair.

With hand signals, he sends two four-man teams forward, into the warren of crates and pallets to each side. The rest he sets in a defensive perimeter around the plane.

Finally, he puts himself behind a low row of crates, with the rear wall of the hangar to his back. From this spot he's got a good look at every avenue of approach.

Now, he only needs to decide: go for the nuke, or get in the plane? Attack, or escape? It will all depend on how things go in the next thirty seconds.

And Tucker's played this game enough times to know that things could still go a hell of a lot of different ways.

***

Rheinhardt moves silently in his assault boots, rifle tight to shoulder, hunched over it, padding forward smoothly, barrel panning and pivoting, scanning the dim angles and alleys, floor to cavernous ceiling, all of it through and around the red target reticule of his sight.

His nerves are basically silly string at this point. He's completely exhausted, body and soul, from days of sleeplessness, combat, and intolerable stress. It's a deep-core tiredness, unlike anything he's ever experienced. But with tens of thousands of hours of CQB behind him, both training and real gun-fights, he's on a rail. All of this is muscle memory.

What's also in memory is the mental sight picture he took of Tucker out at the far end of the hangar, as he and Ali were shooting their way in. Tucker, and that dinosaur rifle of his. *Chekov's M14*, Rheinhardt thinks mordantly. *We saw it over the mantelpiece in the first act…*

Whoever Tucker has sent in after him, they're not stupid enough to expose themselves.

Rheinhardt keeps moving forward.

***

Ali kicks off the sandals thoughtfully provided by the fucking mullahs.

Barefoot, rolling on the outside of her soles, squeezing the black assault rifle by the pistol grip and vertical foregrip, solid yet supple, she moves even more stealthily than Rheinhardt, a dark shadow amidst greater shadows.

She comes upon the first pair of Tucker's men. Heavy rifle reports shout back and forth.

The two move in bounding overwatch, decent fire and movement. The one who is set tries to drive Ali under cover with aimed and evenly spaced single shots while the bounder moves up.

Ali knows the routine. But she likes her odds here. She drops to a knee, rounds snapping over her head, and opens up on the shooter, going for his exposed forehead or eye. She'll need to hit something, because she's exposed and he'll have her zeroed in fractions of a second.

She doesn't hit him, but she does send enough lead downrange, close enough to his face, to drive him under cover. Meanwhile the bounder also reaches his next cover.

And Ali's mag goes dry. At that instant a third shooter appears from around something, right in her path, not three meters away. Switching from primary to secondary weapon is always faster than reloading, and Ali's AK swings down on its strap, her .45 coming up in the same blur. The figure before her goes down with two double-taps to head and center of mass.

O-kay, she thinks. *Cover now.*

She slithers off to one side, into the shadow of pallets piled high.

Reloading the AK by touch, she looks nearly straight up the stack of crates beside her.

* * *

Rheinhardt hears the flurry of shots on the other side.

A head, sights, and barrel pop up, twenty meters away down the rows of piled crap.

He snap-fires two into the man's face.

And the bounder has broken cover, not knowing that his set partner is already dead.

Rheinhardt drops him on the run with two, then puts two more into him on the ground.

Four fast incoming rounds catch him across the cheek, neck, chest, and shoulder.

The force of the volley knocks him over, and he goes with the movement, rolling back and laterally into a side alley.

He touches his cheek, which is just creased, then the side of his neck, which is hit out at the edge, but bleeding freely. A quick pat of his Kevlar at chest and shoulder tells him it saved him and is holding for now.

He pulls out a pressure bandage from the accessible pouch where he keeps it, unpeels the backing, and slaps it across his neck. It seems to stop the bleeding.

Less good is the news that he has absolutely no idea where those four shots came from.

* * *

There's a reason snipers never get in trees. It is a pretty good place to bag a couple of kills. But they will be the last kills you ever bag. Because you will never get out of that tree alive.

Ali bends the rules, as Delta guys do. She's got more mobility up here, and can leap from box to box. She's also only got a few opponents, and can climb down again when they're dead.

As it plays out, she finds she doesn't even have to move.

She just lets them maneuver underneath her, working out their solid small-unit tactics.

One bounds by, then sets under cover. Then the second bounds by. Ali shoots him twice in the top of the head. His buddy, up ahead, spins to his rear. But he's already dead on his feet.

Neither ever thought to look up. Because they knew the rules about getting in trees.

Ali rolls sideways, over and down into one of the dark side spaces, landing crouched on hands and feet. She'll take the last one head on.

She hears two double-taps across the hangar, from her left.

She and Rheinhardt will meet again in the middle.

Goddammit.

Tucker realizes he may have erred when his guys back in the defensive perimeter start getting shot.

Sending out the two hunter-killer teams was probably the right play. But letting the rest of the team, and particularly himself, get stuck in a static posture, and against guys like this – out on some kind of kill-crazy rampage – was perhaps not his most brilliant move of the day.

Maybe he's getting tired. Or frustrated

His guys are dropping on either side of him, only twenty meters away. Then ten.

And he's fast running out of guys.

It looks like he may have to count on Rheinhardt's predictable Galahad impulse – getting himself killed doing something risky to save the girl.

As the whole drama devolves into cliché, Tucker figures he'll at least head off an obvious one. He likes having the Israeli girl as cover. He likes much less the thought of her elbowing him in the nuts at a critical moment. Shifting backward, he knuckle jabs her at a spot between her shoulder blades, a governing vessel pressure point. She slumps forward, half-paralyzed.

He keeps her propped up on the crate before him, still aiming over her shoulder.

He still hasn't gotten a look at anything.

Wait... *there*. That shadow was him.

Fucking Rheinhardt.

And there it is again, more recognizably this time. Tucker fires four rounds, the M14 cracking heavily. But the shadow pivots and slides away.

Musa Harb, emplaced off to Tucker's right, and perhaps last henchman standing, fires at the same movement, while keeping carefully under cover. He knows enough not to show an inch of himself to a Delta shooter.

As Rheinhardt maneuvers around looking for his shot, Tucker continues to aim his rifle around Chaya, looking for his – while keeping his profile down to nearly nothing.

But Tucker's bad fortune is in having opponents on both sides.

Breaking through the last of the defense on his left, Ali gets a look at the side of his torso. She pops him twice in the shoulder, rounds pounding but not penetrating his suit, throwing him off balance and out of position.

He pivots to his left, firing instantly and accurately, driving Ali back under cover.

This exposes his right side though, and with a flick of his thumb, Rheinhardt goes cyclic and pummels Tucker's hip and thigh with the rest of a 5.56 mag.

Released from his grip now, Chaya slumps forward over the crate.

And Tucker tumbles backward, left, and to the ground, from the full-auto pounding.

And in an eye blink, Rheinhardt accelerates like a big cat and leaps over the crates, empty rifle trailing in his slipstream, right-hand .45 coming out of hip leather, left-hand gun from his vest. He flies in a vicious predator flash, his throat emitting some kind of guttural growl.

* * *

Musa Harb, to Tucker's right, and an unflappable son of a bitch, takes some panicking.

But Rheinhardt, black-clad and blood-smeared, snarling and flying forward, pouring left-handed no-look fire into his position, pretty much does the job. Musa ducks and makes a fighting retreat behind the plane. Rheinhardt leaves his empty gun in mid-air then hits the ground again on top of Tucker, who has just sat up and drawn his own .45.

Their four arms come together between their crashing bodies, two of them gun-wielding and trying to elevate for headshots, the other two holding them down with raw arm strength. The pair grapple and roll across the hard floor, both firing point-blank into each other's assault suits, heavy rounds hammering the already raw chest and abdomen flesh beneath.

This all happens in full view of their two lieutenants, Ali and Musa, who are now emplaced on opposite sides, facing in. Both are under good cover, about thirty meters to each side.

The two men in the middle holler in pain and rage, rolling over each other, both .45 slides finally locking back as the guns go dry. Tucker swings Rheinhardt around and off him – or is it Rheinhardt leaping away? – both guns fall to the floor, and both of their right hands flash up and around holding commando knives.

This is a stripping away – of tools, of civilization, of humanity.

They are two beasts.

* * *

Ali watches the brawl over the top of the red-dot point sight on her AK.

She's never seen two human bodies move so fast. *Ever.*

Light catches the six-inch commando blades as they swing and flash and parry.

Both men obviously know the properties of each other's liquid Kevlar suits. They're going almost exclusively for head and neck attacks, with shot-up bits of the suits as secondary targets, and lots of knee and elbow strikes mixed in.

Tucker is the more accomplished martial artist.

But this is a street brawl. Where the meaner man often prevails.

Ali goes back to her sight and tries to track Tucker. She doesn't think she can make a headshot. They're simply moving too fast. And if she goes for one, and misses, she might hit the wrong head, as the two swing and grapple around each other.

So instead she depresses her barrel and shoots Tucker in the legs.

Several times.

* * *

Rheinhardt sees Tucker drop straight out from under him, as he swings his blade at the side of his neck. And it isn't an intentional duck this time.

Seizing the opening instantly, Rheinhardt kicks him with a steel toe in the armpit, then falls straight on top of him. Tucker lets his knife go to deflect Rheinhardt's killing stroke away from his neck.

But then Tucker instantly thumb-pokes him in a nerve point on the inside of the arm, at the crease of the elbow tendon. In addition to triggering fantastic pain, this makes Rheinhardt's whole arm go numb and paralyzed. His knife skitters across the stone floor.

They both roll away and spring to their feet.

Down to bare hands now.

* * *

When she makes her shots on Tucker's legs, Ali also inadvertently identifies her position for Musa Harb, who takes aim across the expanse of hangar floor and around the two writhing, clawing, cursing bodies, and shoots her in the head.

The round catches her across the parietal lobe of the cranium, high and left, furrowing through hair and a few millimeters of skin and subcutaneous fat, before angling off into a dark corner of the huge building. It also knocks Ali to the floor, giving her an instant mind-wrenching headache, and starts bleeding lightly.

She pops back up again instantly, two positions to the left, and with a whole new sense of priorities in her targets.

She finds the guy, Musa.

And she puts *his* head in *her* sights.

But before she can fire, she realizes he's no longer aiming at her.

He's shooting toward the middle.

At Rheinhardt.

* * *

Rheinhardt is back on his feet and trading Jiu jitsu and Krav Maga strikes with Tucker, when his legs rocket out from under him, from the multiple bullet impacts fired by Harb.

It's disconcerting. But this is a good thing, he thinks, in a way. He's lying down now, after not being able to catch a breath in what feels like weeks. Maybe he can take it easy for a second here.

But of course, Tucker comes straight down on him, forearm going for throat.

Rheinhardt blocks the lethal attack with his dead right arm.

With his left, instantly, and by touch, he pulls his multitool from its belt pouch.

Before Tucker can come in with a second strike, Rheinhardt jabs him twice, straight on with the blunt, hard metal end of the multi-tool.

The first jab is to the dead center of his chest, at the sternum, which is the nerve nexus of the pericardium channel. It sets up the second strike, to the nerve gate on the right side of the abdomen, at the eleventh rib.

Rheinhardt only knows a couple of pressure points. But they are all he needs.

The combination renders Tucker instantly and completely paralyzed.

Though this fact won't be evident for a while, because he's also instantly unconscious.

And when he does wake up, he'll probably scream in pain for a while.

* * *

A single shot cracks over Tucker's collapsed body, which is now draped over Rheinhardt's nearly equally lifeless one. Twisting his neck to his left, Rheinhardt can see Musa Harb pointing a rifle directly at his head. But there's already a single perfect hole in the man's forehead and he slumps over dead.

Rheinhardt turns his head back to the right.

And there's Ali, looking calmly over her sights, smoke curling from the end of her barrel.

No more shots are fired. Silence.

Rheinhardt figures he'll just lie here underneath Tucker for a while.

When someone does get around to pulling Tucker off him, that someone is Spider. He's looking a little worse for wear, but still on his feet.

"What, you still alive?" he says to Rheinhardt, helping him sit up.

"You tell me," Rheinhardt croaks, touching his split lips and the raw meat of his cheek.

"Bishop and Grinch have secured the nuke. They had to kill or capture a few Iranian guys."

Rheinhardt nods, and looks around Spider, to where Ali is working on Chaya. He creaks to his feet, and limps over as quickly as doesn't hurt too much.

Chaya is still foggy, but coming around.

"Fancy meeting you here," he says, smiling painfully through split and swollen lips.

She smiles back. "…And what will you be wanting today, Sergeant Major?"

"Shoulder wound's through and through," Ali says, securing two bandages. "She'll be fine."

Rheinhardt turns his head to regard Ali. "And what about you?"

"Me?" She straightens up. "What about me?" Blood streams down her face from her head wound, and the bullet crease on her waist never did get wrapped up.

Spider says, "I got it." He sits her down on a crate and opens his own aid pouch.

* * *

"Retard One, this is Retard X, how copy?"

Rheinhardt didn't even realize his earpiece was still in. But when he tries to answer, he finds his throat mic is MIA.

"Retard One, Retard X is on short final to your location at Doshan Tappeh AB. How copy?"

Rheinhardt lets out a heavy sigh. He brushes Chaya's hair off her forehead, then stands and heads for the door. When he emerges, it's much lighter outside than when he left it.

And in the sky is an insect-like Ghost Hawk, humming its way down toward him.

It settles on its wheels, the side door slides open, and Mike Brown hops out, looking just as spry as you please. No injuries, no powder burn, clean uniform. He looks positively human.

He trots up to Rheinhardt's staggering, bleeding, tattered form, and puts his hand on his shoulder. "Jesus Christ, Sarge… Are you okay?"

Rheinhardt just waves vaguely in response to this. He's actually still trying to catch his breath. "What's going on?" he says, finally.

Mike looks him in the eye. "It's over."

"Who won?"

"The Iranian people. There are tens of thousands of them, maybe hundreds of thousands, flooding the streets of downtown. A whole regular Army division rolled in, sporting green armbands, to help keep order. They linked up with the Kurds and are all working together. Khamenei and the mullahs are under arrest and have been handed over to Moussavi's people."

"Ahmadinejad?"

"Unaccounted for. But they think he'll turn up, if he hasn't fled the country. The whole capital's been liberated. There are gorgeous women draping BJ with garlands in Meidan Sepah."

"Seriously?"

"Totally. You want to talk to him?" Mike hails BJ then hands his headset over to Rheinhardt, who gingerly seats it on his much-pummeled head.

"BJ?"

"Yeah, man! You're alive?!"

"A little bit. You okay?"

"I'm fucking fantastic! I've got hot Persian chicks draping me in Green Revolution flags and trying to kiss me to death."

"Just don't let Captain Johnson find out."

"Yeah. I'm trying to stay off CNN."

While the two are talking, Mike's sat phone goes off. He turns away to take the call.

When he turns back, he's holding the device out for Rheinhardt.

"Um. Colonel Havering for you."

"Oh, hell. Gotta go, BJ. Time for that court martial…"

Rheinhardt swaps the headset for the sat phone. "Go for Rheinhardt."

"Havering here."

"Hello, Colonel."

"Huh. So how'd your training op go, Sergeant?"

"It was pretty realistic."

"Huh. I'm watching some pretty incredible shit here on CNN. Looks like the Arab Spring hit Persia."

Rheinhardt doesn't have the energy to say anything in his own defense.

"They're calling it a popular uprising, backed by the military and the Kurds. Mullahs all in handcuffs and suchlike. Moussavi talkin' 'bout a transition government, then elections."

Rheinhardt almost cracks a smile, but still doesn't speak.

"Nice to see people standing up for their own freedom. Natural rights, blood of tyrants, Jeffersonian democracy. All that."

"Yes, sir."

"I presume your training op is concluded. Expect they'll want to see you back at the Pentagon."

"Roger that."

"Okay, then. You fly safe."

The line goes dead.

* * *

Rheinhardt starts to hand the phone back. Then he remembers something fairly critical that he's lost track of in all the crises. He dials the number of the sat phone he gave Bleep in Balad.

It answers on the first ring. *"Go for Bleep."*

"Bleep, this is Bo Peep. The beards are shaved. Repeat, the beards are shaved. How copy?"

"All received, Bo. Beards are shaved. Standing down. Thank fuck for that. But — Bo, there's something else."

"Yeah?"

"The second missile. Its guidance chip was ALREADY pro-grammed for Tehran. Also for a three-thousand-foot airburst. Another EMP strike."

"What? Did you say the second missile was already targeting Tehran?"

"That's affirmative."

Rheinhardt wrinkles his bloody and grimy brow.

Through the hangar doors, he can see Spider and Ali frog-marching Rod Tucker out in front of them. He's bound hands, feet, and elbows. He can barely walk anyway from the lingering paralysis of the nerve strikes. And he looks like he's still getting used to being conscious.

"Bo out," Rheinhardt says, and hands the phone back to Mike.

Tucker holds Rheinhardt's gaze as he shuffles forward.

Speaking thickly, a bit like a dental patient, Tucker says, "So what's it gonna be for me, then, Bo – a CIA black site?"

Rheinhardt spits blood off to the side. "If you're lucky. Personally, I'm hoping you'll face trial by the Iranian people. The jails won't improve overnight under new management."

Tucker's expression remains inscrutable.

Spider pokes him in the back with his rifle, urging him toward the waiting helo.

"Wait one second," Rheinhardt says. "You've got to tell me something, Tucker. My team who's got your two nukes. On the passenger ship. They say the second one was programmed to airburst over Tehran."

Tucker smiles, his biker 'stache cracking from crusted blood.

"Course it was. C'mon. You don't think I'm stupid, do you Bo?"

Rheinhardt inclines his head. "No, Rod. I don't suppose I do think you're stupid."

Tucker nods, seeming gratified. "I know as well as anybody how evil the mullahs are. While defending Israel has been getting Americans killed, it's mostly IRG that's been doing the killing. Hell, the imperialist Jews and the messianic mullahs are as bad as each other. We needed rid of both. And I was making it happen."

Rheinhardt gives him a look of sheer wonder.

"So you were going to launch EMP strikes on *both* Tel Aviv and Tehran?"

"Shut 'em both down. Set everyone free."

From behind, Mike says, "Wait a minute. What was Bleep doing in the missile targeting?"

Rheinhardt exhales. "Because I tasked him with re-targeting one of the missiles for Tehran. If our assault here failed, I figured we could at least shut everything down with an EMP blast. It might stop the full Iranian military from overrunning us. And it might even allow the Iranians to bring off their revolution. There'd be a lot of rebuilding afterwards. But they'd do it as free people."

Spider, Ali, and Mike now regard Rheinhardt in wonder.

But Rheinhardt is looking at Tucker as he says, "Shut it all down. Set the people free."

"Genius is *so* bloody close to madness," Spider says, shaking his head in awe. He then hands Tucker over to the two crew chiefs on the Ghost Hawk, who trundle him off toward the helo.

"I'll be seein' you, Rod," Rheinhardt calls after him.

"Yeah. See you, Bo," Tucker says over his shoulder.

And Spider carries on shaking his head.

"Jesus, Rheinhardt. You just executed the biggest take-down in Delta history. Not a room, or a building, or a complex. But an entire fucking country. What are you going to do now?"

"Disneyworld?"

Spider laughs out loud. "Axis of Evil: two down!"

The sound of turbo-fan engines draws their eyes upward. Their MC-130 is turning in and lining up to land. Mike says, "We're going to consolidate our wounded here, then fly them direct to Landstuhl."

Rheinhardt nods once, his amusement fading. "How many?"

"Numbers still coming in. Looks like forty KIA across all the teams. Times two wounded."

"Jesus. That's over fifty percent casualties."

"Not bad against a half-million-man military."

Rheinhardt pauses quietly to consider that, for the ones who lived, there'd be no flags, no bands – just a ride back to their home bases, to repack their bags for another no-notice mission, anywhere in the world, at anytime.

"I changed my mind about Disneyworld," Rheinhardt says. "I just want to go home."

Ali steps up and takes his hand. "That jet in the hangar there will go transcontinental. Might need a refueling stop."

"Sounds good." Rheinhardt pauses, leaning on, and around, the others now.

He can see Chaya walking out of the hangar under her own power, hand to her shoulder.

There's sunlight on her face.

After long hours of storm and darkness… the sun has finally battled its way free.

The two lock gazes across the clean open air.

Rheinhardt says, "Think we can refuel at Ben Gurion International?"

Ali smiles. "Don't see why not."

As the clouds part, bright sunlight falls across the runway and the hangar.

It's a new day.

Love this book? Share the love, support independent authors, and make me your best friend forever, by posting a quick review on Amazon. Thanks! - Michael

Want to be alerted when the next D-BOYS book or other title from MSF is released? Sign up for e-mail alerts at michaelstephenfuchs.com/alerts and I'll keep you updated. (And I'll never share your address or use it for anything else.)

And you can follow Michael on Facebook (facebook. com/michaelstephenfuchs), Twitter (@michael-stephenf), or by email (www.michaelstephenfuchs. com/alerts).

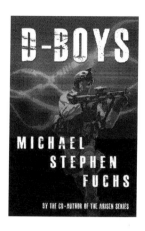

**The world's most elite counter-terrorist operators.
A cyber-security guru suddenly getting shot
at and blown up rather more than usual.
And nuclear-armed terrorists rolling with impunity through a lawless and brutal virtual world.**

The year is now. Islamist terrorists hack into America's most
sensitive defense networks, launch chemical weapons attacks
on Western cities, and stage a raid on the vulnerable nuclear
weapons storage facilities in Pakistan. They are using a massively multiplayer online video game (or "virtual world") as
a platform for planning and rehearsing their attacks – forcing a squad of supremely elite Delta Force Operators (reinforced by a cyber-security expert from the Department of
Homeland Security) to go inside the game to fight them.

But the fight only begins there. Get ready for breath-steal-
ing action in every known battlespace – clockwork urban
safehouse takedowns, combat helicopter assaults, brutal
ambushes in the trackless mountains, waterborne SEAL team

ops, precision close quarters battle sequences, and CheyTac Intervention sniper rifle systems that can kill you from a mile and a half away.

Get ready for D-Boys – where the weapons, tactics, tech, and 21st-century warriors will be unlike anything you've ever read. Available now.

The D-Boys will return in 2016 in **CLOSE QUARTERS BATTLE**

The book in your hand is a work of imaginative fiction. The author would like to stress that – in another illustration of how fiction cannot hold a candle to real life – the imagined exploits of the fictional characters in this novel are a dull shadow of the real-life exploits of our real SOF operators, who train like professional athletes, perform like minor gods, and lay it all on the line every day in the defense of freedom and decency. In a tiny gesture of thanks to them, a portion of the earnings from sales of this book will be donated to the Special Operations Warrior Foundation – which provides college scholarships to the children of SOF personnel who are killed in operational missions or training accidents. Tax-deductible donations to this foundation can be made at www.specialops.org, or to Special Operations Warrior Foundation, P.O. Box 13483, Tampa FL 33681-3483, USA.

BIBLIOGRAPHY

This book would not have been possible without Pete Blaber's *The Mission, The Men, and Me: Lessons from a Former Delta Force Commander* – and particularly Eric L. Haney's *Inside Delta Force: The Story of America's Elite Counterterrorist Unit*. From both books I harvested an enormous number of ideas, facts, vignettes, and other priceless gems regarding Delta practices, theory, tools, tricks, and (in particular) mindset. From both books, I also cribbed a lot of call signs and descriptions and characteristics of real operators. I did this for verisimilitude and as an homage to the real-life superheroes of our special operations forces. The call signs and characteristics are, in most cases, mashed up amongst several characters, so no actual person is represented. You should absolutely buy and read CSM Haney's and Major Blaber's books, which are much, much better than mine.

I also owe a great debt to Dalton Fury's excellent *Kill Bin Laden: A Delta Force Commander's Account of the Hunt for the World's Most Wanted Man.*

I have substantially borrowed from Derek Leebaert's magisterial, thrilling, and surprisingly gorgeously written *To Dare & To Conquer, Special Operations and the Destiny of Nations, from Achilles to Al Qaeda*. I only picked up this book when I was already two-thirds of the way through this one, but it somehow became indispensable. You should definitely buy and read it.

The helo sequence with the IDF guys in the Stealth Hawk flying into Iran under fire was more or less totally cribbed from the heart-stopping rescue and extraction of a Special Forces recon team from the desert in Iraq in 1991, conducted by 160th Special Operations Aviation Regiment pilots and crew CW4 Jim Crisafulli, CWO Randy "Beastman" Stephens, PFC Todd "Diff" Diffenderfer, Bruce Willard, Richard Detrick, and MSG Gordy Hopple, as recounted in *The Night Stalkers: Top Secret Missions of the U.S. Army's Special Operations Aviation Regiment*, by Michael J. Durant and Stephen Hartov, with Lt. Col. (Ret.) Robert L. Johnson. I stole it out of despair that I could ever make up anything half as thrilling as what these guys actually did. The book I got it if from is completely amazing, and filled with the amazing exploits of genuine real-life heroes, the pilots and crew and support guys of the 160th SOAR. You should definitely buy and read it, right this second.

The Chinook evasive maneuvers in response to a missile threat were taken more or less *en toto* from Major Chris Hunter's amazing book *Eight Lives Down: The Most Dangerous Job in the World in the Most Dangerous Place in the World*. He's a genuine hero with some of the most amazing stories in the world to tell, and you should seriously buy and read his book.

The observation about soldiers cleaning weapons being like a ladies' sewing circle is from *Generation Kill* by Evan Wright. The book is utterly awesome, as is the HBO miniseries of the same name, both for the same reason – the real-life recon Marines depicted are as completely hilarious as they are uniquely American (plus deadly).

"Majestic Army base," "Live a lifetime in a second," and "prenuptial agreement with Death" are all phrases that I borrowed from *Nightcap At Dawn: Soldiers' Counterinsurgency in Iraq* by "J.B. Walker" (a group of soldiers returning from Iraq). You can and should buy their wonderful, remarkable book at: http://www.lulu.com/product/paperback/nightcap-at-dawn-soldiers-counterinsurgency/15469136

Air Force CCT Dan Schilling's Five Lessons of Combat are, in fact, from Dan Schilling. You can read them – along with his (and others') amazing, heart-stopping experience of the "Black Hawk Down" incident in Mogadishu in *The Battle of Mogadishu: Firsthand Accounts from the Men of Task Force Ranger*, edited by Matt Eversmann and Dan Schilling. Awesome book.

I also owe big-time – and you'll also definitely, *seriously* want to watch – the television series *The Unit*, created by David Mamet and Eric L. Haney.

Here are some other books that contributed very much to the production of this one:

Never Surrender: A Soldier's Journey to the Crossroads of Faith and Freedom, by LTG (Ret.) William G. (Jerry) Boykin and Lynn Vincent

Delta Force: The Army's Elite Counterterrorist Unit, by Col. Charlie A. Beckwith (Ret.) and Donald Knox

SEAL Team Six: Memoirs of an Elite Navy SEAL Sniper, by Howard E. Wasdin and Stephen Templin

Task Force Black, by Mark Urban

Hellfire, by Ed Macy

Warrior Soul: The Memoir of a Navy SEAL, by Chuck Pfarrer

Lone Survivor: The Eyewitness Account of Operation Redwing and the Lost Heroes of SEAL Team 10, by Marcus Luttrell with Patrick Robinson

The Sheriff Of Ramadi: Navy SEALS and the Winning of al-Anbar, by Dick Couch

Down Range: Navy SEALs in the War on Terrorism, by Dick Couch

Black Hawk Down: A Story of Modern War, by Mark Bowden

Against All Enemies: Inside America's War on Terror, by Richard A. Clarke

No Easy Day: The Only First-hand Account of the Navy SEAL Mission That Killed Osama Bin Laden, by Mark Owen with Keven Maurer

Wired's Danger Room blog, and especially Wikipedia, were also utterly indispensable (perhaps, in the latter case, needless to point out).

The author wishes to thank the following people. You know what you did.

Anna Kathleen Brooksbank

Mark George Pitely

Sara Natalie Fuchs

Richard S. Fuchs

Virginia Ann Sayers-King

Valerie Sayers

Alexander Montgomery Heublein

Amanda Jo Moore

Glynn James

Michael and Jayne Barnard

Robert Gottlieb

Jenn Newark

Slayer 155

GLOSSARY

160th SOAR - Special Operations Aviations Regiment, the "Night Stalkers"

1st SFOD-D - U.S. Special Forces Operational Detachment - Delta

2IC - 2nd In Command

AA - Anti-Aircraft, weapons systems used to shoot down aircraft

AB - Air Base

AC-130 - the Spectre gunship

ACAS - Airborne Collision Avoidance System

ACUs - Army Combat Uniform

AFB - Air Force Base

AH-6 - the attack version of the Little Bird helicopter

AK - the standard Eastern bloc assault rifle

AN/PEQ-15 - infrared laser aiming/illuminating sight mounted on rifles

AO - Area of Operations

APC - Armored Personnel Carrier

AQ - al Qaeda

ASW - Anti-Submarine Warfare

BDA - Battle/Bomb Damage Assessment

BDUs - Battle Dress Uniform

BFT - Blue Force Tracker

Bowstring - the Delta squadron on 60-minute alert

BTR - a Soviet armored personnel carrier

CAG - Combat Applications Group (Delta)

CAS - Close Air Support

CBRN - Chemical/Biological/Radiological/Nuclear

CCT - Combat Control Team, the Air Force personnel who direct air support

CENTCOM - Central Command of the U.S. military, responsible for the Middle East

Charlie Mike - continue mission

CheyTac - the Cheyenne Tactical Intervention sniper rifle system

CIA - Central Intelligence Agency

CO - Commanding Officer

Comms/commo - military communications

CQB - Close Quarters Battle

CSAR - Combat Search and Rescue

CT - Counter-Terrorism

DA - Direct Action, combat operations

DCI - Director of Central Intelligence

DEVGRU - U.S. Naval Special Warfare Development Group, aka SEAL Team 6

DHS - U.S. Department of Homeland Security

DIA - U.S. Defense Intelligence Agency

E&E - Escape & Evade

ECM - Electronic Counter Measures

EMP - Electro-Magnetic Pulse

EOD - Explosive Ordnance Disposal

ETI - Estimated Time to Impact

FBI - Federal Bureau of Investigation

FOB - Forward Operating Base

FPF - Final Protective Fire, when personnel fire everything as a last ditch maneuver

Frago - fragmentary (or partial) order

GEOINT - Geospatial Intelligence, from satellites

Ghost Hawk - the U.S. 3rd-generation stealth helicopter

GIGN - Groupe d'Intervention de la Gendarmerie Nationale, the premier French CT unit

GWOT - Global War on Terror

H&K USP - Heckler & Koch Universal Service Pistol

HDS - Holographic Diffraction Sight

HEU - Highly Enriched Uranium

Hip - Russian Mil Mi-17 helicopter

Hizbullah - the party of God, which runs the Gaza Strip

HK416 - Delta's primary assault rifle, designed by them and Heckler & Koch

HUMINT - Human Intelligence

HVT - High Value Target

IAF - Israeli Air Force

ICS - Inter-crew Communication System, the internal radios on aircraft

IDF - Israel Defense Forces

IED - Improvised Explosive Device

IR - Infrared

IRG - Iranian Revolutionary Guards

JOC - Joint Operations Center

JSOC - Joint Special Operations Command

JSOTF - Joint Special Operations Task Force

LAF - Lebanese Armed Forces

Lima Zulu - LZ, Landing Zone

Little Bird - light helicopter used for special operations

LPI - Low Probability of Intercept, said of communications

M14 - 7.62mm selective fire automatic rifle used by U.S. until 1970

M240 - U.S. standard light machine gun

MG - Machine Gun

MH-6 - The transport and recon variant of the Little Bird helicopter

MIA - Missing In Action

Mikes - military slang for minutes

MLM - Main Line of Resistance

Mossad - National intelligence agency of Israel

MP7 - Sub-machine gun/Personal Defense Weapon (PDW) from Heckler & Koch

MTO - Mission Tasking Order

MWR - Missile Warning Receiver

NCA - National Command Authority

NGA - National Geospatial Agency

NSA - National Security Agency, the U.S. cryptologic intelligence agency

NSC - National Security Council

NVG - Night Vision Goggles

OGA - Other Government Agency, usually meaning the CIA

OP - Overwatch Point

Oscar Mike - On the Move

Pax - Personnel

PC - Precious Cargo, i.e. a rescued hostage

PKM - Soviet light machine gun

QRF - Quick Reaction Force, a unit kept on standby for rescues

ROE - Rules of Engagement

RFN - Right Now, a time designation

RQ-11 Raven - a hand-launched, remote-controlled mini UAV

RQ-130 - a flying wing stealth UAV

RTB - Return To Base

RTU - Returned to Unit, what happens when an operator is kicked out of an SOF unit

SAD - Special Activities Division, the paramilitaries of the CIA

SAFIRE - Small Arms Fire

SATCOM - satellite communications

SCAR - SOF Combat Assault Rifle

SDV - Seal Delivery Vehicle

SEAL - U.S. navy's SEa, Air, and Land Teams

SecDef - U.S. Secretary of Defense

SERE - Survival, Evasion, Resistance, Escape school

Shin Bet - Israel's internal security service

SIGINT - signals intelligence

Sitrep - Situation report

SMG - Sub-Machine Gun

SMU - Special Mission Unit

SOF - Special Operations Forces

SSE - Sensitive Site Exploitation

STARS - Surface-To-Air Recovery System

Stealth Hawk - U.S. 2nd-generation stealth helicopter

SWORDS - Special Weapons Observation Reconnaissance Detection System, an armed robot

Tango - Terrorist or target, an enemy

TF - Task Force

TLA - Three Letter Acronym

TOC - Tactical Operations Center

UAV - Unmanned Aerial Vehicle

USSOCOM - United States Special Operations Command

Victor - Vehicle

VPN - Virtual Private Network

WIA - Wounded in Action

XO - Executive Officer on board a ship

ARISEN

Hope Never Dies.

Fans of the bestselling ARISEN series call it "**Staggeringly good - the most consistently excellent franchise in zombie literature**"…"**Wall to wall adrenaline - edge of your seat unputdownable until the very last page**"…"**totally stunning in its originality**"…"**jaw dropping**"…"**moves like an avalanche**"…"**You can smell the smoke, feel the explosions, and hear the rounds headed down range**"…"**edge of the seat, nail biting, page turning mayhem**"…"**had me holding my breath more times than I could count**"…"**a knock down drag out kick ass read - the best ZA book series**

around, period"…"rolls along like an out of control freight train"…"Left me shaking at the last page…"

Alpha team will return – but so will Spetsnaz Alfa Group – in

ARISEN, BOOK ELEVEN – DEATHMATCH

They are the most capable, committed, and indispensable counter-terrorist operators in the world.

They have no rivals for skill, speed, ferocity, intelligence, flexibility, and sheer resolve.

Somewhere in the world, things are going horrifyingly wrong...

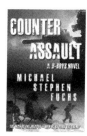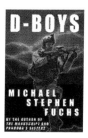

Readers call the D-BOYS series "a high-octane adrenaline-fueled action thrill-ride", "one of the best action thrillers of the year (or any year for that matter)", "a riveting, fast paced classic!!", "pure action", "The Best Techno Military Thriller I have read!", "Awesome!", "Gripping", "Edge of your seat action", "Kick butt in the most serious of ways and a thrill to read", "What a wild ride!!! I simply could not put this book down", "has a real humanity and philosophical side as well", "a truly fast action, high octane book", "Up there with Clancy and W.E.B. Griffin", "one of the best Spec Ops reads I have run into", and "hi-tech and action in one well-rounded explosive thriller."

ABOUT THE AUTHOR

MICHAEL STEPHEN FUCHS, in addition to co-authoring the first eight books of the bestselling ARISEN series with Glynn James, wrote the bestselling prequels ARISEN : GENESIS and ARISEN : NEMESIS (an Amazon #1 bestseller in Post-Apocalyptic Science Fiction and #1 in Dystopian), as well as Book Nine (#1 bestseller in War, #1 in Military Science Fiction) and Book Ten (an Amazon overall Top 100 bestseller). The series as a whole has sold nearly a quarter million copies. He is also author of the D-BOYS series of high-tech special-operations military adventure novels, which include D-BOYS,

COUNTER-ASSAULT, and CLOSE QUARTERS BATTLE (coming in 2016); as well as the acclaimed existential cyber-thrillers THE MANUSCRIPT and PANDORA'S SISTERS, both published worldwide by Macmillan in hardback, paperback and all e-book formats (and in translation). He lives in London and at www.michaelstephenfuchs.com, and blogs at www.michaelfuchs.org/razorsedge. You can also follow him on Facebook (facebook.com/michaelstephenfuchs), Twitter (@michaelstephenf), or by email (www.michaelstephenfuchs.com/alerts).

Made in the USA
San Bernardino, CA
14 October 2016